MURDER ON THE PRINCE REGENT

IRINA SHAPIRO

Storm

Ebook ISBN: 978-1-80508-964-3
Paperback ISBN: 978-1-80508-966-7

Cover design: Debbie Clement
Cover images: Arcangel, Shutterstock

Published by Storm Publishing.
For further information, visit:
www.stormpublishing.co

ALSO BY IRINA SHAPIRO

The Invite

A Tate and Bell Mystery

The Highgate Cemetery Murder

Murder at Traitors' Gate

Murder at the Foundling Hospital

Murder at the Orpheus Theatre

Murder on Platform Four

The Carnival Murders

Murder on Devil's Ridge

Wonderland Series

The Passage

Wonderland

Sins of Omission

The Queen's Gambit

Comes the Dawn

The Hands of Time

The Hands of Time

A Leap of Faith

A World Apart

A Game of Shadows

Shattered Moments

The Ties that Bind

The Summer Solstice

PROLOGUE

Lorna Thorpe hurried down the narrow stairs, a small stack of freshly laundered unmentionables pressed to her chest. Her breath came in short gasps and her heart beat rapidly as she approached the cabin. She hoped to get in and out as quickly as possible, before the Blackstocks returned from their daily walk. She didn't want to be alone with Lord Blackstock, not after... She couldn't allow herself to dwell on it or she would lose her nerve, and ultimately her place.

The first-class saloon was empty, the remnants of the passengers' breakfast already cleared away by the stewards. Lorna wished the lads were still there, to serve as an extra layer of protection, but they couldn't afford to linger, not when they had so much to do and were on their feet from dawn until well past dusk.

Pausing before the cabin door, Lorna stood still and listened for a moment, then, satisfied that the cabin was empty, turned the knob and entered the room. The first thing she noticed was the smell. It wasn't the usual odor of a cramped space occupied by two people who hadn't properly bathed in a fortnight. It was thick and metallic, and overlaid with the acrid stench of sweat. The second thing she noticed was that the room was almost completely dark. The oil lamp on the desk wasn't lit, so, although Lorna could see where she was going by the light that spilled through the door, she couldn't make out any of the particulars of her surroundings. She approached the desk, set down the laundry, and lit the lamp. The light illuminated the windowless room and cast a golden halo onto the unmade bed, which took up most of the space. She started, then froze in panic when she realized the bed wasn't empty.

Lorna clamped a hand over her mouth to stifle the strangled cry that forced its way through her tightly pressed lips as her brain caught up with her eyes and she realized what she was looking at. Taking a hasty step backwards, she collided with the cabinet, then stumbled towards the door, desperate to escape. But she couldn't leave without taking one last look to make certain she hadn't invented this waking nightmare. The figure was still there, unmoving, so Lorna inched towards the bed, terrified but also desperate to get a closer look.

Lord Anthony Blackstock was sprawled on the bed, his eyes open wide and staring at the ceiling he could no longer see. He was completely naked, his lithe body powerful even in death. Lorna's breath caught in her throat when her gaze swept over his hips and the stiff rod that protruded proudly from a thicket of curly dark hair. But Lord Blackstock's arousal was the least shocking aspect of his appearance. His head was encased in an iron contraption that was shaped like a birdcage but constructed of thick black bars and had round openings for the eyes and a slit for the mouth. The word *pig* was carved into his chest, the letters jagged and raw and scored deep into the flesh. Dried blood striped Anthony Blackstock's torso and had saturated the sheet beneath. His hands gripped the fabric, his stiff fingers like white-knuckled claws.

Lorna stood rooted to the spot, unable to move or tear her gaze from the grotesque spectacle before her, but then common sense prevailed and she lurched towards the door, slammed it shut behind her, and sprinted towards the stairs. It was only when she went up on deck and gulped mouthfuls of fresh, salty air that she realized she had to report what she had seen. And there was no way to describe it other than murder.

ONE

MONDAY, JUNE 20, 1859

Gemma Tate pulled on her bonnet, tied the ribbons beneath her chin, then grabbed her reticule and gloves and hastened downstairs. She had planned to leave half an hour ago, but her patient, Mrs. Ramsey, had had a difficult morning, and Gemma could hardly leave until Anne was washed, fed, and ready for the day. The past six weeks had been extremely challenging for them both, as Anne convalesced after a fall down the cellar steps, further complicated by progressive cognitive decline. Not only had Anne been completely bedbound and in round-the-clock pain, but she couldn't recall what had happened or why, and kept asking Gemma why she was in such agony and begging to be brought downstairs, where she could sit by the window and watch the world go by.

Anne's bruises had faded after the first few weeks, and her bones had begun to knit, albeit slowly due to her age, but the emotional damage wouldn't heal as quickly. Anne might not remember the fall, but on some deeper level she recognized that her injury had not been accidental, and that the person who had pushed her had used her to ensure his escape and had not cared if she had been hurt or even killed as a result. The culprit was behind bars now, awaiting trial for the murder of an innocent young woman, but Gemma saw no point in reminding Anne of that awful day. She would forget the answer a few moments later anyway, but those brief minutes of awareness left Anne feeling frightened and shocked to learn that a person she'd had no reason to mistrust had intentionally caused her harm. Anne had broken several bones, but the fall had also impacted her tenuous hold on reality, the shock and pain having seemingly impaired her mental faculties even further.

Gemma's own morale had suffered greatly during the past weeks, and the only happy moments she had had to look forward to were her outings with Sebastian and her occasional walks with her friend Poppy Bright. Poppy, who worked the night shift at an infirmary in Lambeth, had offered to look after Anne on Gemma's days off, and Gemma had readily agreed. She could hardly ask Mabel to both nurse Anne and see to her numerous domestic chores, and she knew too, how much Poppy longed to see Colin Ramsey. In some ways, this was the perfect opportunity for them to spend time together and get to know one another better.

Colin appreciated Poppy's help with his mother and praised her gentle touch, but seemed oblivious to Poppy's feelings for him and resigned to remaining single. Until a few months ago, Colin had still held out hope that Gemma would throw over Sebastian and transfer her affections to himself, but he'd given up, probably because he'd finally realized that they weren't well suited, for which Gemma would be eternally grateful. She couldn't imagine her life without Sebastian, but, although they had spoken about the future, as a favor to Colin, they had agreed to wait to make their relationship official until Anne was up and about and Colin had found a new permanent nurse for his mother.

Gemma was eager to take the next step in her life, but she now realized that she could never be happy with the lot of a conventional wife. And if Sebastian meant to be with her, he would have to accept that. It was early days, and she hadn't yet put her plan into action because most of her time was spent caring for Anne, but she had asked—no, had pleaded with Colin—to instruct her in anatomy. She accepted that she could never become a surgeon—her sex precluded that—but she wanted to learn nevertheless and hoped the new skillset would prove an asset in the future. Gemma thought Sebastian would understand her desire to advance in her vocation. He was no longer shocked by her unconventional ideas and had come to appreciate her input and value her medical expertise. Perhaps she'd discuss it with him today.

Tempted to hurry, Gemma forced herself to walk at a sedate pace. Sebastian would wait, and perhaps he was running a bit late himself. She knew he had planned to stop at Scotland Yard first thing to collect his wages, since he had been working a case in Cripplegate and had not been there to receive this week's pay packet. This was Sebastian's first day off in a fortnight, and, although it fell on a Monday, Gemma had arranged the time off with Colin and Poppy and didn't need to be back until Poppy was due to leave for work. Sebastian and Gemma had agreed to meet by Waterloo Bridge and go to Regent's Park. It was a fine day for a walk.

Gemma hoped the weather would hold, but one never knew. It had been cold and gray yesterday, but today the sky was clear and the sunshine gentle, though there was a stillness in the air, the kind before a storm. It was pleasantly warm but not so hot as to make her perspire in her many layers. Gemma hoped they would have time to stop by her favorite bookshop before Sebastian was due to take her home. It was his birthday on Saturday, and Gemma wanted to buy him a gift. Sebastian loved to read and often said that, if he couldn't spend the evening with Gemma, an engrossing novel was the next best thing. She needed to find out which new releases Sebastian had already read and which books he planned to read next so that she could return the next day and purchase them. It wasn't as personal and as creative a gift as the one he'd given her for her birthday, but she was in no position to track down and purchase an American pistol, complete with a box of cartridges. The gift of entertainment would have to suffice.

As Gemma approached the bridge, her heart lightened, and

her step unwittingly quickened when she spotted Sebastian. He looked handsome and comfortably cool in a tan summer suit and his new brown derby, but, rather than appearing relaxed, he was scowling, his attention fixed on some distant point upriver, his posture radiating tension. As if sensing her gaze on him, Sebastian turned. He smiled, but the smile was apologetic, his gaze full of regret. Gemma's spirits sank as she hurried towards him. She didn't know what had changed, but she was certain this day wasn't going to go as planned.

TWO

Sebastian held out his hands, and Gemma placed her own in them, her eyes filled with uncertainty. He hated to disappoint her, especially as he knew how much these outings meant to her after a week spent indoors nursing an increasingly demanding Anne. He was disappointed himself as well—he'd waited two whole weeks to see her and had planned a very special day for them—but, as usual, life and Superintendent Ransome had got in the way.

"I'm so sorry, darling," Sebastian said, "but I can't stay."

"Why not? What's happened?" Gemma didn't look angry, only worried. "Are you all right?"

Gemma's concern for him made him feel even guiltier for ruining her day. "I'm well. It's just that there's been an incident that might have far-reaching implications, and Ransome has asked me to look into it. Discreetly."

"Can you tell me about it?" Gemma asked, her concern instantly replaced with curiosity.

"I'm afraid I don't have time," Sebastian demurred. "There's a boat waiting for me."

"A boat?" Gemma exclaimed. "Where are you going?"

Sebastian sighed. He didn't have time to explain—he'd wasted nearly an hour already—but he could hardly walk away and leave

Gemma standing there, especially when she looked so breathtakingly lovely, her eyes alight with a desire to help. He had yet to become accustomed to seeing her wearing color after endless months of mourning black, and he marveled at how much younger and more vibrant she looked now, her green eyes and chestnut hair accented by the pale-green silk of her new walking gown and a matching bonnet decorated with ribbons and flowers of deep pink velvet. He longed to see Gemma smile and hear all about her week, and, if he were honest, he enjoyed the admiring looks men cast in her direction as they walked past, Gemma utterly oblivious, her attention only for him.

His ride would wait a few more minutes, Sebastian decided, when deep disappointment shadowed Gemma's gaze despite her best efforts not to let him see her dismay. Neither the corpse nor the culprit was going anywhere, and the least he could do was offer an explanation before he walked away, leaving Gemma to either spend the day on her own or return home and resume her duties until he could make it up to her.

"There's been a suspicious death aboard the *Prince Regent*," Sebastian announced.

"The *Prince Regent*? Is that a ship?"

Sebastian nodded. "It's a packet boat that's owned by an American firm, Grinnell, Minturn and Company. Their Blue Swallowtail line sails from New York to London. The vessel is currently at anchor in Limehouse Reach, near the Isle of Dogs, and a cutter is waiting by Westminster Bridge to ferry me to the ship."

Gemma looked puzzled. "But how could Ransome know about an incident that took place aboard a packet boat?"

"The captain dispatched a messenger to Scotland Yard as soon as the body was discovered. The messenger arrived just before I did."

"But you haven't had a day off in weeks," Gemma protested. "Why did Ransome have to send you?" she demanded, then nodded to herself, as if the answer were evident. "He wanted his best man on this."

Scotland Yard had been in a state of transition since Ransome's appointment two months before, and several inspectors who'd been loyal to the previous superintendent, Lovell, and had been vocal in their opposition had either been transferred to other divisions or had chosen to depart of their own volition. Two men had been promoted from within—Constable Hammond and Constable Bryant—both of whom Sebastian liked and respected, but they were not yet up to the task, not when it came to a case that involved a foreign nation.

"I could hardly refuse," Sebastian explained. "I'll make it up to you. I promise."

Gemma made a dismissive gesture, then slid her arm through his as they began to walk towards the Strand. "Don't worry about me. I'm not a child. I can handle a canceled outing. I'd rather hear more about the case. Who died? And how?"

Sebastian found himself relaying everything Ransome had told him, which admittedly wasn't very much since the message from the captain had been short on the details of the victim's passing. It had, however, supplied an identity, which in this case was particularly important.

"The victim was Lord Anthony Blackstock, a close associate of the British envoy to the United States. He was returning to England after a visit with the ambassador. According to Ransome, Blackstock was being considered for the ambassadorship once the current envoy is recalled to England."

Sebastian stopped walking and held up a hand as an unoccupied hansom trundled towards them, the driver scanning the passersby from his perch in search of a fare. He nodded to Sebastian and pulled on the reins to slow the conveyance. It wasn't far to Westminster, but it would take too long to get there on foot, and time was of the essence since, once they rendezvoused with the cutter from the *Prince Regent*, it would still take at least an hour to reach the Isle of Dogs, or possibly longer, depending on the current.

"Does Ransome think this incident was politically motivated?" Gemma asked. "Do you?"

"I don't know," Sebastian admitted. "The missive was brief, but the urgency was unmistakable. There's much at stake since an assassination of a diplomat could lead to a schism between the two nations."

"Which is why the ship is so far out? The captain is trying to contain the news?"

"And presumably to keep the killer from coming ashore if this is a case of murder," Sebastian replied.

"Well, that hardly sounds like a foolproof plan," Gemma said. "The killer can still escape."

"It's the best that could be done under the circumstances. The vessel had to come in close enough to send a message. Had the captain decided to wait in the estuary, it would have taken more than twelve hours for the messenger to get to Scotland Yard, and then just as long for a detective to arrive on the scene."

"Was Lord Blackstock definitely murdered? It could have been a natural death," Gemma pointed out. "A person doesn't have to be aged to suffer a cardiac infarction or a blood clot in the brain."

Sebastian shrugged. "I won't know for certain until I see the body."

"I'm coming with you," Gemma announced. "You will need someone with a medical background to examine the body."

Sebastian was about to protest but reconsidered. Gemma's gaze was determined, and her chin jutted out in a way that warned him not to challenge her. And she made a valid point. There was likely a doctor aboard, but Sebastian had no idea how skilled or how cooperative the man would be. Gemma's expertise had often proved invaluable, and could be again, especially since the victim might be traveling with members of his family, who might refuse permission to perform a postmortem. Gemma's observations could be the only help Sebastian would have to go on, and, although she wasn't an accredited doctor or a trained surgeon, she had enough practical experience to make a determination on the cause of death.

"All right," he said as the hansom drew up. He called out their destination to the driver. "But I don't want you going off on your own unless I deem it safe."

"Of course," Gemma replied, looking very pleased indeed. "I will follow your lead."

"Where have I heard that before?" Sebastian grumbled as he settled next to her and shut the half-doors at the front of the cab.

"What do you know of this Blue Swallowtail line?" Gemma asked as the carriage merged into mid-morning traffic, which was mercifully light for a weekday.

"Not very much," Sebastian replied. "It's a fairly new route. The Red Swallowtail line sails between New York and Liverpool and has been in operation for several decades now. The London-bound ships sail on a two-week schedule."

"Does it really take only a fortnight to get to London from New York?"

"It would appear so, assuming the weather cooperates, of course."

"To think that one can reach the other side of the world in just two weeks," Gemma mused.

If one reaches it at all, Sebastian thought. An alarmingly large number of transatlantic voyages still ended in tragedy, and, until such a time as ships could call to shore or signal others when a vessel was in distress, the casualties would continue to mount, the ocean floor littered with sunken ships and the remains of those aboard. Travelers were prepared to take their chances, their need to get to their destination greater than their fear, but ocean travel remained a risky proposition, even for the wealthy, who presumably traveled in style.

"Do you know anything about the British envoy?" Gemma asked.

"Richard Lyons, first Earl Lyons, has been in the post since December 1858 and resides in Washington. According to

Ransome, he's an experienced politician who's well liked and respected by his peers. Before his posting to the United States, he was the minister to Tuscany, but that posting lasted less than a year."

"Why?"

"Ransome thought it was because he coveted a more influential position, but he couldn't be sure."

"And is he now ready to return to England? Is that why Lord Blackstock was being considered for the post?"

"I really don't know," Sebastian said.

"What about Lord Blackstock?"

"Lord Blackstock was the lieutenant governor of a Caribbean territory—Grenada, Ransome thought—for several years before returning to England. That's all he knows of the man other than what he could glean from *Debrett's Peerage.*"

The cab came to a stop, and Sebastian helped Gemma out before paying the driver. He scanned the shore, searching for the cutter with the ship's name, and spotted it eventually. Two sailors dressed in dark blue trousers and shirts with red neckerchiefs tied loosely around their throats sat in the boat. Their caps were pushed back, and they were smoking and talking easily, as if they had all the time in the world. One of them, the messenger Sebastian had met at Scotland Yard, who'd introduced himself as Peters, recognized Sebastian and straightened immediately, then flicked his cheroot overboard and adjusted his cap. His counterpart did the same.

Some short distance from the cutter, his back to Sebastian and his gaze fixed on the river, stood Constable Forrest. His hand rested on his hip, and one foot was propped on a discarded pot, the pose reminiscent of a general surveying the battlefield.

"Ransome sent Constable Forrest?" Gemma whispered, lest the young man overhear her exclamation of surprise.

Constable Forrest was the youngest and least experienced constable at the Yard, though he made up for his lack of knowledge with unbridled exuberance. He was like a playful puppy, excited for every new opportunity and eager to learn, but the young man lacked an innate copper's instinct and in some instances was more of a hindrance than a help.

"No one else was available," Sebastian replied in a low voice. "There was an accident at a building site in Millbank. Several men were crushed by falling masonry. Ransome dispatched half a dozen constables to help free the survivors and move them to an infirmary. He thought I could rely on the captain should I require further assistance. I'm glad you're coming."

"Are you ready to leave, Inspector?" Peters asked.

"I am."

"Who's this, then?" the second man asked.

Constable Forrest turned as soon as Peters had addressed Sebastian, and his expression betrayed his shock when he spotted Gemma. He'd met her once before, very briefly, and had heard the derisive comments directed at Sebastian after he had brought her to Scotland Yard following the arrest of the Foundling Hospital killer, whom Gemma had apprehended single-handed. The gossip had died down, mostly because everyone had quickly realized that Sebastian would belt anyone who so much as mentioned Gemma in a way that was disrespectful, but that was probably about to change. Constable Forrest was not likely to omit Gemma's presence from his account once he returned.

"Inspector Bell, I have quite despaired of seeing you," Constable Forrest exclaimed, his gaze sliding uncertainly towards Gemma.

"I had to wait for Miss Tate. She's coming with us," Sebastian replied, loudly enough for the sailors to hear.

Constable Forrest's face turned pink with indignation, and his nearly hairless upper lip glistened with perspiration. "Inspector," he began, his scandalized gaze now alternating between Gemma and Sebastian. "Surely Superintendent Ransome..." His voice trailed off since it seemed he wasn't quite sure how to phrase his complaint without offending his superior or the lady, who didn't appear perturbed in the least and smiled at him beatifically.

"Miss Tate is an experienced nurse and will assist me in assessing the crime scene," Sebastian replied crisply. "Now, if you have no further objections, I suggest you get in the boat."

Constable Forrest shot Gemma a sulky look and clambered into the boat, which was thankfully large enough to accommodate them all. Sebastian had expected a rowboat or a ship's dinghy, but the service cutter was longer and wider and was meant to accommodate a dozen people should an evacuation become necessary and the passengers have to be rowed to shore. Sweeping Gemma into his arms to keep her boots and skirts from getting soaked, Sebastian deposited her in the boat, and jumped in himself just before the next wave rolled onto the bank. Pleased to have kept his boots and trousers dry, he settled next to Gemma, who set her reticule in her lap, adjusted her skirts, and tightened the knot of her bonnet to keep it firmly in place should the wind pick up once they were out on the river.

"How long until we reach the ship?" Gemma asked.

"'Bout an hour, ma'am," Peters said. "Maybe two."

"So, is it one hour or two?" Constable Forrest demanded hysterically.

The cutter had yet to get into open water, but the young man already looked like he was suffering from motion sickness and wanted nothing more than to get out and plant his feet firmly on the ground.

"That all depends on the current, Constable, and the weight," Peters replied patiently. "With two more people aboard..." He made the universal gesture of *what can you expect?* and gripped his oar with both hands.

The second sailor took hold of his own oar, and they began to row, the cutter slicing through the muddy water as it glided towards the center of the river. The wind became gustier once they were on the open water, and the sailors had to mind the traffic, since there were a number of vessels on the river, ranging from rowboats to a massive man-of-war that was moving towards the open sea, its sails taut in the stiff breeze. It grew considerably colder when the cutter came alongside the ship, its hulking form blocking the sun and casting the cutter in deep shadow. Sebastian wrapped an arm about Gemma, and shot Forrest a narrow-eyed look when the constable's eyebrows lifted. If Constable Forrest shared his observations with the men, Sebastian would never hear the end of it.

The two sailors remained silent, rowing in perfect unison and at an impressive pace until they were in Limehouse Reach and the *Prince Regent* finally came into view. The term "packet boat" put one in mind of a weathered dinghy that ferried packages and bags of mail, but the *Prince Regent* was about two hundred feet in length and equipped with three fully rigged masts, a long, pointed bowsprit, and a reinforced hull. It was sleek and solid and sat low in the water, the upper deck bathed in summer sunshine since the sails were furled while the ship lay at anchor. These American clippers being able to cover two hundred miles a day meant that packet boats were now making the crossing faster and more frequently than at any time in history.

The name of the ship was proudly stenciled in gold letters, and Sebastian wondered why an American maritime line would name a vessel after the British monarchy. Perhaps it was out of respect for Her Majesty Queen Victoria, or maybe it was a veiled insult, given the fraught history between the two nations and the fact that the owners had named the vessel after the royal consort rather than after the sovereign herself, which would have been more fitting. Perhaps there already was a *Queen Victoria* in the company's fleet, but, if there was, Sebastian wasn't aware of it.

The hull of the *Prince Regent* towered above them like an unscalable mountain as the cutter drew alongside. Peters called out to someone aboard the ship, and a rope ladder was tossed over the side, two young faces peering down as the sailors waited for the first person to make their ascent. Gemma looked at Sebastian, her eyes wide with apprehension as she realized she would have to climb aboard unassisted. It was a long way up, and Gemma was hampered by a corset, crinolines, and wide skirts. She also didn't possess the upper body strength required to pull oneself up while holding on to a ladder that wasn't affixed to anything and flapped in the breeze, the bottom not quite reaching the cutter beneath.

"You first, Miss Tate," Peters said. "Here, give me your hand."

"I don't—"

"It's the only way to get aboard, miss. If you can't make the climb, we'll have to row you to shore and leave you to find your own way back."

Gemma gazed towards the shore, which had been taken over by the West India docks and was dotted with huge, windowless warehouses, shipbuilding yards, and seedy dockside taverns frequented by rough men. This was no place for an unaccompanied female, and, even if Gemma managed to get to a main road unmolested and found an empty hansom, it would take her hours to get home. Her panic was evident as she turned to Sebastian for reassurance.

"Don't worry. I will be right here to catch you if you fall," he promised.

The sailors chuckled, probably imagining Gemma hurtling down, her skirts lifting to expose her lower extremities. Thankfully, they didn't verbalize what they had to be thinking.

"One rung at a time, and don't look down," Sebastian said.

It would be difficult enough for an inexperienced man to climb up, but, with layers of fabric between Gemma's boot-clad feet and the rungs of the ladder, it would be even more of a challenge. She'd have to free her foot before placing it on the rung, otherwise she'd step on her skirts and possibly lose her balance. Gemma nodded, but the terror in her eyes reminded Sebastian of a condemned prisoner who was about to mount the scaffold.

She pushed her reticule into his hands, then grabbed hold of the sides of the ladder and lifted her foot to the lowest rung. The ladder shifted beneath her, and Gemma nearly lost her balance, but righted herself and held on until the ladder stopped shaking. She slowly brought her other foot onto the rung and hung there for a while, her arms straining beneath her cape as she clung on for dear life. Once she thought it safe, she lifted her right foot, maneuvered it until she'd worked the boot free of the fabric that cascaded down to the tips of her toes, and placed it firmly on the rung above.

"That's the way, Miss Tate," Peters called out encouragingly. He was clearly impatient to get aboard and wanted Gemma to go faster.

She ignored the man and went at her own pace, which was glacial since she took a break between each rung, but as long as she was heading up and not down it was still progress. Sebastian could see her arms quaver as her gloved hands gripped the sides of the ladder, and he prayed she wouldn't look down and lose her nerve. Gemma was halfway up and would get hurt if she let go now and plummeted into the boat. Even if he managed to break her fall, she would not get away unscathed, and neither would he.

Sebastian breathed a sigh of relief when the two sailors who waited on deck grabbed Gemma beneath the arms and hoisted her up and over the side. He waited for her to assure him she was all right, but he couldn't see or hear her and hoped she was simply taking a moment to catch her breath.

"Inspector," Peters said once Gemma was safely aboard.

Sebastian pushed Gemma's reticule into the waistband of his trousers to free his hands and took hold of the ladder. The hemp bit into his bare hands and irritated the skin, but, although Sebastian's gloves were in his pocket, he preferred to climb without them since it gave him a stronger grip. He focused all his energy on maintaining his balance and moved as quickly as he was able up the ladder. The sailors helped him over the side, but he shook them off and turned to look for Gemma, who stood off to the side, her cheeks pink with exertion and her eyes shining with relief and obvious pride.

"Are you all right?" Sebastian asked as soon as he approached Gemma and handed her the reticule.

Gemma nodded. "I can't quite believe I made it. My every muscle is groaning in protest," she admitted.

Sebastian could feel her pain. His arms and thighs still quivered with tension, and he nearly lost his balance as a naval cutter sailed past and the packet boat rocked from side to side in the vessel's wake. Sebastian had to spread his feet further apart to retain his stance.

"You did brilliantly well," he assured Gemma, who had grabbed onto the railing to steady herself.

"I don't think I can manage to get down," she admitted just as Constable Forrest's head crested the side, and then he was helped aboard and stood some distance away as he took a moment to regain his composure, which was clearly shaken.

"You won't have to," Sebastian hurried to assure her. "The *Prince Regent* will dock, and we will disembark with the rest of the passengers."

That seemed to put Gemma's mind at rest, and she looked around with obvious interest. Even though the ship was at anchor, there seemed to be quite a few people on deck, some crew members, others clearly passengers who must have come up for some fresh air. Sebastian couldn't spot anyone who might be a commanding officer, and turned to one of the crewmen who'd helped them aboard.

"I'd like to see the captain."

"Captain Grant is unavailable at present, sir. The first mate, Mr. Reynolds, is the one you need to speak to. If you're both ready, I'll take you down."

It seemed odd that the captain wouldn't be available to speak to Sebastian when he had been the one to summon the police, but perhaps he was occupied with some more immediate problem. Sebastian couldn't think of anything more pressing than murder though, especially as the ship lay at anchor. He took Gemma by the elbow and they moved forward, Constable Forrest walking slowly behind them as he tried to adjust to the rolling of the deck. It took several steps to become accustomed to the swaying motion, but then it got easier, and they were able to move a little faster.

Sebastian had never been aboard a ship and couldn't imagine what it must be like when the sea was rough and the deck heaved beneath one's feet as huge swells crashed against the hull. It had to be frightening, and maybe a little bit exhilarating, as long as one believed the ship could outrun the storm. There were no guarantees of safe passage, but, as Sebastian crossed the deck behind the swaggering sailor, he thought he'd like to cross the ocean one day and see America for himself.

The man led them towards the forecastle companionway. The bright afternoon light was quickly replaced by deep shadows as soon as they descended the steps and were ushered towards what had to be the front of the ship. The rolling was more pronounced belowdecks, and there was a woodsy smell that was tinged with damp and overlaid with something just this side of putrid. There were two doors at the end of the corridor, and the sailor knocked on the left one.

"Enter," a voice called from within.

The sailor pushed open the door and announced, "Inspector Bell of Scotland Yard and his companions, sir." He tipped his cap, turned on his heel, and left the way they'd come.

Sebastian entered the cabin, followed by Gemma and Constable Forrest, who held his tall hat beneath his arm lest it get knocked off by the low lintel. He remained close to the door since there was nowhere for him to go. The cabin was small and economically furnished, and it occurred to Sebastian that Mr. Reynolds did not usually receive visitors in what had to be his private space. But this wasn't a conversation to be conducted in public.

The first mate was seated behind a narrow desk strewn with papers but rose to his feet and nodded in welcome, doing his utmost not to betray his surprise when his gaze settled on Gemma. He was tall and broad, and looked imposing in his navy blue uniform. Reynolds had thick black hair that curled gently away from a high forehead, wide blue eyes, and strong white teeth that flashed bright against his tanned skin when he smiled in welcome.

"Inspector Bell of Scotland Yard, Constable Forrest, and Miss Tate," Sebastian announced. He sounded like a pompous butler announcing morning callers.

Mr. Reynolds held out his hand to Sebastian, but his gaze was still on Gemma, a grin tugging at the corners of his generous mouth.

"Miss Tate is an experienced nurse and will assist me during the course of the investigation," Sebastian added, and wondered why he felt the need to explain Gemma's presence.

Mr. Reynolds walked around the desk and stood before them. He was almost a head taller than Sebastian and towered over Gemma, who tipped her head to look at him from beneath the brim of her bonnet. Mr. Reynolds ignored Constable Forrest and held out his hand to Gemma, who had no choice but to take it. He sandwiched Gemma's hand inside both of his own and smiled into her eyes as if he'd been waiting for her all this time and she had finally come.

"My dear Miss Tate, welcome aboard the *Prince Regent*. If there's anything you need, anything at all, ask, and I will see that you get it."

This sounded oddly forward when said with an American accent and that intimate smile, and Sebastian could have sworn that Gemma blushed before glancing down at their still-joined hands.

"Thank you, Mr. Reynolds," she replied politely.

"It's Shep," Reynolds said. "That's what my friends call me. May I know your name?"

"Gemma."

"I believe that means jewel, does it not?" Shep Reynolds asked. "I couldn't think of a more fitting name for a woman whose eyes sparkle like emeralds."

"Mr. Reynolds," Sebastian interrupted, annoyed with the man's smarmy antics.

Shep Reynolds flashed Gemma a conspiratorial smile that was probably meant to unite them in their scorn for Sebastian's obvious displeasure, but Gemma gently pulled her hand away and drew her gaze away from the man, clearly relieved to no longer be the object of his undivided attention.

"My apologies, Inspector," he said. "I didn't mean to neglect you."

Sebastian ground his teeth in irritation but didn't want to give Reynolds the satisfaction of admitting he'd irked him. "Not at all," he replied. "If you would tell us what happened."

"Of course. But first, allow me to get Miss Tate a chair. A lady should never be left to stand." Shep Reynolds brought over his own chair and set it down. "Miss Tate, please."

Gemma had no choice but to sit. She had to crane her neck to look up at the men, but after the climb aboard she probably welcomed a few minutes of respite.

"This morning, around nine o'clock, Miss Thorpe entered stateroom two, ready to carry out her morning duties."

"Which include?" Sebastian asked.

"Tidying the cabin, making the bed, and collecting the dirty linen. I expect she was also going to finish packing since we were due to arrive this afternoon."

"Go on."

"Miss Thorpe happened upon the body of Anthony Blackstock and immediately went for help." Shep Reynolds cast an apologetic look at Gemma before continuing. "I'm afraid the victim was discovered in rather shocking circumstances."

"Was Lord Blackstock the only passenger in stateroom two?" Sebastian asked.

"No, he was traveling with his wife."

"Where is Lady Blackstock at present?"

"Lady Blackstock is missing, Inspector."

"Missing? How does one go missing on a ship?"

Shep Reynolds' lips quirked in a way that suggested Sebastian was a simpleton. "She's either hidden herself away or she's dead, like her husband."

"What was the cause of death, Mr. Reynolds?" Gemma asked.

"I'll leave you to be the judge, Miss Tate, since I have no medical expertise." Shep Reynolds turned back to Sebastian. "Once I confirmed that Lord Blackstock was beyond help, I locked the cabin, informed Captain Grant, and instructed the crew to drop anchor. That done, I dispatched a messenger to Scotland Yard. Since Lord Blackstock was a British national, Captain Grant thought the matter best handled by British authorities. I am entirely at your disposal for the duration of your investigation, Inspector. And, of course, yours, Miss Tate."

"How much do the other passengers know of what has happened?" Sebastian asked.

"All they know is that there's been an unnatural death. No one except Miss Thorpe is privy to the details, and she has been warned not to say anything for fear of inciting panic."

"Where is the captain?" Sebastian asked.

"Captain Grant is ill. He took to his bed two days ago, so I had to assume command."

"Is there a surgeon on board?" Gemma asked.

Mr. Reynolds' expression became pained. "Our surgeon, Mr. Humphries, did not arrive in time for departure. We had no option but to set sail without him."

"Is there anything I can do to help Captain Grant?" Gemma offered.

"It's kind of you to ask, Miss Tate, but I'm afraid there's nothing you can do for him. Captain Grant suffers from malaria. We don't have the necessary remedy on board since treatment is the province of Mr. Humphries. It's best you leave him to rest."

"Before I examine the body and speak to Miss Thorpe, I would like you to walk me through the specifics of your operation," Sebastian requested.

"How do you mean, Inspector?" Shep Reynolds asked. He seemed eager for Sebastian to leave the cabin, but before he got started Sebastian needed some basic information.

"How many people are on board? How are they distributed? Who has access to the cabins?"

"Ah, I see," Reynolds replied. He sucked in a quick breath and began reciting the details in a manner that seemed exceptionally well rehearsed. Perhaps this was a speech he gave often. "There are one hundred and fifty passengers and fifty crewmen, all of whom have sailed under Captain Grant's command before and, as far as I know, had not come in contact with any of the passengers before sailing. The passengers are divided among three sections: first class, second class, and steerage. There are eight staterooms in first class, and eight second-class cabins that can accommodate two passengers each. The steerage is a communal area with multi-level berths and separate mealtimes, since those in steerage are provided with only two meals instead of the three the others are served."

After a momentary pause, Reynolds continued. "The passengers from the different classes don't normally interact, unless, as was the case with the Blackstock servants, they come to first class to attend to their duties. The aft deck is reserved for first-class passengers, who are allowed to come up during the day if they wish to take the air. On this voyage, Captain Grant had also permitted three passengers from second class on deck, since they're traveling with a first-class passenger."

"Do any other first-class passengers have servants on board?" Sebastian asked.

"They do not."

"And were the Blackstocks traveling on their own?" Sebastian asked. "Aside from their servants? Any family members or friends?"

"No."

"And how many servants do they have?"

"There's just Miss Thorpe and Lady Blackstock's lady's maid, Miss Van Kemp. The women share a cabin in second class."

"That was kind of the Blackstocks," Gemma said approvingly.

"I don't think the decision was made with kindness in mind," Shep Reynolds replied.

"Why do you say that?"

"I don't think the Blackstocks cared to have their servants exposed to the passengers in steerage, who might carry diseases and generally don't bathe or change their garments for the duration of the voyage. I expect the choice was entirely selfish, with their own well-being in mind."

"I see," Gemma said, her mouth pressing into a thin line of disapproval.

Sebastian did not find it surprising that the Blackstocks had attempted to limit exposure to people they would see as no better than vermin. But there was something in what Mr. Reynolds had said that had surprised him.

"Did Lord Blackstock not have a valet?" he inquired.

"No."

"That's rather odd, isn't it?" Sebastian asked, addressing Gemma instead of Shep Reynolds.

"Yes, it is," Gemma agreed. "I would expect him to travel with at least one manservant. If not a valet, then someone to see to the luggage and transportation while abroad."

"And what about the first-class stewards?" Sebastian asked. "Did they assist him in any way?"

"There is Mr. Hendon and Mr. Sims. They see to meal service and the general cleanliness of the cabins, but they return to their quarters immediately after supper and do not set foot in first class until breakfast the following morning. I have already spoken to them both, and they didn't see or hear anything suspicious either yesterday or this morning."

"Does anyone else have access to the staterooms?" Sebastian inquired.

"There's Mr. Abrahms. His sole job is to empty the chamber pots."

"Did you speak to him as well?"

"Erm, no. I didn't think anything he had to say would be pertinent."

Sebastian didn't bother to ask why. He'd speak to the stewards himself and make sure to question Mr. Abrahms.

"Do you know the Blackstocks' home address, Mr. Reynolds?" Sebastian inquired.

"Blackstock Hall, Oxfordshire. Lord Blackstock mentioned it over a drink one evening."

"Did he mention any family? Any children?"

Reynolds looked thoughtful. "I believe the Blackstocks were recently married and had no children, but don't quote me on that."

"And Lady Blackstock? Do you know anything about her background?"

"It never came up."

"What is she like?" Gemma asked. She resolutely used the present tense, clearly refusing to believe Lady Blackstock was also dead.

"Beautiful. Self-effacing," Reynolds said, and something in his face softened.

"Were they happy?" Gemma asked.

"I don't think I'm best placed to offer an opinion on their union, Miss Tate."

"Who is?" Sebastian asked.

"The servants, I suppose. I doubt the other passengers know the truth of the Blackstocks' marriage."

"Has anyone shown animosity toward Lord and Lady Blackstock?" Sebastian asked. "Any disagreements or arguments while on board?"

"Not that I'm aware of, but I don't spend much time in first class. I have no call to come downstairs until it's time for me to snatch a few hours of sleep before returning to my duties, Inspector. But given the damage inflicted on the victim, I would have to say that someone must have felt a burning hatred toward the man."

"Damage?" Gemma echoed.

Reynolds nodded slowly and averted his gaze. "Perhaps it's best if Inspector Bell goes in first."

Gemma looked all set to argue, but Sebastian forestalled her by saying, "I will examine the scene in due time, Mr. Reynolds. But first, I'd like to know if you have searched the vessel for Lady Blackstock."

"We did, Inspector, to the best of our ability."

"What do you mean, *to the best of your ability?*" Sebastian challenged.

"Exactly that. The hold is fully loaded. There's freight, an enclosure for the animals, as well as foodstuffs and water stores. There are the crew's quarters as well as a storage space for canvas, lumber, tools, and barrels of tar should the ship require urgent repairs. If Lady Blackstock managed to squeeze herself between two crates or burrowed into a haystack meant for the goats in the hope of remaining hidden until we dock, she would be rather difficult to locate. There is, of course, another, much grimmer possibility."

"You think Lady Blackstock is no longer on board," Sebastian concluded.

Reynolds nodded. "The night watch heard a loud splash off the port side just after midnight. They tried to see what it was, but there was thick cloud cover last night, and we were still in the estuary. They couldn't say with any certainty that it was a person, but, as they didn't hear any cries for help or see anyone struggling to keep their head above water, if it was a human being then it was one who was already dead."

"Would the port side be closest to shore?" Sebastian asked.

"No. That would be the starboard when sailing towards London."

Sebastian hated to praise the man—he was full of himself as it was—but he had to admit that Reynolds had acted precisely as he himself would have done in the circumstances. Had the ship continued to London and docked, the culprit would have had no difficulty getting off and melting into the crowds in the pandemonium that reigned at the docks. With cargo being loaded and offloaded, animals led on and off the vessels, stores replenished, and passengers and their servants boarding and disembarking with their luggage, the killer could walk off the ship and wave a bloodied axe above their head, and no one would take any notice.

As long as the *Prince Regent* remained at anchor, the killer was trapped aboard, unless they had been the one to jump overboard and had attempted to swim to freedom. Their chances of getting to shore on an overcast night though, and while the ship was still in the estuary, were slim to none, in Sebastian's estimation. The killer had probably realized that as well and was even now biding their time until the *Prince Regent* was cleared to dock.

"Is anyone besides Lady Blackstock missing?" Sebastian asked.

"Not that I'm aware of," Reynolds replied.

"When was the last time the Blackstocks were seen?" Gemma asked.

"They took supper with the rest of the first-class passengers yesterday evening. Lady Blackstock retired around nine o'clock. Lord Blackstock enjoyed a drink with several fellow passengers and returned to his cabin around eleven. According to the stewards, everyone was in high spirits during supper and eager to arrive in London."

"How many passengers are in first class?" Sebastian asked.

"Nine. Well, seven now, I suppose," Reynolds replied morosely.

"What can you tell us about them?"

"Mr. and Mrs. Caldwell are American. From South Carolina. Mr. Caldwell's father is Truman Caldwell of Caldwell Steel." Mr. Reynolds paused, as if trying to recall the names of the other passengers, then went on. "Mr. and Mrs. Glenn are also American, from Vermont. They're older, late fifties perhaps. Mr. Glenn claims to be a well-known poet. Can't say I ever heard of him myself."

"Who are the other three?" Sebastian asked.

"Mr. and Mrs. Ringwood are British. They are returning home after a year spent abroad. Very pleasant young couple," Mr. Reynolds opined. "And the last is Miss Hobson. She is a violinist, and she's traveling with the Bennett String Quartet. The remaining members of the quartet are in second class."

"Why?"

"I expect they couldn't afford three first-class staterooms,"

Mr. Reynolds replied with a shrug. "And since there's only one woman, they decided she should travel in comfort."

"I will need to speak to all the first-class passengers. And I would like my constable to carry out his own search of the ship. Can you spare someone to accompany him, Mr. Reynolds?"

"Of course. Petty Officer Maitland will take you around, Constable. And I will assist you in any way I can, Inspector. And Miss Tate." Reynolds beamed at Gemma. "If you would like to rest, my cabin is at your disposal for as long as you require."

"Miss Tate and I will begin by examining the Blackstocks' stateroom," Sebastian announced. "Then I will have a clearer understanding of what we're dealing with."

"What we're dealing with is murder, Inspector Bell," Mr. Reynolds said, his expression grim. "In all my years in the merchant marine, I have never seen anything so horrific."

"Thank you, Mr. Reynolds," Sebastian said. "Now, if you would unlock stateroom two."

"Of course. Please follow me."

Constable Forrest and Gemma were the first ones through the door, followed by Shep Reynolds. Just as Sebastian was about to follow, he spotted a folded newspaper on the first mate's desk. The *New York Herald*. The paper was dated March fifteenth, more than two months out of date. Sebastian didn't think Reynolds would miss an old newspaper, and he was curious to peruse the articles and learn something of life in New York, so he reached for the paper, folded it, and stuffed it into the pocket of his coat, to be examined at a later date.

THREE

They didn't have far to go to reach first class. The staterooms were just beyond the short corridor that culminated in the captain's and first mate's cabins. The communal space in between was bisected by a long table and served as a dining hall for the passengers, but at the moment it was empty, first class deserted. Stateroom two was the second door on the left, with three more staterooms on that side and four staterooms opposite. Gemma heard sounds coming from within, but all the doors remained firmly shut. Once Constable Forrest was dispatched to find Petty Officer Maitland, who'd take him down to the hold, Mr. Reynolds extracted a key from his pocket and unlocked the door but did not open it. He stepped aside, held the key out to Sebastian, and gestured towards the door, inviting him to enter.

Gemma stood next to Sebastian. She wouldn't admit as much to Shep Reynolds, but she was nervous and needed a few moments to prepare for whatever horror awaited them inside. She had seen her share of wounded men and mangled corpses during her time in Crimea, but she had quickly learned to concentrate on what she could do for the wounded men and not how much damage had been inflicted on their bodies. And when some of her patients had died, she had viewed them only as lost young men whose lives had been cut short by a senseless war—and whose injuries might have had a chance to heal had they received timely medical assistance or had not been operated on in a filthy, inadequately lit room by surgeons who had been so exhausted, they had barely been able see straight, much less hold a scalpel.

But what she was about to encounter in stateroom two would be vastly different. Gemma had seen the horror and incomprehension in Shep Reynolds' eyes and had sensed his relief when he had handed responsibility over to Sebastian. She didn't get the impression that Reynolds scared easily. Transatlantic travel was not for the faint of heart, and he must have crossed the ocean more times than he could count, but he had been shocked by what he had seen and had described the scene as nightmarish. Surely it took much to shock such a man.

"Shall we?" Sebastian asked as he placed his hand on the knob, and Gemma nodded, as ready as she would ever be to get the gruesome task over with.

Sebastian unlocked the room, turned the knob, and pushed open the door. The first thing Gemma became aware of was the odor. She knew that smell well, and it brought her right back to Scutari, where the wards and corridors had reeked of blood, all manner of human secretions, and death. She moved a little further into the stateroom. The reek of urine here was overlaid with the tang of blood and the sharp smell of sweat, but death had already set about its work, and there was also a putrid whiff of the decay that set in as soon as the heart stopped beating.

There was no window, but someone had left an oil lamp burning, and the halo cast the tableau in a wavering light. The cabin was not what Gemma would have expected of first-class accommodation, but she supposed it was quite luxurious compared to the cheaper quarters, which were reserved for single travelers, servants, and immigrants. She supposed some of the passengers in steerage were returning home, having either made their money in America or grown too homesick to remain in a foreign land.

The stateroom was sparsely furnished. The bed had a plain

wooden headboard and footboard, the washstand appeared to be bolted to the floor, and a tall cupboard was fitted into the corner. There was also a tiny desk, one chair, and a traveling trunk at the foot of the bed. Gemma absently noted the items in the room, but her attention was fixed on the bed. She must have let out an involuntary gasp because Shep Reynolds was instantly at her side, offering to take her on deck for a breath of air in a tone so solicitous it made her angry. She didn't care to be patronized, nor was she about to faint.

"I'm quite all right, but thank you for your concern, Mr. Reynolds," she snapped, and noticed Sebastian's mouth twitch.

"I left him as he was," the first mate said apologetically. "I had no way of knowing a lady would be present."

"I've seen worse," Gemma said, and moved towards the bed.

She felt grateful to Sebastian for not trying to shield her from the gruesome sight. Instead, he turned to face Shep Reynolds. "That will be all, Mr. Reynolds. I'll find you if I have need of you."

Thus dismissed, Reynolds bowed stiffly to Gemma and departed. Gemma thought he was relieved to be spared another examination of the scene and could probably do with some fresh air himself. Once Reynolds was gone, she returned her attention to the bed. The victim was naked, his skin a sickly shade of gray in the lamplight and completely at odds with the stiff, purplish male member that pointed straight up like a mast. Lord Blackstock's chest, arms, and legs were covered with crisp black hair, the hair on his chest matted with dried blood where three letters were carved into his chest. *PIG*.

The victim's facial features were almost entirely obscured by a metal contraption that encircled his head, with openings for the eyes and the mouth between the vertical bars. Horizontal strips of metal pressed against the man's forehead and encircled his neck, and a short metal pole extended from the top of the cage, but its purpose wasn't evident. Wide blue eyes stared through the round eye openings, the man's expression one of absolute horror.

"What the...?" Sebastian didn't finish the sentence out of respect for Gemma, but she had a fairly good idea what he had been about to say.

It took much to rattle Sebastian, but he was clearly as appalled as she was. He carefully turned the man's head to the side to reveal a lock at the back of the cage. There was a small keyhole but no key. Gemma stared at the mask, her breath coming in short gasps as she imagined how it would feel to get locked into the iron contraption. She had to turn away, afraid she would be sick if she allowed herself to give in to the feelings of suffocating dread.

Who would make such an object, and why? The cage had to be a torture device, but why would someone bring it aboard or lock it around the victim's head? And what had happened to Lady Blackstock? The sheets on the empty side of the bed were rumpled, an indentation of the woman's head still visible on her pillow. Had someone murdered her husband, then spirited her away in the middle of the night? Had they killed her as well and thrown her body overboard to conceal their crime? Then why leave Lord Blackstock here, like this? And what exactly did the message mean to convey? The immediate answer was obvious. Most people thought of a pig as the lowest of the low, an animal that wallowed in its own waste and indiscriminately ate whatever it could find.

There were plenty of individuals who referred to policemen as pigs, believing the men to be sellouts and tools of a government that did nothing but oppress them. But since Lord Blackstock was not affiliated with the police service, that probably wasn't relevant. Whoever had scored their message into Lord Blackstock's chest had clearly meant to imply that he was no better than filth and deserved to be treated as such. The gore had crusted at the edges, but the deep wounds were still moist on the inside, the blood dark and glistening like freshly sliced liver. Another, stronger wave of nausea assaulted Gemma, and she lifted her hand to her nose and shut her eyes to block out the grisly sight.

"Perhaps you should take Mr. Reynolds up on his offer of a breath of air," Sebastian suggested gently when Gemma leaned against the door to steady herself. "I'll have a closer look on my own."

Gemma opened her eyes, but avoided looking at the victim and fixed her gaze on Sebastian, who was looking at her with concern. "I just need a moment. I wasn't expecting..."

Sebastian crossed the cabin in two strides and pulled her into his arms. He held her close, his nearness and the faint aroma of his spicy cologne helping to dispel the awful stench that had settled in Gemma's nostrils. She breathed in his familiar scent, then gently pushed him away.

"I'm all right. Let's focus on the task at hand."

"Are you sure you don't require smelling salts, Miss Tate?" Sebastian asked, mimicking Shep Reynolds and making Gemma smile despite the unspeakable awfulness of the scene.

"Why? Do you have any?" she asked.

Sebastian shook his head. "If you pass out, I'll have to give you mouth to mouth," he replied cheekily.

Just as the nurses at Scutari had sometimes resorted to gallows humor at the most inappropriate moments, so, Gemma had learned, did policemen. It was a way to distance themselves from the horror and remember that they were still living, breathing men able to make jokes, banter with their colleagues, and flirt with the ladies.

Gemma took a deep breath, steeled herself, and turned her attention to the victim once more. There was much one could learn from a corpse, and this body had its own story to tell. Gemma peered at the man's head and tried to look past the iron bars to see what she could make out. Having drawn her conclusions, she moved downwards, with the intention of examining every inch of the victim's flesh. Sebastian left her to it and focused on his own investigation, the two of them working in silence like partners of long standing, which they were quickly becoming. The thought heartened her, and Gemma felt something loosen in her chest as she went about her examination, an unflappable professional once more.

FOUR

While Gemma focused on the body, Sebastian set to searching the room. He hoped to locate the key to the cage and the implement that had been used to carve the letters into the man's chest, but didn't find either object on the bed or on the floor beneath. He did identify the source of the sharp smell. Someone had knocked over the chamber pot and spilled its contents, which had completely dried.

Having finished with the bed, Sebastian checked inside the cupboard and the trunk but didn't notice anything out of the ordinary. The trunk was full of clothes, which were of excellent quality and appropriate for different seasons and occasions. There was a hat box, and several pairs of shoes stood lined up against the wall. The cupboard had two shelves and a deep drawer. On the top shelf were a silver-backed mirror and hairbrush, and a bar of soap. The shelf below held two towels. The drawer held Lady Blackstock's unmentionables and her corset, which she must have taken off while changing for bed. Two hooks were nailed to the wall and had been used to hang the Blackstocks' outerwear and Lady Blackstock's bonnet, which hung suspended by the ribbons. Lord Blackstock's silk top hat sat atop the cupboard. Sebastian did not find a razor or any other toiletries that would belong to a man.

The surface of the desk was devoid of writing implements, but Sebastian was more interested in the two drawers. When he opened the top drawer, he finally found what he had been looking for. Lord Blackstock's leather billfold was stuffed with notes and lay next to a red Oriental lacquer box that contained a solid-gold pocket watch, a ruby and diamond tiepin, and two sets of gold cufflinks. In the drawer below was Lady Blackstock's jewelry box, a beautiful piece made of inlaid walnut that held several exquisite and clearly valuable items. Sebastian lifted out a blue velvet box that contained a three-strand pearl choker with a diamond clasp. The remaining compartments were devoted to two pairs of earrings, three rings, and an enamel brooch studded with emeralds and a light purple stone that could have been amethyst.

"I can safely say that robbery wasn't the motive," Sebastian said as he closed the jewelry box and set it on the desk, then stacked Lord Blackstock's belongings on top. He would ask Reynolds to hold on to the items until the ship docked and the valuables could be returned to the Blackstock family. Even if the Blackstocks didn't have any children, there had to be someone—parents, siblings, or maybe children from a previous marriage.

"What are your thoughts?" he asked when Gemma didn't reply.

"I think Lord Blackstock was asphyxiated."

Sebastian returned to the bed, where Gemma stood holding a pillow in her hands. There was flaky brown residue on the pillowcase that matched the rust on the bands and corresponded to the shape of the iron cage.

"Someone held the pillow over the victim's face until he suffocated. And the nasal bone appears to have been crushed."

"It could have been Lady Blackstock," Sebastian ventured.

"Why would you say that?" Gemma exclaimed, clearly shocked by the suggestion.

"There's no evidence of forced entry, nothing of value appears to have been taken, and the lady is missing."

"She might be a second victim."

"Possibly, or she may be our killer."

"So, where is she, then?" Gemma demanded.

"She may have gone into hiding or jumped overboard when she realized she'd hang for the murder of her husband."

"Or both Blackstocks were murdered, and Lady Blackstock's body was thrown overboard," Gemma argued.

"Why dispose of only her?" Sebastian asked.

"For one, Lord Blackstock would be too difficult to move. For another, Lady Blackstock's disappearance throws suspicion on her and diverts attention from the real killer."

"That is indeed a possibility, but if they were both murdered, what did the killer have to gain by their deaths?"

"I think the killer wanted to send a message, at least in the case of Lord Blackstock," Gemma replied.

Sebastian nodded. "The cage and the carving on his chest speak for themselves, but perhaps there's more to this message than we realize, particularly when we take Lady Blackstock's disappearance into account."

"What is this contraption, and where did it come from?" Gemma asked, not bothering to hide her revulsion.

"I don't know, but the killer could have simply smothered Lord Blackstock in order to kill him. To leave the man naked, mutilated, and wearing that horrible mask speaks to burning anger and a desire to humiliate the victim, even in death."

Gemma nodded in agreement. "The wounds are deep, so the killer applied considerable force when scoring the letters into the chest."

"Was he still alive, do you think?" Sebastian asked as he studied the blood on the victim's chest and the bedlinens beneath.

"If he was—and given the amount of blood, that's a distinct possibility—Lord Blackstock had to be unconscious, or everyone would have heard his screams."

"*Could* he have been murdered by a woman?" Sebastian asked, his mind still on Lady Blackstock.

"Yes, I think so," Gemma said.

"What is your best guess as to the sequence of events?" Sebastian inquired as he looked around the cabin, which was too orderly to make him think there had been a physical altercation.

"Given the traces of rust on the pillowcase, the only thing I can say for certain is that the cage was already in place when the victim was suffocated."

"He doesn't appear to have struggled."

"Perhaps he was drugged," Gemma suggested.

"I didn't find any opiates, but the killer could have taken the bottle away, as they took whatever they had used to slice the flesh."

"I expect both are now at the bottom of the sea," Gemma replied.

"You're probably right, unless the killer assumed that the ship would continue on to London and they had nothing to fear."

"Whoever killed Lord Blackstock probably imagined they'd be long gone by the time an investigation was launched," Gemma allowed.

"How long would you say he's been dead?"

"Longer than six hours, since rigor has fully set in. The postmortem will tell us more, and it's imperative that we remove the mask."

"Why?"

"I think there might be something in his mouth, but I can't be sure. The opening is not wide enough to push my fingers through."

"We'll deliver the body to Colin as soon as we disembark, but I cannot give Reynolds leave to dock until we know more of what happened."

"How do you wish to proceed?" Gemma asked. She pulled the coverlet over the body, offering the dead man a belated measure of dignity.

"I think you should be the one to speak to Miss Thorpe," Sebastian mused. "She might find it easier to confide in a woman. I will interview the other first-class passengers and see what I can learn about the Blackstocks."

Gemma nodded. "I will ask Mr. Reynolds to introduce me to Miss Thorpe."

Sebastian didn't like the idea of leaving Gemma alone with the glib Mr. Reynolds, but he could hardly object based on his personal dislike of the man. Gemma would resent the insinuation that she couldn't look after herself, and there was no reason to think Reynolds would behave in a way unbecoming of a gentleman, even if he was clearly interested in Gemma.

"All right. Let's reconvene in about an hour," Sebastian said, and opened the door, finally allowing in some much-needed fresh air.

Gemma stepped outside, and Sebastian shut the door behind them, turning the key and pocketing it so no one could interfere with the crime scene.

FIVE

Mr. Reynolds was on the bridge, engaged in a discussion with the man at the wheel, but a fair-haired man in uniform approached Sebastian and Gemma and nodded stiffly.

"Inspector Bell, Miss Tate. Jim Brock, second mate. If I can be of assistance?"

"It's nice to meet you, Mr. Brock," Gemma said.

"The pleasure is all mine, ma'am," Mr. Brock replied smoothly.

"Have you seen Constable Forrest?" Sebastian asked.

"He's in the hold. He will be a good while if he means to conduct a thorough search."

"I would like to speak to Miss Thorpe, please," Gemma informed him.

"Of course. I can bring her to you."

"I would rather speak to her in her cabin, if I may."

Mr. Brock nodded. "Very well. I'll take you down. Inspector Bell?"

"I need to speak with the first-class passengers, but first I'd like a word with the stewards and Mr. Abrahms. In private."

Mr. Brock nodded and called out to a passing sailor.

"Mr. Jarome, get Hendon, Sims, and Abrahms and bring them to first class."

"Right away," the sailor replied, and strode off.

Sebastian gave Gemma a searching look, and she smiled up at him. "I'll see you later. I'll be fine."

"Shall we, Miss Tate?" Mr. Brock invited as soon as Sebastian returned downstairs to interview the stewards.

Gemma turned towards the stairway they had just ascended, but Mr. Brock forestalled her. "We'll take the stairs by the main hatch. There's no way to access second class from first-class accommodation."

Gemma followed Mr. Brock towards the hatch, then down the narrow stairs. If first class was somewhat spartan, second class was just a row of narrow cupboards in a passage adjacent to steerage. The space was dim, and dank air wafted through the low doorway, the odors of sweat, urine, and damp seeping into the corridor. Gemma caught a glimpse of narrow, multistoried berths that resembled a honeycomb. The berths were occupied mostly by men, who were in various stages of repose and whose bedding looked soiled and wrinkled. The women, who were mostly young and many with children to look after, congregated at the center, all industriously occupied with minding their bored, fractious offspring, washing clothes in shallow basins, mending, and darning socks. There was no time for them to rest, not even on a transatlantic voyage.

The overcrowding and low thrum of conversation further reminded Gemma of a beehive, but there was no lovely scent of honey or the soothing buzzing of bees. This beehive was a slum that would clear once the ship docked, and then a new batch of travelers would claim their berths, most likely without the benefit of fresh bedding or a good airing out.

Mr. Brock led Gemma to one of the cabins, knocked on the slatted door, then yanked it open without waiting for a response. The cabin contained two berths separated by a space barely wide enough to traverse sideways. There were two hooks near the door, one on each side, where the women could hang their clothes, and their cases were stowed beneath the foot-ends of the berths, which didn't look long enough to allow the passengers to straighten their legs while lying down. One woman was asleep. She was curled into a ball beneath the drab blanket, her braided white-blond hair the only visible attribute since she faced the wall and had pressed her face into the pillow. The second occupant was awake. She sat with her back to the wall and her knees pulled up to her chest, her stockinged feet peeking from beneath the hem of her skirts. She started when the door opened but seemed to relax when she recognized Mr. Brock.

"Miss Thorpe, forgive the intrusion," Mr. Brock said, sounding anything but apologetic. "This is Miss Tate. She is here with the inspector from Scotland Yard and would like a word."

Miss Thorpe nodded, then swung her legs over the side and pushed her feet into well-worn leather shoes. She was about twenty and had light brown hair and soft brown eyes fringed with long lashes. Her nose was a bit long and her lips too thin, but overall she had a pleasant, open face. Her complexion was sallow, but if she had been confined to this tiny cabin for two weeks she was probably in desperate need of fresh air and sunlight. When she stood, Gemma noted that Miss Thorpe was quite tall for a woman and very thin.

"Is there somewhere more private where we can talk?" Gemma asked. She could hardly question Miss Thorpe inside the cabin, with her cabinmate mere inches away, but to speak to her in the communal area where everyone could overhear wouldn't do either.

Miss Thorpe shook her head. "If it's privacy you want, Miss Tate, you won't find it here."

"Perhaps we can take a walk on deck?" Gemma suggested.

"Only first-class passengers are permitted on the upper deck," Miss Thorpe said.

"These are extenuating circumstances, I'm sure no one will mind," Mr. Brock said from the doorway.

Miss Thorpe nodded and followed Gemma down the corridor and up the stairs. Mr. Brock walked behind them but excused himself as soon as they reached the deck. Gemma looked around, then pointed to a relatively private spot in the stern. From her vantage point, she could see several passengers on the aft deck, but there was no sign of Sebastian. Miss Thorpe gripped the railing and turned her face up to the sky. She drew in a long breath, then another. After the stultifying fug below, the air smelled fresh and sweet, and the tang of brine was refreshing. Miss Thorpe's hair looked dark blond in the sunlight, and when she turned to face Gemma there were golden flecks in her eyes that Gemma hadn't noticed inside the dim cabin.

"Thank you for this," Miss Thorpe said. "I've barely seen the light of day since boarding in New York."

"It's not me you have to thank."

"Mr. Brock wouldn't have allowed it if you weren't there," Miss Thorpe replied flatly. She seemed to accept the limitations of her position and appeared too tired to chafe against them.

Gemma couldn't help but wonder how this timid woman must have reacted when she came upon the nude, mutilated corpse of her employer.

"How long have you worked for the Blackstocks, Miss Thorpe?" Gemma asked once the maidservant seemed ready to answer her questions.

"It's Lorna," Miss Thorpe said. "And almost six months. I started a few weeks before we left for New York."

"Were you forewarned when you were offered the position that you would be leaving the country?"

"No, I wasn't, but I didn't mind. I've always wanted to travel. And I knew the Blackstocks meant to come back."

"What were they like, Lord Blackstock and his lady?"

Lorna's expression became pained, and Gemma realized she had asked a difficult and clearly unwelcome question. It wasn't surprising; few servants cared to speak frankly about their employers. Their honesty could come back to haunt them, even if their employers were dead and past caring. Lorna sighed and gazed out over the water.

"Lady Blackstock is kind, or as kind as a woman in her position can afford to be. Lord Blackstock is... was handsome, intelligent, and charming when it suited him."

"And when it didn't?"

Lorna shrugged. "He could be short-tempered and impatient."

"You were the one to find him this morning."

Lorna nodded. "It was horrible. The most awful thing I have ever seen."

"Did you expect the cabin to be empty?" Gemma inquired.

"In first class, breakfast is served at eight, and then the passengers go up on deck for their morning constitutionals around nine," Lorna said, her nose wrinkling with disdain. "In other words, they leave their cabins so that the servants and stewards can take out their night soil, make the beds, and put away the clothes they'd worn the day before."

"Did you normally see to your morning duties by yourself?"

"Greta Van Kemp—my cabinmate—is Lady Blackstock's lady's maid, but she didn't come with me this morning."

"Why not? Does she not help Lady Blackstock dress for the day and arrange her hair?" Gemma inquired.

"Normally, yes, but Greta took to her bed yesterday. I offered to see to Lady Blackstock until Greta felt well enough to resume her duties, but her ladyship said that wasn't necessary and she would dress herself."

"Is Miss Van Kemp ill?"

"She said her stomach hurt and she was bilious. I thought it was seasickness, since the sea was rather rough yesterday, but today the water is calm."

"How long has Miss Van Kemp been Lady Blackstock's lady's maid?"

"She started a week before we sailed for London. Miss Hewson, the previous lady's maid, ran off with his lordship's valet a month ago. They left without giving notice or collecting their wages."

"Do you know why?" Gemma asked, scandalized by the audacity of the couple.

"They wanted to remain in America. If they had come back to England and then returned under their own steam, they would have spent all their wages on their passage anyhow."

"Was his lordship angry?"

"Of course he was, mostly because he wasn't able to find a new valet before we sailed. It was sheer luck that her ladyship took to Miss Van Kemp, or I would have had to see to her myself on top of my other duties."

"So, who was looking after Lord Blackstock during the voyage?"

"Mr. Sims and Mr. Hendon polished his shoes and helped him to shave, but otherwise his lordship was forced to fend for himself."

"Do you know what became of his lordship's razor? It is missing from the room."

Lorna shook her head. "It was there yesterday, when I tidied the stateroom after breakfast. Maybe one of the stewards took it away, to sharpen it."

"Lorna, did you ever see the cage Lord Blackstock was wearing on his head before today?"

Lorna nodded. "I saw him showing it off to Lord Lyons. The Blackstocks were guests of the British envoy while we were in Washington," she explained.

"Did Lord Blackstock bring the mask with him from England?"

"No," Lorna said with a shake of her head. "He found it in some antique shop in Alexandria and couldn't believe his luck. He said it was called a scold's bridle and had been used in centuries past to punish women who spoke out of turn or nagged their husbands. The proprietor told him the mask was from the seventeenth century and had originally come from Jamestown Colony, so it was one of the earliest examples of colonial governance. Lord Blackstock joked that he would use it on Lady Blackstock once they got home because she was prone to nagging."

"*Was* it a joke?" Gemma asked.

"His lordship was fond of history and liked to collect rare artifacts," Lorna said, but Gemma noticed that she hadn't actually answered the question.

"Was Lord Blackstock ever cruel to his wife?" Gemma pressed, determined to get an answer.

"He doted on her. Lady Blackstock said it was a love match, and his lordship had sacrificed quite a lot for her."

"What had he sacrificed?"

Lorna shook her head. "I really don't know. She never said."

"Did she love him as well?"

"Her ladyship was devoted to her husband's well-being and comfort. She had a way with him and always knew how to quiet him when he was in ill temper."

"Did Lord Blackstock frequently lose his temper?" Gemma asked.

"Sometimes, but his anger didn't last long, and then he'd carry on as if nothing had happened."

"Did Lord Blackstock ever lose his temper with you?"

Lorna nodded but didn't elaborate. "He did do one nice thing for me, though," she offered, as if she suddenly felt the need to defend her temperamental employer.

"Oh?"

"His lordship permitted me to borrow books from the library. I like to read," Lorna explained.

"That was kind of him."

"He had great respect for learning and said that every person, no matter how lowly, should try to better themselves in whatever way they could."

"I can't say I disagree," Gemma said. "Lorna, who do you think murdered Lord Blackstock?"

Lorna recoiled, the question clearly taking her by surprise and frightening her out of her wits. "I don't know, Miss Tate, and I don't think I should speculate. After all, whoever did it must still be aboard, mustn't they?"

"What about Lady Blackstock? Where do you think she is?"

The maidservant's eyes brimmed with tears. "I don't know,"

she whispered. "But she must be dead, or she'd be here. I'm almost glad she isn't. It'd break her heart if she saw his lordship like that."

"Did the Blackstocks keep any medicines in their stateroom?" Gemma asked, changing tack again.

"What sort of medicines?" Lorna gaped at her.

"Anything that might contain laudanum. Or morphine."

"Oh, no," Lorna exclaimed, clearly shocked by the very suggestion. "Lord Blackstock was a great one for natural health. He never allowed anything of that sort in the house, not even a health tonic or foreign wines, like that port wine or madeira. The only thing he permitted was whisky. He called it the elixir of life."

"What about Lady Blackstock? Did she take anything, perhaps without her husband's knowledge?"

"Not that I ever saw. You should ask Greta. She might know."

"Lorna, if Lady Blackstock had witnessed her husband's murder and had been overcome with grief, might she have taken her own life?"

Lorna sniffled and shook her head. "I wouldn't have said so, but what do I know of someone's mind, Miss Tate? I barely know my own these days."

"What will you do now?" Gemma had sympathy for the woman's plight.

"What can I do? I'll look for a new position, but once news of what happened gets out no one will want to take me on. Some think tragedy is contagious, and maybe it is. After this, I'll be untouchable."

"I don't think that's true," Gemma said.

"And how would you know?" Lorna demanded sharply. "Have you ever been tainted by murder?"

"Yes, I have."

"Can you honestly tell me it hasn't changed your life and how you see your future?"

Gemma considered the question. Lorna was right. Gemma's life had not been the same since Victor's tragic death; but, although she'd give anything to have spared her brother such a horrific end, she also knew that if it wasn't for Victor's death she would never have met Sebastian or Colin and would probably still be taking care of Mrs. Gadd, her life as small and dull as if she were a bedbound invalid herself.

"Few people's lives are devoid of tragedy, but it's what you do after that counts. If you believe yourself to be tainted, others will think so too. What happened to your employers was not your fault, nor does it reflect on your character."

Lorna shot her an irritated look but didn't bother to argue. "Are we done here, Miss Tate?"

"We are."

Lorna nodded and walked away, disappearing into the shadowy stairwell. A few moments later, Gemma followed. She needed to speak to Miss Van Kemp, and if the woman was still asleep Gemma would have no choice but to wake her.

SIX

Sebastian returned to the communal area, and a few minutes later three sailors descended the narrow stairs. He had no difficulty guessing which one was Abrahms and why he had been charged with taking out the chamber pots. He was a frightened-looking black youth of about sixteen and hung well behind the two white sailors, who looked impatient and self-assured.

"Mr. Abrahms, if you would wait on deck a moment," Sebastian said. The poor lad looked like he was going to soil himself at the sound of his name but nodded and scurried back up the stairs.

Sebastian gestured to the chairs opposite. "Sit down, lads."

The sailors took a seat. They were both in their early twenties, tall, fit, and blandly handsome. Sebastian thought they had probably been chosen for their looks, much like the footmen who served at table at wealthy houses. First class might not be luxurious, but it was the best the *Prince Regent* had to offer, and it was helpful to have attractive, non-provoking stewards to attend the passengers and make them feel looked after.

"I expect you've heard what happened," Sebastian said.

Both men nodded in unison.

"Shocking," the fair one said.

"What is your name?"

"Hendon, sir."

"Did either of you see or hear anything during supper or afterwards last night?" Sebastian asked. "An argument, a threat, a physical altercation?"

Sims and Hendon shook their heads.

"Everyone was civil, but it was obvious they couldn't wait to see the back of each other," Sims said.

"But that's nothing unusual," Hendon chimed in. "Just how it is after two weeks aboard. People want to get where they're going. It's nothing personal."

"Was there anything personal in the passengers' interactions with each other during the voyage?"

Both sailors shook their heads.

"Nothing that stood out," Hendon said. "They were aloof at first, but then they got to talking, as people do when they're stuck together for hours on end."

"Can you tell me about Lord Blackstock? What was he like?"

"Pompous, entitled, a typical British aristocrat who thinks he's the next best thing to royalty. No offense, Inspector," Sims said when he must have recalled that Sebastian was British.

"None taken. And Lady Blackstock?"

"A real looker," Sims said with a fond smile. "But quiet as a mouse."

"I think she was unwell." Hendon gave Sebastian a meaningful look. "Could be seasickness, or she might have been in the family way."

"You think she's dead?" Sebastian asked when Hendon spoke of Lady Blackstock in the past tense.

He nodded. "We know every inch of this boat, and she's nowhere to be found."

"Can you think of anyone who held a grudge against either of them?" Sebastian asked desperately.

Sims shrugged, but Hendon looked uncomfortable, his gaze sliding away from Sebastian in a way that suggested he was conflicted about revealing what he knew.

"Mr. Hendon, a man was brutally murdered. If you know something..."

Hendon sighed. "I don't want to point fingers, Inspector, but two days ago Miss Thorpe lost her footing while carrying a basin of water and accidentally spilled a bit on Lord Blackstock's sleeve. She caught herself and immediately apologized."

"How did Lord Blackstock react?" Sebastian asked.

"He slapped her, hard, and called her a careless slut."

"Strong words. What did Miss Thorpe do?"

"She mumbled another apology and hurried off. I think she wanted to put as much distance as she could between herself and her employer."

"And do you think Miss Thorpe could be responsible for Lord Blackstock's death?" Sebastian had yet to meet the woman, but he was curious if Mr. Hendon thought her capable.

Hendon shook his head. "I don't suppose that was the first time Miss Thorpe was treated harshly or unfairly, but I find it hard to believe that she could murder a man."

"How well do you know Miss Thorpe?" Sebastian inquired.

"Not at all, sir," Hendon hurried to explain, "but you get a sense of people, don't you?"

"Yes, you do, but that doesn't mean you can't be wrong," Sebastian replied. "Dismissed. Please ask Mr. Abrahms to come down."

"Yes, sir."

SEVEN

"Sit down," Sebastian invited when Mr. Abrahms stood stiffly before him.

The young man looked apprehensive, then lowered himself into a chair but sat on the edge, his back ramrod straight, his eyes darting around as if he were looking for the nearest exit, even though he knew precisely where it was. Abrahms was thin and wiry, and had soulful dark eyes and full, pouty lips. A ropy scar ran from his right ear to the corner of his mouth, and his right index finger was crooked, probably the result of not being set properly after it had been broken.

"What's your name, son?" Sebastian asked.

"Abrahms."

"Your Christian name."

"Joseph, sir."

"I hear you have the best job on board, Joseph," Sebastian teased.

He hoped the young man would make a face to show his displeasure or complain about taking out buckets of piss and shit, but Joseph's expression remained stony.

"I'm the youngest member of the crew," he replied carefully, as if this were some sort of test. "It's only right that I should get the lowliest job."

"How long have you been a sailor?"

"Eight months, sir."

"And before that?"

Joseph Abrahms drew into himself, his mouth quivering and his eyes radiating such fear and pain that Sebastian instinctively backed off. The boy's past wasn't likely to have any bearing on the case, and, unless Sebastian heard otherwise, there was no sense in opening up old wounds. He assumed Joseph Abrahms was a free man, if he was part of a Northern crew, but perhaps freedom was a privilege he hadn't been born to, and he might have started his life as a slave. London newspapers didn't devote too much space to American politics, but there were occasional articles about the abolitionist movement in the North and the unyielding resistance of the Southern states, which depended on slave labor for nearly all aspects of their economy. The tension that had been brewing for decades was escalating, and the rhetoric was growing more militant as the states came to loggerheads.

"How often did you come down to first class, Mr. Abrahms?" Sebastian asked, deciding that any hint of familiarity might be perceived as condescending.

"Three times a day."

"And did you ever witness or overhear any altercations?"

Abrahms shook his head. "I tried to come down when all the passengers were out."

"How did you know when they'd be out?" Sebastian asked.

The young man shrugged. "These people can't stand to be cooped up. They go up on deck whenever they can. Makes them feel free."

The word was uttered with such bitterness, Sebastian thought freedom meant something vastly different to the young sailor than it did to passengers who were listless and bored.

"But I bet you observed them," Sebastian said. "I think you're probably a good judge of character." Frightened people usually were, since they always needed to know where the next threat was coming from.

Abrahms shrugged again. "They were much like any other group of passengers, sure of their place in the world and eager to get to their destination."

"What about the Blackstocks?"

Abrahms looked away, but not before Sebastian saw a shudder pass through him.

"Did Lord Blackstock say something to you, lad?"

Abrahms shook his head but wouldn't look at him.

"And Lady Blackstock?"

Abrahms looked up then, and his dark eyes glittered with heartfelt sympathy. "She was frightened, sir. Terrified for her life."

"What was she frightened of?"

"I don't know." But Sebastian was sure he did, just as he was certain that Joseph Abrahms knew something of visceral fear.

"May I go now?" the sailor pleaded.

"Go on, son. Find me if you need to speak to me."

"Yes, sir."

Abrahms hurried up the stairs, and Sebastian followed. It was time he met the first-class passengers.

EIGHT

When Gemma entered the cabin, Lorna Thorpe wordlessly left and shut the door behind her. Gemma had no choice but to sit on Lorna's berth, since she could hardly stand between the two berths and lean over Miss Van Kemp, who was now awake and staring at Gemma fearfully. She was terribly pale, her lips were dry and peeling, and there were dark smudges beneath her eyes, but beneath the sickly pallor Miss Van Kemp was a beautiful young woman with wavy blond hair, dark blue eyes, and a pert nose lightly sprinkled with freckles.

"I'm sorry to disturb you, Miss Van Kemp," Gemma said. "Miss Thorpe tells me you've been unwell. I'm a nurse, so if there's anything I can do to help..."

Miss Van Kemp shook her head. "It's seasickness."

"Have you been suffering the entire voyage?"

"No, just these past two days."

They both knew Miss Van Kemp was lying, since it was unlikely she'd suddenly become severely seasick after two weeks aboard, and right before they arrived in London.

"You should have a drink. I think you might be dehydrated," Gemma observed. "When was the last time you had something to eat?"

"Not since yesterday morning."

"Have you been vomiting?"

Greta Van Kemp shook her head. "Not after the first time."

Whatever was ailing the woman, she appeared to be on the mend and would feel better once she had a cup of sweet tea or even just water and some food. But Gemma wasn't there to dispense medical advice. She needed to ask Greta about the Blackstocks, and there seemed no obvious way to bring the conversation around to the murder.

"I expect you heard what happened," Gemma said, watching Greta closely.

"Yes. Lorna told me."

Gemma expected Greta to say something more, as one would in such a shocking situation. When faced with sudden and violent death, people usually expressed horror, made sure to say something kind about the victim, or even asked endless questions, needing to understand the death and to feel reassured, but Greta Van Kemp remained silent and fixed Gemma with a baleful stare, clearly wishing she'd leave.

"Miss Van Kemp, I'd like to ask you a few questions about your employers."

"I don't have to answer your questions," Greta retorted, her nostrils flaring with outrage. "You are not the police."

"You are absolutely right, I'm not, and you don't have to answer my questions, but if you refuse Inspector Bell will speak to you instead."

Greta Van Kemp turned even paler, if such a thing were possible, and Gemma thought she might be weighing her options. Sebastian would be gentle; he had no reason not to be, but Greta didn't know him and, based on her reaction, probably feared that he would try to bully and intimidate her.

"All right," she conceded sulkily. "I'd rather speak to you, then."

"Thank you. I appreciate your cooperation."

"As if I have a choice," Miss Van Kemp muttered under her breath, but Gemma pretended not to hear.

"Miss Thorpe tells me the Blackstocks hired you while they were visiting New York."

"Yes. The previous lady's maid left without warning shortly before they were due to sail."

"I hear the valet left too."

Miss Van Kemp nodded. "They saw their chance and took it, and I can't say I blame them. America is the land of opportunity. They'll be all right as long as they're prepared to work hard and don't expect the streets to be paved with gold, as some fools imagine them to be."

"How did you come to work for the Blackstocks?"

"The agency I had registered with sent several applicants to the hotel. Lady Blackstock chose me over all the others."

Gemma had never had a lady's maid and never would, but she thought the hiring of a lady's maid was usually the province of the housekeeper. Since the Blackstocks had been traveling and there had been no one available to vet the candidates, Lady Blackstock would have had to interview potential maids herself, unless she had asked a member of the hotel staff to conduct the preliminary interviews and weed out anyone they deemed undesirable.

"Did Lady Blackstock interview you herself?"

"I had to see the manager first. Once he was satisfied that I was qualified, he sent me up to speak to Lady Blackstock."

"Was Lord Blackstock present during the interview?"

"No, but he came in at the end."

"And how did he seem?" Gemma asked.

"He was charming and friendly. I think his approval helped Lady Blackstock to make up her mind."

Several questions instantly sprang to Gemma's mind, and she was surprised by how cynical she had become over the past months. It wasn't necessarily a bad thing that she was more aware of people's motivations, but it was sobering to realize just how much went on behind bland smiles and innocent gazes, and how often people had a secret agenda.

Looking at Greta Van Kemp, who was stunningly beautiful even when she was clearly unwell, Gemma couldn't help but wonder if hiring her had been a deliberate choice, but if it had been, which Blackstock had stood to benefit? Had Lord Blackstock instructed his wife to hire the lovely young woman because she'd caught his eye, or had the decision lain with Lady Blackstock, who might have devised an experiment intended to test her husband's loyalty? Or might it have been something even darker? Had Lady Blackstock intentionally chosen Greta to tempt her man? If Lord Blackstock had been taken with the new maid, then perhaps he would have shifted his attention to her and left his wife in peace.

Gemma couldn't get the memory of Lord Blackstock's horrified gaze as he stared through his cage out of her mind. Someone had wanted him to suffer in his final moments, and he clearly had. If Gemma was a betting woman, she'd put money on this murder having to do with a woman's wrath. Dragging her mind back to Greta Van Kemp, who now seemed even more impatient for her to leave, Gemma asked, "Do you like working for Lady Blackstock, Miss Van Kemp?"

The maid shrugged. "It's a job, and I need the money. Girls in my position can't afford to be too picky."

"Do you have family in New York?"

"I have a sister. She's also in service."

"What can you tell me about the Blackstocks' marriage?" Gemma asked.

"I can tell you that Audrey Blackstock was not a happy woman."

"You speak of her in the past tense," Gemma pointed out.

"*Is* not a happy woman," Greta Van Kemp amended.

"What makes you think she's unhappy?"

"She sometimes confided in me. I think it's because she was— is lonely and was desperate for another woman to talk to."

"What did she say?"

Greta looked like she would refuse to answer, then seemed to recall that the alternative to Gemma was an inspector from Scotland Yard and relented. "She didn't want to marry Anthony Blackstock. She loved another man, but her father forced her to accept Lord Blackstock's proposal. Her father was flattered that a peer—that was the term she used—would wish to marry his daughter and thought he might benefit from the arrangement."

"Benefit how?"

"Socially. Financially," Greta said with a shrug.

"Did Lady Blackstock tell you how they met?"

It wasn't often that a nobleman married a commoner, even one that was exceptionally pretty. There were plenty of women with pedigree to choose from, so perhaps it really had been a love match, at least for Anthony Blackstock.

"Yes, she told me," Greta replied warily. "She wouldn't stop talking, especially that first week while we were still at the hotel, and we were left alone together while Lord Blackstock went downstairs to have a drink at the bar. Sometimes I wished she'd just be quiet and let me do my job so I could go to bed."

Greta sighed. She no longer seemed defiant or frightened, only annoyed to have to recall the details of her mistress's life. It was clear she didn't like Audrey Blackstock and didn't seem to care what had happened to her. Greta's concern was entirely for herself.

"Lady Blackstock's father—I forget his name," Greta said with a dismissive wave of her hand, "is a professor at Oxford. His area of interest is divinity during the Middle Ages." She made a face that seemed to imply that she couldn't think of anything more boring. "Lord Blackstock was interested in history, and the two men met when the professor—Stack, that's his name—was invited to give a..." Greta paused, looking to the low ceiling as she tried to remember the name. "Bampton lecture," she finally recalled. "That was it."

"Bampton lecture?" Gemma asked. She wasn't familiar with

the term and hoped Lady Blackstock had offered an explanation that the maid could recollect.

"Audrey said it was a series of theological lectures funded by some wealthy benefactor. Must be nice to have so much money you can afford to waste it on something so pointless," Greta said bitterly. "I don't suppose he ever went to bed hungry." A heavy sigh escaped her, then she recalled that Gemma was still waiting for an answer. "Lord Blackstock wished to continue the discussion, so Professor Stack invited him to dine. That's how he met Audrey."

"So, the marriage was not a happy one for Lady Blackstock?"

"She never said so outright; she wouldn't dare, but I think she loathed the man," Greta said.

"And was he loathsome?"

Greta sighed again. "He was all right, as far as I could tell. But what do I know of marriage? The Blackstocks were the first married couple I'd worked for. My previous position was with an old woman who was completely bedbound for more than a year before she finally passed. She was kind and left me a small bequest, but I gave the money to my sister when she got with..." Greta looked away, clearly embarrassed to admit that her sister had become pregnant out of wedlock.

"Was Lord Blackstock ever unkind to you?" Gemma asked.

"He hardly noticed me," Greta replied stonily. "He's not the sort of man who likes women."

"How do you mean?" Gemma asked carefully.

"He preferred the company of men."

Greta's answer could be interpreted in a number of ways, but Gemma decided not to press her since neither her tone nor her facial expression appeared to hint at anything untoward. Some men simply preferred to spend time with other men because they found the conversation more stimulating and thought women inferior in all the ways that mattered to them.

"When was the last time you saw Lady Blackstock?" Gemma asked instead.

"Yesterday, in the morning. I helped her to dress."

"And then you took ill?"

Greta nodded. "I could barely keep anything down."

There was another reason, besides seasickness, which would account for Greta Van Kemp's symptoms, but Gemma didn't think she had the right to ask. Greta had been with the Blackstocks mere weeks, so even if she was with child it could hardly be Anthony Blackstock's, and she now found herself in an untenable position, possibly out of a job and on her way to the other side of the globe. Gemma didn't envy the woman and hoped for her sake that it really was just some kind of sickness.

"What do you think happened to Audrey Blackstock?"

"I don't know," Greta whispered. "I really don't."

"What will you do if she doesn't turn up?" Gemma asked.

Greta shook her head, and her eyes brimmed with tears. "I haven't been paid, and I will be alone in a foreign country with no one to turn to."

"Do you think Lady Blackstock will come back?"

"I think Lady Blackstock is dead," Greta finally admitted. She jumped to her feet, pushed open the door, and fled, leaving Gemma to ponder her parting words.

She wasn't sure what to do next, so she exited the cabin and looked up and down the passage. There was no sign of either Greta Van Kemp, Lorna Thorpe, or Mr. Brock.

NINE

Sebastian blinked several times when he emerged from the shadowy first-class hatch onto the deck. He looked around, curious if there were other free blacks on the ship's crew and if they were as terrified as Joseph Abrahms. He spotted two men, both considerably older than Joseph, who were talking easily with other crew members as they went about their work. Sebastian supposed that was a good sign, but until he knew more about life aboard the *Prince Regent* he would reserve judgment.

He turned the other way and spotted several well-dressed couples promenading on the aft deck, their faces shadowed from the sun by hats and bonnets. Despite their leisurely pace and apparent calm, their heads periodically swiveled towards the bridge, their tense expressions indicative of their concern. One of their own had been murdered, and they clearly wanted to know if they were safe.

"If you will wait a moment, Inspector, Mr. Reynolds will make the introductions," said Mr. Sims, who either happened to be passing or had been spying on Reynolds' orders. "Mr. Reynolds needed a word with the coxswain."

"I can introduce myself," Sebastian replied, and was about to walk away when Mr. Reynolds approached them, his expression irritatingly ingratiating.

"Were you able to learn anything from the stewards?" Reynolds asked.

"Not too much."

Reynolds nodded, having clearly expected as much, then gestured towards the passengers, who had stopped walking and had formed a loose circle as they watched Sebastian with trepidation.

"You can use my cabin if you wish," Reynolds offered.

"I will interview the passengers in the saloon."

There was some risk of being overheard, and the passengers would be facing the door behind which Anthony Blackstock's corpse awaited transport to shore, but the passengers had sat at that table every day for nearly a fortnight, and the open space would render them more forthcoming than the tight, low-ceilinged confines of the first mate's cabin, where they would have to stand unless they were to sit on Reynolds' bed.

Once Reynolds had performed the introductions and the exclamations of horror and sympathy were out of the way, Sebastian decided to start by speaking to the Caldwells. Jeffrey and Marilyn Caldwell were a handsome couple, their clothes and Mrs. Caldwell's extravagant jewelry indicative of their wealth. Mrs. Caldwell was around twenty-five, possibly a bit older. Her fair hair was parted in the middle and arranged in a low knot secured with a black velvet ribbon. She had a round face, and her snub nose and wide blue eyes that peered anxiously from beneath pale, wispy eyebrows put Sebastian in mind of a child with a nervous disposition. Although not stout, Mrs. Caldwell was a bit plump, her figure further thickened by the wide skirts and full sleeves of her dark blue satin gown.

Mr. Caldwell was tall, lean, and dark in his coloring. He couldn't sit still for long without fidgeting, and his gaze kept straying to the Blackstocks' door, unlike that of his wife, who made a point of not looking in that direction and focused her worried gaze on Sebastian's face, clearly hoping he could provide the answers she needed. Unlike the British upper crust, who didn't bother to hide their disdain for the police, the Caldwells were friendly, and Jeffrey Caldwell had held out his hand to Sebastian and had pumped it enthusiastically when they had been introduced, as if they had met at a social function and were part of the same circle rather than two strangers thrown together by a murder inquiry.

"Please, call us Jeff and Marilyn," Jeffrey said as soon as they were seated. "We are not ones to stand on ceremony."

"What's your Christian name, Inspector?" Marilyn asked, and smiled apologetically, having probably realized she had just violated some basic rule of British conduct.

"Sebastian."

"That's a fine name," Marilyn gushed. "So strong and masculine. Like Heathcliff. I read *Wuthering Heights* three times. Oh, and *Jane Eyre*," she added, her hands going to her bosom. "So romantic."

"*Wuthering Heights* is one of my favorites as well," Sebastian replied.

It wasn't, but he wanted to keep Marilyn talking, and a common interest tended to predispose one favorably upon first meeting. As it happened, Sebastian had developed a lasting dislike of Heathcliff and hadn't thought very much of Mr. Rochester, but the authors who'd written *Wuthering Heights* and *Jane Eyre* seemed to revere selfish, brooding men whose misguided actions were viewed as romantic rather than inexcusable and at times downright cruel. Sebastian briefly wondered if Gemma shared Marilyn Caldwell's sentiments, then realized that Marilyn was still speaking, and he had not been paying close attention.

Sebastian had heard American pronunciation before, and he'd had no difficulty understanding either Mr. Reynolds or the stewards, but the Caldwells were clearly not from New York and spoke in some sort of regional accent. Their speech was slower, the vowels drawn out, and Sebastian found that he had to concentrate on every word to make out what they were saying.

"I beg your pardon?" he said, hoping Marilyn would repeat what she had just said.

"I was just saying that it's tragic what happened," Marilyn said. "Absolutely tragic. Anthony Blackstock seemed such a charming man. And Audrey..." She dabbed at her eyes with a lace-trimmed handkerchief. "The thought of Audrey..."

Marilyn choked up and needed a moment to compose herself. Once she was able to speak without crying, she fixed Sebastian with that childish stare and whispered, "Do you think Audrey is dead?"

"Mary, stop badgering the man," Jeffrey admonished. "He only just got here. He doesn't know what happened to Anthony or if Audrey is dead." He turned to Sebastian. "If there's any way we can help, please don't hesitate to ask, Inspector."

"Thank you. For now, I would just like you to answer a few questions."

Sebastian thought it telling that the Americans had used the Blackstocks' Christian names rather than their titles, bringing Lord Blackstock and his wife to their level rather than acknowledging the social divide. He supposed that was common in America, where there were no noble titles or centuries-old estates that had been passed down from generation to generation. Everyone was equal, at least in theory, but no society could completely eradicate the class system, not when there were individuals who were unbelievably wealthy, millions who were enslaved, and everyone in between. Call it what they would, but in some ways the United States were even more discriminatory than England.

"We'll be happy to answer any questions you might have," Marilyn said, her fair head bobbing.

"Is this your first visit to England?" Sebastian asked.

"It is. We could have sailed from Charleston—that's in South Carolina—but we thought we'd spend a few weeks in New York first," Jeff said. "We've never been that far north."

"And it was so worth it," Marilyn drawled. "We had a wonderful time, didn't we, Jeffy?"

"We sure did. An absolutely fizzing town," Jeffrey agreed, the words not quite matching the scowl that crossed his face and was immediately replaced with an amiable smile.

"Had you met the Blackstocks before you boarded the *Prince Regent* in New York?" Sebastian asked.

He had no concept of the distances involved, or how close Charleston might be to Washington, where the Blackstocks had spent several weeks. But he did know that Washington was somewhere between Charleston and New York, so it was possible that the two couples had met in a social setting.

"No, we hadn't," Jeff replied. "We met the Blackstocks at South Street seaport, just before we came aboard."

"What was your impression of them?"

"They were good company," Marilyn said. "And that's saying a lot on a voyage that has felt like a month of Sundays."

"It's been two weeks, Mary," Jeffrey pointed out. "Really not that long at all."

"Yes, but there's nothing to do. We're trapped here all day long," Marilyn complained. "And the first-class accommodation leaves much to be desired." She made an expansive gesture meant to encompass the dim, narrow communal hall, and the staterooms beyond. "Why, our servants have more comfortable quarters." She sucked in a shuddering breath. "I simply can't bear to spend another night aboard this ship. You must allow us to dock, Inspector Bell."

Jeffrey shot her a warning look, then turned to Sebastian. "Mary is frightened, Inspector. We all are. To think that Anthony was murdered mere feet from where we slept is unsettling to say the least. We're anxious to put this tragedy behind us."

"I quite understand, Mr. Caldwell, but I cannot allow anyone to leave until I know what happened. Your testimony may help me. Did you notice any tension between Lord Blackstock and Lady Blackstock these last few days?"

"You think Audrey killed Anthony?" Jeffrey exclaimed, his gaze going towards the Blackstocks' stateroom.

"I never said that," Sebastian replied. "But given that Lord Blackstock is dead, and Lady Blackstock is missing, it's a question that needs asking."

"Audrey went quiet sometimes," Marilyn said. "I thought she was sad, but when I asked if she was all right she'd brighten immediately and blame her mood on seasickness. Morning sickness, more like," she scoffed.

"Mary," Jeffrey hissed. "You shouldn't say such things."

"I'm sure a man in Sebastian's job is not easily shocked," Mary replied, unperturbed by her husband's criticism and referring to Sebastian as if he were an acquaintance rather than an inspector with the police. "And it could be important, especially since Audrey didn't seem pleased."

"Did Lady Blackstock tell you she was with child?" Sebastian asked. Marilyn seemed entirely too sure for someone who'd nothing to go on but a pensive mood.

Marilyn's expression turned defensive. "Audrey never said she was expecting, and I didn't ask, but I did hear her retching yesterday morning."

"Are you certain it was Audrey Blackstock you heard? It is my understanding that her lady's maid was taken ill," Sebastian replied. "She might have been in the Blackstocks' stateroom."

"I suppose it may have been the maid," Marilyn said with a shrug. "Pretty little thing," she added with a lift of one eyebrow. "Too pretty, if you ask me."

"He wasn't asking, and you shouldn't have said anything unless you were sure, Mary," Jeffrey chastised his wife.

"I thought it might be important," Marilyn replied warily. "I only wanted to help Audrey."

"I know, my dear. I know." Jeffrey squeezed Marilyn's hand. "You've such a kind heart."

Marilyn smiled at her husband, and it was clear that all was forgiven.

"Are we finished, Inspector? We could use some air," Jeffrey said, and looked meaningfully at stateroom two again.

Even with the door shut, an unpleasant odor was wafting through the door slats and permeating the unventilated space. Sebastian would have no choice but to leave the door that led to the stairs open during the next interview.

"A few more questions, and then you will be free to leave," Sebastian promised. "Was there anyone who didn't get on with Lord Blackstock? Anyone he had an altercation with?"

"He didn't care for Mr. Reynolds, I'll tell you that," Jeffrey said. "He thought the man insolent."

"Why would he think that?"

"Mr. Reynolds didn't appear to be sufficiently impressed with Lord Blackstock's pedigree."

Marilyn shook her head. "That's not why."

"Why, then?" Jeffrey asked, turning to face her wife.

"Mr. Reynolds was sweet on Audrey. It was obvious from the way he watched her, and he was always trying to engage her in conversation, especially when she was on her own. Did you not notice, Jeffey?"

Jeffrey Caldwell nodded slowly. "I did catch him looking at Audrey, but I didn't think it was admiration I saw in his gaze."

"What was it, then?" Sebastian asked.

"Lust."

"Did Lady Blackstock respond to his advances? Did she seem flattered?"

Jeffrey Caldwell shook his head. "She went out of her way to avoid him. I think he frightened her. And to be honest, Sebastian, I had considered reporting Mr. Reynolds to Captain Grant, but then the poor man took ill, and I didn't want to disturb him."

"Admiration or desire, Mr. Reynolds' behavior towards Audrey was wholly inappropriate," Marilyn stated. "I wouldn't be surprised if Anthony had words with the man."

"Was Anthony Blackstock aware of Mr. Reynolds' interest?" Sebastian asked, directing the question to Jeffrey.

"I think so," Jeffrey replied. "He seemed to find it amusing at first, but as Mr. Reynolds grew more persistent I think Anthony became annoyed, then understandably angry."

"Did either of you witness a set-to between them?"

"No," Jeffrey replied for them both. "But Mr. Reynolds did give Anthony a wide berth, didn't he, Mary?"

"He did," Marilyn confirmed.

"Thank you," Sebastian said. "Please come find me if you think of anything else."

"We will be sure to do that, Sebastian, but we told you everything we know," Jeffrey said. He was already halfway out of his seat, his hand extended to Marilyn.

"Can you kindly ask Mr. and Mrs. Glenn to come down? And leave the door open."

"Of course," Jeffrey called over his shoulder as he guided Marilyn towards the stairs.

TEN

As soon as Gemma emerged on deck, she spotted a well-dressed woman standing by herself by the stern. Her gloved hands gripped the railing, and she looked unbearably sad as she gazed longingly at the city skyline just visible in the distance. Several other passengers milled on deck, their gazes periodically straying towards the first-class hatch, either because they had yet to be interviewed by Sebastian or maybe because they expected him to materialize and announce that he'd solved the case, Audrey Blackstock had been found, and the culprit had been apprehended and would be taken away in chains.

Gemma hesitated for only a moment, then made her approach to the lone woman. If she could learn anything while she waited to confer with Sebastian, so much the better.

"Hello," Gemma said. "My name is Gemma Tate. I'm here with Inspector Bell."

The woman turned but didn't smile or immediately return the greeting. She was around thirty and so thin, her shoulders and elbows poked sharply through the fabric of her gown, and her face was pointed and angular. She had a patrician nose, pale blue eyes, and reddish hair that was mostly covered by her bonnet. Despite her gaunt appearance, the woman had the potential to be attractive, but the downward cast of her mouth and her speculative gaze were a bit off-putting. But then again, she was on her own mere hours after a brutal murder had been committed. She had little to smile about.

She studied Gemma for a long moment, then finally said, "Yes. I saw you arrive. Cora Hobson. Miss." The last word was thrown down like a gauntlet, and Gemma felt a stab of pity for this woman who was probably reminded daily that she was not married and likely had no hope to ever be.

"It's a pleasure to meet you, Miss Hobson."

"There's nothing pleasurable about this situation."

"No, I suppose there isn't," Gemma agreed. "May I ask you a few questions?"

"As it happens, I have a question for you. Why are you here, Miss Tate? What's your role in this?" Miss Hobson didn't appear hostile, simply curious.

"I'm a nurse. I was in Crimea, and I'm here to help Inspector Bell assess the crime scene."

"Is that the only service you perform for your inspector?" the woman asked rather snidely.

"I'm sure I don't know what you mean, Miss Hobson."

"Oh, come now, Miss Tate. There's no need to be coy." Miss Hobson's eyes suddenly shimmered with tears. "You seem like a nice woman, so permit me to offer a word of warning. Don't let him take advantage of you. Men are like that. They will single you out for attention, make you feel seen, and then, just like that, their affections will shift to someone else. No explanation. No apology. Just a wall of politeness you will never be able to breach."

"I'm sorry your hopes were disappointed, Miss Hobson."

Gemma wondered who Miss Hobson was referring to and if her heartbreak was recent, but didn't want to ask outright. Maybe she would reveal the information on her own, since she seemed eager to talk, or maybe she had been reflecting on the past as she anxiously waited for news and wished more than anything that she didn't have to face life alone.

"Thank you," Miss Hobson said, and turned away, her focus returning to the hazy skyline on the horizon.

From the deck of the ship, London looked like a mirage, the glittering river and impressive architecture disguising the filth and poverty that killed thousands every year. As summer advanced, the temperatures were rising, the sun warming the contaminated river water and accelerating the spread of contagion that slowed during the winter months. It had been particularly bad last year, the stench from the river so awful it had been dubbed the Great Stink. Londoners had been forced to keep their windows closed during the hottest days of the year and use lime chloride on windows and curtains to combat the smell. Already the water was beginning to smell, a fact the passengers had clearly noticed, as someone behind Gemma made a comment about the odor.

Before Miss Hobson became aware of the miasma and returned to her cabin, Gemma's eagerness to learn as much as she could prompted her to try again.

"Miss Hobson, did you know the Blackstocks?"

Miss Hobson nodded without turning around.

"How well?"

"As well as one can get to know someone after spending nearly a fortnight in close quarters."

"Are you traveling alone?"

"I'm traveling with members of a string quartet."

So, this was the violinist Mr. Reynolds had mentioned. Gemma wasn't sure how to politely inquire about the arrangement. It seemed odd that an unmarried woman would be traveling with three men, but perhaps societal restrictions didn't apply to working women.

"My brother plays the viola," Miss Hobson supplied rather haughtily. "He acts as chaperone when we travel."

"You must come from a very talented family if you're both musicians," Gemma said.

"There's no need to romanticize it, Miss Tate. It's a way to make a living, but the life of a troubadour is never an easy one, especially for an unmarried woman." Miss Hobson chuckled bitterly. "After all, even the reputation of a spinster must be safeguarded against malicious insinuations since any hint of scandal can lead to canceled engagements and a decrease in bookings."

Gemma wasn't sure why the woman was so antagonistic, but, given her unhappy expression, Miss Hobson's demeanor likely had nothing to do with Gemma and everything to do with whatever awaited her once the ship finally docked. Had they met in a social setting, Gemma would have excused herself and walked away, but she'd come aboard to investigate a crime, and she wouldn't be so easily fobbed off.

"Did you hear anything last night, Miss Hobson?" she asked. "Sounds of struggle or perhaps cries for help?"

"I didn't hear anything, but I take a few drops of laudanum at bedtime. I'm afraid I'm unable to get to sleep without it."

The laudanum would ensure that Miss Hobson had fallen asleep quickly and remained asleep through the night, her slumber deep and her dreams vivid. Even if she thought she had seen or heard something, she would hardly make a reliable witness since she could have dreamed the whole thing and not realized it.

"Was there anyone who didn't get on with Lord Blackstock?" Gemma tried again.

"I wouldn't have said so until last night," Miss Hobson said.

"What happened?"

Miss Hobson looked around, as if worried that someone would overhear and retaliate against her, which wasn't entirely far-fetched given what had happened to Lord Blackstock and his lady.

"The gentlemen in first class liked to play cards after supper. It gave them a way to pass the time and allowed their wives time to prepare for bed."

'What did they play?"

"Mr. Caldwell taught the gentlemen an American card game called poker."

"Did they play for money?" Gemma asked.

"Indeed they did, and it is my understanding that the stakes were quite high. Last night, a terrible quarrel broke out. I didn't see what happened for myself, you understand, but I heard every word."

"Between whom did this row take place?"

"Lord Blackstock and Mr. Caldwell. Lord Blackstock lost several hands in a row and became terribly upset."

Gemma knew nothing of the rules of poker or any other card games gentlemen with a penchant for gambling played for money, but she did understand just how easily a player could lose their shirt if they didn't walk away from a losing streak. She had been an unwilling witness to several such games during her night shifts at Scutari, where the doctors and surgeons had sometimes gathered after hours and had played well into the night despite their obvious fatigue. The men had longed to forget the horrors they'd seen and the patients they'd lost, and had often allowed their frayed nerves to get the better of them when they had lost hand after hand and had been forced to part with their wages as well as watches, cuff-links, and even articles of clothing. Driven to despair by bad luck, they had been determined to win back what they had lost, and their refusal to walk away had inevitably led to greater losses and, at times, substantial debt.

"Can you tell me what happened?" Gemma pressed.

Miss Hobson seemed reluctant to discuss last night's fracas but probably realized it was important that someone close to Sebastian know the truth, since what had occurred might very well be the motive for the murder.

"Mr. Caldwell won a considerable sum. He had also won big the night before. I don't think it was about the money," Miss Hobson said, a speculative look in her gray eyes when she turned to look at Gemma. "Lord Blackstock seemed to be well off, or at least he liked everyone to believe he was. For him, it was a matter of principle, and honor."

Miss Hobson seemed to have gleaned quite a lot of what had transpired for a woman who hadn't been present and had only heard the argument through the slats in her door, but Gemma was eager to hear the woman's opinion, since she had clearly formulated one and was willing to share her observations. Miss Hobson was more animated now, her hands no longer gripping the railing but clasped loosely before her.

"Was the row limited to angry words?" Gemma asked.

Miss Hobson shook her head. "Lord Blackstock threw back his chair, leaned across the table, and jabbed a finger into Mr. Caldwell's chest. He accused him of cheating and called him some very unflattering names indeed."

"What sort of names?"

Gemma was convinced that Miss Hobson had not only heard what had been said but had been a witness to what had happened. She couldn't have known that Lord Blackstock had leaned across the table and jabbed a finger in Mr. Caldwell's chest unless she had opened the slats just enough to allow her to peer into the saloon without being seen. Perhaps the other ladies had done the same, since it had to be impossible not to be aware of a violent argument in such close quarters.

"Lord Blackstock accused Mr. Caldwell of cheating and called him a pig. He said men like Mr. Caldwell are nothing more than colonial upstarts who have no morals or breeding and are no better than their slaves, whose lifeblood supports their owners' depraved lifestyle."

"Good God," Gemma exclaimed, shocked by the vitriol losing a game of cards had brought out in Anthony Blackstock. "Does Mr. Caldwell really own slaves?"

"He does, and quite a few at that."

"How do you know? Has he admitted to it?"

Gemma was frankly horrified, but she supposed it wasn't completely unexpected that an American passenger might be from the South and own other human beings as if they were horses or dogs.

"I think the Caldwells preferred not to talk about it while on board, but Mrs. Glenn told me during one of our walks. She's very active in the abolitionist movement in her native Vermont and found it difficult to remain civil in the presence of unrepentant slavers. Especially in view of Mr. Abrahms' obvious terror when in the vicinity of the Caldwells. Mrs. Glenn had approached him, and, once he felt he could trust her, he had shared something of his experiences with her."

"Mr. Abrahms?" Gemma asked, trying to place the name.

"The young man who takes out the night soil. He's originally from Georgia and, from what Mrs. Glenn said, had suffered horribly before he managed to escape with the aid of the Underground Railroad." Seeing Gemma's confusion, Miss Hobson hurried to explain. "It's not an actual railroad, Miss Tate, it's a group of individuals who smuggle out escaped slaves and help them get to the Northern states."

"Surely Mr. Abrahms is safe now," Gemma said, wondering if the Caldwells could somehow arrange for the man's return to Georgia.

"I don't think these poor people are ever safe, Miss Tate, and Mrs. Glenn shared with me in confidence that the boy's mother and sister were hanged as punishment for his escape. He will have to live with that for the rest of his days, even if he is free."

Gemma's hand flew to her bosom, her heart racing with shock. In England, slavery had been abolished more than twenty years before, so she had never met an enslaved person, but, thinking on it now, she realized that it wasn't so long ago at all, and the world was still a cruel and savage place.

"Did Lord Blackstock have strong opinions on slavery?" Gemma asked once she had recovered her composure. "Was that why he verbally attacked Jeffrey Caldwell?"

Perhaps it was his disdain for Mr. Caldwell's way of life and not Lord Blackstock's personal losses that had been at the root of the argument, especially after he had spent time with the British envoy and might have been privy to discussions relating to the abolition of slavery in the United States.

Miss Hobson shook her head and smiled at Gemma scornfully, as if she had missed the point entirely. "I don't think Lord Blackstock much cared about the plight of the slaves. In fact, he had called Mr. Abrahms a dumb Negro when the boy got in his way a few days ago. I think Lord Blackstock simply wanted to rile Mr. Caldwell. Perhaps he even wanted Mr. Caldwell to strike him."

"To what end?"

"If Mr. Caldwell physically assaulted a British nobleman, Lord Blackstock could demand that Mr. Caldwell spend the night in the brig. Perhaps he'd hoped to recoup his losses by way of apology."

"Did he succeed? Did Mr. Caldwell throw a punch?"

Miss Hobson shook her head. "Mr. Caldwell collected his winnings, stood, and wished Lord Blackstock and everyone else present a pleasant evening. He then retired to his cabin and, as far as I know, did not leave it until this morning. But, as I said, I was asleep."

"How soon after Mr. Caldwell returned to his cabin did you take the laudanum, Miss Hobson?"

"As soon as I undressed for bed and changed into my night-dress. I was deeply upset by what I had heard and wanted only to get to sleep."

"Was Lady Blackstock present for this confrontation?" Gemma asked.

"No, she was in her stateroom, but I'm sure she heard it. Everyone did."

Gemma couldn't wait to share what she had learned with Sebastian, but, much as she would have liked to declare the case solved, she knew from experience that the process was rarely so straightforward. Having suffered grave insult, Mr. Caldwell might have had a motive, but he would be very foolish indeed to murder Lord Blackstock a few hours later and carve the word *pig* into his chest. However, it seemed that several people had overheard the argument, and a killer who was clever and impetuous might make use of the opportunity and point the finger at Mr. Caldwell without saying a word.

And Miss Hobson had also mentioned that Lord Blackstock

had insulted Mr. Abrahms, who might have been triggered by the man's cruelty and snapped and responded in kind.

"How did Lord Blackstock react to Mr. Caldwell walking away?" Gemma asked.

"He was furious. In some respects, Mr. Caldwell had doled out the greater insult by simply ignoring Lord Blackstock. He likely made him feel like a right fool."

"Do you think Mr. Caldwell is capable of murder?"

Miss Hobson scoffed. "I know Mr. Caldwell about as well as I know you, Miss Tate. Are you capable of murder?"

That was a good question, one that Gemma didn't care to ponder, since there was no easy answer. Most people would say they weren't capable of murder, but Gemma had seen enough, both in Crimea and since then, to know that everyone had a breaking point and, once they'd reached it, there was no telling what they might do.

ELEVEN

Gemma was just about to ask Miss Hobson if she had spent any time with Audrey Blackstock during the voyage and what impression she might have formed when a tall, dark-haired man approached them and tipped his silk top hat.

"Ladies," he said, and smiled disarmingly. "I do hope I'm not interrupting."

Miss Hobson tensed, and Gemma caught a flash of longing in her eyes before she rearranged her face into an expression of polite interest. The man didn't appear to notice her reaction, probably because his attention was fixed on Gemma. His eyes were the color of strong tea, his manner warm and inquisitive.

"Ezra Pennington," he offered when Miss Hobson failed to introduce him, and bowed from the neck.

Gemma couldn't help but wonder if Mr. Pennington was the man who'd lost interest in Miss Hobson and had moved on without a word of explanation. He was certainly worthy of notice, and, if he was a member of the string quartet and Miss Hobson had spent countless hours in his company, it wasn't difficult to imagine why she'd fallen so hard.

"Gemma Tate," Gemma replied when Miss Hobson remained resolutely silent.

"A pleasure to meet you, Miss Tate. We saw you come aboard, didn't we, Miss Hobson? I do declare, you are a brave soul. Few ladies would attempt to make that climb."

"And with good reason," Gemma replied. "It was quite terrifying."

"Mr. Pennington plays the cello," Miss Hobson interjected woodenly.

"For my sins," Mr. Pennington said, and rolled his eyes.

"Why do you say that?" Gemma asked.

She couldn't see how making music could be seen as a punishment, but what did she know about the life of a musician? Or troubadour, as Miss Hobson had referred to herself.

"It's very heavy, and very large." Mr. Pennington's tone was confidential. "I suppose I should be grateful. I don't need to spend money on joining an exercise gymnasium. Not when I lug around such a great weight every day of my life."

"Both exercise and music offer wonderful health benefits," Gemma said.

"Indeed they do, but the cello is not beneficial for my pocket. I was forced to pay for an additional berth just so I could store my instrument. I wasn't about to allow the crew to stow it in the hold, and there's no space for it inside the cabin."

Having been inside Miss Thorpe and Miss Van Kemp's cabin, Gemma could certainly believe that. There was barely room for a satchel, much less an unwieldy cello case.

"Do you like music, Miss Tate?" Mr. Pennington asked.

"Yes, very much, although I don't get to see it performed very often. What's in the quartet's repertoire, Mr. Pennington?"

"Mostly Schubert, Beethoven, and Bach. And, of course, Mozart. Very unpatriotic, I know, but no English composer can compare to the greats."

"How did you come to perform in the States?"

Gemma turned to Miss Hobson, but she didn't seem inclined to join in the conversation and made a point of not looking at Ezra Pennington.

"An American businessman approached us after a concert one evening. He was visiting his younger brother, who's at Oxford," Mr. Pennington explained. "He enjoyed the music and asked if we might be interested in performing abroad. He would cover the cost of the crossing, provide us with modest accommodation, and book several engagements."

"That sounds like an exciting opportunity," Gemma said. She assumed the quartet's benefactor had profited from the arrangement but didn't think the terms were germane to the case.

"That's what we thought," Mr. Pennington said. "Miss Hobson took some persuading, but as the only woman among us her opinion carried double the weight."

"They talked me into it in the end," Miss Hobson said. "And I must admit, it was the right decision."

"Mr. Abbott—that's the gentleman I mentioned—held a dinner party a few days after our arrival, and we played for his friends. As he had hoped, a number of guests inquired if we might be available to perform at their upcoming events, and our schedule filled rather quickly."

"We were even invited to Newport," Miss Hobson said, and smiled for the first time. She was surprisingly lovely when she let down her guard. "What a marvelous place. If I lived in New York, I would summer in Newport every year."

Ezra Pennington chuckled good-naturedly. "If you could afford it. You should see the mansions, Miss Tate. The residents refer to them as summer cottages, but they are nothing short of palaces. Many of them were still closed up since it was barely the start of the season, but a few families arrived in late May since it was already very warm in the city." Mr. Pennington sighed wistfully. "I would have loved to see it on the Fourth of July. There were to be lavish parties and fireworks on the beach."

Miss Hobson looked horrified. "We can't be seen to celebrate America's independence."

Ezra Pennington made a dismissive gesture. "I don't think our participation would make a jot of difference to anyone."

"But there is such a thing as loyalty, Ezra."

A tense look passed between them, and Gemma thought the comment must refer to a previous conversation, but neither said anything further about either Newport or the Fourth of July. Instead, both Miss Hobson and Mr. Pennington turned to Gemma. It seemed it was up to her to keep the conversation flowing.

"Did you play for the passengers during the crossing?" she asked.

"We did," Ezra Pennington replied. "We set up right here, on the aft deck, and performed for an hour after dinner one evening."

"The music was carried over the dark waters of the Atlantic and seemed to float right up to the twilit heavens," Miss Hobson added dreamily. "It was beautiful. A truly gratifying experience."

Despite her obvious resentment of Ezra Pennington, she seemed lighter around him, whimsical even. Perhaps he brought out the best in her, or the more likely possibility was that she refused to let him see her pain and worked hard to appear untouched by his desertion. She almost succeeded.

"Were the passengers in second class allowed to attend?" Gemma inquired.

"No, of course not," Ezra replied, "but we held a performance for them as well, and the passengers in steerage were able to hear. Everyone deserves a bit of joy, don't they?"

"They certainly do," Gemma agreed. "Did the Blackstocks attend your concert?"

"Yes. They were sat right over there." Miss Hobson pointed to a spot across the deck. "Lord Blackstock brought up a chair for his wife and stood behind her the entire time, his hand on her shoulder. He complimented us afterwards and even asked if we might be interested in playing at a garden party they were planning to host in August."

"And were you?"

"As much as we like to pretend we're all about the music, we still have to eat," Ezra Pennington said. "So yes, we would have happily accepted and performed Lord Blackstock's favorite pieces."

"He said he was partial to Vivaldi," Miss Hobson explained.

"Will you be returning to America next year?" Gemma asked.

"I don't know about that," Ezra Pennington said. "It would be too risky to undertake a tour on our own, but it would be nice to be invited back. Wouldn't it?" he asked, turning to Miss Hobson.

Miss Hobson nodded. "Yes, it would, but I could do without the crossing. Or the murder," she added with a shudder.

"Plenty of people get murdered in England," Ezra reminded her.

"I'm sure they do, but they don't generally get asphyxiated while I'm sleeping next door."

"How did you know Lord Blackstock was asphyxiated?" Gemma asked, surprised by Miss Hobson's admission. Ezra Pennington looked taken aback as well and took a small step away from Cora, as if to distance himself from any unpleasantness.

"I heard you speaking to Inspector Bell, Miss Tate. I was in my cabin while you examined the body." She glared at Ezra Pennington scornfully. "Do you honestly think I'm capable of murder, Ezra?"

"I have no idea what you're capable of, Cora dear," Ezra replied with a teasing smile, but Gemma sensed a dark undercurrent beneath the rather telling quip.

The tension was broken by a tall, elegant man who strode towards them across the deck. Miss Hobson and the newcomer resembled each other so much, Gemma was in no doubt that the man was her brother.

"Miss Tate, may I present my brother, Michael Hobson," Cora Hobson said as soon as the man joined their group.

"Good day to you, Miss Tate," Michael Hobson said, and bowed politely. "A pleasure to meet you."

"Likewise, Mr. Hobson," Gemma replied.

The Hobsons appeared to be close in age, and glanced at each other in a way that told Gemma everything she needed to know.

They knew each other so well, they could read each other's thoughts, much as she and Victor had done since they were children. Victor had been gone seven months now, but at times Gemma thought she could still sense his presence and hear his words of advice. She knew it was her own mind supplying the sentiments Victor would have expressed based on her intimate knowledge of his character, but she fervently wished it wasn't so, and that she could still communicate with her twin despite the unbreachable divide wrought by death.

"Are you twins?" Gemma asked.

Michael Hobson grinned. "Is it that obvious?"

"It is to me."

"Cora is older by twenty-two minutes, and she never lets me forget it."

"I am a twin as well. Was a twin," Gemma amended, and felt the sting of tears.

"We're very sorry for your loss, Miss Tate. Losing a sibling is unspeakably painful, but losing a twin..." Michael Hobson's gaze was warm with sympathy and understanding. "Do you have any other siblings?"

"No, it was just Victor and me."

Gemma was grateful no one had made the connection to the Victor Tate who had been murdered in the Strand last November. She didn't want to talk about Victor's death, especially when a murder had taken place aboard the *Prince Regent* only a few hours before. She was more interested in what else Miss Hobson might have overheard last night and wasn't saying.

The fourth member of the quartet, Clyde Bennett, joined them then. He was also a violinist and the founding member, after whom the quartet had been named. Unlike the other two men, Mr. Bennett was short and stocky, and had reddish hair, bright blue eyes, and a broad face bracketed by thick whiskers.

"Miss Tate is here with the police inspector," Mr. Pennington explained after the introductions had been made.

"Are you really?" Mr. Bennett exclaimed, staring at Gemma as if he suddenly saw her in a whole new light. "Do they permit women to join the police service these days?" His gaze radiated curiosity and, Gemma suspected, genuine respect.

"They do not, but they do engage the services of surgeons unaffiliated with the police to carry out postmortems and assess the crime scenes," Gemma replied.

"Surely you're not a surgeon, Miss Tate," Mr. Pennington said, looking dubious in the extreme.

"No, but I am a nurse. I was in Crimea."

"Is there no end to your bravery, Miss Tate?" Miss Hobson exclaimed, but although the words were flattering, her expression was one of disdain. "Nothing would compel me to go to a war zone and tend to scores of wounded men." She wrinkled her nose.

"I can't conceive of what you must have endured," Mr. Bennett said. "My brother was in Crimea. He was wounded during the Battle of Inkerman. Might you have looked after him, Miss Tate? Captain Clarence Bennett. Second Infantry Division."

"I'm sorry, but the name is not familiar to me."

"Well, no matter," Mr. Bennett said. "If it wasn't for the dedicated surgeons and selfless nurses at Scutari, my brother would have surely died."

"I'm very glad to hear your brother recovered, Mr. Bennett," Gemma said. "So many didn't."

Bennett nodded. "Yes. I've heard awful stories from Clarence, and I'm not ashamed to admit I was terribly glad I was never tempted to take the Queen's shilling. I'd rather play my fingers to the bone than forfeit my freedom and quite possibly my life."

Mr. Hobson, who had been watching Gemma intently during this exchange, interjected as soon as there was a pause in the conversation. "We heard that Lord Blackstock died under suspicious circumstances, but that's all we know really. Did you see it— the body, I mean? Is that why you're here, Miss Tate?"

Either the Hobsons had not had a chance to speak since this morning or Michael Hobson was playing dumb for Gemma's benefit, possibly to see what he could learn.

"I did, yes," Gemma replied.

"Can you tell us about it?" Mr. Hobson pressed. "What happened?"

"I'm afraid I'm not at liberty to discuss the details of the case." Gemma didn't think it right to divulge what she had seen, but, since Miss Hobson had already revealed the probable cause of death, she didn't see any harm in admitting the truth. "But I do think Lord Blackstock died by asphyxiation."

"But was he murdered?" Mr. Bennett cried. "Is it all right if I ask you that? It's only that when the circumstances are described as suspicious, murder instantly springs to mind."

"Yes, he was murdered, Mr. Bennett," Gemma replied.

There was no point in dissembling. Everyone would find out eventually, if they hadn't already. The arrival of a Scotland Yard detective was bound to give it away, since Sebastian would not have been called in if Lord Blackstock had died a natural death. It wasn't surprising that the passengers were curious about the details. People enjoyed gruesome tales of murder as long as the crime was far removed from their own lives, and they could treat the case as a shocking story.

Sebastian's new landlord, Bertram Quince, had a profitable sideline writing penny dreadfuls under his nom de plume, B.E. Ware, and was currently working on a full-length novel that featured a Scotland Yard detective, Samuel Knell, who by Mr. Quince's own admission was loosely based on Sebastian. Sebastian seemed both flattered and appalled by Quince's fictional inspector. Gemma thought he secretly hoped the novel would be rejected by Quince's publisher since a full-length detective story would be something of a novelty in literary circles and might not appeal to the public.

"Did you know Lord Blackstock?" Gemma directed the question to the men since Miss Hobson had already admitted to knowing the victim.

"Only to say good morning to," Michael Hobson replied. "The passengers from second class are not permitted to mix with the first-class ticket holders. We are only allowed to come up on deck because of Cora."

"I would have preferred to travel second class," Miss Hobson said reproachfully. "But Michael insisted I should have a proper cabin."

Michael smiled at his sister affectionately. "Three months of traveling and staying in separate boarding houses took a toll. Cora needed to rest, and we're just fine in second class, aren't we?"

The men nodded.

"As long as I have a place to lay my head and can count on at least two meals a day, I'm as happy as a man can be," Ezra Pennington said.

"I wouldn't have said no to first class," Clyde Bennett admitted, "but since Mr. Abbott covered the cost of the voyage and was willing to pay for a first-class stateroom for Cora, I will say thank you and leave it there."

"Too bad his generosity didn't stretch to paying for a berth for my cello," Ezra said with a chuckle, "but I'm still grateful for the opportunity to perform in the United States. It was truly eye-opening."

"I'm glad to be heading home," Miss Hobson said. "I am ready to sleep in my own bed and eat good, English food again."

"I can't say I missed the food, but I look forward to seeing my mother and sister, and longtime friends," Ezra said.

"What about you?" Gemma asked, turning to Mr. Bennett and Mr. Hobson. "What are you looking forward to?"

"I'm going to visit my brother. He's written to tell me I have a new nephew," Mr. Bennett said, his face breaking into a joyful smile.

"And I am excited to not hear Cora complain anymore," Michael Hobson said with an indulgent smile. "She's not a natural traveler. Are you, Cora?"

"Foreign travel is better suited to men," Cora replied.

Gemma would have liked to speak privately with Miss Hobson again. She was sure the woman knew more than she had thus far admitted, but the men did not look like they were about to leave, and Gemma didn't think she should question Miss Hobson in front of them. Perhaps she'd find a moment alone with her later in the day, after conferring with Sebastian.

Excusing herself, Gemma headed towards the hatch that led to first class, but was waylaid by Mr. Reynolds, who smiled broadly and slid his arm through hers in a way Gemma found entirely too familiar. Perhaps Americans didn't stand on ceremony when it came to social interaction, but like it or not, Gemma was now trapped and had no choice but to walk with him.

TWELVE

"Miss Tate, how are you getting on?" Mr. Reynolds asked once he'd drawn Gemma far enough from the members of the Bennett quartet to converse privately.

The question was not unreasonable, but Mr. Reynolds gazed at her like a man eager to claim a slot on her dance card rather than an officer who was in charge of a murder inquiry in the absence of his captain. Perhaps all Americans were so cavalier, or maybe it was just an act, meant to disarm and inspire confidence.

"Very well, thank you, Mr. Reynolds," Gemma replied politely.

"Shep, please."

"Shep," Gemma replied obediently.

"I was hoping I might steal you away for a cup of tea. I know how you English like your tea. I prefer coffee myself."

"A cup of either would be most welcome," Gemma said.

It had been hours since breakfast, and she didn't expect she and Sebastian would have anything to eat until they returned to shore. Sebastian had to be starving. He was always hungry, probably because he was perpetually in motion and expended more energy than someone whose work kept them behind a desk.

"Then please join me in the mess, and I will ask Cook to brew us a pot of coffee. You look a bit pale, if you will forgive me saying so."

"It's been years since I've been on a ship," Gemma said. She became queasy and felt a little unsteady on her feet as they navigated the narrow passages belowdecks that led to the mess hall.

"You'll get your sea legs by tomorrow."

"I very much doubt I'll still be here tomorrow," Gemma replied, and hoped that was true.

Shep Reynolds guided her through a door that led to a room furnished with a long table and a dozen chairs. Gemma's gaze slid to the wall, where several framed portraits hung in a row at eye level. A small plaque was affixed beneath each. Joseph Grinnell, Robert Bowne Minturn, and Preserved Fish.

"Preserved Fish?" Gemma exclaimed, and turned to Shep Reynolds. "Is that a joke?"

He laughed softly. "The accent is on the last e. It's from the Bible. As in preservéd from sin."

"And was he?"

"I very much doubt it."

Shep Reynolds held out a chair and invited Gemma to sit. "You must have great faith in Inspector Bell's abilities if you think he can solve a murder in one day," he said conversationally as he settled in a chair across from her.

"He's a very capable man."

"Are you his spy, Gemma?" Shep Reynolds asked once he'd instructed the steward to bring a pot of coffee and some bread and butter.

Gemma was annoyed that Reynolds had used her Christian name without being invited to do so, but she wasn't going to chastise him for his impropriety. She wanted to keep things friendly.

"What makes you say that, Shep?" she asked with a coy smile.

"Well, it's a shrewd ploy, isn't it? Set a beautiful, intelligent woman among the passengers and let her see what she can glean. Perhaps even force a confrontation to flush out the killer." Shep smiled slyly. "A cat among the pigeons, as you British like to say."

Gemma was torn between feeling flattered and indignant, but she could hardly fault the man for arriving at the obvious conclusion. She was questioning the passengers in order to help Sebastian; she could hardly deny that, but it wasn't her intention to cause a disturbance, only to learn the truth. And at that moment, the truth was that she couldn't be sure Shep's admiring gaze was genuine. Perhaps he really did find her intriguing, or perhaps he was doing his best to disarm her and worm his way into her confidence. If there was one thing she'd learned in Crimea, it was that men were nothing like what she had thought them to be before she'd had the wool pulled from her eyes.

As a respectable young woman, she had only been exposed to members of her family and family friends, who had treated her with kindness and respect and had always given the impression of being honorable and trustworthy. It was only once Gemma had been on her own and surrounded by men of different ilk and from all walks of life that she had understood just how duplicitous and self-serving they could be.

It wasn't that all men were immoral, they were simply human, with human failings. And when thrust into a situation where the veneer of respectability was torn away, their true natures inevitably began to emerge. Just as there were selfless individuals who risked their lives to help others, there were always those who found ways to profit, and there were some, like Shep Reynolds, who used their wit and charm to manipulate the people around them to do their bidding, especially women, who might be flattered by their attentions. One thing was certain, Gemma had to tread carefully around this man, lest he lull her into a false sense of security.

"Since you have divined my purpose on the ship, perhaps you will answer a few questions," Gemma said, and offered Shep her most beguiling smile.

"But Inspector Bell has questioned me already."

"But I haven't."

"All right. Ask away," Shep said, and his smile was slow, warm, and entirely too familiar.

Gemma felt heat rise in her cheeks as his gaze caressed her as if he could see through the layers of fabric down to her very skin, which prickled with unease at such unwelcome intimacy. Desperate to regain control, Gemma fixed Reynolds with a steady gaze, forcing him to meet her eyes.

"It seems there was a rather nasty confrontation between Lord Blackstock and Jeffrey Caldwell last night," she said.

"Was there?"

"Were you not aware of the argument?"

Shep shook his head. "With Captain Grant indisposed, I spent the better part of the last two days on the bridge. And for what it's worth, I don't think Mr. Caldwell could hurt a fly. I have never met a more even-keeled gentleman."

"Is that a nautical term?"

"It is, and I couldn't think of a more apropos way to describe the man."

"And how would you describe Lord Blackstock?"

"Tempestuous would probably do the job."

"Did he row with anyone else?"

"Why, Miss Tate, I believe you're resorting to nautical metaphors yourself, but we pronounce row differently."

"Row as in argue, Mr. Reynolds, not as in row with oars."

Shep Reynolds laughed. "I forget that for all intents and purposes, we speak a different language. You pronounce the same word differently and give it an entirely different meaning."

"You didn't answer my question."

"Anthony Blackstock had a short fuse. It was only a matter of time until he blew up at someone. I can't say I'm surprised it was at Mr. Caldwell."

"Did he take issue with Mr. Caldwell specifically? I was told he called the man a pig."

"The Caldwells own a good portion of South Carolina, as well as Caldwell Ironworks. I think Lord Blackstock felt a bit inferior despite his exalted title. From speaking to the man, I got the impression that he was land rich but cash poor."

"Was there anyone else Lord Blackstock took umbrage with? It has come to my attention that he was unkind to Mr. Abrahms."

"Unkind how?"

"He insulted him."

"And you think Mr. Abrahms retaliated by murdering Lord Blackstock and carving his own insult into the man's chest?"

"I don't know. Did he? People have killed for less."

"You'd know better than me, but I really don't think so. Mr. Abrahms has had to endure much worse than mere insults. Sticks and stones, Miss Tate. Sticks and stones."

"Are you suggesting that only physical harm can induce someone to react violently?"

"No, but I would stake my life on Joseph's innocence."

"Was there anyone else Lord Blackstock clashed with?"

"Not that I know of, but like I said, I spent most of my time on the bridge."

"You're not on the bridge now," Gemma observed.

"We're at anchor. The coxswain will send for me if my presence is required or if someone else wishes to board."

Recalling her own ordeal when boarding the ship, Gemma asked, "Mr. Reynolds—Shep—could someone have come aboard without your knowledge?"

Reynolds appeared surprised by the question but seemed to give it due consideration. "It's not very likely, but it's not impossible," he said at last.

"Would there be no way to stop them if they tried?"

"Do you suggest we pour boiling oil on the heads of all trespassers?" Shep asked, and grinned, flashing those perfect white teeth again. "Isn't that what you British do?" He was teasing her and clearly enjoying himself, but Gemma found his glib tone and the medieval reference galling. They weren't savages, although, recalling some of the mangled bodies of young men she'd tended to at Scutari, perhaps she was being naïve, and mankind never truly evolved, and the only things that changed were the weapons and the uniforms.

"We don't normally engage in barbaric behavior, if that's what you mean," she replied defensively. She still found the jibe upsetting and felt the need to defend her countrymen. "Boiling oil was used when a stronghold was under siege, and only as a last resort. And no one has relied on such antics in centuries, Mr. Reynolds."

"Forgive me. I didn't mean to offend," Shep replied, his expression now contrite. "I was joking."

"This is a serious matter." Gemma had no right to upbraid the man, but he seemed infuriatingly unconcerned. "A man has been brutally murdered, and his wife is unaccounted for, most probably dead."

"You're right, of course. Please accept my sincerest apology. I tend to resort to levity when faced with situations I am helpless to control. To answer your question, I don't believe anyone has come aboard. There's always someone on the bridge, and several sailors standing watch. So, although it's not completely impossible, I don't think that's what happened."

"Which means the killer was someone already aboard this ship."

"That would be the most logical assumption."

Gemma cocked her head and fixed Shep Reynolds with a piercing gaze. "Pardon me for saying so, Shep, but, levity aside, you don't seem very upset Lord Blackstock was murdered."

Shep's gaze grew even more serious. "I'm of the opinion that we all get what's coming to us."

"Are you suggesting that the victim brought the murder upon himself and deserved such savagery?"

"I'm suggesting that Anthony Blackstock hurt someone badly enough to make them lose control," Shep replied. "Which, in my eyes, makes him partly responsible. And I'm also of the opinion that there's only one likely suspect."

"And you think that's Audrey Blackstock," Gemma concluded.

"She was best placed to murder Anthony Blackstock during the night."

"But why would she do it here and now?"

Shep Reynolds tilted his head to the side and fixed Gemma with a melancholy look. "Even a faithful dog will bite its owner if kicked hard enough."

"Have you witnessed this alleged abuse of a woman you have just compared to a dog?"

Shep Reynolds waited until the steward set a tray before them and unloaded the items onto the table. There was a pot of coffee, milk, sugar, a plate of sliced bread, butter, and a dish of something blackish-purple that filled Gemma with deep suspicion.

"What on earth is that?"

"Grape jelly. Try it. I think you'll like it."

Gemma had heard of grape jelly but had never tasted it, and, although it sounded harmless enough, she found the color off-putting. Shep took a slice of bread, buttered it, then added a spoonful of jelly and spread it about before putting it on a plate and handing it to her. It seemed churlish to refuse, so Gemma accepted the offering and took a bite. The jelly was both sweet and tart, and absolutely delicious.

"It's made with home-grown Concord grapes. Captain Grant always makes certain there are several jars on board. He eats grape jelly every morning."

"It's lovely," Gemma said. "But I think you're avoiding my question."

Shep buttered a slice of bread for himself and added a bit of jelly, then said, "I've crossed the Atlantic dozens of times, Miss Tate, and have served with and known all sorts of men. I don't have to be a witness to abuse to know that someone is capable of it."

"So, you condemned Anthony Blackstock based on a hunch?"

"I condemned Anthony Blackstock based on the fear he inspired in the women he was meant to protect."

"Are you referring to the Blackstocks' servants?"

Shep nodded. "You've seen the mask, Miss Tate."

"Lord Blackstock was something of a historian, was he not? This was an artifact. Are you suggesting he meant to use the mask for its intended purpose?"

Shep Reynolds gave Gemma a knowing look. "There are three types of men, Miss Tate—those who love women, those who hate and fear them, and those who are utterly indifferent to them. Anthony Blackstock did not like women. It was obvious, despite his mostly charming demeanor. It was feigned. He was a man who thought a woman should know her place, and her place was right after his horses and dogs and before his livestock."

"Is this opinion based on evidence?"

"Captain Grant invited the gentlemen from first class to take an after-dinner drink with him several times during the voyage. The captain is a lifelong bachelor and has no use for women unless they're there to cook, clean, and do his laundry, but he does enjoy the company of men, and he likes his drink. Some would say too much to be in a position of authority."

Gemma thought that was a bit disloyal, but this was a murder investigation, and she wasn't about to turn down the revelation Shep Reynolds was about to share.

"Over brandy and cigars, Anthony Blackstock regaled us with tales of torture in the Middle Ages. He described devices invented with the express purpose of punishing women and said that collecting such objects was something of a passion with him. That was when he told us about the scold's bridle he had found during his visit, which is now locked around his head. It seems he kept a number of such devices at his home, and from the way he described them I got the distinct impression that he had found occasion to use them."

Gemma couldn't take another bite and set down the uneaten bread. Her throat seemed to close, and the queasiness had turned into full-blown nausea as her mind supplied images she would rather not see. The very notion of being locked inside the iron cage stole her breath, and terror welled in her breast as she imagined the fear a woman might feel when at the mercy of a man who was capable of inflicting such torture.

"What sort of devices?" she choked out.

"There was the yoke, something called a cucking stool, and a drunkard's coat, which Blackstock described as a barrel with an opening for the arms and head. All these were used to punish disobedient women. And he was also in possession of a centuries-old Judas cradle, a torture device used during the Inquisition on both men and women and intended to tear the area between the legs when the victim was lowered onto it. Lord Blackstock brought the cradle back from some Caribbean island, where he discovered it at a sugar plantation. He thought it was brought over by Spanish pirates."

Shep Reynolds shook his head in disgust. "Anthony Blackstock told these stories with relish and went so far as to suggest that the women of today have too much freedom and need to be periodically reminded of their obligation to the men in their lives." He sighed. "He mentioned breaking his riding crop over a spirited filly. And I don't think he was speaking about a horse."

Gemma swallowed hard, then took a gulp of her cooling coffee in an effort to dislodge the lump that had formed in her throat. If a man was capable of such cruelty, he wouldn't stop with his wife. He would inflict his brand of discipline on any woman who found herself in his power, and possibly every man.

Perhaps that was the reason Audrey Blackstock's lady's maid and Anthony Blackstock's valet had run off. Few individuals in service would simply leave. They would give at least a few weeks' notice, ask for a character reference, and collect their wages. The maid and valet had forfeited both the references and the wages, since servants were usually paid quarterly and the two had left sometime in May. Perhaps they had seen a chance of a better life and had taken it, or perhaps one or both could no longer suffer the abuse and had been willing to forgo the references and the money that would help them start fresh in favor of getting away unimpeded.

And if that were the case, it was just as possible that Lorna Thorpe and Greta Van Kemp had been Lord Blackstock's victims as well. But neither maidservant bore signs of abuse, and both were still aboard, whereas Lady Blackstock was missing and had presumably been inside the stateroom when her husband was killed.

"The watch heard something heavy drop in the water around the time of the murder," Shep Reynolds said once the silence had stretched on too long. "And the manner of Anthony Blackstock's death appears to be a final message from a woman who couldn't take any more. Audrey Blackstock wanted the world to know what sort of man she had married."

Shep Reynolds' theory made an awful kind of sense, and Gemma couldn't help but wonder if Sebastian had come to the same conclusion after speaking to the other passengers. But before she accepted Shep's version of events, she had to be sure to rule out anyone else who might have borne Lord Blackstock a grudge.

"Is there anyone else aboard the ship who might have wanted to punish Lord Blackstock?" she asked.

"What reason would someone who barely knew him have to lock his head in a torture device and carve a slur into his chest? As far as I can see, Audrey Blackstock is... was the only one who could have managed that, and she's gone. Sad as I feel for the poor woman, to my mind, the case is solved."

"So, what do you propose?"

"I propose you allow us to dock."

"That's really not up to me," Gemma protested.

"No, but Inspector Bell clearly listens to you, so a word in his ear—"

"Will have to wait," Gemma finished the sentence. "If what you say is true, then Inspector Bell will arrive at the same conclusion. Until then, the investigation must remain active."

Shep Reynolds smiled indulgently. "I thought you might say as much, but it was worth a try."

"Why are you in such a hurry to dock, Mr. Reynolds?" Gemma asked.

Shep's about-face wasn't lost on her. Less than half an hour before, he had suggested they remain on board long enough for Gemma to get her sea legs. Now, he was urging Gemma to convince Sebastian to accept his explanation and close the case. Perhaps Shep Reynolds was right, and the solution was obvious, but until Sebastian was satisfied that there was sufficient evidence to accuse Audrey Blackstock of murder he would not be willing to walk away. Nor should he, since to Gemma's mind Jeffrey Caldwell was the more likely suspect.

"We have a schedule to keep, freight and mail to deliver, and passengers to discharge. We can't afford to delay much longer. And I need to get home."

"Why?" Gemma asked, and wondered who was waiting for Shep Reynolds at home.

She'd noted that he hadn't mentioned Captain Grant or the man's urgent need for medical attention. Did Shep think a bout of malaria would simply run its course, or did he hope to captain the ship in Grant's absence and perhaps show his superiors at Grinnell, Minturn and Company that he was ready for a ship of his own? He'd said himself that he'd crossed the Atlantic a great many times. Perhaps this unexpected situation was interfering with his personal plans and needed to be resolved quickly.

"I have personal business to attend to at home," Shep said, but did not elaborate.

They had finished their coffee, and there seemed nothing left to say, so Gemma pushed away from the table and stood primly, waiting for the first mate to escort her upstairs. He thanked the steward, who immediately began to clear away the dirty crockery, and held the door for Gemma.

"Whom would you like to speak to next, Miss Tate?" Shep Reynolds asked as soon as they emerged on deck.

Gemma would have liked to feel a fresh breeze on her face after the windowless stillness of the mess, but the air was warm and moist, the sky no longer bright blue but a washed-out aqua that looked grayer the closer it got to the horizon. The skyline that had looked sharp that morning was now murky, the buildings dissolving into the shimmering haze of the still summer afternoon.

"I need to speak to Inspector Bell," she said, then turned on her heel and went in search of Sebastian.

THIRTEEN

Sebastian was still in first class. He looked tired, cross, and a bit green around the gills, and with good reason. Even with the open door, the narrow space was beginning to smell like a dead house, the combination of the rising temperature, the Blackstocks' windowless stateroom, and the dead body responsible for the pronounced odor of decay.

"I need some air," Sebastian said as soon as he saw Gemma. "Let's find a spot where we can speak privately."

That was easier said than done since the deck was crowded with passengers and crewmen. Presumably each sailor had his job when the ship was at sea, but when the vessel was at anchor all they could do was bide their time, much as if they were in the doldrums and didn't know when they would be on their way again. The mood was somber, and countless pairs of eyes turned towards Sebastian as soon as he and Gemma came up on deck, everyone hoping for news or at least an update on when the ship would be permitted to continue on to the port.

Gemma and Sebastian carefully navigated around masts, overhanging rigging, several hatches, and the forecastle until they found a spot near the prow. It wasn't very private, nor was it particularly quiet, but at least it was outside, and none of the passengers could come near without being spotted. Gemma relayed everything she had learned and watched Sebastian's face darken with anger.

"I'm certain Reynolds was aware of the altercation between Jeffrey Caldwell and Anthony Blackstock but chose not to mention it," he said.

"What could he hope to gain by not telling you?" Gemma asked.

"Time," Sebastian replied. "He's astute enough to realize that someone will mention the argument sooner or later, but in the meantime he's cozying up to you in order to manipulate the investigation."

"How? And why would he need to cozy up to me?" Gemma asked, not bothering to hide her annoyance. Did Sebastian really think she was so easily led?

"If what Reynolds said about Anthony Blackstock is true, then the man was a nasty piece of work who had a short fuse and a penchant for cruelty. Reynolds was hoping to influence the outcome of the investigation by playing on your sympathies." Sebastian smiled tenderly and reached out to cup Gemma's cheek when she opened her mouth to protest at the injustice of this insinuation. "But he didn't realize how clever you are," he said before Gemma had a chance to reprove him.

"Reynolds thought that if he offered a neat solution to the problem, I would see the logic of his argument and persuade you to close the investigation, but, although his theory is plausible, I'm not convinced Audrey Blackstock is the killer," Gemma said.

"Neither am I."

"But why would Shep Reynolds attempt to manipulate the outcome?" Gemma asked. "Do you think he's somehow involved?"

Until that moment, it hadn't occurred to her to include Shep Reynolds in the list of suspects, but now she wasn't so sure. Reynolds' cabin was a few feet from first class. He probably had obtained, or could easily obtain, a key to the Blackstocks' stateroom, and no one would question his presence if they saw him near the staterooms in the middle of the night, but would assume he was on his way back to his own quarters. He would have the strength to subdue Anthony Blackstock and to carry Audrey Blackstock up on deck if he intended to dispose of her body. But what would be his motive?

Gemma could conceive of several possibilities. Perhaps Anthony Blackstock had insulted Shep Reynolds as well, or had made a threat Reynolds couldn't afford to ignore. And if Reynolds had murdered the Blackstocks, the best way to deflect suspicion would be to send for the police and head up the investigation in lieu of the captain. But if Anthony Blackstock had threatened Shep Reynolds, why would Reynolds murder the man's wife, then blame her for her husband's death, unless he had murdered her for just that purpose? It didn't quite make sense unless the man was a remorseless killer who was utterly devoid of any shred of humanity. Despite his cocky manner and apparent lack of sympathy for Anthony Blackstock, Gemma did not think Shep Reynolds lacked a soul.

The other possibility was that Anthony Blackstock had been the one to murder his wife and throw her body overboard. Was it possible that Shep Reynolds had caught him in the act and killed him to avenge Audrey, whom he'd singled out for his attention? But then why try to blame her for Blackstock's murder, unless Shep Reynolds feared the investigation was getting too close and his own liberty was at stake?

Unless Audrey Blackstock wasn't dead. But if she was alive and Shep Reynolds was hiding her somewhere on the ship, why would he attempt to pin the murder on her? As soon as Audrey emerged, she would have to face the consequences. And she would have no choice but to reveal herself if she hoped to lay claim to her husband's estate. Otherwise, the woman would not only be a fugitive but a destitute one.

Gemma supposed such a scenario was possible, but it didn't seem very likely, not when most people were ruled by greed and self-preservation. Neither Audrey Blackstock nor Shep Reynolds would benefit financially from the crime, and, if they'd conspired to kill Anthony Blackstock with a view to setting Audrey free, they could have made his death look like natural causes by simply holding a pillow over his face. Audrey would raise the alarm, there'd be no proof that Anthony Blackstock had been murdered, and the coconspirators would get on with their lives without the threat of imprisonment and execution. Putting Anthony Blackstock in that horrible mask and cutting letters into his chest precluded even the most incompetent policeman from mistaking his death for anything other than murder.

"There's no reason to think Reynolds was involved, at least not yet," Sebastian said once Gemma had outlined her theories, "but he might have his own motive for wanting the case closed quickly."

"Do you think he's protecting someone?"

"Yes, himself and his future prospects."

"I'm afraid I don't understand," Gemma said. "Do you think that a murder aboard the ship will somehow derail his career aspirations?"

"Not so much the murder, but the delay the investigation will cause."

"The delay was unavoidable."

Sebastian nodded. "Reynolds had no choice but to follow Captain Grant's orders and alert the police. Anthony Blackstock was a British national who was murdered aboard an American vessel. He was a respected politician and a member of the nobility, and happened to be closely associated with the British envoy to Washington. If the shipping line was accused of mismanaging the case, the repercussions could be dire; the line could be banned from docking at any British port. The ensuing backlash might even lead to diplomatic tensions between the two nations."

"That being the case, why would Shep Reynolds wish to manipulate the outcome?" Gemma asked. "Surely it's in everyone's best interest that the investigation is as thorough and complete as possible in order to absolve the shipping line of any culpability."

"If it is my finding that Audrey Blackstock murdered her

husband and took her own life in a fit of remorse, then no one else is at fault and the *Prince Regent* is free to proceed, which is what Shep Reynolds is after. And if the *Prince Regent* docks today, she will be recorded as having arrived two days ahead of schedule, which will be a feather in Reynolds' cap."

"Will docking today really make that much difference?"

Gemma still couldn't comprehend why that should matter in the face of what had transpired on board. There was no bringing Anthony Blackstock back from the dead, nor was there much likelihood of finding Lady Blackstock's body if she was in the water, unless the current deposited it on the banks of the Thames, but finding out what had happened had to take priority over arriving ahead of schedule.

"It will make a difference to Reynolds and Captain Grant," Sebastian replied wearily. "Individuals on both sides of the Atlantic place bets on transatlantic clippers, and notable crossing times are posted in certain papers in the Shipping Intelligence columns, much like the results of horse races. The captains who achieve the fastest crossing times are rewarded by the owners of the shipping lines, and those who'd bet on the right horse, so to speak, collect substantial winnings."

"People bet on sailing ships?" Gemma asked, bemused, but then realized she shouldn't be.

Individuals susceptible to gambling would bet on anything and root passionately for their champions. In Scutari, Gemma had seen patients betting on how quickly a rat or a roach could cross the ward, or placing wagers on which patients would live and which would die. It was a grim, awful thing to do, but for some men it was a way to defy their fear and focus on something other than their own mortality. And when someone survived the odds and managed to live another day, it gave the other men hope and allowed them to believe they might also live long enough to see their loved ones again.

Sebastian's gaze went to the tall masts and the web of rigging overhead. "Betting on crossing times is more popular than you might imagine. It began in earnest in the Thirties, after the East India Company's monopoly on the tea trade was abolished and the competing merchants were desperate to be the first to deliver their shipments of tea from China.

"And in 1851, the *Flying Cloud*, a clipper owned by the same line as the *Prince Regent*, set a record when it sailed from New York to San Francisco in under ninety days. What made the crossing even more notable was that the clipper was navigated by a woman," Sebastian explained when Gemma gaped at him.

Sebastian wasn't a gambler, and she was amazed he'd know this, but perhaps it wasn't so surprising. Despite not having a university education—Sebastian had attended the village school until he'd left to help his parents on the farm when he turned fourteen—he was well read and liked to keep abreast of what was happening in the world. In his line of work he had to remain well informed, but, more importantly, he had to comprehend the vagaries of human nature if he hoped to unravel the motives and spot the lies people told so he could get to the truth.

Sebastian read a variety of newspapers and sometimes stopped for a pint at some of the seedier public houses, where he could rub elbows with the lower orders and hear what occupied their minds and roused their ire. It was his innate curiosity and understanding of his fellow man that made him such a good detective, and such a dangerous enemy should someone dare to cross him.

"So, that's what Shep Reynolds is concerned with?" Gemma asked, now even more repelled by the man.

"The London-bound ships' two-week schedule makes it easy to track their crossing times. Betting on ocean crossings is extremely popular in the United States and has been at fever pitch since gold was discovered in California ten years ago, but there are those who bet on the New York to London route as well. If the *Prince Regent* docks two days early, she can return earlier than expected, which will no doubt result in a bonus for Reynolds and Grant."

"To try to force your hand for the sake of arriving a few days earlier is contemptible and underhanded, but I must admit that

Mr. Reynolds makes a valid point about Audrey Blackstock," Gemma mused. "At first glance, Jeffrey Caldwell is the obvious suspect, but, unless the man is a complete fool, he wouldn't murder Anthony Blackstock the very night the two men engaged in a heated exchange. And if not Caldwell, then who, besides Lady Blackstock, would have reason to murder the man in such a grisly way?

"Even if Lorna Thorpe, who made it sound like her employer's anger was fleeting and harmless, or Joseph Abrahms, who had to have been called much worse names while enslaved, had borne Reynolds a grudge for the way he had treated them, why go to the trouble of putting Blackstock in a bridle and carving an insult into his chest? And the fact that Audrey Blackstock is missing could speak to her involvement."

"Until we know more, we must treat Audrey Blackstock as a second victim," Sebastian replied. "Perhaps the killer had no choice but to murder her because she was a witness to the crime, or perhaps the killer wanted everyone to think that she murdered her husband and then killed herself because she couldn't bear to face the gallows. It's also possible that Audrey Blackstock is still on this ship, and she could be alive or dead, her body safely hidden until the ship docks."

"What do you propose?" Gemma asked. Her head was swimming with all these possibilities, and her frustration mounted as they considered and discarded each one in turn.

"I need to question the Caldwells about last night's altercation, and I have yet to speak to the Glenns and the Ringwoods, since a couple of sailors had come to take away the remains and I wasn't able to interview them until the sailors left. And I'd like to get the body to Colin today. The postmortem might reveal something we have yet to consider."

"Such as?"

"What if asphyxiation was not the cause of death? Anthony Blackstock may have pressed his caged head into the pillow, which would account for the rust on the pillowcase. He could also have suffered a heart attack or died of an overdose of laudanum or morphine before the letters were cut into his chest, which would explain why no one heard anything."

"Yes, a postmortem will definitely tell us more," Gemma agreed. "In the meantime, I should reinterview Greta Van Kemp and Lorna Thorpe. As Lady Blackstock's lady's maid, Greta might know if Audrey Blackstock was with child and, if so, whether the child's paternity might have been in question. And since Greta was unwell yesterday, Lorna would have been the one to assist her mistress as she prepared for bed. She would have overheard the altercation between the two men and might have something important to add. I wonder why she didn't mention it when I spoke to her earlier."

Sebastian nodded in approval. "Can you find your way back to the servants' cabin?"

"I think so."

"All right. Let's meet in the first-class saloon in an hour," Sebastian suggested as they made their way towards the hatches that would take them belowdecks once again.

FOURTEEN

Sebastian watched Gemma disappear as she descended the stairs that led to second class and steerage. He had yet to visit either, but he dreaded returning belowdecks. It was the closeness of the space that bothered him. The windowless passages, low ceilings, and tiny cabins stole his breath away, and he tried to imagine what it would feel like to be confined to quarters for two whole weeks, especially in inclement weather. He would brave any discomfort if he decided to emigrate to America—after all, a person could tolerate anything for two weeks—but, now that he had decided to remain in England, he was glad he didn't have to.

As he made his way down, Sebastian realized he'd never asked Gemma about the voyage to Scutari. It must have taken weeks, if not months, and the route would have been determined not only by distance and geographic impediments but by whichever power controlled the various ports at the time of the journey. Once they disembarked, Florence Nightingale's nurses would have also had to travel over land and been on the road for days before they reached the out-of-the-way hospital and finally settled into their accommodation.

Not for the first time, Sebastian reflected on how brave Gemma was and how stoic in the face of life's hardships. Few women of his acquaintance would subject themselves to such an ordeal or risk their safety to help others, while living in unspeakable conditions and working practically around the clock. Sebastian smiled when he recalled Mr. Reynolds' observation that Gemma's name meant "gem." She really was a gem, and, if he didn't secure her affections, some other man would be sure to snatch her up. The only thing that worked in Sebastian's favor was that, for some unfathomable reason, Gemma loved him and wanted to be his partner both in life and in his work. Despite the heartbreak life had dealt him, he really was the luckiest of men, and he would tell Gemma so as soon as an opportunity presented itself. But just now, he had to focus on the matter at hand.

"Back so soon?" Marilyn Caldwell asked as soon as Sebastian walked through the door. She was just coming out of her stateroom, having changed into an afternoon dress of blue and cream striped satin.

It was odd that a couple as wealthy as the Caldwells would be traveling without servants, but perhaps all their servants were slaves, and the Caldwells had no wish to bring them to England and open themselves up to derision and judgment. It was easy enough to manage without servants if one stayed at luxury hotels that could provide whatever service their guests required. It was certainly a less incendiary decision than bringing along enslaved people and setting them among servants who, although frequently disgruntled and underpaid, were at least free and might put ideas of revolt in their heads.

"You failed to mention that your husband and Lord Blackstock quarreled last night," Sebastian said as soon as he approached the stateroom and saw that Jeffrey Caldwell wasn't there. He was probably waiting for Marilyn on deck.

Marilyn waved a dismissive hand. "It was nothing, Inspector. No harm done."

"I was told Lord Blackstock accused your husband of cheating and called him a pig. That doesn't sound like nothing to me."

"Anthony was frustrated at having lost," Marilyn explained

calmly. "These things happen when men's blood is up. He instantly regretted his outburst."

"Did he offer your husband an apology?" Sebastian inquired.

"Not in so many words, but Anthony looked mortified when he realized how unfair he'd been. Jeffrey was upset, I won't lie, but he prayed on it and decided he wasn't going to hold a grudge. As good Christians, we believe in the power of forgiveness, Inspector, and try to turn the other cheek, as the Bible teaches us. Matthew 5:39," she added for good measure.

"The Bible also talks about an eye for an eye, and a tooth for a tooth." Sebastian couldn't remember the exact verse, he'd never been particularly devout, but he was fairly certain it came from Deuteronomy. "The word *pig* was carved into Lord Blackstock's chest. That's quite a coincidence, since he'd called Jeffrey a pig last night."

Marilyn Caldwell looked suitably horrified. "You never said."

"Would it have mattered if I had?" Sebastian countered. "Where's your husband, Mrs. Caldwell?"

"Right here," Jeffrey Caldwell said as he came down the stairs. "And no need to repeat yourself, Inspector. I heard what you said."

"And what have *you* got to say?"

Jeffrey smiled indulgently. "If I was to murder every man who caused me offense, I would have left a trail of bodies from Charleston to New York."

"You expect me to believe that you simply shrugged off such a grave insult?"

"I did, yes. Tempers flare when men lose money. Even more so after they have been confined to close quarters for two weeks. I took my winnings and left. That was the end of it. I fully expected Anthony to apologize once he'd had time to cool down, but even if he didn't I was prepared to forgive him, as Mary said."

"So, you didn't go to his cabin during the night and teach him some manners?" Sebastian asked.

"Unequivocally, no. And to allay any doubts, I invite you to search our stateroom. I expect whoever mutilated Anthony Blackstock would have incurred a number of bloodstains and probably used a sharp object. You will not find any soiled garments or knives in our cabin."

"You could have easily disposed of the evidence," Sebastian said. *Much as you could have disposed of the only witness*, he added silently.

"Yes, I could have, but I still have my pocketknife and shaving razor."

"Which you could have cleaned."

Jeffrey sniggered, his demeanor one of a man completely unafraid, since he probably never had occasion to be, and Sebastian caught a glimpse of someone who wasn't nearly as affable as he liked to pretend. "I would have to be an absolute moron to murder Anthony Blackstock right after he attacked me in full view of several witnesses, and do it in a way that would point directly to me. And I can assure you, Sebastian, I'm no moron. And I think neither are you. I'm not your man, but I will humor you until you prove otherwise." Caldwell gestured towards the stateroom. "Shall we?"

Sebastian walked past the man and entered the stateroom, which was a mirror image of the Blackstocks'. The room was tidy, the bed neatly made, and the Caldwells' possessions economically organized within the small space. Sebastian searched the room thoroughly while Marilyn and Jeffrey looked on from the doorway, but he found nothing to implicate Jeffrey Caldwell in Anthony Blackstock's murder. That didn't mean Caldwell was innocent, only that there was no evidence to prove his guilt.

FIFTEEN

Having completed his search, Sebastian asked the Caldwells to go on deck and requested that Mr. Hendon, who'd come to inquire if lunch may be served, find the Glenns. They returned to the first-class saloon a few minutes later and immediately introduced themselves as Francesca and Chester. Mrs. Glenn, who was probably in her early fifties, was an imposing woman. She was elegantly attired in a morning gown of pale marigold, and her pearl necklace and earbobs glowed richly in the soft light of the oil lamp. She had wide, dark eyes and chestnut hair that was gently threaded with silver. Laugh lines fanned from the corners of her eyes and bracketed her mouth, but her cheeks were unlined, and her jowls were still firm above the high collar of her gown.

Chester Glenn's hair and short beard were shot through with strands of gray, but otherwise he showed no signs of impending old age. He was tall and erect and had the lean physique of a much younger man. His whimsical maroon waistcoat and silk cravat hinted at a flair for fashion, and the thick gold chain of his pocket watch and the cabochon ring he wore on his pinky reinforced Sebastian's assumption that the Glenns were comfortably off.

Francesca and Chester joined Sebastian at the table, their faces reflecting their desire to be of service.

"We have been waiting for our turn to speak to you, Inspector," Chester Glenn said, and reached for his wife's hand, which he squeezed affectionately.

"Why is that? Do you know who murdered Lord Blackstock?" Sebastian asked.

To be handed the identity of the killer was too much to hope for, but the Glenns clearly knew something, or thought they did.

"We don't know who did it, of course," Chester Glenn said. "If we did, we would have said so as soon as you came aboard, and we certainly don't want to accuse anyone, but Franny saw something she thought was important for you to know. Go on, tell him, Franny," Chester urged his wife when she failed to speak.

"What did you want to tell me, Mrs. Glenn?" Sebastian prompted.

Francesca leaned forward, even though they were quite alone. Sebastian leaned in as well, eager to hear what she had to say. When she spoke, Francesca's voice was low and husky, and her hands were clasped before her on the table, her knuckles white with tension.

"Yesterday, after breakfast, Chester and I went up on deck. All the first-class guests usually did the same, since it gave the stewards an opportunity to clear away the breakfast dishes and clean our cabins. It was chillier than I had anticipated, and after a time I became quite cold. Chester offered to fetch my shawl, but he was engaged in conversation with Mr. Hobson, and I saw no reason to interrupt, so I nipped downstairs myself," she explained. "The stewards had finished. They're very quick. A few minutes per cabin at most, since there's not that much to do and the guests don't like it when they handle personal possessions. All they do is make the beds and give the floor a perfunctory sweep. And Mr. Abrahms empties the chamber pots."

"Get to the point, Franny," Chester said gently.

Francesca nodded. "I didn't think there was anyone here. I grabbed the shawl and had just come out of our stateroom."

"Whom did you see, Mrs. Glenn?" Sebastian asked when Francesca paused.

"I didn't see anyone at first, but I heard them, Inspector. There was..." The woman colored slightly and looked to her husband, who nodded reassuringly. "There was grunting and a sort of whimpering coming from the Blackstocks' stateroom. I returned to our cabin, shut the door, and opened the slats just enough to see out. Then I waited."

Mrs. Glenn looked deeply embarrassed and clasped her hands even tighter. "I'm not the sort of person to spy on others, Inspector, and normally, if I saw or heard something I wasn't meant to, I would keep walking, but there was just something about that whimpering that made me think someone was in terrible pain."

Chester Glenn placed a hand over his wife's, as if silently shoring her up.

"The truth is, I thought it might be Joe Abrahms, and I wanted to make certain he was okay. The poor boy is terrified, and every time he comes down here and comes face to face with Mr. Caldwell not only is he reminded of his tragic past and the people he's lost, but he fears for his very life."

"Does Mr. Caldwell have the power to harm him?"

Francesca nodded. "Of course he does. If he writes to Joe's owner—and it wouldn't be very difficult to discover who his owner is—and tells him where the boy is, the man can try to reclaim ownership."

"How can he do that if Joseph never returns to Georgia?" Sebastian asked.

"He doesn't have to cross the Mason–Dixon line to be in danger. There are people, bounty hunters, who track down runaway slaves, kidnap them, and bring them back to their owners. By the time anyone realized Joe was gone, he'd be on some boat, hog-tied and gagged, and on his way to Georgia."

"I see," Sebastian said quietly. He hadn't realized how fraught with risk Joseph Abrahms' new life really was or how easily he could be returned to the hell he'd fled and lose the freedom that had cost him so much.

"Did Mr. Caldwell make any threats?"

"I'm not certain, but, given Joe's obvious fear of the man, I think he must have said something," Francesca replied.

"And was it Joseph Abrahms you heard in the Blackstocks' stateroom?"

"I wasn't sure, so I waited," Francesca said, still reluctant to name the person.

"Did you think it might have been Audrey Blackstock?" Sebastian tried again.

Francesca shook her head. "Audrey was on deck. I saw her before I came downstairs. She was speaking to Mr. Reynolds. That man was always cornering her when she was on her own. I think he made her quite uncomfortable."

"So, who was it?"

Sebastian was growing frustrated with this drawn-out account, but he had to allow Francesca Glenn to tell him in her own time. She was clearly embarrassed and would have never admitted to snooping had a murder not taken place and made her feel it was her duty to reveal what she knew.

"The door eventually opened, and a young woman stumbled out. Her clothes were in disarray, and there were red marks on the lower half of her face. Finger marks," Francesca added. "Like someone had held their hand over her face to keep her quiet. The poor thing looked haunted and ran towards the door, even though she was clearly unsteady on her feet. What happened in that cabin had not been done with her consent, Inspector. She had been viciously violated."

"Who was the woman, Mrs. Glenn? Had you seen her before?"

Francesca nodded. "It was Audrey Blackstock's lady's maid. We were never properly introduced, but I heard Lady Blackstock address her. The name sounded Dutch. Van Sant or Von Kent, or something similar."

"And the man?" Sebastian asked.

He assumed Mrs. Glenn was referring to Anthony Blackstock, but it was possible that someone else had been in that stateroom. One of the stewards, perhaps. Sailors were a rum bunch, and, although they would never dare assault a first-class passenger, a maid was of no account and would probably not be believed if she made a complaint.

"It was Anthony Blackstock, Inspector Bell," Francesca whispered. "I saw him. He emerged a few moments later, and," she looked absolutely mortified, her gaze resting on her clasped hands, "he was still buttoning his trousers as he walked towards the stairs."

"Had you seen Lord Blackstock accost any other women?" Sebastian asked. "Or men?"

"No, but there was something about him." Francesca made a show of thinking, then said, "Predatory. He was the sort of man women instinctively fear, even if he's the soul of politeness and good manners. It's all an act. Beneath the veneer of respectability hides a barbarian. There, I said it," she cried. "It was important you know what sort of man Anthony Blackstock was."

"Thank you, Mrs. Glenn. I know that wasn't easy, but what you told me casts my investigation in a whole new light."

"Does it really?" Francesca asked, her face alight with hope.

"It most certainly does."

Then, having realized that she had exposed Miss Van Kemp to scrutiny and embarrassment, Mrs. Glenn added, "Please, be kind to the young woman, Inspector. I daresay she suffered enough at the hands of that man."

"You have my word," Sebastian assured her as she stood wearily. "Mr. Glenn," he said, turning to Chester. "Did you happen to notice if Joseph Abrahms was in the vicinity when the quarrel between Mr. Caldwell and Lord Blackstock broke out last night?"

"Erm, yes, he was, actually."

"Had he come down to empty the pots?"

"No," Chester Glenn said. "In his rage, Anthony Blackstock

knocked over a bottle of whisky, then called to Mr. Abrahms, who'd come down to bring Miss Hobson a glass of water, to wipe it up."

"And did he?"

Chester Glenn nodded. "He crouched beneath the table and mopped up the whisky as quickly as he could. He was very frightened."

"Was Mr. Abrahms there when Lord Blackstock called Mr. Caldwell a pig?"

"Yes, he was. Why?" Chester Glenn asked.

"No reason. I'm just trying to get my house in order."

"Your house?" Mr. Glenn asked confusedly.

"I just need to establish who was there."

"Joseph Abrahms had nothing to do with Lord Blackstock's death," Francesca Glenn said hotly. "And I will not have you accusing him. Not if I can help it."

"I have not made any accusations, Mrs. Glenn," Sebastian replied calmly. "I simply need to know who was where at the time of the altercation. Did you overhear the argument?"

Francesca nodded. "Yes, I did. It was vicious. And I must admit that, even though I don't like Jeffrey Caldwell and cannot respect what he stands for, he acquitted himself admirably and conducted himself as a gentleman should, unlike Anthony Blackstock, whose behavior was abominable." She drew herself up. "And now, if you don't mind, I need some air. It's awfully close in here."

Francesca Glenn didn't seem to fully grasp that by sharing what sort of man Anthony Blackstock was she had given Greta Van Kemp a motive for murder. A woman who had been brutalized by a man on whose goodwill her livelihood depended would feel pain, rage, humiliation, and an all-consuming desire for vengeance. And to lock his head in a device meant for tormenting women and carve the word *pig* into his chest would certainly be appropriate, but Sebastian wasn't ready to rule Jeffrey Caldwell out as a suspect.

Sebastian would speak to Greta Van Kemp in due course, but first he intended to ask Chester Glenn a few questions. Francesca

Glenn walked towards the stairs, then stopped and turned. Her husband made to follow, but Sebastian forestalled him.

"A moment, Mr. Glenn."

Chester paused. "I really should see to my wife."

"Just a few questions, and then you can join Mrs. Glenn on deck."

Chester nodded reluctantly. "All right. Go on without me, my dear," he called out. "I'll join you in a moment."

"Lord Blackstock was found with an iron cage on his head and the word *pig* etched into his chest. The cage could represent bondage, and I was told that he had called Mr. Caldwell a pig, so the circumstances of his death fit with the insults he had hurled at his opponent."

Chester Glenn appeared shocked by the image Sebastian had just supplied, but then shook his head slowly. "I know how it looks, Inspector, and of course you must investigate every angle, given what's happened, but I would be hard-pressed to believe that Mr. Caldwell would go to such lengths to avenge an insult. Besides, no one heard a thing last night. Surely, if Jeff Caldwell had broken into the Blackstocks' stateroom and gone for Lord Blackstock, there would have been a commotion. And poor Audrey would have been frightened out of her wits. But I didn't hear a peep from either of them."

"So, what do you imagine happened?" Sebastian asked. He had to agree with Chester Glenn's assessment. The lack of a struggle and Audrey Blackstock's silence were puzzling.

"The maid, Miss Van something, had a key to the Blackstocks' stateroom. She came to lay out Audrey's gowns and tidy the cabin. Given what that man did to her..."

"You think Miss Van Kemp murdered Lord Blackstock?" Sebastian asked.

"She must have. She had reason enough, didn't she?"

"You think she could have done that all by herself?"

"I don't know," Chester Glenn demurred, clearly realizing how far-fetched that sounded, then added, "Well, maybe not by herself, but if she had help..."

"Help from whom?"

"The other maidservant perhaps? She must have suffered at Blackstock's hands as well. A man like that doesn't just do something like that once."

Sebastian had to acknowledge that it wasn't an unreasonable suggestion, except for one thing. "And Lady Blackstock? What do you reckon happened to her, Mr. Glenn?"

"Perhaps the women blamed her for not protecting them from her husband."

"What could she have done?"

"Probably nothing, but that doesn't matter to someone who's angry enough to kill and who will most likely hang for murder if there's an eyewitness." Chester Glenn pushed to his feet. "If you will excuse me, Inspector."

"Of course."

Sebastian watched Chester Glenn leave, then leaned back in his chair, his gaze finding the closed door of the Blackstocks' stateroom. He only had Francesca Glenn's word for what had happened between Lord Blackstock and Greta Van Kemp, but Sebastian didn't doubt that Mrs. Glenn had told him the truth of what she had seen. Her husband made a valid point. Victims looked for someone to blame, and they might have held their mistress responsible for her husband's actions. And if the two maids had joined forces and murdered the man who'd abused them, they could either trust that their mistress wouldn't report them to the police or do away with her as well since Audrey Blackstock would have the power to see them hang. It would be a matter of kill or be killed.

But what if Mrs. Glenn had misinterpreted what she had seen and heard? Greta Van Kemp might have been a willing participant, and what Mrs. Glenn had taken for whimpers of pain may have been exhalations of pleasure that Anthony Blackstock had tried to mute by putting his hand over his lover's mouth. Lord Blackstock certainly wouldn't be the first man to carry on with the hired help, and Greta Van Kemp wouldn't be the first woman to find her employer attractive. Perhaps she had enjoyed his attentions, or maybe she hoped to profit in some way. But if Audrey Blackstock had got wind of the affair, she would have motive to murder her philandering husband and to humiliate him in death the way he had humiliated her in life.

It was easier to believe that Anthony Blackstock was the aggressor, given what Sebastian had heard of the man thus far, but he had to keep an open mind until he could rule out one or both scenarios. What puzzled him the most was why the killer had chosen to murder Anthony Blackstock aboard the ship. The *Prince Regent* was a day away from docking in London, a city of millions, where it would be that much easier to disappear. Why murder the man in his bed and in such a brutal fashion? The evidence spoke to a crime of passion rather than a premeditated act of violence, but the killer would still have had to plan the attack and make certain they weren't seen in a space where there was nowhere to hide should they be spotted. The captain's and first mate's cabins were just through the passage, and the other staterooms were within shouting distance. How was it that no one had heard a thing?

And there was another possibility, one that he wasn't yet ready to act on but would have to consider further. Sebastian still needed to question the Ringwoods, but first he had to speak to Miss Van Kemp and see if she'd corroborate Mrs. Glenn's account. He mounted the steps to the deck and was surprised to see that, while he had been below, the sky had turned a menacing shade of violet, and the wind had picked up. The first-class passengers held on to their hats as they hurried towards the stairs, eager to take shelter. Sebastian stepped aside to allow them to pass, hurried towards the stairs, and descended into the second-class corridor, where he nearly collided with Gemma.

"Did you find Greta Van Kemp?" Sebastian asked.

"No one has seen her."

"I must speak to her straight away."

"Why? What's happened?"

Sebastian was about to relay what Mrs. Glenn had shared with him when the first mate hurried down the steps and strode purposefully towards them. His shoulders blocked the light, leaving the passage in deep shadow, but a chill breeze filled the corridor, and the floor was rolling beneath their feet.

"Inspector, Miss Tate, I'm afraid I must ask you to leave," Shep Reynolds said without preamble.

"Why?" Sebastian demanded.

"A storm is brewing, so if you hope to make shore before it breaks you must get on your way."

"I would prefer to remain on board," Sebastian said.

"The storm promises to be a bad one, and as acting captain I will order everyone to their cabins, for their own safety. We are at capacity, so the only place you can reasonably wait out the tempest is the Blackstocks' stateroom. I assure you, Inspector, that no one is going anywhere, and you will be able to resume your inquiries first thing tomorrow. Unless, of course, you're prepared to permit us to dock, in which case you can disembark once we make port."

Reynolds' reason for wanting them gone was flimsy at best, and Sebastian thought the man was simply trying to force his hand to allow the ship to dock, but he could hardly refuse to leave. The *Prince Regent* sailed under an American flag, which under maritime law meant that the vessel was American territory. Sebastian wasn't sure if the ship was considered a sovereign domain, but there was no one he could ask, and he instinctively knew that Ransome would advise him to not make waves in a situation that was already delicate and could escalate further if the murderer was an American citizen.

As long as Greta Van Kemp wasn't aware she was now a possible suspect, the interview could wait until tomorrow morning.

"I would like Constable Forrest to remain on board, as a precaution," Sebastian said.

"And I would like you to remove the body."

Sebastian inclined his head. He had every intention of taking the body with him.

"Is there anyone you'd like me to put in the brig until you return, Inspector?" Shep Reynolds asked, his mouth quirking with amusement.

"I don't think that will be necessary."

"Then I will instruct the crew to prepare the body and lower the cutter. It is my only concern that you get back safely."

"Yes, I can tell," Sebastian muttered under his breath. Reynolds clearly wasn't as concerned for his own men, who would be out on the open water during a storm.

"Thank you, Mr. Reynolds," Gemma said, and smiled up at the first mate, probably in an effort to defuse Sebastian's anger.

Shep Reynolds reached out and took Gemma's hand, bringing it to his lips. "Until we meet again, lovely Gemma."

A stab of resentment pricked Sebastian in the heart, but he could hardly behave like a jealous husband and reprimand the man. And Gemma didn't seem to mind the attention. She was looking up at Mr. Reynolds with something akin to admiration.

"I expect your part in the investigation is at an end," Shep Reynolds said softly. "Perhaps I might be permitted to call on you when I'm next in London?"

"I expect you will be seeing me again sooner than you imagine, Mr. Reynolds," Gemma replied, and Sebastian felt gratified by the amusement in her voice. "I trust you can manage without me until then?"

"I will do my best."

"Goodbye, then," Gemma said, and swept past the man, Sebastian at her heels.

Shep Reynolds had not been exaggerating. A massive storm cloud was moving towards London, and the sky that had been clear a few hours ago was now the color of a livid bruise. Thunder boomed in the distance, and lightning split the sky somewhere above the estuary. There were whitecaps on the river, and the wind-whipped water rushed past the hull in a murky torrent. The larger vessels looked ready to brave the storm, but the smaller craft that usually made up a good portion of river traffic were gone, the boats moored and the ferrymen safe on dry land and probably already at some nearby tavern, enjoying a well-deserved jar of ale.

Sebastian and Gemma waited on deck while the canvas-wrapped body of Anthony Blackstock was carefully lowered into the cutter. Constable Forrest, whose head was adorned with laurels of cobwebs and whose hands, tunic, and shoes were covered in grime, joined them at Sebastian's behest and drew in several deep breaths, his face turned to the stormy sky, his eyes closed with pleasure. It seemed the constable didn't enjoy closed spaces or noxious odors either.

"Anything?" Sebastian asked once Constable Forrest got his fill of ozone-tinged air.

The constable shook his head, setting off a halo of dust around his head. "The cargo is tightly stacked, sir, to avoid the crates shifting during the voyage. Not even a child could crawl in between the barrels and chests. There are other, less crowded areas, like the animal enclosure and the brig, but there was no one there that I could see, and I didn't smell nothing suspicious either," the constable said, wrinkling his nose in distaste.

"What were you expecting to smell, Constable?" Mr. Reynolds asked.

"If Lady Blackstock is down there and has been since last night, then surely she would have had to relieve herself at least once, sir."

"Yes, I suppose she would have," Reynolds allowed, "but as I told you before, Inspector, we searched the hold, and there was no one there. I never expected your man here to prove otherwise."

"It's not that I don't trust you, Mr. Reynolds, but I had to be sure," Sebastian lied. He didn't trust the man as far as he could throw him.

"Do I have to go back down there, sir?" Constable Forrest whined.

"You don't. However, you are to remain on board until I return.

Keep an eye on things, Constable, and report any unusual activity to Mr. Reynolds."

"Yes, sir. Any chance of a mug of tea, Mr. Reynolds?" Constable Forrest asked. "It's only that I'm gasping after spending hours in the bowels of the ship."

"Of course," Reynolds replied, and called out to a passing sailor. "Take Constable Forrest to the mess, Roberts, and have Cook make him a cup of tea and something to eat. I daresay the poor man has earned it."

Constable Forrest looked vastly relieved to be excused from his hold-searching duties and eagerly followed Roberts to the mess. Watching him walk away, Sebastian thought perhaps he should have instructed the constable to keep a particular watch on Miss Van Kemp, but, if Mr. Reynolds was confining everyone to their cabins, there was nowhere for her to go, and he doubted she would try to get to shore in a storm, even if she happened to be a competent swimmer. The rushing river was a long way down, and, even if Greta Van Kemp was brave enough to dive in and swim for it, Limehouse Reach was home mostly to docks, warehouses, and shipbuilding yards, which would be no help to a woman on the run. And if Constable Forrest hovered next to Miss Van Kemp and Miss Thorpe's cabin, he might tip his hand and give the woman reason to flee. It was best if Miss Van Kemp and Miss Thorpe suspected nothing and thought they had only to bide their time until the ship finally docked, probably tomorrow since Sebastian couldn't hold it up for much longer than that.

Once the rope ladder was lowered, Sebastian took Gemma's reticule and stuffed it into the waistband of his trousers to free her hands, then spoke a few quiet words of reassurance, most of which were snatched away by the gusts of wind, and made his way down. He positioned himself at the center of the boat, directly beneath the ladder, while Gemma carefully descended the hempen steps, her gloved hands gripping the sides as the ladder writhed like a snake in the gathering wind that tore at her skirts and pulled at her hair.

Gemma breathed a sigh of relief when Sebastian took hold of her waist and she was able to let go and step down onto the cutter. She trembled with tension and gripped his hand as Sebastian guided her towards the stern of the rolling boat. There was hardly room to move with the victim's remains lying in the bottom and the two sailors, who looked none too pleased to have been ordered to ferry them back to shore, occupying the middle bench.

Sebastian waited until Gemma was seated, then squeezed in next to her on the narrow bench, removed his hat and set it in his lap, and wrapped a protective arm about her shoulders. He hoped they would outrun the storm, but when a fat raindrop fell on his bare head, slid down his temple, and dripped into the collar of his shirt, and thunder boomed again, closer this time, he knew his hope was in vain. The heavens were about to open up, and they would be caught on the open water.

SIXTEEN

"Goodness me! Just look at the state of you," Mabel exclaimed when Sebastian and Gemma finally made it back. "I'll put the kettle on. Miss Tate, get out of those wet clothes before you catch your death. Inspector, I'm certain Mr. Ramsey will be happy to lend you something dry. I don't think his trousers will fit, though." Mabel gave Sebastian's solid form an appraising look. Colin was both thinner and a little shorter. "A dressing gown, perhaps."

"I'll be fine," Sebastian replied stoically.

"You're shivering and dripping water on the floor," Gemma said, looking at him with concern.

She was shivering herself, her teeth chattering with cold. The sodden skirts of her gown were so heavy the fabric clung to her legs, making it difficult to walk. Her boots squelched, and, although her hair had remained dry, her bonnet resembled a shapeless wet blanket. Droplets of water hovered on Gemma's lashes, then rolled down her cheeks when she momentarily shut her eyes. Her corset stuck to her damp skin, and she longed only for dry clothes and a warm fire.

"Perhaps you could wear something that belonged to the late Mr. Ramsey. You are about the same size," Mabel mused. "There's a trunk full of his things in the attic. Let me see what I can find."

"Thank you, Mabel," Sebastian said, then turned to Gemma. "Go on. I don't want you to get ill."

"Is Poppy still here?" Gemma asked before heading upstairs.

"She left about two hours ago," Mabel said. "Miss Bright couldn't afford to wait any longer, since she's on shift at the infirmary tonight and will have a devil of a time getting out to Lambeth in this filthy weather."

Gemma would have liked to have seen Poppy and thanked her for looking after Anne, but she could understand her reasons for leaving.

"I'll be right back," she told Sebastian.

She hitched her skirts and hurried to her room, where she began to strip off her wet garments as soon as she shut the door. Despite the discomfort of the interminable journey to Blackfriars, she was grateful to be on dry land and in her own bedroom, which seemed the height of luxury after the close quarters she'd visited on the ship. Braving a storm in Limehouse Reach wasn't nearly as terrifying as facing a storm at sea, but she could still recall the squall the troopship she had sailed on had encountered on the way to Crimea. She would never want to relive those moments of sheer terror as the vessel was tossed on the huge swells and the wind tore at the sails as if they were nothing more than a lawn handkerchief rather than sturdy swaths of canvas. Gemma still thought of the young man, boy really, who'd lost his grip on the rigging when he'd tried to adjust the storm jib and had fallen to the deck, landing with a thud beneath the mizzen mast. The boy's death rattle echoed in Gemma's mind as she recalled his pleading gaze and his bloodstained mouth moving urgently as he attempted to speak, his final words dying with him as Florence Nightingale knelt by his side, the boy's hand in hers.

So many souls perished at sea, which made it all the more ironic that the Blackstocks had made the crossing safely only to be met with a tragic end a day before arrival. Or maybe not so strange, Gemma mused as she stepped out of her crinolines and hung them on the footboard to dry before rolling down her stockings. Sebastian was working on the assumption that something that had occurred within the past few days had provoked the killer to lash out. But what if this murder had been planned in advance and the culprit had bided their time and waited for the ship to reach London before executing their plan so they would have a way to escape?

As far as Gemma and Sebastian were aware, the Blackstocks had not known anyone except their two female servants when they'd boarded the *Prince Regent* in New York. Once he and Gemma were in the hansom and couldn't be overheard by the sailors, Sebastian had shared what Mrs. Glenn had told him, but, having spoken to the two maids, Gemma found it hard to believe they could be responsible. They would certainly have a motive if Lord Blackstock had made free with them, and Mrs. Glenn's account went a long way towards explaining why Miss Van Kemp's predecessor had left without giving notice, but how could a woman, even an angry, vengeful woman, overpower a man of Lord Blackstock's size and murder him without anyone hearing a thing? And where had Lady Blackstock been during the attack? Could Greta Van Kemp have incapacitated Audrey and somehow managed to get her up on deck and over the side? That didn't seem very likely, even if she and Lorna Thorpe had been working together.

And could the two maids be so skilled at deception as to act so unperturbed after committing a double murder? Greta Van Kemp had said she'd been unwell, which could be the result of her encounter with Anthony Blackstock, but Gemma couldn't bring herself to believe that the small, fragile woman who'd sat across from her that morning could manage such a brutal attack, even if aided. And if the killer was Lorna Thorpe, how could she have managed to murder Lord Blackstock and dispose of Lady Blackstock's remains without anyone hearing the sounds of a struggle? It simply didn't add up.

If the Blackstocks had not known anyone else before boarding, then Jeffrey Caldwell was the only possible suspect. He'd had motive and opportunity, given that his stateroom was just across from the Blackstocks' cabin, and he was strong enough to murder Anthony Blackstock if he'd attacked the man in his sleep and had the element of surprise on his side. And as the *Prince Regent* had been due to dock the following day, last night had been his only chance to avenge his honor before the passengers disembarked and went their separate ways. This theory had gaping holes, but to Gemma's way of thinking, it was more plausible than killer maids.

Was it possible that all the staterooms could be opened with the same key? Gemma wondered as she closed the last hook of her spare corset and reached for the bodice of a dry gown. Mr. Reynolds hadn't checked if he had the right key before inserting it into the lock, but perhaps he had been certain it was since he'd been the one to lock the stateroom and hold on to the key until the police arrived. Also, and this was a question that seemed to arise again and again, where had Audrey Blackstock been during the attack, and why had she not cried out or called for help?

Was it possible that Audrey Blackstock had died first? Gemma paused, considering this interesting new possibility. Yes, that had to be how the killer had managed it. He or she had entered the stateroom to find the Blackstocks asleep. If the killer had gone for Lord Blackstock first, Lady Blackstock would have woken and called for help, but if they'd hit her over the head and either knocked her unconscious or killed her outright, that would have left only Anthony Blackstock, and if the man was a deep sleeper...

Shaking her head, Gemma nearly growled with frustration. How deeply did a man have to sleep to not realize that his wife had just been murdered and that someone who had no business being in his stateroom was fitting an iron cage around his head? Blackstock would have had to be comatose, and, even if he had been so deeply asleep, he would have woken when the killer placed a pillow over his caged head and pressed it down hard. They had to be missing something, a vital clue that would explain how the murders had been carried out and by whom.

Gemma buttoned her collar, rewound her hair and pinned it

into place, then hurried downstairs, spurred on by the wonderful aroma of soup. Her clothes were dry, and she had stopped shivering once she'd dried off before putting on a fresh camisole and bloomers, but deep inside she still felt a persistent chill, and needed a hot meal to warm her through. Sebastian was in the kitchen. He had changed out of his wet things and his hair had begun to dry, the locks curling into gentle waves. He was seated at the pine table but stood to greet Gemma when she arrived, his gaze sweeping over her to make certain she was all right before he held out a chair for her and she took a seat opposite, happy to be in Colin's warm, dry kitchen.

George Ramsey's things suited Sebastian rather well, except for the elaborately embroidered waistcoat that was entirely too fanciful for a man of his simple tastes. But Sebastian seemed at ease in his borrowed clothes, which reminded Gemma of his ability to adapt. He was as comfortable in a dockside tavern as he was in a nobleman's drawing room, and she'd seen him hold his own in either setting and converse easily with his companions.

Mabel ladled vegetable soup onto plates, then cut slices of bread and poured them cups of strong tea. "This should tide you over until dinner. I cannot believe those ill-mannered Americans did not offer you a spot of luncheon," she grumbled. "But what can you expect from someone who'd send you out in a dinghy in the middle of a raging storm? And you two, turning up here looking like drowned rats and with a dead body in tow. Shameful," she sputtered.

"Mabel," Gemma tried to cut in, but Mabel wasn't quite finished.

"And Mr. Ramsey, God bless him, can never say no to a fresh corpse. Already down in the cellar, working on the poor sod, despite the time and the long hours he already put in this afternoon. I suppose we should be grateful he didn't invite half a dozen students to observe. Thank the Lord for small mercies, or I'd be mopping the floor all night and trying to air out their scent."

Several of Colin's students drenched themselves in flowery

cologne to counteract the reek of death in Colin's basement, but, although this tactic seemed to help them, it filled the downstairs with a cloying stench that lingered long after they left and annoyed Mabel no end, especially on rainy days, when the students also tracked mud into the corridor and left their wet things to drip on the foyer floor.

Mabel poured another cup of tea, added milk and sugar, and set the cup on a tray next to a plate of digestives. "I'll just take this up to Mrs. Ramsey. She'll be ready for a cup of tea, not to mention a bit of company, since she would have forgotten by now that Miss Bright was ever there. I reckon it will raise her spirits once she can finally come downstairs for a spell. Stuck up there all day by her lonesome," she said with a shake of her head.

Anne was hardly on her own all day. Gemma spent most of her time in the older woman's room, reading, playing simple card games that Anne could still follow, and cajoling her to eat. Although Poppy had come by to mind Anne, Mabel had clearly had a frustrating day and was in a mood.

"Don't tell her about the murder, Mabel," Sebastian said.

"As if I would. It's sure to give her nightmares after what happened last time." Mabel shook her head in dismay. "The mad things people do," was the last thing Gemma heard her say as she left the kitchen.

Once Mabel had gone Gemma and Sebastian applied themselves to the soup, each becoming lost in their own thoughts, then Sebastian laid his hand over Gemma's, his gaze searching her face.

"Not quite the day I had planned for us," he said apologetically.

"No," Gemma replied. "But at least we got to spend it together."

"There is that." Sebastian smiled. "Finish your soup, and let's get down to the cellar. This day is not over yet."

SEVENTEEN

Colin had already prepared his instruments and was about to start on the postmortem when Gemma and Sebastian joined him in the cellar. The body of Anthony Blackstock was laid out on the dissecting table, a sheet modestly draped over his hips, and the damp canvas he had been delivered in folded neatly and left on the floor by the wall. The corpse looked no less horrifying in familiar surroundings, the iron cage around his head truly the stuff of nightmares, especially since the man's eyes were still open, and he stared through the round eye openings as if he were fully aware of what had been done to him.

Colin gaped at Sebastian's borrowed waistcoat as they approached, then shook his head, as if trying to dispel the memory of his father wearing it in happier times, and turned towards the body. "I've seen my share of gory corpses, especially while I was a student in Edinburgh and the remains were at times in an advanced state of decomposition, but this..." He gestured towards the body on the table. "This is profoundly disturbing. The victim must have stirred up some very strong emotions to drive someone to such extremes."

"From what we've heard of the man, he wasn't a very pleasant individual," Sebastian replied with a sigh.

"Every human being deserves sympathy and understanding," Gemma admonished, then recalled what Sebastian had done to the man who'd murdered Louisa. There were times when Sebastian chose moral justice over legal fairness, and in some instances she couldn't say she blamed him, but until she knew the truth of what had happened to Anthony Blackstock, she wasn't going to judge.

"I don't know about that," Sebastian replied. "I will investigate Anthony Blackstock's death to the best of my ability and ensure justice is served, but I'm not sure I can spare sympathy for a man who was said to abuse the women in his care and who hurled vicious insults at a fellow passenger and a vulnerable boy."

Colin seemed surprised by Sebastian's admission and peered at him curiously. "And are you able to investigate his death fairly if you think he was a cad?"

"Just because Anthony Blackstock wasn't a likable man doesn't mean he should be murdered, and his killer is just as guilty of breaking the law and deserving of the consequences. I have a duty to the dead, and I take it very seriously," Sebastian said stiffly, and Gemma thought Colin had wounded him by questioning his integrity.

Colin inclined his head in acknowledgment of Sebastian's rebuke. "Perhaps you could walk me through what you've uncovered," he said, clearly keen to redirect the conversation. "It might help contextualize my own findings."

Sebastian laid out both the facts and their theories, beginning with Lorna Thorpe's discovery of the body and their belief that Anthony Blackstock had assaulted Greta Van Kemp.

"I see what you mean about the victim," Colin allowed. "He certainly sounds like a blackguard of the first order."

"Are you able to narrow down the time of death?" he asked, ignoring Colin's veiled apology.

"Based on rigor, lividity, and the warm temperatures during the day, I'd say eighteen to twenty-four hours, since rigor has almost completely passed." Colin also seemed glad to return to more solid ground. Morality and justice were weighty subjects and probably meant something different to each man.

"We know the victim was still alive after dinner, and, although he wasn't discovered until about nine this morning, I doubt the killer would have risked murdering him once the sun was up and the sailors had set about their morning duties."

"I'd say your window is twelve to three," Colin said.

"Which lines up with our estimate," Sebastian said, making sure to include Gemma in the assessment.

"Was there much blood at the scene?" Colin inquired as he peered at Anthony Blackstock's mutilated chest.

"The bedlinens were bloodied but not soaked," Sebastian replied.

Colin nodded, as if his suspicions had just been confirmed, and said, "I will not be able to remove the mask without the aid of a blacksmith, but I can tell just by looking at the victim that his nose was broken."

"Do you think someone hit him?" Gemma asked.

"The most obvious answer is that the nasal bone was crushed when the pillow was held over his face and the middle bar was pushed into the bone."

"Is there anything else you can tell by looking at the body?" Sebastian asked. "Was he conscious at the time of death?"

"Impossible to tell at first glance, I'm afraid. Especially when I am unable to examine the head."

"His hands are balled into fists," Sebastian said.

"Yes, but that could have been an involuntary, subliminal reaction to pain. It doesn't mean he was fully conscious."

"Might he have been drugged?" Gemma asked. "It's hard to believe he wouldn't have put up a fight if he was aware of what was happening."

"Again, difficult to tell." Colin leaned over the victim and sniffed the area near his mouth. "There's no obvious odor of opium, but that doesn't mean an opiate wasn't present at the time of death. I might be able to tell you more once I've opened him up."

"Were the letters carved into the victim's chest after death?" Gemma asked, hoping Colin would disagree with her suspicion that they hadn't been, but Colin shook his head.

"Given the amount of blood on the body and the blood that was soaked into the bedlinens, I would have to say that the heart was still pumping when the killer went about mutilating the body. Which is not to say that the victim was conscious and aware of what was being done to him."

"Poor sod," Sebastian said under his breath. "That must have hurt."

Colin nodded in agreement, but his expression was thoughtful. "I know someone who might be able to get the mask off," he suddenly said. He walked over to the stairs and called out to Mabel, who appeared in the doorway above a few moments later.

"Mabel, can you pop next door and ask Jacob to come? And ask him to bring whatever tools he thinks necessary to force a lock."

Gemma couldn't see Mabel's expression from her vantage point, but she was sure the maid was torn between irritation and elation. She was in the midst of preparing dinner and would not care to be interrupted, especially if she had something on the stove or in the oven; but Gemma also knew that Mabel harbored tender feelings for the neighbor's coachman and would welcome an opportunity to see him.

"Yes, sir. I'll go right over," Mabel chirped, and shut the door.

"Jacob is a handy lad, and always eager to help," Colin explained as he returned to the dissecting table. "He might be able to get the mask off, which would go a long way towards helping me reconstruct the events of last night."

Gemma nearly offered to try to unlock the cage with two hairpins, but decided not to alert Colin to the fact that Sebastian had taught her to pick locks. Colin would most definitely not approve, and the lock looked too compact and sturdy to manipulate with a pin. It would probably require a lock-picking tool or something that could pry the two halves apart. Best to wait for Jacob and see what he might suggest.

"I think there's something inside the victim's mouth," Gemma pointed out to Colin as he prepared to examine the rest of the body.

Colin moved the oil lamp closer to Anthony Blackstock's face and peered inside. "Ah, yes, I see it now. I don't think I will be able to extract the object without removing the mask. The slit is too narrow."

Colin busied himself with examining Blackstock's hands, then asked Gemma to hold the lamp aloft and carefully scraped the scalpel beneath the victim's fingernails. Having finished and deposited the residue onto a glass slide, he turned the corpse onto its side and checked the rectum while still managing to keep the sheet in place in case Gemma should give in to the vapors if she saw the man's arse and erect member.

Colin rolled the corpse onto its back once again. "There's no blood beneath the fingernails, so I expect the incisions into his chest were made once the victim had lost consciousness, but there are traces of foreign matter, which could be skin particles from his assailant. There are also dark fibers beneath the nails of the right hand," he said slowly as he peered at the slide through a magnifying glass.

"Which would suggest that he was conscious at the time of the attack," Sebastian concluded.

"Not enough to put up a good fight," Colin replied. "None of the nails are broken, so perhaps he only managed to rake his fingers over the other person's skin, but he most definitely did not draw blood or try to claw at the mask, since I see no rust or iron residue."

"Was he sexually violated?" Sebastian asked when Colin failed to mention the rectal examination.

"I see no evidence of sodomy," Colin said, his gaze sliding away from Gemma in obvious embarrassment. "There's no tearing, bruising, or semen inside the rectum."

"And what of his arousal?" Sebastian asked.

Gemma was grateful for Sebastian's matter-of-fact tone and his refusal to avoid difficult questions because she was a woman and might be shocked by the mention of the victim's obvious arousal. He acknowledged her experience and wasn't put off by the fact that she had seen men in various stages of undress and physical conditions.

"That sometimes happens at the moment of death," Colin explained. "Blood surges to the extremities. I'm sure you've seen it in victims of hanging."

Sebastian nodded. "Yes, I have. It's always a great source of entertainment for the crowds," he added with disgust. "The men comment on the size of the poor bugger's appendage, and the ladies giggle and point, like the poor man is some creature at the zoological gardens."

Even in the pale light of the oil lamp Gemma could see the crimson flush that stained Colin's cheeks. He was saved from further embarrassment by the arrival of Jacob, who was followed by a giddy-looking Mabel, her earlier vexation clearly forgotten. Jacob was a strapping lad of about twenty-five whose dark blue eyes and slow smile were sure to appeal to any young woman. His dark hair was damp from the rain, and he hadn't bothered to put on a coat before following Mabel into the stormy night. His biceps were clearly outlined beneath the fabric of his damp shirt, and the sleeves were rolled up to reveal sinewy forearms. Jacob smelled of tobacco, horse, and straw, his scent a powerful aphrodisiac if Mabel's expression of longing was anything to go by. Gemma thought that Jacob had come running for her, not Colin, and had probably missed dinner in the servants' hall in his eagerness to impress Mabel with his lock-picking skills.

It never ceased to both pique and reassure Gemma that even in the face of violent death people were still consumed with their own feelings. She was honest enough to admit that, despite the body on the table and the gruesome manner of the victim's death, she still found her gaze straying to Sebastian and longed for his undivided attention. She wanted to walk into his arms and feel his stubble against her cheek as he held her close. And she wanted to be alone with him, free to express her affection for him without trying to avoid Colin's watchful gaze or Anne Ramsey's pointed and surprisingly lucid observations about the nature of their relationship.

Gemma's attention snapped back to the victim when Jacob asked Colin to turn the body onto its stomach and bent low to examine the lock, concentrating his attention studiously on the head.

"This is a box lock," he said.

"Can you open it?" Sebastian asked.

"I can try, but you'd have better luck if you could find someone who's proficient with a lockpick," Jacob replied as he straightened.

"We don't have time to look for a thief."

Jacob shrugged. "Shall I give it a go, then?"

"Do, but try not to lacerate the skin," Sebastian replied.

Jacob's brows knitted at what had to be an unfamiliar word, but he got the gist of Sebastian's instruction and went to work, inserting the chisel he'd brought between the two halves of the lock and working it back and forth until the seam widened a little. He reached for the hammer and drove the chisel deeper into the lock, repeating the back-and-forth motion again and again. Colin sucked in his breath every time Jacob hammered on the chisel handle, as if expecting the instrument to penetrate the victim's skull, but Jacob seemed to know what he was doing and kept at it until the lock finally snapped open and he was able to pull apart the hinged sides of the cage.

"Good man," Sebastian said, and patted Jacob on the shoulder.

Jacob breathed a sigh of relief and set down his tools, his gaze sliding to Mabel, who beamed at him and clapped her hands in delight. One would think Jacob had performed a clever magic trick rather than busted a lock on a medieval torture device locked around a dead man's head. Colin went to remove the mask, while Sebastian reached into his pocket and drew out a couple of coins, which he held out to Jacob.

The man shook his head. "No need, Inspector. I was happy to help."

"Mabel, perhaps you can offer Jacob a drink," Colin suggested. "You should join him, of course. A small sherry?"

Mabel blushed and looked at Jacob, who nodded in approval. "A drink would be most welcome, Mr. Ramsey." *Especially with Mabel*, his gaze seemed to say. Jacob collected his tools, and the two headed upstairs to enjoy their drinks in the parlor.

"Good thing Jacob is sweet on Mabel, or we'd have had to wait until we found a locksmith to get this contraption off," Colin observed as he parted the sides of the mask and lifted Anthony Blackstock's head in order to remove the object entirely.

"He's a fine man," Sebastian said. "Mabel could do worse."

"Good with his hands," Gemma added, and was surprised when both men turned to stare at her as if she'd said something inappropriate.

"Indeed," Colin muttered under his breath as he returned the body to a supine position.

He reached for a long tweezer, inserted it into the mouth, and carefully maneuvered out the object. It was nearly as large as Gemma's fist, and was black and slimy with blood and saliva. At first glance it looked like a leather ball.

"It's a glove," Colin said once he had pulled apart the folds .

"A man's glove with deep toothmarks in the leather, which suggests that Lord Blackstock was alive and awake when the glove was shoved into his mouth," Sebastian replied as he peered over Colin's shoulder.

"Why would someone stuff a glove in the victim's mouth?" Colin looked dismayed and swallowed hard, as if he could imagine his own mouth filled with leather.

"The killer wanted to silence the man. A handkerchief wouldn't do the job, and a towel wouldn't fit. The glove not only stopped the victim from calling out but also prevented him from breathing through his mouth," Sebastian explained.

"He must have been in a panic and tried to bite through the leather. Can you tell anything from the glove?" Colin asked, turning to Gemma.

She picked up the glove and examined it carefully, turning the leather inside out at the opening and peering inside.

"The leather is soft, and the stitching is fine, but I don't see a maker's label," she said.

"The glove in itself doesn't tell us very much," Sebastian interjected. "It could belong to Lord Blackstock or to anyone aboard the ship. The killer could have used their own glove or stolen it from someone who could afford a sturdy pair of gloves."

"Did anyone report a glove missing?" Colin asked.

"Not that I'm aware of, and I very much doubt they'd have noticed it was gone. This is the sort of glove a man would wear during the colder months. It would probably be in his luggage."

"Why would a man who's traveling to London in the summer pack winter gloves?" Colin mused.

"He could be returning home after months or years spent in the States, or he could be planning on remaining in England until it's cold enough to need heavy gloves," Gemma said.

Sebastian nodded in agreement. "I still don't understand why Blackstock didn't put up a fight if he was conscious."

Colin didn't reply right away but moved his fingers over the victim's skull, carefully probing every inch. He nodded to himself once his fingers paused at the back of the head.

"There's a sizable contusion on the parietal lobe. The blow doesn't appear to have broken the skin or cracked the bone, but it must have stunned the victim long enough for the killer to stuff the glove into his mouth and fit the mask around his head. If I had to guess, I'd say that Anthony Blackstock was in deep sleep, lying on his side or his stomach, when he was struck on the back of the head."

"Perhaps Lady Blackstock was struck as well," Gemma suggested. "That would explain her silence."

"Yes, that does seem likely," Sebastian said once he'd probed the swelling on the back of Lord Blackstock's head. "And perhaps the second glove was used to gag her. Any idea what Blackstock was hit with?"

"Could have been anything. With enough force, it's easy to stun someone, especially when they are asleep, but I don't think the killer intended to murder the victim right away. He or she clearly wished to torment him first, hence the mask, and they must have used a very sharp instrument for the final act."

"Any guess as to what it was?" Sebastian asked.

"A knife or a razor. The cuts are thin and deep, so not something as thick and blunt as Jacob's chisel, and definitely not serrated since the edges are straight. Do you have any suspects or working theories?" Colin asked as he reached for a scalpel.

"There are several possible suspects, but I'm woefully short on facts. It's the first mate's theory that Audrey Blackstock murdered her husband, then threw herself overboard rather than face the consequences."

Colin nodded without looking at Sebastian as he pressed the point of the scalpel into a spot by the victim's shoulder and made the initial cut in what would be a Y incision that was the first step in opening the body.

"And is that plausible?" he asked.

"It is," Sebastian conceded. "It's the theory that makes the most sense and fits the facts, but without a motive it's difficult to prove."

"Gemma, what do you reckon?" Colin asked as he continued to slice into the body.

"I think Mr. Reynolds is keen to close the investigation."

"Why?"

"For one, he's eager to dock as soon as possible," Sebastian answered in Gemma's stead, "and for another, he seems to have been sniffing around Audrey Blackstock for the duration of the voyage. Perhaps matters came to a head and Anthony Blackstock confronted him last night."

"From what I heard, Audrey Blackstock did not welcome Shep Reynolds' attentions," Gemma cut in. "And there is a possibility that she was with child. Would it be possible for her to swim to safety if she managed to escape?"

"It takes approximately twelve hours to sail from the estuary into London. Given that Lord Blackstock was murdered sometime last night, the ship had to be somewhere in between. The Thames is quite wide and deep, and the currents are strong and subject to the tides. So, to answer your question, someone would have to be an exceptionally strong and experienced swimmer to risk it," Sebastian replied. "And they would have to be prepared to risk illness and possibly even death from the contamination in the water."

"I doubt a woman would attempt it, even if the water was crystal clear," Gemma said. "Even if she happened to be a strong swimmer, her skirts would become waterlogged, and a corset would make it difficult to breathe. Unless she went over in nothing but her undergarments, which would put her in rather an awkward position if she made it to shore."

"If Lady Blackstock had been planning this, she might have tied her clothes into a bundle and strapped it to her back. Her things would still get wet, unless she wrapped them in oilskin, but at least she'd have something to wear if she made it to shore. Do you know if any of Lady Blackstock's things are missing?" Colin asked.

"No, but that's a question I will put to the Blackstock servants tomorrow," Sebastian replied.

Colin reached for the rib-spreader and looked all set to fit it into the chest cavity. "Let's talk over dinner. You two look like you could use a rest, and I need to concentrate on the postmortem."

On any other day, Gemma might have asked to stay and watch, since this was a learning opportunity not to be missed, but she was too worn out and emotionally overwrought, and wanted only to sit down and shut out the ghastly images that had been seared into her brain.

Sebastian pulled out his watch and checked the time. "Ransome will be expecting an update. If I leave now, I'll probably be able to catch him. I should be back by dinner, so I'll see you both then."

He hurried up the steps and was gone without another word.

Tiredly, Gemma trudged upstairs. Colin preferred to dine at seven, but tonight dinner would be late since he'd want to finish the post-mortem before he came up. Gemma thought she should spend some time with Anne, but when she peeked into the room Anne was asleep, so Gemma continued to her own bedroom. She didn't bother to light a lamp, just kicked off her shoes and reclined on the bed. She thought she should probably review the facts of the case, but after the din and crowded bowels of the ship her room was blessedly quiet, steady rain beat on the roof and the wooden shutters, and no sounds of carriage traffic came from outside. Try as she might, Gemma's thoughts refused to crystallize into ideas, and her eyelids fluttered with fatigue, her body sinking deeper into the mattress as she allowed herself to relax. She was asleep in moments.

EIGHTEEN

About the last thing Sebastian wanted to do was go back out into the storm. The streets were deserted. Anyone who had a home to go to was hunkered down behind solid walls and closed shutters. Those who didn't, mostly street children, who were barefoot and dressed in rags, sheltered in doorways and beneath the awnings of shuttered shops, their pale faces staring out of the gloom. The sky was nearly as dark as if it were night, forceful gusts of wind whipped the trees into a frenzy, and the rain came down in sheets, turning the road into a shallow river of mud.

His predecessor would have left hours ago, but Ransome would still be at his desk, his dark head bent over some report as he waited for news. Ransome wasn't the sort to agonize over every investigation, but he was a clever man who instinctively knew which cases had the power to take him down or raise him up, and this was one of those instances. As soon as the newspapers got wind of Lord Blackstock's death, the headlines would scream that Scotland Yard had failed to solve the murder of a British peer and had permitted the Americans to give sanctuary to a killer.

Most London papers, particularly the *Illustrated London News*, relied on stories of murder and mayhem to draw in their readers, and Sebastian could just imagine the images that would grace the *Illustrated News*'s front page when they discovered that the victim had been left buck naked and wearing an iron mask. That kind of sensationalism not only sold papers but pointed an accusing finger at the police service, using tales of horror to terrify the public and underscore the shortcomings of the force. The revelations were inevitable, but due to the isolation of the ship there was little risk of the story breaking tonight, which afforded Sebastian and, in turn, Ransome a brief reprieve.

As the Yard's new figurehead, Ransome had quickly learned that, even if he never left his office, all criticism and dissatisfaction would be laid at his door and he had to safeguard his reputation if he hoped to last in the job, unlike Lovell, who'd left under a cloud and was no longer spoken of by the men he had disappointed. And at this point, Sebastian's own career prospects were directly tied to Ransome's, since Ransome tended to saddle him with cases that inevitably made it into the papers and shone a spotlight on the Met.

And there was another reason Sebastian felt a duty to Ransome. He genuinely believed that Ransome had the power to revolutionize the service and, given enough autonomy by the commissioner, would increase the Yard's solve rate through intelligent police work conducted by dedicated and well-trained detectives rather than appointments based on familial connections and called-in favors. Which made it all the more galling to have to tell Ransome that Sebastian didn't know who had murdered Anthony Blackstock and that the killer was still safe aboard a vessel that flew American colors and would no doubt sail into port tomorrow in defiance of Sebastian's directive. Such defiance would not benefit either relations with the United States or the police commissioner, who would be called to account by the Home Secretary.

There was one person this case would benefit, Sebastian thought wryly as the hansom he'd been lucky to find crawled along the washed-out road. Bertram Quince would thank his lucky stars when he learned the details of the case. There was nothing to stop him appropriating the particulars for his own purpose, and, as long as he changed the names and amended a few details, no one was likely to bring a complaint against him. This made Sebastian inexplicably furious, and he acknowledged that he was probably directing his anger towards Quince because there was no one he could reasonably blame for the murder just yet. He could hardly be expected to solve the case in a few hours, and he couldn't hold Shep Reynolds responsible. The man had done the right thing and had given Sebastian run of the ship, but he couldn't keep the *Prince Regent* from docking indefinitely and had a duty not only to the men who paid his wages but also to the passengers, who were anxiously waiting to arrive at their destination.

Sebastian was also irritated with Ransome. The man had unwittingly thwarted Sebastian's marriage proposal, and now he would have to wait for another opportunity to finally declare himself to Gemma and solidify their plans for the future. He'd lived at the Quinces' boarding house for over three years, and, although his lodgings had never felt like home, they had served his needs and had given him a place to bide in solitude. Now that a vastly different life was finally in sight, he couldn't wait to move out of the boarding house and into a home of his own. And having unexpectedly inherited a tidy sum from an uncle he hadn't seen since he was a child, Sebastian finally had the financial freedom to offer Gemma a comfortable home in a respectable neighborhood.

Sebastian imagined her pleasure at decorating the rooms of their house with furnishings she had chosen, and grew uncomfortably warm at the promise of the privacy that had been denied them thus far. To share his life with Gemma was the most intimate thing he could conceive of, and as he pictured her sleepy face as she woke, her hair fanned out on the pillow, and her smile dreamy as he reached for her, his anger dissipated, and all he felt was a deep longing laced with long-forgotten optimism. That life was finally within his reach. All he had to do was wait a little bit longer, and it would be his. But just now, he had to concentrate on the job at hand.

Sebastian dashed towards the door as soon as the hansom came to a stop and he'd paid the driver, and hurried inside before his borrowed clothes got soaked. He had a case to solve.

NINETEEN

The duty room was empty of the usual assortment of drunks, brawlers, and thieving prostitutes, who loudly proclaimed their innocence as they were dragged off to the cells, where they would remain until they were either charged or released. And it seemed the respectable citizens who came by to make a complaint or report a missing person weren't willing to brave the weather. The few constables who were still in the building were in the breakroom, enjoying a mug of tea and a friendly chat, their muffled laughter drifting down the deserted corridor.

"All right, Inspector?" Sergeant Meadows asked when Sebastian walked past the reception desk. The sergeant raised an eyebrow at Sebastian's garish waistcoat, but, either through prudence or fear of causing offense, offered no comment.

"Fine. You?"

"A bit bored, if I'm honest, but at least I'm warm and dry, and it's not too long till supper," Sergeant Meadows said and smiled wistfully.

Mrs. Meadows was a talented cook who sent in a cake every week, making Sergeant Meadows the most popular man at Scotland Yard. The men joked that if Mrs. Meadows was as skilled in the bedroom as she was in the kitchen, it was a wonder he made it to work and managed to keep his mind on the job when such delights awaited him at home. Sergeant Meadows ignored the ribbing, but Sebastian thought he secretly enjoyed the speculation about his home life and was exceptionally proud of his missus.

"Ransome still here?" he asked.

"Still here," Sergeant Meadows confirmed. "Hasn't left his office in several hours, in fact."

"Mood?"

"Grim."

"Right," Sebastian muttered as he set off down the corridor towards Ransome's office. The superintendent looked tired and frustrated, and laid down his pen as soon as Sebastian knocked on the doorjamb.

"Good, you're back," he said, and leaned back in his chair. "Murder or natural causes?"

Sebastian settled in one of the guest chairs and faced Ransome. "Most definitely murder, committed while the ship was in the estuary. The victim was knocked out, asphyxiated, and left naked except for an iron cage on his head. The word *pig* was carved into his chest. His wife hasn't been seen since she retired last night, and the watch heard a loud splash around the time of the murder."

"Bloody hell," Ransome exclaimed. "Please tell me Lord Blackstock wasn't murdered by an American. The diplomatic nightmare that could spawn..." He went quiet as another thought seemingly occurred to him. "Is there any reason to suspect the murder was politically motivated?"

"Not that I can see," Sebastian replied.

"Thank the Lord for small mercies," Ransome grumbled. "So, what happened?"

"I don't know."

"Surely you must have formulated a theory."

"The most obvious conclusion, and the one suggested by the acting captain, is that Lady Blackstock murdered her husband, then jumped overboard."

"Acting captain?"

"Captain Grant suffers from malaria and took to his bed two days ago."

"And is this acting captain a competent man?"

"He appears to be, but he's driven by his own agenda, as most people are."

"Judging by your sour expression, you don't buy this murder-suicide theory."

"Audrey Blackstock had means and opportunity, and if she was the killer, that would explain her disappearance, but I can't see a plausible motive. And the timing is questionable."

"Why?"

"Unless she planned to commit suicide the entire time, I can't see why she would choose to murder her husband aboard a ship and in such a vicious manner."

"Perhaps he was a brute."

"By all accounts, Anthony Blackstock was a thoroughly unpleasant man, but if Audrey Blackstock valued her life and hoped to benefit from her husband's death she could have resorted to a less public way of ridding herself of him. A pillow over his face would have sufficed, and she could have acted the bereaved widow and insisted he died of a heart attack."

"Where did the cage come from?" Ransome asked.

"The cage belonged to Blackstock. It would appear he collected medieval torture devices."

"Charming," Ransome grumbled. "Has the vessel been searched?"

"Yes, by both the crew and Constable Forrest."

"And?"

"No trace of her."

"You think she was a second victim," Ransome concluded.

"I think that's very likely."

Ransome growled with frustration. "Are there any suspects besides Lady Blackstock? Did anyone have motive to want both Blackstocks dead? Give me something, Bell. I will have to alert Sir

David to the situation first thing tomorrow, and it would help if I had something to tell him."

"A few hours before he was murdered, Anthony Blackstock accused another passenger of cheating at cards. He insulted him and called him a pig. He also disparaged the man's way of life."

"Which is?" Ransome inquired, drawing out the words.

"He is from South Carolina and owns a number of slaves."

Ransome's face rearranged itself into lines of incomprehension. "That's your man, then. Why didn't you arrest him?"

"There's no physical evidence to suggest that Jeffrey Caldwell murdered Blackstock."

"What evidence do you need? The man suffered a grave insult at the hands of Blackstock and wanted to avenge his honor. He carved *pig* into his chest in return and perhaps used the cage to show that, despite his rank and wealth, Anthony Blackstock was at Caldwell's mercy, much like his slaves."

"As you said yourself, sir, to charge an American would invite undue scrutiny, and I am not convinced he's guilty."

"Based on what?"

"Based on gut instinct and years of experience."

"You must be joking," Ransome erupted.

"Jeffrey Caldwell did not strike me as either impulsive or foolish. To murder the man who insulted him hours after the altercation and carve the very word Blackstock had used into his chest would be the height of idiocy."

"People do dumb things when driven by injured pride."

Sebastian shook his head. "It's too neat, too staged."

Ransome's breath came out in a gush of aggravation. "Is there anyone else?"

"There is another possible suspect, but someone else who may have a motive has also come to my attention. This is far-fetched, and I don't know how plausible this theory is, but it would be remiss of me not to at least consider it."

"Go on."

"The youngest member of the crew is a Negro lad called

Joseph Abrahms. He was born a slave in Georgia and escaped to the North via a network that aids escaped slaves. It is my understanding that he suffered terribly, and his mother and sister were murdered as punishment for his escape."

"What does this have to do with Anthony Blackstock?" Ransome asked, clearly not following.

"According to the Glenns, who are active in the abolitionist movement, Joseph was terrified to come face to face with a known slave-owner. It's unlikely that many Southern plantation owners sail from New York, so this was probably his first encounter of this kind. Mrs. Glenn explained that all Caldwell would have to do would be to alert someone to Joseph's whereabouts, and he could be snatched and brought back to Georgia."

"Again, what does this have to do with Anthony Blackstock?"

"If Jeffrey Caldwell was murdered, Joseph Abrahms would be an obvious suspect, but if a man who'd insulted Caldwell was found murdered and Jeffrey Caldwell was charged with the crime, Joseph would be safe."

Ransome's eyebrows lifted in astonishment. "So, you think that this Joseph Abrahms used the row to his advantage, murdered Anthony Blackstock, and disposed of his wife, all in the hope that Jeffrey Caldwell would be accused and arrested?"

"Desperate men do desperate things," Sebastian replied.

"Would he know about the cage Blackstock had in his possession, and would he have the strength to overpower Anthony Blackstock and carry his wife up on deck and throw her overboard?"

"He did, and he would. And he could safely assume that I would find out about the altercation between the two men and draw the obvious conclusion."

Ransome nodded. "All right. You said there was someone else?"

"According to Francesca Glenn, Anthony Blackstock raped his wife's lady's maid the morning of his death. He also called the other servant a slut and slapped her when she spilled a bit of water on his sleeve. The previous lady's maid left the Blackstocks' employ without giving notice. She was so desperate to get away, she forfeited her wages and character."

"Did you question the maids?" Ransome asked.

"I haven't had a chance to speak to either woman. Miss Tate and I were made to leave."

"You brought Miss Tate aboard?" Ransome asked, one dark brow lifting in censure.

"Not intentionally."

"And why were you asked to leave?"

"Mr. Reynolds used the impending storm as an excuse, but I think he wanted me off the vessel and hoped that I would accept the neat solution he'd presented and not return."

"Was he not the one who sent for the police?" Ransome asked. "Or was that the actual captain?"

"Mr. Reynolds sent for the police after consulting with Captain Grant, but it seems he had hoped that the inquiry would be a mere formality. I don't think he expected me to launch a lengthy investigation."

"What did he hope for, then?"

"He wanted me to take possession of the body and clear the ship to dock, thereby avoiding any unpleasantness or questions from his superiors."

Ransome chuckled. "I expect you thoroughly ruined his day."

"For which he paid me back by obstructing my investigation."

"Do you mean to go back tomorrow?"

"I do. I have yet to learn the results of the postmortem, but I doubt anything Mr. Ramsey finds will alter my conclusions."

"I trust you will leave Miss Tate at home this time?" Ransome asked pointedly. And when Sebastian didn't reply, he added, "Have you made arrangements for the ship's cutter to collect you in the morning?"

"I will find my own way. I don't trust Reynolds to follow through on his promises."

Ransome sighed heavily. "I need a result, Bell. If this case causes Sir David and the Home Secretary embarrassment, I will not be able to guarantee your place on the police service."

"I will not be made a scapegoat, John," Sebastian ground out.

"And I would rather you not be, but such is the nature of professional politics, Sebastian. Someone has to take the blame, and, given that the Met is hanging on by a thread and there are those who're eager to cut our funding or even disband the force altogether, I must do whatever it takes to safeguard the future of the Met. It's nothing personal," Ransome added after a pause.

"It never is," Sebastian said, and pushed to his feet.

"Report back tomorrow."

"Yes, *sir*," Sebastian replied, his bitterness on full display.

Ransome glanced towards the window, where the rain was lashing against the panes and the sky was as black as Sebastian's mood. "I won't be leaving for at least another hour. Tell my driver I said to take you home."

Sebastian was about to refuse the offer of a ride, then checked his pride and nodded his thanks. He was eager to get back to Blackfriars, see Gemma, and hear what Colin had to say. Perhaps something Colin had found would tip the scales in favor of a particular suspect.

TWENTY

Despite Ransome's offer of his carriage, it took Sebastian more than an hour to get back to Blackfriars, since a wagon had lost its wheel on the Strand just as the brougham turned into it, and it took a long while to right the conveyance and move it to the side of the road to let the traffic pass. Sebastian returned just in time for dinner, and a good thing it was too. He was starving. It had been hours since he'd eaten the thin vegetable soup, and his belly felt as hollow as if he hadn't had anything since breakfast.

The dining room was awash with gaslight, there was a succulent aroma of beef, and the two people at the table were the only individuals Sebastian cared to be with on this dark night. Gemma seemed rested, but Colin looked preoccupied, his mind obviously still on his work.

"Do either of you have any objections to discussing the results of the postmortem over dinner?" Colin asked once Mabel had delivered the first course, which thankfully wasn't more soup, and departed. Sebastian studied the tiny mounds of salmon mousse presented on slivers of toast and served with a slice of cucumber and a sprig of dill. He rarely got to enjoy such elegant fare, and made a mental note to compliment Mabel as soon as she returned.

"I'm very eager to hear what you have discovered," Gemma said, and looked to Sebastian.

"It takes a lot to put me off my food," he said, and popped a triangle of toast into his mouth, savoring the delicate flavor of the mousse.

Colin took a sip of water, then set down his glass. His mousse remained untouched. "Gemma correctly identified the cause of death as asphyxiation. There's a petechial hemorrhage in the lungs, but there's also another, more obvious sign of strangulation. In their frenzy, the killer applied a considerable amount of pressure." Colin pointed to a spot beneath his chin. "The hyoid bone is just here, and it was crushed by the base of the cage. Judging by the victim's facial expression and the residue beneath his fingernails, I'm almost certain he was conscious during the attack and tried to fight off his assailant but didn't have enough purchase to get a good grip on their hands."

Gemma winced, and Sebastian thought that she was imagining Anthony Blackstock's final moments and the agony he must have experienced as his neck was crushed and the life was squeezed from his lungs. No one deserved such a frightening, brutal end, not even a man who had seemingly been fascinated with torture and collected objects that should have been displayed in a museum to warn future generations about the cruelty of man and what it could lead to when left unchecked.

"Would it require the strength of a man to crush the hyoid bone?" Gemma asked.

"I shouldn't think so. If a woman put all her weight into pressing the pillow down on the victim's face, the iron band would do the rest."

"If the victim was conscious during the attack, how is it that he wasn't able to throw off his assailant?" Gemma asked. "Anthony Blackstock was a big man. Even if he couldn't manage to grab the killer's hands and force them to release the pillow, surely he could have shoved his attacker hard enough to ease the pressure or used his knees to create a barrier between himself and the killer. The only explanation I can think of is that the victim and the killer were evenly matched."

Colin sighed and shook his head. "Not necessarily. The victim's last meal of fish and potatoes was almost entirely digested, but what remained was soaked in spirits. Anthony Blackstock had been drinking heavily, as must have been his wont. There was scarring and liquid around the liver, his abdomen and ankles were noticeably swollen, and there was a red cast to his palms, which are all symptoms of liver damage. I would wager that he had lost weight recently and had been suffering from stomach pains, fatigue, and occasional nausea. He may have attributed these symptoms to prolonged travel, seasickness, and the fare aboard the ship, but if he continued to drink heavily the damage would most likely have led to cirrhosis of the liver."

Colin took a sip of water. "To answer your question, Gemma, I think Anthony Blackstock was insensible with drink and only woke when the pressure on his nose and neck turned excruciating. He would have experienced a momentary surge of vitality, brought about by panic, but by the time he would have fully understood what was happening and tried to save himself, it would have been too late. And if a woman, even a slight one, had straddled him and put all her weight into holding the pillow down, I very much doubt Blackstock would have been able to shift her even if he bucked, since the pressure on his neck would cut off all air supply within moments."

"Was there anything else?" Sebastian asked once Mabel, who had been very pleased when he'd complimented the mousse, had served the roast and left them once more.

Sebastian had hoped Colin would give him something more to go on. The symptoms of liver damage provided context for Anthony Blackstock's overall condition at the time of death but didn't help Sebastian identify his killer, since it could have been anyone aboard the ship, male or female, working alone or with an accomplice. Perhaps the killer had even offered Anthony Blackstock his favorite whisky to make certain he was well and truly drunk by the time they made their move.

Colin sampled the beef, nodded in approval, and speared a piece of potato. "I examined the residue I had collected from beneath the victim's fingernails and noticed a number of black fibers trapped within the organic matter."

"Do you think the killer wore a garment made of black wool?" Gemma asked eagerly.

"Worsted, more like," Colin mused. "The fibers appeared to be longer and smoother than those normally found in wool and would have become embedded under the fingernails when the victim clawed at the killer's sleeves in his final moments."

"I doubt Audrey Blackstock would be wearing worsted in the middle of the night," Gemma mused. "But a maidservant might."

"That's what I was thinking," Colin said. "It had to be the lady's maid, Greta Van Kemp."

"What brought you to that conclusion?" Sebastian asked.

"Since Miss Thorpe discovered the body and reported it to the crew, she couldn't be the killer," Colin explained, as if that should be obvious. "The only other maidservant is Miss Van Kemp, and, if Anthony Blackstock had forced himself on her, she had a compelling motive to want him dead."

"If Anthony Blackstock forced himself on Greta Van Kemp, it's just as likely that he had assaulted Miss Thorpe. Perhaps that was part of her plan," Sebastian argued. "Reporting the crime would make Miss Thorpe look like an innocent bystander and allow her to hide away in second class until the ship made port. The killer, be it Miss Thorpe, Miss Van Kemp, or some other person, had no way of knowing that the captain would instruct Reynolds to drop anchor and involve Scotland Yard. They probably assumed that the Americans would perform a cursory investigation, fail to solve the case, and allow everyone to disembark."

"What about Shep Reynolds?" Gemma suddenly asked.

"What about him?"

"Could he be the murderer?"

"He could," Sebastian replied, "but what would be his motive?"

"He took a marked interest in Audrey Blackstock. And his coat is black worsted," Gemma announced.

"That doesn't mean he's the killer," Colin replied.

"No, it doesn't, but there are other factors. His cabin is near the Blackstocks' stateroom. He could get a spare key to the stateroom. And he even went so far as to proclaim that the man got what he deserved. He's also a tall, powerfully built man who'd have no difficulty murdering an inebriated sleeping one."

"But he was the one to alert Scotland Yard," Colin protested. "Why would he do that if he was guilty?"

"Shep Reynolds sent a message to Scotland Yard at the behest of Captain Grant," Gemma countered. "He could hardly have ignored a direct order from his captain, or he would have incriminated himself. Perhaps he assumed that no one would ever suspect him and all he'd have to do was offer his assistance and wait for the detective to come up empty and leave. When Sebastian was taking too long for Reynolds' liking, he used the storm as an excuse and forced us off the ship."

"What do you think, Sebastian?" Colin asked.

"Reynolds' black coat, the location of his cabin, and the spare key are all circumstantial. And his dislike of Anthony Blackstock is hardly motivation for such a frenzied attack. I highly doubt he murders every man he thinks deserving of a lesson in manners or whose wife he finds attractive. I wager he finds a woman to flirt with on every crossing just to make things more interesting. He even made sheep's eyes at you," Sebastian teased Gemma.

"Perhaps Audrey Blackstock took offense," Colin suggested.

"Perhaps, but that doesn't explain why Audrey Blackstock is missing. Presumably, Shep Reynolds would have no reason to murder her."

"Maybe they fell in love and Reynolds promised to marry her if she were free."

"Let us say that's a possibility," Sebastian allowed. "What

would be the sense in hiding her if she was innocent of any wrong-doing? She would have a lot of explaining to do once she reappeared, and she would have to reappear to claim her husband's estate. And why kill the man in such a gruesome fashion? Blackstock was drunk. All Reynolds had to do was hold a pillow over his face."

"Not if he wanted to frame someone else for the murder," Gemma chimed in.

"What reason would Shep Reynolds have to frame Jeffrey Caldwell?" Sebastian countered.

"Reynolds could be an abolitionist."

"There are people whose commitment borders on fanaticism, but this would be taking it too far," Sebastian replied. "And Reynolds doesn't strike me as someone who'd risk his own life for a cause. He's too self-serving."

"It was a stroke of genius on Captain Grant's part to bide in Limehouse Reach," Colin said.

"Yes, it was," Sebastian agreed. "The killer is trapped aboard the *Prince Regent,* and unless they decide to swim for it they have no choice but to brazen it out."

"If they didn't swim for it already, I doubt they'll do so tonight," Gemma said, her gaze going to the window. The storm continued to lash the city with unrelenting ferocity, the night beyond dark and dense as coal.

"The killer has a much better chance of survival if they remain aboard the ship," Colin mused. "Ingesting even a small amount of river water would introduce deadly parasites into the system, especially now, when it's so warm and the Thames is a breeding ground for putrefaction."

"But would an American know that?" Gemma asked. "Perhaps their rivers are not as polluted."

"Possibly not, but the night watch would have spotted a swimmer."

"Would they not have spotted a body?" Sebastian asked.

"A corpse will sink due to its density, which is greater than that of the water. It will only become buoyant once the gasses build up and propel it to the surface," Colin explained.

"And how long would that take?"

"Several days."

"By which time Audrey Blackstock's remains could be anywhere, if it was her body that was thrown overboard," Gemma concluded.

She looked deeply troubled, and Sebastian thought that, as far as Gemma was concerned, Audrey Blackstock was the true victim of whatever had happened on the *Prince Regent*, whether she had been the perpetrator or an innocent bystander who'd simply got in the way of someone else's rage. Only her remains would tell her story, but without a body there could be no answers, and they would likely never find out how Audrey had died.

"What's the next step?" Colin asked.

Sebastian sighed. He'd been driven by his need to keep Gemma safe, since he hadn't trusted the sailors alone with her if he'd sent her back with the body, but he should have challenged Shep Reynolds and insisted they be permitted to remain aboard. He'd lost valuable time, been forced to admit his failure to Ransome, and learned little of real value from the postmortem. Every man and woman aboard that ship probably owned a garment of black wool or worsted, so he was no closer to identifying the killer or conclusively ruling out Audrey Blackstock. Every theory led to more questions, and, the more Sebastian thought he understood the nature of the perpetrator, the more he believed their actions had been fueled by rage, a need for retribution, and a desire to maim. Given the killer's volatile mindset, Sebastian feared they would do something drastic, much like an animal that would chew off its own paw to set itself free from a trap.

With the storm still raging, there was no way to return to the ship tonight, but he would set off first thing tomorrow morning, and he would go alone. There was nothing more Gemma could do to help, and, if the killer was growing as frantic as Sebastian suspected, they might try to take their chances and attempt to fight their way out, which could lead to innocent casualties.

"I'm not sure," Sebastian replied, then folded his napkin and laid it on the table. "Thank you for dinner, but I must get back before Quince locks the door."

Before her marriage, Mrs. Poole used to keep a key hidden by the back door, but her new husband had done away with the spare, proclaiming that the lodgers had to return by the time he locked up for the night. Quince usually didn't retire until ten o'clock, but given the weather it would take Sebastian some time to find a hansom and get to Clerkenwell. "I will collect my things tomorrow, if that's all right."

"Sebastian, why don't you stay?" Colin invited. "It's a deluge out there, and I just received a very fine bottle of brandy from a student who's been offered a place on St. Thomas's surgical ward." He turned to Gemma. "Perhaps you'll join us for a small sherry?"

Both the promise of an after-dinner drink and a bed for the night were extremely appealing. Sebastian kept his alcohol use in check, but there were times when he permitted himself a much-needed brandy, and tonight was an occasion that called for a drink. And if he remained in Blackfriars, he would save himself hours of travel, both this evening and tomorrow morning.

Sebastian stole a peek at Gemma. Would she object to him staying the night? He would never abuse Colin's hospitality by giving in to his yearning, or disrespect Gemma in any way, but she was still an unmarried woman whose reputation could suffer needlessly if it was put about that she had spent the night under the same roof as a man who was neither her husband, fiancé, nor employer. Sebastian tried to read Gemma's expression, but her head was bowed, her gaze on her plate, and her cheeks stained a rosy pink. She had clearly had similar thoughts and was probably uncomfortable with Colin's spontaneous offer.

"I really should get back," Sebastian repeated. "Gustav has been alone all day."

"Mrs. Quince will feed Gustav, if he hasn't already stuffed

himself full of mice," Colin protested, seeming oblivious to his companions' emotional torment. "Gemma, tell him he must stay. It's silly to go out in this weather when there's a perfectly adequate guest room upstairs."

"Please, stay," Gemma said quietly, and finally looked at Sebastian, her gaze soft in the gaslight. "Colin is right. It makes no sense to go out in that storm."

Sebastian knew he should protest but said only, "Thank you. That's very kind."

TWENTY-ONE

The conversation at dinner left Gemma feeling tired and melancholy. She'd had her fill of murder and wanted only to retire to her room, where she could read for a while in an attempt to force the ugliness from her mind and concentrate on less gruesome subjects, such as the pursuit of love and the inevitable turmoil such a quest entailed. She thought *Sense and Sensibility* would do the job. It was one of her favorites and could always be relied on to soothe her troubled spirit.

"Won't you stay for a drink?" Sebastian asked when Gemma rose from the table and bid the men goodnight.

She shook her head. "I'm rather tired."

"May I escort you upstairs?" Sebastian asked as he followed her out the door.

Gemma would have preferred that Sebastian remain downstairs, where she wouldn't be tempted to walk into his arms. She was in need of comfort, but such thoughts were dangerous, especially when Colin had invited him to stay and Sebastian would be just next door on this dark, wild night, his proximity as comforting as it was unsettling. It would be best if she was already asleep by the time he came up and she didn't eagerly listen for his step on the stairs or imagine him undressing for bed on the other side of the wall.

Sebastian would never take advantage of the situation and come to her room, but Gemma wasn't sure she could trust herself. She was so tired of waiting for her life to begin, and knew all too well that nothing was guaranteed. A year ago, such brazen longing would have shocked her, but now she was older, and wiser, and ever more conscious of the passage of time. She had watched everyone she had loved die. Victor and his young bride had passed before they had even made thirty.

As long as she was alive the future was always in view, but, much like the horizon, it seemed to keep shifting and remained tantalizingly out of reach. Gemma was twenty-eight, a woman grown in years but not in experience. She knew the facts and she so longed for physical intimacy with a man she'd come to love deeply. It sometimes scared her how much power Sebastian held over her heart, but she was as innocent as an adolescent bride when it came to practical knowledge.

She was ready, not only for love but for motherhood. How many more years did she have before she was deemed too old to have a child? She realized she was up against societal norms, but there was also the science. A woman was only in bloom for so long, and then she began to wilt, like a flower that had had its time in the sun and would soon return to the earth from which it had sprung. Dust to dust. Ashes to ashes.

"Yes, you can escort me upstairs," Gemma said softly as she lifted her gaze to his face and felt the warmth of his hand as it enveloped hers.

Propriety would be observed; she wouldn't have it any other way, but who could fault her for seeking Sebastian's comforting embrace or giving herself up to a goodnight kiss? They were walking up the stairs in silence, Gemma savoring the anticipation of their rare moment of privacy, when she heard Anne calling to her from her bedroom.

"Is it all right if I come in?" Sebastian asked when they reached the landing. "I'd like to say hello."

"Of course. Mrs. Ramsey will be glad to see you," Gemma said woodenly, her hope for an uninterrupted moment with Sebastian quickly evaporating.

She knocked, then pushed open the door. The air in the room was stale with the odors of prolonged convalescence. Anne lay propped up against the pillows, her face as pallid as the linen behind her head. Her hair had turned even grayer these past few weeks, and lines of pain were etched into the papery skin beneath her eyes and around her mouth. She looked older than her sixty years, and her gaze was as clouded as if she were in the early stages of cataracts. Her eyes seemed to clear when she spotted Sebastian, and her gaze slid towards her late husband's waistcoat that Sebastian was still wearing.

"George," she choked out, her eyes glowing with hope. "Darling, is it really you?"

Sebastian was about to correct her when Gemma laid a gentle hand on his wrist. There was no longer any point in reasoning with Anne. She either forgot the answers as soon as the words were spoken, or became tearful and confused when she realized she couldn't recall the events or the people that had mattered to her. What was the harm in letting her think George had come to see her? Perhaps it would soothe her and help her rest.

"You look well, Anne," Sebastian said softly.

Gemma could tell he was uncomfortable with the lie, but he understood the value of offering peace to a person who had nothing else to hope for.

Anne's bottom lip began to tremble, and she lifted her hand, reaching out to Sebastian. "Please, take me with you," she pleaded. "Life has become such a sore trial of late."

"It's not your time, but I will be there, waiting for you, when it is."

"I don't want to stay here by myself," Anne wailed tearfully. "I'm lost, and I can't find my way back. My mind has become a labyrinth of dark passages and blind corners. I'm so frightened, George."

Sebastian sat on the edge of the bed and took Anne's hand in his. "I know, Annie, but we don't decide when it's time for us to go."

"Why not?" she demanded. "Why should we be forced to go on when life has lost all meaning? None of it means anything without love or hope for the future."

"There are people who love you, Annie," Sebastian said.

Anne shook her head miserably. "You're not here to help me through this, and I'm a burden to our son."

"Never. Colin adores you."

"I'm only holding him back. It's time Colin was married and had a family of his own. I don't want him to be alone, George. He's such a sensitive boy. He needs love and support. And Gemma won't have him," Anne said bitterly. "She doesn't think he's good enough for her."

"It's really not that, Mrs. Ramsey," Gemma interjected, but Anne glared at her, her lips pursing in anger.

"I've told you time and time again that policeman is no good for you, Gemma. Men like him can't help but court trouble. It's the darkness in their soul. Pain calls out to pain, and blood invites blood. He'll drag you down into the mire, and you will drown in his filth," Anne snarled. She was gripping Sebastian's hand, her nails digging into his flesh. "Why won't you listen, you foolish girl?"

"That's quite enough," Gemma said sternly.

She hated to rebuke Anne and understood that the woman couldn't control her mounting fears, but her dire predictions always unsettled Gemma, and she wished Anne's fixation would find another target. Just as quickly as Anne's wrath had come, it seemed to pass, leaving her startled and confused. She yanked her hand away, and her mouth opened in a scream when she realized that the man wearing her husband's waistcoat was not George but someone who, at the moment, seemed a stranger.

"Who are you, and what are you doing in my room?" Anne

shrieked. She looked to Gemma, her eyes pleading for help. "Who is this man?"

"It's all right, Mrs. Ramsey. I'll go now," Sebastian said, and sprang to his feet.

"Where's my Colin?" Anne cried. "I don't trust his nursemaid to keep him safe."

"Colin is well, Mrs. Ramsey. I just saw him downstairs," Gemma said. "Should I ask him to come up?"

"What's he doing downstairs?" Anne demanded. "He should be in bed. It's past his bedtime."

"I'll go check on him as soon as you get to sleep," Gemma promised.

Sebastian backed out of the room, but Gemma sat with Anne until the older woman finally calmed down and fell asleep, her fingers still wrapped around Gemma's as if Gemma were a life raft that could ferry her to safety.

"She's getting worse," Sebastian said once Gemma finally tiptoed from the room and found him waiting in the corridor.

He hadn't bothered to turn on the lamp, and the only light came from the floor below, the gaslight shimmering faintly and diffusing like gold dust along the narrow corridor.

"Physically, Anne's improving," Gemma replied wearily, "but her memory slips a little more each day, and her sense of time is no longer linear. It's like a spiral that keeps twisting and turning without beginning or end."

"But her heart knows," Sebastian said sadly. "It understands what's happening."

Gemma nodded. "Yes, it's as if there's a deeper layer of cognizance that's desperately trying to fight its way to the surface."

"She's right, though. To live without love and hope is to merely exist."

In the dim light, Sebastian's eyes were a bottomless brown, and shadows painted hollows on his face and darkened his hair. He was achingly familiar but also different, more intense, on edge. There was something in his gaze that was weighty and deep, but it wasn't mere desire for physical intimacy. It was something solemn and all-encompassing.

"Gemma, I wasn't going to..." he began. His voice was low, almost hoarse, and he seemed to be weighing his words carefully, afraid to say the wrong thing. "That is, I—" The sound of footsteps put paid to whatever he had been about to say.

Colin trudged up the stairs. His shoulders drooped, he'd loosened his tie, and he wore an expression worthy of a sulky child.

"I waited and waited," he complained.

"I'm sorry," Sebastian said. He'd clearly forgotten all about the drink he was going to share with Colin after dinner. "If it's not too late..."

Colin made a dismissive gesture. "Another time. I'm rather tired, actually."

Postmortems were physically taxing, needing a lot of sheer physical strength to saw through bone and slice through muscle. And then there was the emotional cost. No matter how many bodies Colin had autopsied, he still treated each victim with care and respect, never forgetting for a second that, not very long before, they had been a human being with feelings and needs, and had people who loved them. The weight of responsibility for their final moments on earth rested with him, and he never shirked his duty to them, not until they were decently buried and could rest in peace.

Gemma knew just how Colin felt. She had felt that way about every patient in her care, and although after a time she had learned to erect an emotional barrier, if only to protect her sanity, she couldn't detach herself completely. Anne's plight left her feeling emotionally drained and crippled with guilt every time she lost patience at having to repeat herself or had to battle with Anne to eat or wash or change out of her soiled nightdress. Anne needed her as much as any wounded soldier had done, except this casualty had the mental capability of a child and needed to be treated with all the gentleness and love of a devoted mother whose patience never ran out and whose kindness was the only thing keeping the darkness at bay.

"Did you go in to say goodnight to Mother?" Colin asked, looking from Sebastian to Gemma.

"Yes. She's asleep."

"Oh, good. She's had a difficult day." Colin's gaze narrowed as it slid towards Sebastian. "What are you two doing skulking in a dark corridor?"

"Just saying goodnight," Sebastian replied evenly.

"Goodnight, then," Colin said, but made no move to leave.

He waited until Gemma entered her room and was about to shut the door before walking away, his heels clicking on the wooden boards as he strode towards his own bedroom at the end of the corridor.

TWENTY-TWO

Sebastian removed George Ramsey's waistcoat and tossed it over a chair, then pulled off his damp boots, but didn't bother to undress fully. He wasn't ready to go to sleep, and needed something to read to take his mind off Gemma and the awful things Anne had said about him. Was it true? Would he bring Gemma nothing but pain, and would Gemma suffer the same fate as Louisa because of him? He had tried to speak to Gemma about his fears, but Colin had interrupted, and now, as Sebastian listlessly paced the room, all he could think was that, if he truly loved Gemma, he would walk away and leave her to live her life in peace. The very thought of never seeing her again hurt so badly, though, he decided that now wasn't the time to make such a life-altering decision.

Instead, he checked the pocket of his coat and was gratified to find that the newspaper he'd taken from Shep Reynolds' cabin was still dry, probably because he'd held Gemma against that side and no rainwater had penetrated the pocket. Sitting on the bed, Sebastian leaned against the headboard and unfolded the *Herald*, desperate for a distraction. He skimmed through articles devoted to finance and politics, read a gripping account of the mounting tensions between the Northern and Southern states, and greatly enjoyed a story about a runaway heiress whose father had employed the Pinkerton Detective Agency to track her down and bring her back. The errant heiress had been found in the Dakota Territory with a man who was decidedly unsuitable and who had engaged in a shoot-out with the Pinkerton agent. Both men had been wounded, while the young woman had managed to steal a horse and ride hell for leather, leaving the frontier town in the dust and disappearing without a trace.

It was on the next to last page that Sebastian spotted the name Minturn, and he read the brief article. It began as an innocuous engagement announcement but then became decidedly more interesting, the tone of the reporter surprisingly irreverent given the grim postscript. The announcement read:

Mr. Robert Bowne Minturn of Grinnell, Minturn and Company, has announced the engagement of his beloved niece, Leah Minturn, to Shepard Reynolds, son of Lionel Shepard Reynolds of Islip, Long Island. The marriage will take place on Saturday, July 16, 1859, at Astor House Hotel in New York City.

Miss Minturn is the sole heiress to her uncle's shipping fortune and was previously engaged to Cyrus Rutherford III. Her unfortunate bridegroom was murdered two weeks before the wedding, his mutilated remains discovered in a seedy dockside brothel on South Street. The victim was asphyxiated, the word "scum" carved into his chest. The culprit was never apprehended, and Mr. Rutherford's remains were returned to his family for burial.

The disillusioned bride decided to forgo a period of mourning and quickly transferred her affections to Shepard Reynolds. We hope she will be luckier this time.

Sebastian folded the newspaper and tossed it aside, a whole new set of questions swirling in his mind. Had Shep Reynolds been responsible for the death of this Cyrus Rutherford, and, if he had, why had he kept the newspaper on his desk? Was it because of the engagement announcement, because he wanted a souvenir of his crime, or because he wasn't guilty and didn't see the article as incriminating? And if Reynolds was the killer, why would he murder Anthony Blackstock in almost exactly the same way? He'd have to be very stupid, very cocky, or just insane.

On the other hand, if someone was aware of what had happened to Leah Minturn's fiancé, and it was probably safe to say that every member of the crew had heard what had happened, to murder Anthony Blackstock in a similar fashion would be sure to incriminate Reynolds when the details came out and the obvious conclusions were drawn.

Attractive as it might seem to accuse Shep Reynolds of the murder and close the case, Sebastian wasn't convinced. Reynolds was slippery, smooth-talking, and ambitious, but that didn't make him a killer. However, learning that Reynolds was about to be married did provide a hitherto elusive motive. Leah Minturn was the sole heiress to what had to be a sizable fortune and most likely a stake in the shipping company. Shep Reynolds would not take kindly to someone threatening his future, and, if Anthony Black-stock had been about to accuse him of inappropriate behavior towards his wife, both Blackstocks would immediately become a threat that would need to be eliminated, since Audrey Blackstock would be able to point the finger at Reynolds if allowed to live. By suggesting that Audrey had murdered her husband, then killed herself, Shep Reynolds had offered Sebastian a neat solution that if accepted would ensure he was in the clear.

Getting up, Sebastian undressed down to his drawers and got into bed. His mind had been buzzing like a hive all day, and he needed a few hours of rest. He turned out the oil lamp and shut his eyes, determined not to think about Gemma or this maddening case.

TWENTY-THREE

Unable to sleep, Gemma needed all her strength of will not to pull on her dressing gown and tiptoe down the corridor to Sebastian's room. What had he been about to tell her when Colin interrupted? Sebastian had looked so serious, and—now that she thought about it—had seemed filled with trepidation. Had he been about to officially declare himself? Flipping onto her stomach and pummeling the pillow with all the frustration of a woman who'd come within an inch of her heart's desire, Gemma told herself that this was neither the time nor the place to have that conversation. They were in the middle of a murder investigation, and she couldn't and wouldn't leave Anne now. Anne and Colin needed her, and she would not let them down. She had given her word that she wouldn't leave before Anne was back on her feet.

Desperate to not think about Sebastian, Gemma redirected her thoughts to the investigation. The one aspect of this case that truly troubled her was the fate of Audrey Blackstock. What had happened to her and why? The only thing Gemma was certain of as her mind began to drift and her body relaxed into the mattress was that this was a crime driven by emotions so raw and passions that ran so deep, the killer couldn't possibly be a random acquaintance. Whoever had killed Anthony Blackstock was a person whose pain was etched as deeply into their heart as the letters that had been carved into the victim's chest. This was personal, and nothing less than a human sacrifice would do. And Audrey Blackstock was the key to unraveling the mystery.

When she finally slipped into unconsciousness, Gemma's dreams were dark and menacing, a pervasive feeling of entrapment bringing her to the edge of panic as she found herself wandering about in the bowels of a ship. She traversed one corridor after another, desperate to find a way out, but the ship was a maze of twisting corridors and closed doors, a mass grave of people who were still alive but packed together like pilchards in a barrel. As she pounded on a door she thought might lead her to the deck, she realized she was Audrey Blackstock, and she knew in her bones that, if she didn't escape, she would surely die. The door was yanked open, and Audrey fell headlong into another passage, but her relief was short-lived. She was seized by strong, masculine arms, and a large, calloused hand clamped over her mouth as she was dragged, struggling, onto the deserted deck.

Audrey's heart—or was it Gemma's?—hammered against her ribs as the man lifted her easily and hurled her over the side, her scream caught in her throat as she hurtled towards the roiling river beneath. There was a moment of paralyzing shock as the cold water closed over her head, and then she was sinking, her skirts heavy and wet and clinging to her legs like weighted restraints. She fought desperately to rise to the surface and draw a lifesaving breath, but the water sucked her into its depths, the river refusing to relinquish its hold. Audrey's flailing arms grew tired, and her lungs burned with the need for air. Unable to keep her mouth closed, she parted her lips and filthy, muddy water rushed in, filling her nose and mouth and stinging her eyes. She had no more strength to fight, and the will to live seemed to have deserted her, the watery grave's embrace suffocating as she sank to the silty bottom. She thought her lungs would burst as her heart fluttered in her chest, and then she was floating, weightless, as the river claimed her for its own.

Gemma sat bolt upright, her heart hammering with terror as she tried to vanquish the nightmare that continued to play in her mind even now that she was awake. She had not drawn the curtains last night, preferring to greet the dawn from her bed, and now she was desperate to see a glimmer of the rising sun and the reassuring sliver of daylight on the horizon. But there was nothing but the pale crescent of the moon that hung high above the chimney of the house across the street. The rain had stopped, and the wind had died down, and, after a series of deep, calming breaths, Gemma was finally able to quiet her racing heart and focus on what was real.

She slipped out of bed, pulled on her dressing gown and belted it tight, then padded towards the door in her bare feet. All was quiet. Even Mabel was still abed in her attic room, the floorboards that creaked loudly as soon as she was up still undisturbed. Gemma stopped before Sebastian's room, her heart leaping into her mouth as she raised her hand and knocked lightly.

Sebastian opened the door almost immediately. His face was bone white in the silvery light of the moonlit corridor, and his eyes resembled hollow dark sockets. His hair was tousled, and dark stubble shadowed his jaw. He wore nothing but trousers that he must have hastily pulled on before he opened the door. His chest was bare, the smooth skin pale except for the golden hair that curled on his pectorals and snaked down towards the navel and beyond.

The muscles of Sebastian's stomach were taut, and his jaw tightened when he took in Gemma's anxious face. Propriety be damned: she walked into his embrace and rested her head against his shoulder, her arms going around his waist and holding him tight. He was warm and solid and safe, and she wished she could remain in the fortress of his arms forever, but then she heard the moaning of floorboards in Colin's room and immediately pulled away, stepping as far back as she was able without encountering the wall.

"Gemma, are you all right?" Sebastian demanded as he hastily grabbed his shirt and pulled it on, buttoning it lest Colin emerge from his bedroom and arrive at unwarranted conclusions based on the hour and the state of their undress.

"What's happened?" Colin asked as he yanked open his door and stepped out into the corridor, a flickering oil lamp in his hand.

He held it before him, illuminating Gemma and Sebastian and peering at them like a put-upon parent who'd just been woken from his well-deserved slumber. He seemed relieved to find Sebastian dressed and Gemma securely belted into her modest dressing gown, but it was clear he had questions about the nature of this nocturnal meeting and was about to assume the role of a strict chaperone.

"We must go back to the ship," Gemma cried. "Before it's too late."

Colin's sorrowful expression reminded her it was too late already, and the body of the victim even now reposed in the cellar, but an inexplicable sense of urgency seemed to drive Gemma on. She didn't believe in portents or prophetic dreams, nor did she believe that she had somehow seen what had happened to Audrey Blackstock, but she did believe in the powers of observation and the unerring veracity of a woman's intuition. She couldn't put her feelings into words or quantify her fear, but she must have seen or heard something that had bloomed into a subliminal warning when her mind had relaxed in sleep. All she knew was that she sensed imminent danger.

"We must return to the ship," Gemma tried again.

"Gemma, it's half past three," Colin said as he peered at the pocket watch he must have grabbed along with the lamp.

"Sebastian, please," Gemma pleaded, turning all her considerable powers of persuasion upon him. "I think Audrey Blackstock is at the center of this case, not her husband."

Sebastian nodded. "All right. I'll meet you downstairs in fifteen minutes. And Gemma..."

"Yes?"

"Bring the pistol."

"Why?"

"Just in case."

"Gemma, perhaps you should let Sebastian go on his own—" Colin began, but Gemma cut across him.

"I'm going, Colin. If you need help, perhaps you can ask Poppy to come by before her shift. Tell her I'll make it up to her."

Gemma didn't bother to wait for Colin to reply. She hurried to her room, where she opened the drawer of the bedside table and took out the polished case that contained the Colt 1849 pocket revolver Sebastian had given her for her birthday. The pistol was a thing of beauty and, despite its compact design, was as deadly a weapon as any Gemma had seen in Crimea. She would have been happy to leave it in its case forever, but Sebastian had insisted on teaching her how to use it, and they had practiced at an out-of-the-way copse in Hyde Park until Gemma had been able to hit the target three times in a row.

It had felt surprisingly empowering to fire a weapon and see the lead ball find its mark, but Gemma still hoped she would never have to point the gun at a human being. She would rather not bring it now, but she could understand Sebastian's concern. Whoever had killed Anthony Blackstock had not shied away from brutality and would no doubt try to fight their way out if cornered. Constable Forrest had his truncheon, but Sebastian was unarmed, and Gemma knew how he worried for her safety.

Taking out the pistol and the box of paper cartridges Sebastian had purchased for her, Gemma realized there wasn't enough room in her reticule for both, so she decided to leave the spare cartridges behind. She had asked Sebastian to load the pistol after their last target practice since she was still slow and clumsy when it came to loading the cartridges and securing the percussion caps. And if they needed more than five shots, they'd have much greater problems than the lack of ammunition. Besides, she needed to leave room in her reticule for one more item.

Gemma dressed hastily, then wound her hair into a knot before pulling on and lacing her boots. She would have loved a cup of strong, sweet tea to steady her nerves, but the sense of urgency prevailed, and she hurried downstairs and made for the cellar door, the flame of her candle just barely slicing through the viscous darkness when she descended to the cavernous space below. Colin kept an array of instruments and remedies in the cabinet in the corner. He used to keep the medicinals upstairs, but, since Anne had unwittingly helped herself to half a bottle of castor oil because she had mistaken the mixture for tea, Colin had moved the supplies to the cellar for safety.

Gemma opened the cabinet and ran her finger along the vials and jars, hoping she'd find what she'd come for. She breathed a sigh of relief when she spotted the Howard & Sons label, and dropped the stoppered bottle into her reticule. She inwardly apologized to Colin for helping herself to his stock without permission, and vowed to replace the bottle before he realized it had gone.

Sebastian was dressed in his own clothes and waiting for her by the door. Gemma drew on her short cape and pulled on her bonnet, then Sebastian unlocked the door and they stepped out into the darkness. She was grateful he hadn't asked her to explain herself or suggested she remain at home. On some instinctive level, he shared her urgency and was willing to put his trust in her intuition, and, as he reached for her hand, Gemma felt even more strongly that time was of the essence.

TWENTY-FOUR

The night was desolate, the houses that lined the streets black silhouettes against the sky, the clumps of chimneys like pointy scales on the backs of slumbering beasts. A lone streetlamp cast a pool of light onto the cobblestones, but the shadows beyond were impenetrable. Gemma thought she saw a furtive figure dart into a narrow alleyway, and a mangy cat with a dead mouse clamped between its jaws ambled across the road, but otherwise all was silent and empty until a hansom rattled down the street. The driver was hunched on his perch, his hat pulled so low all Gemma could make out were bushy muttonchop whiskers separated by a narrow strip of clean-shaven chin. The driver slowed when he saw them, no doubt hoping for an early morning fare, but Sebastian wordlessly waved him on as they headed towards the river.

The Thames shimmered in the barely-there moonlight and wound into the distance, mostly empty of traffic, but there were always those who were abroad during the night. Several small craft bobbed on the surface, the lanterns flickering like glowworms, their light diffusing in the mist rising off the water in an otherworldly haze. One glowing orb began to move, and, with a gentle splash of oars, a rowboat glided out of the mist towards the shore.

"Slow night?" Sebastian asked once the boat drew nearer.

The ferryman was an older man, whippet-thin, lank-haired, and dressed like a medieval peasant, complete with a woolen hood to keep the chill of the night at bay. His long face looked skeletally pale in the meager light, and, when he opened his mouth, he appeared to be missing half his teeth.

"Not much luck tonight, guv. But ye look like ye're in a rush to get somewhere."

"Can you take us to the Isle of Dogs?"

The man pushed back his hood and scratched his head. He probably wondered why a respectable-looking couple would wish to go out to the Isle of Dogs in the middle of the night, but he didn't ask, too fearful of losing the hefty fare he would no doubt name. He called out, "Get in."

The bottom squelched against the silty shore as he brought the boat as close to the bank as he could and waited for them to board. Sebastian lifted Gemma and set her carefully in the prow before getting in himself and settling on the narrow bench at the stern. The boat wasn't big enough for them to sit together, and with the three of them there was barely any room to move.

The ferryman shifted a boat hook away from Gemma's feet. Gemma couldn't help but shudder as she stared at the glinting three-pronged metal hook affixed to the end. This man was one of many who came out on the river each night in the hope of reeling in a floater. They didn't much care about the identities of the men and women who wound up floating down the Thames. They could be victims of a crime or individuals who'd been unable to make it through one more day and jumped from one of London's many bridges. Once the Thames claimed them, they were no longer human beings but coveted prizes for the scavengers who hunted the waterway. The suicides were preferable to victims of crime, since they usually still had their valuables on them and were fully dressed. A good night's work could yield jewelry, coins, boots, and clothes that could be sold to a rag-and-bone man. The garments would be sopping wet and reeking, but they would still fetch a few bob once they dried out. One man's rubbish was another man's treasure, and London's many poor weren't very picky.

The man grunted with every pull of the oars as he guided the small craft away from the shore. If he'd already been out most of the night, he had to be exhausted, but the current appeared to be in their favor, and the little boat moved with surprising speed. The Tower of London loomed over them, its massive shadow obscuring the barely-there crescent of the moon as they rowed past. The arch of Traitors' Gate yawned darkly, the water lapping against the stone lip and the metal grille putting Gemma in mind of another investigation and another gruesomely mutilated victim. Her insides quavered as she recalled the details of her dream. She didn't know why she felt such a sense of urgency. Audrey Blackstock had to be dead, but some primal instinct urged Gemma on, and she offered up a silent prayer that they would get to the *Prince Regent* in time.

After more than an hour on the water, Gemma was chilled to the bone, the velvet of her cape doing little to keep the cold and damp at bay. Her skirts were dewy with morning mist, and her skin felt clammy and moist. She should have felt relieved when the vessel finally came into view, but the hull that rose darkly above the water cast the tiny rowboat in deep shadow, and the deck seemed as high up as the roof of Buckingham Palace. Gemma felt sick with dread when she recalled the perilous ascent of the day before, and her muscles quivered in protest at the prospect of navigating the twitching rope ladder once again, and so soon. But there was no other way to get aboard, and it was too late to change her mind, even though, despite her premonition, everything seemed calm.

In fact, the *Prince Regent* looked deserted, a ghost ship eerily lit by a single lantern. The ferryman pulled up within a few feet of the prow, and Sebastian got to his feet and hollered, "*Prince Regent*, permission to come aboard."

Nothing happened, and Gemma wondered if anyone had even

heard him. Sebastian called out again, then, after a few tense moments, someone finally leaned over the railing and peered at them in the darkness.

"Permission denied," the person called out.

"I am Inspector Bell of Scotland Yard. Please summon Mr. Reynolds."

The man stepped away from the railing and engaged in a muffled exchange with someone Gemma couldn't see, then finally reappeared a few moments later.

"Who's with you, Inspector Bell?"

"Nurse Tate."

"I'll lower the ladder now," the sailor called, and tossed the rope ladder overboard.

Gemma felt queasy with apprehension as she grasped the sides of the ladder. She could feel the rough fibers of the hemp through her gloves, and the step twisted out of her way like an eel, but she refused to give in to fear and firmly planted her boot on the rung. She would have liked to say that it was easier the third time around, but it wasn't, and, by the time she finally made it to the top and was pulled over the side by strong, masculine hands, her thighs trembled with the strain and her heart was ready to explode out of her chest. Gemma's kid gloves were beyond repair, and her bonnet had come off during the climb and now hung around her neck by the ribbons, strands of hair that had come loose whipping in the breeze.

Gemma exhaled slowly, grateful for the solid deck beneath her feet. She looked to the east, where a gauzy streak of mauve had appeared in the sky. It grew brighter and wider as the sky lightened and the sun prepared to crest the horizon. Now that she was finally aboard, she felt foolish, her earlier panic replaced by doubt. The deck was empty, the damp wood glinting in the pearly light and the miles of rigging creaking overhead. Everyone except the night watch was probably still asleep, the shock of discovering there had been a murder in the night replaced by the very human desire to get on with their own lives. For most people aboard the ship, Anthony and Audrey Blackstock would have already receded into the past, their unfortunate passing nothing more than a shocking story to tell their friends and family once the passengers came safely ashore and arrived at their destinations.

Sebastian had intended to return to the ship anyway, so it hadn't been a wasted journey, but in retrospect getting him up in the middle of the night and demanding they leave immediately seemed like the actions of an alarmist. Gemma had simply been overwrought and had allowed her fears to get the better of her, especially at that time of night when life seemed at its most frightening—the witching hour. Gemma recalled the quote from *Hamlet* that had terrified her the first time she'd read the play when she was fifteen.

"'Tis now the very witching time of night, when churchyards yawn and hell itself breathes out contagion to this world: now could I drink hot blood, and do such bitter business as the day would quake to look on."

And that was what had frightened her so badly, Gemma realized. She had glimpsed hell itself in the actions of the killer. The taking of life was distressingly common, but giving vent to such brutality was something else entirely, the actions of an unbalanced mind and the hallmark of true evil. And until the killer was behind bars, she would not be able to rest, and neither would Sebastian. That was why he had not questioned her plea to return. He was driven by the same need to contain evil, and, even though the light of day took the edge off Gemma's dread, she knew the killer was still there, biding their time until they could vanish into the crowd and escape all responsibility for their deeds.

Gemma adjusted her bonnet, tucked in the loose strands of hair, and pulled off her shredded gloves. She would need to purchase a new pair, but these gloves would see her safe if she needed to climb down one more time.

Sebastian had just come aboard and was speaking to the night watch when a shrill cry rent the still air. It seemed to be coming from the aft deck, and as calls for assistance, presumably by a member of the crew, reached them, Gemma was able to make out only one word—"murder."

TWENTY-FIVE

The shouting was followed by the sound of running feet. The night watch who'd helped Sebastian and Gemma aboard sprinted towards the back of the ship, and several other sailors who must have been woken by the noise had come running, erupting from the hatch that led to the crew's quarters below and heading towards the stern. Sebastian and Gemma exchanged looks of alarm, and the two of them rushed after the sailors, arriving at the aft deck moments after the first men.

The sight that greeted them was truly shocking. A woman hung from the boom, her body rotating slowly on her makeshift noose. In the gentle light of dawn, she looked hardly more than a child, her feet only a few inches above the deck and her hands hanging limply at her sides.

The woman's hair was loose, and her thin nightdress billowed in the breeze, the fine lawn fabric clinging to the delicate curves of her bosom and whipping about her legs. A shawl was trapped in the rigging, the colorful woolen square fluttering in the breeze like the wings of a frantic bird. One shoe had fallen and lay on its side, and the woman's bare foot looked heartbreakingly pale and small. Gemma cried out in shock. She thought the victim had to be Audrey Blackstock, but, when the chalk-white, horrified face rotated towards her, Gemma realized she had met the victim less than twenty-four hours ago. The dead woman was Greta Van Kemp.

Gemma's hand flew to her mouth and tears blurred her vision as the men grabbed the body by the legs and held it up, while one of the sailors climbed up on the boom and shimmied down the length of the beam until he reached the rope. He pulled out a sharp knife and began to frantically hack through the hemp, but there was no longer any reason for urgency. The body slumped just as the final strands were severed, and the men lowered Greta to the deck and laid her on her back. One of the men fell to his knees and began to blow air into her lungs, but Gemma was certain it was too late, and, having realized the same thing, the sailor gave up and pushed laboriously to his feet, then wiped his mouth with the back of his hand in revulsion.

Gemma sensed a presence at her side and turned to find Constable Forrest, his eyes wide with shock and his hairless face creased with sleep. He looked like a little boy who'd been woken in the middle of the night. Forrest didn't say anything, just stared at the dead woman, then bowed his head and looked down at his feet, either in sorrow or in shame, since Greta Van Kemp had died on his watch.

"Clear the deck, and fetch Mr. Reynolds," Sebastian shouted, then turned to Gemma and Constable Forrest.

Lines of sorrow were etched into his face, and the weight of responsibility seemed to rest heavily on his shoulders. Even though he had not been on board when Greta had died, Sebastian clearly blamed himself and had probably already catalogued all the ways in which he had failed her, first by not identifying the killer and then by allowing Shep Reynolds to evict him from the ship. He would carry Greta's death with him as he carried so many others, the faces of the victims forever burned into his brain.

Gemma knew just how he felt and didn't bother to try to convince him that it wasn't his fault. It hadn't been her fault when patients had died in her care, but she still grieved for the young men she'd lost and could recall their faces, not as they had been in death but as they had been in life, their eyes pleading for help and their bodies bleeding and broken. Such was the lot of the people who dedicated their lives to the welfare of others. There were those they saved and those they couldn't, and no win ever made up for the loss.

Not bothering with pointless platitudes, Gemma marched across the deck and knelt next to the body. All she could do was assess the damage and help Sebastian find the person who had done this, and in order to do that he needed to know as much as possible about what had happened to Greta Van Kemp.

"Her nightdress is damp from the mist but not wet," Gemma said as purpose overrode the horror and she focused on the victim. "It wouldn't have had time to dry if she had been murdered during the storm."

"So, she hasn't been dead long," Sebastian observed woodenly.

"A few hours at most." Gemma shut Greta's bulging eyes and tried not to look at the swollen tongue that protruded from her mouth. "The neck did not break during the fall, so she would have taken a long while to die," she said, trying not to envision what the poor woman must have endured before death had finally set her free.

Sebastian looked up at the beam, his eyes narrowing as he performed mental calculations and took in his immediate surroundings. Gemma answered his question before he had a chance to ask it, since she had wondered the same thing herself.

"I don't believe this could have been suicide. There was nothing for her to stand on, and I highly doubt Miss Van Kemp climbed into the rigging, affixed the noose, and then jumped to her death. There's nothing here that could have been kicked out from beneath her feet, and the rope is thick and rough. Miss Van Kemp had small, delicate hands and would not have been able to fashion a noose without assistance."

Sebastian nodded. "Any evidence of a struggle?"

"All the nails are broken, and there are scratches on her neck.

Greta must have clawed at the rope in her desperation to save herself. There are also bruises on her wrists and forearms. I expect someone grabbed her and dragged her until she was just beneath the beam, then tried to hold on to her while they fitted the noose around her neck."

Gemma hated to violate the woman's privacy and expose her to searching male gazes, but she had to be certain she had painted the whole picture and not just a partial sketch of what had befallen Greta Van Kemp when she had either come up or been dragged on deck. She blocked Greta from view as much as possible with her wide skirts, then lifted the nightdress and examined Greta's thighs and narrow pelvis for any evidence of sexual violence. She then laid her hands on Greta's abdomen and palpated gently, but the stomach was flat and taut. Carefully turning the body onto its side, Gemma studied the milky buttocks and the backs of Greta's thighs. There were bruises on the hips and thighs, but they were too faint to have been inflicted within the past few hours. Satisfied, she rolled Greta onto her back, smoothed the fabric over her legs, and tucked it underneath so that a gust of wind would not leave her exposed up to her waist.

"Is there any evidence of rape?" Sebastian asked when Gemma remained silent.

Gemma shook her head. "I don't see any fresh bruising or signs of bleeding. Colin will be able to tell you if there's any tearing," she said without meeting Sebastian's gaze. She didn't think she should probe the victim's most intimate areas, especially while she was still laid out on deck. "I don't see any signs of pregnancy, but if she was only a few weeks along there wouldn't be anything to see."

"So, she came up on deck sometime after the storm had passed, either to get a breath of air or possibly to meet someone. The killer grabbed her, dragged her beneath the boom, and strung her up," Sebastian summarized.

"They would have to have had a noose ready if they intended to hang her," Constable Forrest offered quietly, speaking up for the first time.

"Yes, that's a valid point, Constable. The killer must have prepared and lain in wait."

Gemma was certain Sebastian had already considered the noose and arrived at the conclusion that the attack on Greta Van Kemp had been premeditated, but this was his way of including Constable Forrest in the discussion and wordlessly absolving him of guilt. He couldn't have known Greta Van Kemp had been in danger, nor could he have saved her, unless he'd just happened to be on the aft deck in the middle of the night. This was Sebastian's case, and he was the only one who would accept the blame. Constable Forrest was too young and inexperienced to be held to account, and he could not have been expected to remain awake the whole night on the off-chance that another murder might take place.

"The killer had to be a man," Constable Forrest said. "A large man." He sounded a little more confident this time, and, when Sebastian cocked his head and looked at him, the constable did not look away.

"What makes you say that, Constable?"

Constable Forrest knelt next to the body and took hold of the noose, wrapping his large hands around the rope. "There's no way someone with small hands could have tied the noose so tightly. The rope is too thick and stiff."

Sebastian nodded. "Miss Thorpe has larger hands than Miss Van Kemp, and she might have also had an accomplice."

"But why would Miss Thorpe murder Miss Van Kemp?" Constable Forrest asked, his brows furrowing in confusion.

"Perhaps Miss Van Kemp knew something that could implicate Miss Thorpe, and maybe she hoped Miss Van Kemp's death would be mistaken for suicide and the investigation would be closed, leaving her free to get on with her life," Gemma replied.

Forrest didn't argue the point, but his expression was dubious.

"You don't think that's a possibility?" Gemma asked.

He was about to reply when Shep Reynolds exploded onto the deck. His hair was damp, the top button of his coat was undone, and he wasn't wearing a tie. There was a dab of soap beneath his left ear and a smear of fresh blood on his chin. He must have been shaving when he was summoned, and the shocking news had caused him to nick himself. Reynolds looked horrified as he stared at Miss Van Kemp's body, his hand trembling as he ran it through his hair, making it stick up at the front.

"I'm sorry you had to see that, Miss Tate," he muttered, as if he had suddenly recalled that Gemma was there. He didn't look at her, nor did he turn towards Sebastian. He continued to stare at the woman at his feet, his face frozen in horror and disbelief. He was either truly shocked or an exceptionally fine actor who wanted to convey all the right emotions in front of the one person who had the power to accuse him and undermine his command.

"Where was she hanging?" he asked at last.

Sebastian pointed to the spot. "Just there."

"She must have done it herself," Reynolds concluded with a satisfied nod. "Perhaps finding herself alone in a foreign country and with no job or money to fall back on proved too much and she gave in to despair."

"Miss Van Kemp did not kill herself, Mr. Reynolds."

"You don't know that," Reynolds argued.

"I do. She's covered in bruises, she clawed at the rope in her final moments, and the logistics of her death speak to a second person who had come prepared."

"She could have found a way to hang herself if she was determined, and might have incurred the bruises if she had climbed up. And it's not uncommon for suicides to change their mind at the last second. Unfortunately, it's usually too late to save themselves, especially when it comes to hanging. I'm ruling Miss Van Kemp's death a suicide," Shep Reynolds said firmly.

"You are not in a position to rule anything," Sebastian snapped. "Two people, possibly three, have now died on your watch. Will you still refuse to acknowledge that the killer is still on board?"

"Erm, no, but—"

"There are no buts here. This woman was murdered, right here on deck, while your men kept watch. How is such a thing possible?"

Shep Reynolds seemed to recover from his initial shock and took an angry step towards Sebastian, jabbing a finger in his direction. "Don't you dare accuse my crew, Inspector. Their job is to maintain and sail this vessel and get it safely to port. They're not here to guard the passengers or solve murders."

"How could the watch not notice that two people had come up on deck in the middle of the night?" Sebastian demanded.

"Have you ever traveled by ship, Inspector Bell?"

"No," Sebastian admitted with obvious reluctance.

"I didn't think so." Reynolds pointed in the direction of the prow. "The head is over there, in the bow. Do you know what the head is? The privy, as you would call it. Every member of the crew, except the captain, and all the passengers, except those in first class, use the head. If someone gets up in the middle of the night and crosses the deck to get to the head, the night watch have no reason to suspect them of anything other than a full bladder."

"Miss Van Kemp was murdered at the *back* of the ship," Sebastian reminded Reynolds sharply.

"Yes," the man agreed. "And the night watch have no reason to patrol the aft deck during the night. There's no one there."

"Clearly someone was," Sebastian countered.

"Clearly. And if you had done your job and arrested the culprit yesterday, then this woman would still be alive."

"Perhaps I would have done so had you not demanded that I disembark."

"We have protocols for a reason, Inspector Bell, much like the police."

"What do you know of police protocols?"

"More than you might imagine."

"Is that because this is not your first investigation?"

Shep Reynolds looked confused. "What are you talking about?"

"I'm talking about Cyrus Rutherford III."

Gemma had no clue what Sebastian was referring to, but Shep Reynolds clearly did. He went pale, then took a step backwards, as if suddenly desperate to put some space between himself and Sebastian.

"How do you know about that?"

"Were you interviewed in connection with Rutherford's death?"

"No, I wasn't," Reynolds ground out. "He was murdered in a brothel. I have no doubt the whores would remember me if I had been there."

"Yet you benefitted from his death," Sebastian pressed on.

"I did, yes, but, last I heard, offering a grieving woman comfort was not a crime. Nor is proposing to her."

"It's awfully convenient that the grieving woman happened to be the sole heiress to a large fortune and could aid your rise in her uncle's company. And the fact that Anthony Blackstock was murdered in almost exactly the same way is surely not a coincidence."

"I didn't murder either of them."

"Until I know that for certain, I'm watching you," Sebastian hissed, and jabbed a finger into Reynolds' chest.

Gemma let out a weary sigh. The two men were like snarling dogs. She supposed it was to be expected, given the situation, but the first mate's next statement took her completely by surprise.

"You have until noon, Inspector. Then we lift anchor."

"You can't do that," Sebastian retorted.

"Yes, I can. This vessel sails under an American flag, which means you're on American soil when you're on board. You have no jurisdiction here, and I have a schedule to keep."

"You mean a record to set."

"There are people who depend on us, and we can't idle here until you figure this out. By all means, continue your investigation on dry land, but the *Prince Regent* will leave for New York in three days' time."

"Once the killer gets off the ship, they will be out of my reach," Sebastian said, his tone calmer now, more reasonable.

"Perhaps, but I have great faith in Scotland Yard," Reynolds said, not bothering to hide his sarcasm. "You'll get your man. And if you don't, it's nothing to do with me."

"Unless you murdered them, then it's everything to do with you," Sebastian shot back.

"You'll never be able to prove my guilt, because I didn't do it," Reynolds said wearily. He turned to Gemma, his expression rueful. "Please accept my apologies, Miss Tate. None of this is down to you."

With that, Shep Reynolds turned on his heel and strode towards the forecastle.

TWENTY-SIX

Sebastian looked like he would have liked to follow the man and teach him a thing or two about international cooperation, but he sucked in a deep breath, nodded, as if assuring himself that he was calm enough to proceed, and turned to Constable Forrest, who looked on in stunned silence.

"Constable, did you see or hear anything suspicious last night?"

Forrest shook his head. "No, I didn't. Mr. Reynolds ordered everyone to their quarters once the storm broke, so I hardly saw anyone all evening. I was given supper in steerage, and then I bunked in stateroom two. Miss Thorpe was kind enough to change the sheets," he explained.

"Did you hear anything during the night? An argument? A scuffle? A cry for help?" Sebastian tried again.

Constable Forrest looked like he was about to weep. "I slept like a baby, guv. The rolling motion, you know."

"It's not your fault, Constable," Sebastian conceded. "You wouldn't have heard sounds of an altercation from the aft deck unless Miss Van Kemp screamed for help."

"Which she didn't," Gemma said. "Because evidently the night watch didn't hear anything either."

Sebastian's gaze slid towards the body, his expression thoughtful. "If Miss Van Kemp had been accosted in second class, someone would have heard even if everyone was in their cabins. It's a tight space that's adjacent to steerage. The more likely scenario is that Miss Van Kemp had come up on deck of her own volition. It was once she was here that someone attacked her. Why did she not fight back or call for help? She would have known that the night watch were about."

"I think I can answer that," Gemma said as she sank to her knees next to the body.

She pushed back Greta's fair hair, exposing the spot just above her left ear. She hadn't noticed it before but, now that the sun was fully up and the deck was awash in daylight, she could make out a livid bruise beneath the hair.

Sebastian bent over the body and examined the bruise. "Would the blow have stunned her?" he asked as he helped Gemma to her feet.

"Very probably. It would have given Greta's attacker enough time to get her in position and fit the noose over her head. She must have come to when the rope tightened about her throat, but by that stage she would have had no chance of saving herself or the ability to call for help."

"Why her?" Sebastian asked of no one in particular. "What did the killer have to gain by murdering Greta Van Kemp?"

"Perhaps she knew something that would incriminate them," Constable Forrest suggested.

"If she was going to incriminate the killer, she could have done so yesterday," Gemma pointed out. "And who is Cyrus Rutherford?"

"I helped myself to a newspaper when we were in Reynolds' cabin yesterday," Sebastian explained. "I didn't think he'd miss it. It was from March, and there was a short article that mentioned Reynolds. He is to be married in less than a month, and his fiancée is none other than the niece of one of the partners of Grinnell and Minturn, and she is her uncle's sole heir. Her previous fiancé, Cyrus Rutherford III, was found dead in a brothel near the seaport. Asphyxiated, with *scum* scored into his chest. No one has been arrested for the crime."

"Blimey!" Constable Forrest exclaimed. "That's one hell of a coincidence. Begging your pardon, Miss Tate," he hurriedly added.

"It's not a coincidence," Sebastian retorted. "Either Reynolds murdered both men and possibly Miss Van Kemp, or someone is trying to fit him up."

"Who?"

"I don't know, but whoever it is obviously felt Greta Van Kemp was a threat."

"Perhaps the killer was her accomplice," Constable Forrest said, "and decided that she was a loose end."

Sebastian gazed out towards the Isle of Dogs, where warehouses were beginning to open and men could be heard calling out to each other on the docks as they set about their work. Traffic on the river was picking up as well, with small craft and several larger vessels navigating to and away from London. The sky was clear blue, the sun was shining, and the breeze filled the sails of a passing ship. Ship life aboard the *Prince Regent* was about to resume in earnest as the passengers woke, dressed, and waited for their breakfast. Sailors swarmed the deck, several men were already in the rigging, and the coxswain appeared to be in consultation with Shep Reynolds, who glanced nervously towards Sebastian before returning his attention to the other man.

"To date, we have several suspects for the murder of Anthony Blackstock," Sebastian theorized. "I'm inclined to think that the killer is a man, but I cannot rule out the women, since they could have been working in tandem or had a male accomplice. The two people with the strongest motive are Jeffrey Caldwell and Greta Van Kemp, assuming what Mrs. Glenn said was true and Greta really was assaulted by her employer. But if Jeffrey Caldwell murdered Anthony Blackstock in a fit of anger and then killed Audrey Blackstock to silence her, what reason would he have to harm Greta Van Kemp, who wouldn't have been in first class in the middle of the night?

"And if Greta Van Kemp murdered Anthony Blackstock because he had raped her, who would have reason to kill Greta, and where's Audrey Blackstock?" Sebastian sighed heavily. "Shep Reynolds had means, opportunity, and a possible motive, if his upcoming marriage to Leah Minturn was in jeopardy, but now that I know about Cyrus Rutherford there's also the possibility that someone is trying to frame Reynolds for the crime."

Sebastian went quiet, his gaze following Joseph Abrahms, who had appeared on the other side of the deck, a bucket and mop in his hands. Joseph hadn't seen them and went about mopping the deck near the forecastle, entirely focused on his task. His head was down, his shoulders hunched and his movements jerky. He had the look of someone who wanted to disappear, or at the very least not draw any attention to himself, and Gemma didn't think it was because he had something to hide. He might legally be a free man, but inside he was still a slave, a young man who lived in fear and did everything possible not to invite undue scrutiny for fear of getting punished.

Sebastian's thoughts appeared to be running on the same track because he said, "I don't believe Joseph Abrahms is either cunning or brazen enough to murder an innocent man to fit up Jeffrey Caldwell, but Lorna Thorpe would have reason to kill both Anthony Blackstock and Greta Van Kemp."

"Why, sir?" Constable Forrest asked, his eyebrows knitting in confusion.

"If Anthony Blackstock assaulted Greta Van Kemp and had made her predecessor's life a misery, it stands to reason that he would have abused Lorna as well. She's an attractive young woman who wouldn't be likely to escape his notice. If Lorna had reached the end of her tether and murdered her employer, she would have no choice but to kill Audrey Blackstock as well, since Audrey would have the power to send Lorna to the gallows. The only other person who would be able to incriminate Lorna would be her fellow maid and cabinmate, Greta Van Kemp, who had either been Lorna's accomplice or had seen her returning to the cabin covered in blood and held the power of life and death over her. Perhaps Lorna decided to silence Greta before Greta had a chance to betray her, or perhaps Greta realized she was in a position of power and made demands."

"After all, she was out of work and had yet to be paid," Gemma put in. "She would need funds to bide until she found new employment in England or enough money to return home to New York."

"But how do we prove it?" Constable Forrest asked.

Sebastian's gaze went to the noose around Greta's neck. "It would take considerable strength to toss the noose over the boom, then pull on the rope hard enough to lift Greta off her feet and keep her suspended until she was dead. Then Lorna would have to tie the rope to the beam before returning belowdecks," he mused. "Unless she wore gloves, her hands will be red and chafed from the hemp."

Gemma nodded. "Even if she wore gloves, they would be ruined." She reached into the pocket of her skirt and pulled out her own damaged gloves to show Sebastian. "The hemp is too rough for kid gloves. And I doubt she would have used Greta's gloves, since they would be too small."

"I need to speak to Lorna Thorpe," Sebastian said. "Constable, please question the other second-class passengers and see if anyone saw or heard something last night."

"Yes, sir."

Constable Forrest seemed relieved to have something to do and hastened towards the stairs.

"We can't leave Miss Van Kemp here," Gemma said, looking down at the pitiful remains.

She knew Greta Van Kemp was past caring, but Gemma couldn't help but wonder what would happen to her body once a postmortem had been carried out. Had she died at sea, Captain Grant or Shep Reynolds would have held a small service and consigned her body to the deep, but since Greta had died a stone's throw from London such a thing would not be possible. She had no family or friends to claim her remains, and it was unlikely that the *Prince Regent* would ferry the body back to New York. For one, they would probably demand the price of passage, and for another, to stow a body on board for several weeks, even in a coffin, would not only be unsanitary but also dangerous, since the corpse would begin to leak and bodily fluids would contaminate other goods in the hull, possibly precious foodstuffs if they were near. Greta's body would need to be disposed of as quickly as possible, particularly now that the weather was so warm.

Gemma was about to suggest they appeal to Mr. Reynolds to see to the burial when two sailors appeared on deck, a length of canvas in one's arms.

"Mr. Reynolds has instructed us to move the body," the man said. "Where do you want her?"

"Leave the body on her berth for the time being," Sebastian replied. "I will see to it that Miss Van Kemp's remains are removed once the ship makes port."

"As you say, sir," the sailor with the canvas replied.

He spread the canvas on deck. The piece was hardly larger than a child's blanket, and Gemma's heart squeezed with sorrow as the two sailors grabbed the body beneath the arms and by the ankles and laid it in the center. Golden sunlight lit Greta's fair hair and pale face and shone through the thin fabric of her nightdress to reveal the outline of a young, healthy body. Greta Van Kemp would have had years, possibly decades, had she not accepted a position with the Blackstocks. And now she would undergo a post-mortem and then be consigned to a pauper's grave in a foreign land. The sailors deftly wrapped the body and tucked in the ends of the canvas before carrying the bundle towards the hatch that led to second class.

Sebastian came to stand next to Gemma, his expression a combination of simmering frustration and shamefaced contrition.

"I'm sorry," he said quietly. "I behaved badly."

Gemma knew he was referring to the exchange with Shep Reynolds and felt a wave of sympathy. For a man like Sebastian, there was nothing worse than to feel powerless, and, although he was a representative of the law, on this vessel he was as helpless as any of the passengers.

"No you didn't," she protested. "I was tempted to have a go at Mr. Reynolds myself."

"I would have liked to see that," Sebastian said with a rueful grin. The smile slid off his face as he looked at the sun, which was steadily rising in the cloudless sky. "We don't have much time."

"No," Gemma agreed.

"Let's question Lorna Thorpe."

"Actually, there's someone else I'd like to have a word with," Gemma said. "I'll find you later."

She marched off the deck before Sebastian had a chance to stop her and headed towards the aft hatch.

TWENTY-SEVEN

Sebastian made a conscious effort to tamp down his anger. There was nothing he could do to counteract Reynolds' orders, and, annoyed as he was, he could understand the man's urgency. Sebastian didn't know much about sailing, but he knew what it took to run a successful business, and this was a business—a very profitable one. The *Prince Regent* couldn't afford to delay when every additional day at sea ate into the company's profits. And to solve this case might take days, especially now that there was a third victim. If he was no closer to making an arrest by the time the vessel docked, he would have no choice but to round up the remaining suspects and resume his investigation at Scotland Yard.

Sebastian headed belowdecks. Even at such an early hour, steerage was heaving with humanity. The stench was overpowering, the reek of unwashed bodies, soiled nappies, and dirty linen creating an almost solid barrier. Some passengers were still in their berths, lounging until breakfast was served, while others were in the act of washing, shaving, and helping their children prepare for the day. Several women nursed their babies, while others arranged their hair and attempted to tidy their tiny space.

From the whispered conversations and fearful glances directed at Sebastian, it was obvious that news of Miss Van Kemp's death had already spread and people were frightened. Greta Van Kemp wasn't a faceless noblewoman. She had been one of them, a simple person who'd earned her living through sacrifice and hard work. As he passed, several individuals called out to Sebastian, challenging him to answer their queries and asking him to put their minds at rest. But all Sebastian could do was assure them that an investigation was in progress, and they were safe. And they were. As far as Sebastian was aware, no one in steerage had had any dealings with the Blackstocks, and Miss Van Kemp had bunked in second class with a woman who may have murdered all three people.

When Sebastian located Miss Thorpe's cabin, he found the door unlocked. Miss Van Kemp's canvas-wrapped remains occupied the berth on the right, while Miss Thorpe, who was still in her nightdress, her hair in disarray and her eyes red and swollen from crying, huddled on the left-hand berth, a crumpled handkerchief gripped in her trembling hands. She yanked the blanket up to her chin to cover up her state of undress and pulled in her head like a turtle.

"Miss Thorpe, I'm Inspector Bell of Scotland Yard. May I come in?" Sebastian asked from the doorway.

Lorna Thorpe nodded. Sebastian entered the cabin, shut the door behind him, and sat at the foot of Miss Van Kemp's berth. There was hardly any room, but he wanted to be face to face with the suspect, not looking down on her as he hovered above her berth. Lorna looked at him fearfully before her gaze crept to the closed door.

"I shut the door for your own protection, Miss Thorpe," Sebastian explained. "So that no one can overhear what you have to tell me."

"I don't have anything to tell you," Lorna Thorpe moaned. "I don't know anything." She continued to sob, her voice reedy and breathless as she wailed, "I don't understand. Who would want to hurt Greta? She was such a kind soul, so gentle and unassuming. To think that someone would..." The sobs grew louder, Lorna's eyes and nose streaming.

Her gaze slid to Greta's body, and she shuddered, the tears sliding down her cheeks and dripping from her chin. Lorna used a hand to swipe at her eyes, and Sebastian noted that Gemma had been right. Her hands were considerably larger than Greta's.

Sebastian reached into his pocket and pulled out his handkerchief, then handed it to Miss Thorpe, holding it just a bit out of reach so that she had to stretch out her arm. She set aside the sodden one she had been using and accepted the square of linen. Lorna's hands were neither reddened nor chafed. Her palms were pale and unblemished, not the hands of a woman who had hoisted a body that weighed at least seven stone and kept it suspended until the victim was dead.

"May I see your gloves, Miss Thorpe?" Sebastian asked.

"My gloves?"

"Yes. Do you own a pair of gloves?"

"Yes," Lorna muttered.

She bent down and extracted an embroidered velvet reticule from her satchel, from which she withdrew a pair of beige gloves. The gloves looked well used, and the leather was worn and stretched in places, but there was nothing to suggest that they had been used to haul rope. Sebastian handed the gloves back to Lorna, watching her all the while. She looked confused, then pushed the gloves back inside the bag.

"Is that your only pair?"

"Yes," Lorna whispered. "Why do you want to know?"

"No reason," Sebastian replied.

He supposed Lorna could have taken Audrey Blackstock's gloves, just as she could have used Anthony Blackstock's gloves to silence him, but, now that he sat across from the woman and looked her in the eye, he simply couldn't see Lorna as a cold-blooded killer. He'd arrested his share of female murderers. Some were tough, remorseless executioners who were ready to face the consequences of their actions, but most were delicate, weeping women whose fear and misery had tugged at his heart and who had been driven to the edge of sanity by their tormentors. Those types of women tended to distance themselves from the crime, unable to face their victims' suffering, and resorted to poisons or carefully contrived accidents to kill their enemies. It took a particular sort of person to get up close and personal and look into their victim's eyes as they subdued their prey and dealt the final blow. Just as it took a strong stomach to watch someone die, particularly a person they had known. Lorna would have to have been raging to go through with the hanging, but the only thing Sebastian saw in her swollen eyes was terror and grief.

"May I ask you a few questions, Miss Thorpe?" he asked gently. Lorna nodded and sniffed tearfully. "What happened last night?"

"Once the storm broke, we were instructed to remain inside, not that we had anywhere to go. We're not permitted on deck, and there are few common areas."

"So, what did you do?"

"I darned a stocking that had a ladder in it."

"What about Miss Van Kemp? Was she here with you?"

Lorna looked thoughtful. "She didn't come right away. I saw her in the passage, talking to Mr. Reynolds."

"Do you know what they spoke about?"

"No, but Greta seemed upset when she returned to the cabin. She lay with her face to the wall, then suddenly got up and went out."

"Where did she go?"

"I don't know."

"When did you see her next?"

"At supper. There's a table for the passengers in second class. We had fish stew."

"Where did Miss Van Kemp sit?"

"She sat next to Mr. Bennett, and I sat on her other side."

"Who was across from you?"

"The other two gentlemen from the quartet, Mr. Hobson and Mr. Pennington."

"Were those your regular seats?" Sebastian asked.

"No. We normally sat at the other end of the table with the Misses Galen and their parents."

"So, why did Miss Van Kemp suddenly switch seats?"

"She said she couldn't bear the Galens for one more moment. All they talked about was how glad they were to be coming back. They hated everything about America and said the journey had been a waste of time and money. But that wasn't really true," Lorna said, lowering her voice confidentially. "Marian Galen told us that they had gone to visit her father's elderly aunt on Long Island. She'd been ill, and passed while they were there. She left the entirety of her estate to Mr. Galen. He found a buyer to take the lot, and Marian said they were now quite wealthy, but Mr. Galen didn't want anyone to know about his good fortune. That was why he'd decided to travel second class."

"And how did the members of the quartet react to Miss Van Kemp changing seats?" Sebastian asked.

"The gentlemen seemed pleased. Greta was so lovely, they couldn't take their eyes off her," Miss Thorpe said wistfully. "Mr. Bennett and Mr. Hobson kept up a lively conversation, mostly with Greta, but Mr. Pennington was a bit quiet."

"What did they talk about?"

Lorna shrugged. "Music, mostly. Greta said she was very fond of music and asked the gentlemen about their tour. Then she complimented them on their performance last week and asked if they might play for us after supper. Mr. Bennett liked the idea, but Mr. Hobson and Mr. Pennington didn't seem keen."

"Did Miss Van Kemp say anything else?"

"She asked if it would be very difficult to replace their instruments if they got damaged or lost," Lorna said. "Mr. Bennett said their instruments are precious to them, and they treat them like dear friends."

"What happened then?" Sebastian asked.

"Mr. Bennett suggested the quartet practice a new piece, but Mr. Pennington said he had a dreadful headache and excused himself. He took the remainder of his supper to his cabin since he'd hardly eaten."

"And Miss Van Kemp?"

"After supper, Greta and I returned to our cabin, and we went to sleep a short while later."

"Miss Thorpe, did you hear Greta leave the cabin during the night?"

Lorna nodded. "Greta went up every night at half past twelve."

"Really? Why?" Sebastian had not expected to receive such a precise answer, but at least now he could estimate the time of death, since Greta had been dead for several hours by the time her body was discovered.

"The night watch ring a bell at twelve-thirty. It's how they mark time," Lorna explained. "When they'd rung the bell, Greta would go to the necessary."

"Why did she not go before she retired?"

Miss Thorpe gave Sebastian a look that suggested he understood nothing about life aboard a ship.

"There are two hundred people on board, and only one head. There's a long line after supper, and it could take up to an hour to get to the front. There's no privacy, and everyone watches and calls for the person to hurry up. Greta didn't want to wait and was too embarrassed to see to her personal needs in front of all those people, so she'd go to sleep, then go up when no one was there."

"But surely there was no line last night, since Mr. Reynolds had instructed everyone to remain belowdecks."

"After supper, the sailors came around with buckets." Lorna's puffy face reflected her disgust. "Greta wouldn't come out of the cabin when they did and went up as usual."

"Did you hear anything after she left the cabin at twelve-thirty?"

Lorna shook her head. "I must have fallen into a deep sleep. I was worn out with worry," she explained tearfully. "Until yesterday, I had a job and a home, and now suddenly everything has changed. I don't know what to do or where to go."

"Did you and Miss Van Kemp discuss the future? Did she tell you what she planned to do once the ship docked?"

Lorna sniffled and dabbed at her eyes. "Greta meant to return to New York. She had a sister, I think."

"Did she have money to pay for her passage?"

Lorna looked confused. "I don't know. The wages are quarterly, so neither of us would have been paid until the end of June."

"Surely you will be recompensed," Sebastian said.

"Do you really think so?" Lorna's dull gaze sparked with hope for the first time since Sebastian had entered the cabin. "You're right," she said, her tone firmer now. "I'm entitled to my pay. I will return to Blackstock Hall and appeal to Mrs. Front, the housekeeper. I will ask for what's owed to me and ask her for a character. After all, what happened to the master and mistress has nothing to do with my work, does it?"

"I shouldn't think so," Sebastian replied, but his mind was no longer on Lorna Thorpe's immediate future. "Do you mind if I search the cabin, Miss Thorpe?"

"I don't expect you'll find anything, Inspector. Greta and I had one case each. We were permitted to bring just the bare essentials."

"If you would just step outside," Sebastian asked when Lorna remained seated.

Lorna slid off the berth, wrapped the thin blanket about her shoulders, and left without another word. A few moments later, Sebastian followed her outside. As Lorna had predicted, he hadn't found anything helpful, not even an address for Greta's sister in New York. The poor woman would never know what had become of Greta.

TWENTY-EIGHT

Gemma rapped on the door of the captain's cabin and was bidden to enter. The cabin had to be the largest on the ship and was furnished with a tester bed, an elegant desk with a matching chair, and a tall wardrobe. There was a washstand with a pitcher and ewer, and a comfortable armchair had been placed next to the row of windows that spanned the stern and bathed the room in summer sunshine. The windows did not appear to open, which was a shame since the air was thick with stale sweat and vomit, the latter emanating from the bucket that had been left next to the bed. Captain Grant reclined against the pillows, his face and neck flushed with fever, his graying hair matted with perspiration, and thick stubble shadowing a lantern-shaped jaw. His eyes were glazed and narrowed against the bright light, and the coverlet was pulled up nearly to his chin.

The captain appeared surprised to find a stranger in his cabin but didn't ask Gemma to leave, probably because he was overtaken by a coughing fit that lasted several seconds and left him breathless.

"Forgive the intrusion, Captain," Gemma said once the captain had recovered. "My name is Gemma Tate. I'm a nurse, and I'm here with Inspector Bell."

Captain Grant nodded and shivered beneath the blanket. He likely had chills.

"I offered to check on you yesterday, but Mr. Reynolds wouldn't permit it."

"There's nothing you could have done," Captain Grant said hoarsely. It was obviously an effort for him to speak, and his lips were colorless and chapped, a clear indication of a lack of fluids in the body.

"Malaria, is it?" Gemma asked conversationally.

The captain nodded weakly. "Compliments of my time in South America. I was lucky to survive, but the illness plagues me still."

Gemma approached the bed, poured a cup of water from the carafe on the nightstand, and handed it to the captain, who drank thirstily.

He gave the cup back and Gemma refilled it, only this time she didn't hand it to him. She extracted the bottle she had brought from her reticule, added a spoonful of crystalline powder to the glass, then stirred the mixture until the crystals dissolved.

"I happen to know something of malaria," she explained as she held the cup out to Captain Grant. "In Crimea, we had several patients who had been exposed to malaria while serving in India. Unfortunately, we didn't have quinine on hand, but one of the surgeons was able to procure Jesuit's bark from a local chemist, and we brewed it into tea."

"Did it help?" Captain Grant asked. He downed the remedy and set the cup on the nightstand with a shaking hand.

Gemma nodded. She didn't see any point in telling the captain that the patients had died of their injuries before the Jesuit's bark had a chance to do its work. She only wanted to illustrate that she understood the nature of the disease and knew what was required.

"How many doses of quinine do you normally take before the symptoms begin to abate?" she asked instead.

"I require the full seven-day treatment once I'm ill, but Dr. Humphries doses me regularly during the summer months to avoid a recurrence. He missed the sailing," Captain Grant said miserably. "And because he did, I expect the voyage home will be my last." There was deep sadness in his gaze, and Gemma thought that perhaps the man had been forced to face some harsh truths while confined to his sickbed.

"It doesn't need to be," she said soothingly. "A few more doses and you'll begin to feel better."

Captain Grant shook his head. "I was unable to captain my ship, Miss Tate. Mr. Reynolds will make his report to Grinnell and Minturn as soon as we get back to New York, and I will be made to retire. That man has been gunning for my position since he was first assigned to my crew. After this, he is sure to be made captain."

"I expect he will be made captain anyway," Gemma replied. "Were you aware he's to be married to Leah Minturn?"

The captain nodded. "I was, but only because I saw the engagement announcement. Reynolds didn't tell me himself."

"Do the members of the crew know as well?"

Captain Grant shrugged. "I don't know. Perhaps. Some of them read the papers."

"But it's not common knowledge?" Gemma verified.

"I couldn't tell you for certain, but a ship's crew is like a gaggle of gossipy women. They do nothing but yammer once they're in their hammocks at night."

"Was Mr. Reynolds aware that you suffer from malaria before this voyage?"

"He was, and it is my belief that he intentionally furnished Dr. Humphries with the wrong sailing time. He was hoping I would become ill so that he would have legitimate reason to report me."

"What a despicable man," Gemma exclaimed.

"Mr. Reynolds is an ambitious man, so ambitious in fact that he's happy to marry a woman whose reputation was in tatters only a few months ago so that he can get at her fortune."

"Why was her reputation in tatters? Was it to do with a man?"

"Yes, but not in the way you think. Miss Minturn's fiancé was murdered last year. The circumstances were rather sordid, and Miss Minturn was the target of some vicious speculation."

"Could Mr. Reynolds have been involved?" Gemma inquired carefully.

The captain's answer could alter the course of the investigation and either solidify Sebastian's suspicions or put Shep Reynolds in the clear.

"Mr. Reynolds was at sea when the poor man was murdered. He couldn't have had anything to do with it, but he didn't waste any time paying a condolence call on Miss Minturn and turning himself into a very comfortable shoulder to cry on," Captain Grant said spitefully.

"Surely marrying into the Minturn family will guarantee his future with the company," Gemma observed. "Why would he also need to discredit you?"

"Mr. Reynolds likes to hedge his bets, and his greatest ambition is to make a name for himself. He will push the crew beyond their endurance to beat the current record. Mark my words, Miss Tate, in a few years' time his name will be on everyone's lips. If he doesn't destroy his own prospects, that is."

"How could he do that?"

"The man is inordinately fond of the ladies, and they are of him. If his wife or her uncle get wind of his dalliances, he just might find himself behind a desk in some dusty back office."

"What will happen to you if you lose your place with Grinnell and Minturn?" Gemma asked.

Captain Grant's bitterness was palpable, as was his obvious dislike for Shep Reynolds.

"Perhaps I can still captain a whaler. There's a demand for experienced men in New England and Nova Scotia. Just now, I need to get back on my feet so I can sail the *Prince Regent* back to New York."

"I will leave this with you," Gemma said, and gestured towards the bottle of medicine. "There's at least three days' worth of quinine in there, and you should make certain to purchase more while the ship is in port. You should be able to attend to your duties if you take regular doses."

The captain's fever-glazed eyes lit with hope. "Bless you, Miss Tate. Your kindness will not be forgotten."

The quinine appeared to be doing its job already, and Captain Grant was no longer shivering so violently. Gemma poured some water into the ewer, wet a linen towel, then squeezed out the excess water and gently mopped the captain's clammy face and neck. He allowed her to tend to him, grateful for the unexpected assistance.

"How is Inspector Bell getting on?" he asked once Gemma had finished.

"There's been another murder," Gemma said.

"Mr. Brock told me. That poor young woman."

"Captain, have you been able to sleep these past few nights?" Gemma asked as she plumped the pillows behind the captain's head and straightened the blanket.

"Not very well. I managed to doze for a few minutes at a time, but I was never deeply asleep."

"Surely you must have heard something. Your cabin is not so very far from stateroom two, and the aft deck is directly above."

"I don't recall hearing anything out of the ordinary. There were all the usual nighttime sounds of a sailing ship—the creaking of timber, the snapping of sails, the calls of the watch."

"What about footsteps?" Gemma asked.

Captain Grant made a show of thinking. "I thought I heard something around midnight the night Lord Blackstock was murdered, urgent whispers in the corridor, but I was feverish. I might have imagined the entire thing."

"Can you tell me anything about the voices you heard?"

The captain shrugged. "A man and a woman, perhaps. That's all I can reasonably say."

"And last night?"

Captain Grant shrugged again. "I might have heard footsteps

sometime after the first bell and the sound of something being dragged, but I couldn't swear to it."

"Thank you," Gemma said. She didn't think there was anything more to learn from Captain Grant and was eager to leave, but she felt a responsibility towards the ill man. "I will ask Mr. Brock to bring fresh water and some breakfast. You really must eat, Captain."

Captain Grant smiled dreamily. "I would like fried eggs, bacon, and toasted bread with butter and grape jelly."

"Can the cook not make that for you?"

The captain chuckled. "By the final day of the voyage, the galley is down to porridge and salt pork, at least for the crew. We must resupply before we set off for New York. We can't delay arrival any longer, Miss Tate," he said. "Perhaps you can have a word with Inspector Bell?"

"Of course," Gemma promised. It seemed Captain Grant wasn't aware that Mr. Reynolds intended to dock at noon.

Gemma asked one last question before leaving Captain Grant to rest. "Do you think Mr. Reynolds is capable of murder, Captain?"

"We're all capable of murder when we have something to lose."

TWENTY-NINE

By the time Sebastian left Lorna Thorpe's cabin, the crew was all set to serve breakfast. A pot of porridge had been placed on the table in second class, and an even larger pot had been delivered to steerage. A stony-faced sailor dished the unappetizing mush into wooden bowls, while a second man poured black coffee from a kettle and handed around the pewter mugs. The passengers accepted their food and silently retreated to their berths to eat.

Sebastian wouldn't have said no to a cup of coffee himself. He was hungry, tired, and frustrated, and felt trapped by the grimy walls, the low ceiling, and the oppressive press of humanity in steerage. He went up on deck, and his heavy heart lifted a fraction when he spotted Gemma. She stood leaning against the railing, her skirts billowing in the breeze and her hair shining like copper in the sunlight. She reminded Sebastian of a ship's figurehead, her proud profile stern yet entirely feminine. He smiled at the sight of her, reminded once again how beautiful and capable she was. The perfect woman.

Sensing his presence, Gemma turned and smiled, and for a moment Sebastian wished the two of them were alone together, en route to a new life, and not trapped on this ship of death. This was a seemingly unsolvable case, the details of which would enter the public domain as soon as the ship docked and the press got wind of the story. The newspapers would have a field day with the shocking details and jump at the opportunity to impugn the police service and crow once again about how Scotland Yard had failed to apprehend the killer. The arrests regularly made the papers, but it was the cases that baffled the detectives that helped to increase the papers' circulation, the incendiary rhetoric of the journalists stoking fear and dissatisfaction with the police. Ransome would be expecting a result, but Sebastian had nothing to tell him.

"You look cross," Gemma observed.

"Nothing about this case makes sense, and no two pieces of information form a discernible pattern," Sebastian exclaimed, finally giving vent to his frustration. "I can connect the three victims, since they were members of the same household, but that's where the facts end and speculation begins. I can't see who would benefit by murdering all three."

"You no longer suspect Lorna?"

"Lorna Thorpe may have had reason to kill her employer if he had abused her, but I'm hard-pressed to find justification for her to murder two women and dispatch them in a way that would require the strength of a man. The deaths of the Blackstocks also leave her unemployed, homeless, and with her professional reputation forever tainted by scandal. Unless Lorna has appropriated something of great value, she's considerably worse off than she was when she set off on this journey."

"What about Mr. Caldwell?" Gemma asked.

"Jeffrey Caldwell had motive to murder Anthony Blackstock but, even if he murdered Audrey Blackstock to cover up his crime, he had no reason to harm Greta Van Kemp. Greta would have no call to go to her employers' stateroom in the middle of the night and, even if she did go to the privy just after midnight, she would have walked from the center of the ship towards the prow rather than backwards towards the stern, where the first-class cabins are situated."

"Unless she had been on deck and had seen Jeffrey Caldwell

toss Audrey Blackstock's body over the side," Gemma pointed out. "That would make Greta Van Kemp a target."

"It would, but I can't explain Caldwell's decision to dispose of Audrey's remains, not when her husband's body was left on display. Bringing her body on deck would endanger him considerably more." Sebastian sighed wearily. "That leaves Shep Reynolds. The man clearly has an agenda, but unless Anthony Blackstock had threatened him, I can't conceive of a motive to murder two people in cold blood. Where did you go?" he asked when he'd reached the end of his tirade.

"Shep Reynolds seemed reluctant to let us to speak to Captain Grant, so I thought I'd go to see him, if only to offer my services as a nurse."

"Clever girl," Sebastian said approvingly. "And is the captain really ill?"

"He's in a bad way, but he's also angry and bitter. He believes Shep Reynolds is trying to push him out and intentionally prevented the surgeon from coming aboard."

"To what end?"

"To feed his ambition. If Captain Grant is forced to retire, Reynolds is sure to be made captain of the *Prince Regent*. Captain Grant did alibi Reynolds for the murder of Cyrus Rutherford, though. He said Reynolds was at sea when Rutherford was murdered."

"So, you don't believe he's a likely suspect?"

Gemma looked thoughtful. "According to Captain Grant, Mr. Reynolds is something of a ladies' man and has had numerous dalliances. If Mr. Minturn were to discover that Reynolds had been carrying on with a passenger, he might choose a different man to marry his niece and captain his ship."

"If Shep Reynolds had a shipboard fling with Audrey Blackstock and her husband found out, Anthony Blackstock would have the power to destroy Reynolds' life," Sebastian agreed.

"Yes, and if Greta Van Kemp was aware of the relationship she would have enough ammunition to blackmail Shep Reynolds, especially now that she would be trapped in a foreign country with no means to get home."

"Lorna Thorpe saw Greta engaged in a heated conversation with Shep Reynolds. She was deeply upset when she returned to their cabin."

"Perhaps Shep Reynolds refused to pay," Gemma suggested.

"Perhaps he did. He would have the opportunity and the physical strength necessary to murder Greta Van Kemp, therefore eliminating any threat to his plans. And no one would think anything if they saw him on deck in the middle of the night."

"Shall we have a word with the first mate?" Gemma asked eagerly.

"I think we should," Sebastian agreed. He offered Gemma his arm, and they strolled across the deck, looking for all the world like a married couple taking the air.

THIRTY

"I'm rather busy," Shep Reynolds snapped when Sebastian and Gemma found him a short while later. "We're about to get on our way."

"This will only take a moment, Mr. Reynolds," Sebastian promised. "Shall we talk here?" he asked, glancing at the coxswain, who was pretending not to listen, "or would you prefer somewhere more private?"

"Let's speak in my cabin," Reynolds replied, having clearly sensed that it would be in his best interests to keep the conversation confidential.

They followed the first mate down to first class and crossed the passage towards his cabin. Gemma nodded to Mr. Brock, who had just exited the captain's cabin, a wooden tray in his hands. On it was an empty bowl and a china teapot with matching cup and saucer.

"Was the captain able to eat his breakfast?" Gemma asked.

"Captain Grant seems better this morning," Mr. Brock confirmed. "Perhaps he's finally on the mend."

"Perhaps," Gemma replied. She wasn't about to reveal that she had furnished the captain with quinine, in case Mr. Reynolds should see fit to take it away and hinder his progress.

Once inside his cabin, Shep Reynolds settled behind the desk, while Gemma and Sebastian remained standing since there was nowhere to sit except for the bed. The cabin was bathed in sunlight, and someone had tidied up and dusted.

"So, what's this about, Inspector?" Reynolds demanded.

"Did you furnish Mr. Humphries with the wrong sailing time?" Gemma asked. She was angry on behalf of Captain Grant and needed to know if Shep Reynolds had taken advantage of the man's affliction.

Shep Reynolds gaped at her. "The wrong time?"

"Please answer the question," Sebastian said.

Reynolds scoffed. "The *Prince Regent* sails on the eighth and twenty-second of every month from South Seaport. Pier 16. Loading of cargo begins at eight a.m., the passengers start boarding at noon, and we cast off at three p.m. unless a weather system is rolling in, in which case we wait for it to pass. Mr. Humphries knows this, as does every member of the crew. If Captain Grant has made an accusation against me, I'm afraid it was brought about by delirium, Miss Tate."

"Mr. Reynolds, what did Greta Van Kemp wish to speak to you about yesterday afternoon?" Sebastian asked.

"Heard about that, have you?" Reynolds looked annoyed, but there was no fear in his gaze. "Miss Van Kemp asked me to take her back to New York. She was unable to pay her passage but offered to compensate me in other ways if I were to provide her with a berth and board in steerage."

"And did you agree to her terms?" Gemma asked.

"I did not. For one, I didn't care to compromise my reputation, either with the crew or with Misters Grinnell and Minturn. For another, we're usually fully booked on the way to New York, and I could hardly offer her a berth I didn't have. It is true that I could have offered her a hammock in the crew's quarters, but putting a woman among two dozen male sailors is a recipe for disaster." Shep Reynolds' face creased with sorrow. "Had I known what was about to befall the poor woman, I would have given up my own cabin and slept in the hold, but I doubt such a promise would have saved her life."

"Did Greta Van Kemp blackmail you, Mr. Reynolds?" Gemma asked. She watched the man closely, but all she saw was genuine surprise.

"Blackmail me with what?"

"Perhaps you had engaged in a tryst with Audrey Blackstock," Sebastian mused. "If her husband found out and threatened to report you to your superiors, you would have motive to murder both Blackstocks and have ample cause to silence Miss Van Kemp if she tried to blackmail you."

Shep Reynolds' mouth tightened into a thin line, his nostrils flared, and a muscle jumped in his jaw. He took a moment to steady himself, then fixed Sebastian with a narrow-eyed glare.

"Unless you have proof of this alleged affair, I suggest you keep your theories to yourself, Inspector Bell. Otherwise, I will be the one to report *you* to your superiors. I will not have my character assassinated or my future torpedoed by either you or a bitter old man who seeks to blame me for the onset of his illness."

"Let us say I believe you, and Captain Grant has an axe to grind with you," Sebastian replied calmly. "If not you, who would have cause to murder Miss Van Kemp?"

"Why don't you ask Mr. Bennett? Miss Van Kemp seemed eager to speak to him after I refused her request. Now, if we're done here, I must return to the bridge." Shep Reynolds pushed to his feet and gestured towards the door. "After you."

Sebastian and Gemma had no choice but to leave the first mate's cabin and watch him walk away, the two of them left standing in the dim passage as the first-class stewards began to lay the table for breakfast on the other side.

"Would you care for a cup of coffee?" Mr. Hendon asked.

"Not for me, but you go on," Sebastian said to Gemma. "You look exhausted. I'll find you once I've had a word with Mr. Bennett."

Gemma nodded. Having hardly slept, she was tired and

needed a few minutes to sit and think. She settled at the communal table and accepted a mug of bitter-smelling brew, just as strains of a violin drifted towards her from Miss Hobson's cabin.

THIRTY-ONE

Sebastian found the male members of the quartet at breakfast. They sat at the long table, their expressions grim as they applied themselves to their coffee and porridge.

"Good morning, gentlemen," Sebastian said, and wedged himself between Mr. Hobson and a bewhiskered gentleman who sat next to him on the narrow bench. The man huffed at Sebastian's presumed insolence, pushed his bowl away, and stalked off, which was just as well since Sebastian hoped to speak to the men without interruptions.

"Good morning, Inspector," Mr. Bennett replied. "Are you any closer to solving the case? We would all dearly like to go home."

"You will go home this afternoon," Sebastian promised.

Mr. Hobson brightened, while Mr. Bennett's and Mr. Pennington's expressions remained closed, as if they suspected Sebastian of trying to hoodwink them.

"Your quarters are near Miss Thorpe and Miss Van Kemp's cabin—" Sebastian began.

"The poor woman," Mr. Bennett interrupted. "We sat with her just last night. She seemed so delicate, so innocent."

"Did you speak with her much during the voyage, Mr. Bennett?"

Mr. Bennett appeared surprised by the question but answered readily enough. "Not really. Miss Van Kemp and Miss Thorpe kept mostly to themselves. Last night was the first time we'd conversed at any length."

"Why was that?"

"Miss Van Kemp asked if she might join us for supper. Miss Thorpe was there as well."

"And how did Miss Van Kemp seem?" Sebastian addressed the question to all three men, but it was Mr. Hobson who answered.

"She seemed worried and distressed but tried her best to hide it. It was perfectly understandable, of course. The poor woman was anxious about her future."

"How do you know that, Mr. Hobson?" Sebastian asked.

"Well, she asked if we might be in need of a maidservant," Mr. Hobson replied.

"And were you?"

Mr. Hobson shook his head. "My sister and I have a charwoman who comes in twice a week, Clyde lodges at a boarding house in Beaumont Street, and Ezra lives with his mother and sister. They already have a maidservant."

Both Ezra and Clyde nodded.

"Besides, Miss Van Kemp was a lady's maid. To accept a position as a maidservant would be a step down for her," Clyde Bennett said. "She was desperate to secure employment before the ship docked, but I don't expect she would have remained in the job for very long, had she lived, that is."

"Mr. Bennett, were you ever alone with Miss Van Kemp?"

Clyde Bennett stared at Sebastian, uncomprehending. "Alone? Well, yes, I suppose I was, but very briefly. We met on deck a few nights ago. It was just after the watch rang the first bell."

"And how did Miss Van Kemp seem then?"

"She became frightened," Mr. Bennett replied, and Sebastian was gratified to see that he looked deeply uncomfortable.

"Frightened of you?"

Clyde Bennett nodded. "I didn't mean to scare her. I had unintentionally blocked her path when she tried to return to her cabin, and she became alarmed."

"I trust you apologized and stepped aside?"

"Yes, of course, but I couldn't help but notice her terror."

"Do you think someone had hurt her?"

Mr. Bennett nodded. "I do. I did," he amended. "And I think it happened on board. Miss Van Kemp seemed different when we first boarded."

"Different how?"

"Happier, I suppose. She smiled and said good morning when our paths crossed, but after a few days aboard she began to avert her eyes and scurry away."

"What about Miss Thorpe? Had she undergone a similar trans-formation?"

"Not that I noticed," Clyde Bennett said.

Sebastian turned to the other two men. "Did either of you notice this change in Miss Van Kemp?"

"I don't know if she was frightened exactly, but she did seem sad," Mr. Hobson volunteered. "I spoke to her briefly at breakfast the other day, and she mentioned that she regretted her decision to come to England and wished she had found a position closer to home."

"What about you, Mr. Pennington?"

Ezra Pennington's dark gaze was thoughtful. "Miss Van Kemp and I conversed for the first time last night. She did seem nervous, but surely that's understandable, given every-thing that had happened. Miss Thorpe looked anxious as well. They had lost their places and were facing an uncertain future."

"I do hope someone will see to Miss Van Kemp's burial," Mr. Hobson said. "It seems wrong that she should be consigned to a pauper's grave."

"Miss Van Kemp is not our concern, Michael," Mr. Bennett replied sadly. "We have our own struggles to face once we get home."

"Oh? What struggles are those?" Sebastian was quick to inquire.

"Ezra has decided to leave us," Mr. Bennett announced. "He is not happy with my style of management and seeks to find a new situation. We will have to urgently find a replacement if we hope to accept bookings for the summer."

"I don't think Inspector Bell is interested in our creative differences, Clyde," Ezra said. He seemed reluctant to discuss the business of the quartet in front of Sebastian.

"Is that the reason, creative differences?" Sebastian inquired.

"That's not the primary reason," Ezra Pennington backtracked. "I have decided to relocate. That's the real reason I'm leaving. It has nothing to do with any sense of dissatisfaction."

"Where are you relocating to, Mr. Pennington?"

"I've been considering a move to America. I was offered a place with a theater orchestra while we were in New York, and I think I would like to accept."

"It's a wonderful opportunity, Ezra," Mr. Hobson said, and shot Mr. Bennett an imploring look.

"It is," Clyde Bennett conceded. "We wish you much success, Ezra, even though we hate to lose you."

"Thank you, both," Ezra Pennington said stiffly. "Now, if you will excuse me, I need to pack."

He lifted his still-full mug of coffee, reached for a piece of bread left on a platter at the center of the table, and walked towards his cabin.

"Will it be difficult to find a new cello player?" Sebastian asked once Pennington had disappeared through the cabin door.

"Not so very difficult, no, but we have played with Ezra for several years now, and we work well as a quartet," Clyde Bennett explained. "It's not just about finding someone who's trained, you understand. It's also about personalities and work ethic. Ezra is a hard worker, and until now he has always deferred to my creative choices."

"It's for the best, really," Michael Hobson said. "I think Ezra is leaving to spare Cora any further embarrassment."

"Did something happen between them?" Sebastian asked.

Michael Hobson nodded unhappily. "My sister has feelings for Ezra, has done for some time now. I don't believe he ever encouraged her, at least not intentionally, but Cora had begun to build her hopes around him and thought that their close working relationship might result in mutual affection."

"And Mr. Pennington never felt the same?"

"Ezra tends to turn on the charm when in the company of women. His affable nature can sometimes be mistaken for romantic interest," Clyde Bennett supplied.

"Cora became despondent when Ezra paid attention to any other woman, and there were plenty of women who'd approached Ezra in Newport and New York. He just has that effect on the fairer sex," Mr. Hobson said. "Cora was furious when Lady Blackstock sought him out after the concert we gave on deck."

"I don't think she had any reason to be upset," Clyde Bennett said. "We met Lord and Lady Blackstock at a recital in Washington Square. They were among the guests, and Lady Blackstock recognized us immediately when we met again."

"You had met the Blackstocks before?" Sebastian clarified. This was news to him. It could be important that not everyone aboard the *Prince Regent* was a stranger to each other.

"Yes, but very briefly," Clyde Bennett replied. "We met a great many people these past few months. It was a whirlwind, really, and I think the attention went to Ezra's head, especially once he received an offer of work over there. I don't blame him for wanting to go back. I wouldn't mind playing with an orchestra, but I wouldn't accept anything but first violin," he announced self-importantly.

"Perhaps that's not such a bad idea, Clyde," Michael Hobson interjected excitedly. "Cora was happy in New York, and if we go back with Ezra perhaps the Bennett Quartet can remain intact."

Clyde Bennett shook his head. "I'm sorry, but I really couldn't leave, Michael. I would get homesick after a time. I'm surprised Ezra is willing to leave his family. He's quite close with his mother and sister."

"Perhaps he means to bring them over once he's settled," Michael Hobson said.

"Perhaps."

"It must have come as a surprise when you met the Blackstocks aboard," Sebastian observed. "Did you know they would be sailing on the same ship?"

"No, of course not," Clyde Bennett replied. "In fact, we didn't know we would be sailing on the *Prince Regent* either. We had planned to sail on the *Columbia*, but when Ezra went to book our passage there were no second-class cabins left. The *Prince Regent* was the next outbound boat. But it worked out in the end, since the delay enabled us to visit Newport."

"What's the price difference between first and second class?" Sebastian asked. It wasn't really relevant to the investigation, but he was curious what it cost to cross the Atlantic and how much more one had to pay for privacy and comfort.

"First-class staterooms go for one hundred and fifty to two hundred dollars," Clyde Bennett said. "And second-class cabins go for sixty to one hundred dollars. The fares are cheapest during the winter."

"Thank you. Good to know," Sebastian said.

"Are you planning a trip to America, Inspector?" Michael Hobson inquired.

"I have considered it, but my plans have changed recently."

"Shame," Clyde Bennett said. "It's a fascinating place, as long as you keep to the cities. Anything goes in the Territories, however, and the men who feel no remorse and who are quick with their guns are the ones who make the rules."

Michael Hobson finished his coffee and set down his mug. "If you will excuse me, gentlemen. I'm eager to disembark, so I had best get ready."

"Will we really be permitted to dock today, Inspector Bell?" Clyde Bennett inquired eagerly.

"I think so, Mr. Bennett. I think so," Sebastian said, and stood to leave.

"Does that mean you know who the culprit is?" Bennett asked, clearly assuming that the only way the *Prince Regent* would be permitted to dock was if Sebastian got his man.

"I believe I do," Sebastian said, and strode away before the man could ask any further questions.

THIRTY-TWO

The coffee was strong and bitter, but with a splash of cream and two lumps of sugar—there were definite advantages to paying for first class, Gemma reflected—it was palatable and wonderfully reviving. The passengers didn't seem in any rush to sit down to breakfast, so she was left on her own to enjoy her coffee and the music that continued to drift from Miss Hobson's cabin. The piece was soothing and contemplative, and the notes tugged at Gemma's heartstrings. She thought it might be Vivaldi, but she couldn't be sure, since she didn't get to hear music very often.

The melody was conducive to analysis, but for the life of her Gemma couldn't extract any fresh nuggets of understanding from everything she and Sebastian had learned. They had spoken to nearly everyone who may have seen or heard something, but all the potential witnesses had done was send them round in circles, evaluating and reevaluating the same few suspects without settling on a name.

Gemma highly doubted Sebastian would learn anything from Mr. Bennett or the other members of the quartet. What possible motive could Bennett have to murder Greta Van Kemp, and what reason to harm Anthony or Audrey Blackstock? The only connection between the members of the Bennett Quartet and the Blackstocks was Miss Hobson, who occupied a stateroom in first class, but that hardly made her a suspect.

Gemma's musings were interrupted by the stewards, who returned with platters of food. Unlike the travelers in second class and steerage, the first-class passengers were treated to boiled eggs, crisp slices of bacon, and toasted bread served with dishes of butter and jars of jam. Gemma's stomach growled with hunger, but it would be terribly rude to help herself to a piece of bread. She'd have to wait until she disembarked. Perhaps she could purchase a pork pie or a cup of soup from the vendors who were sure to descend on the docks at lunchtime.

"Breakfast is served," Mr. Sims called out.

The music stopped abruptly, and the first-class passengers began to emerge from their staterooms. Although they looked surprised to find Gemma at the table, no one questioned her presence or asked about the progress of the investigation, which was a relief, since she didn't think she should reveal any of the details.

"Miss Tate, won't you join us for breakfast?" Mrs. Caldwell asked after Mr. Caldwell and Miss Hobson had muttered a subdued good morning and taken their seats. "There's more than enough food."

Gemma was about to refuse, then realized that this was an opportunity not to be missed to observe the first-class passengers and speak to the Ringwoods, whom Sebastian had not had time to interview the day before.

"Thank you. If you think there's enough..." Gemma demurred.

"Or course. Mr. Sims, a plate for Miss Tate," Mrs. Caldwell instructed.

"Of course," Mr. Sims murmured, and took a clean plate and cutlery from a small cupboard fitted into the wall.

Gemma accepted the plate with thanks and allowed Mr. Hendon to refill her cup. Mrs. Caldwell passed the platter of bacon, and Gemma helped herself to a boiled egg and a slice of bread. The Caldwells and Miss Hobson applied themselves to their breakfast, talking in the way of people who were accustomed to taking their meals together. The final guests to join them at table were the Ringwoods, who emerged from their stateroom and slid into their seats after a polite greeting. They were around Gemma's age and had the graceful and effortlessly confident air of the wealthy and entitled.

"Good morning," Gemma said shyly. "You must be Mr. and Mrs. Ringwood."

"Miss Tate, I presume?" Mrs. Ringwood asked with a friendly smile. "We've heard all about you and your dashing inspector."

"Really, Winnie," Mr. Ringwood said, and peered at his wife indulgently.

"No one is as dashing as you, my dear," Winifred Ringwood replied with a coy smile. "But Miss Hobson did mention that Inspector Bell is rather striking."

Miss Hobson nearly choked on her toast, coughed into her fist, then went puce to the roots of her hair and stared into her plate.

"It's quite all right, Miss Hobson," Mrs. Ringwood hurried to reassure her. "There's nothing wrong with noticing a handsome man. To what do we owe the honor, Miss Tate?" she asked, her head swiveling in Gemma's direction once again.

Mr. Ringwood cut in before Gemma had a chance to respond. "I heard it said you were in Crimea. Good God, what a debacle," he exclaimed. "Once it was all over, I was glad my father had refused to purchase a commission for me. As the oldest son, I couldn't be spared, but my brother wasn't so lucky."

"I quite understand," Gemma replied with a nod.

She had met plenty of second and third sons, young men whose only opportunity for advancement lay with the army or the navy since they didn't stand to inherit unless their older brothers died. They'd had nowhere to go to drown their sorrows other than the gaming dens and the brothels, and had little value on the marriage market, where ambitious mamas sought titles and estates for their daughters.

"Where's your brother now?" Gemma asked.

"Calcutta," Mr. Ringwood replied with a heavy sigh. "He was

in Meerut during the mutiny of fifty-seven. We were all very worried about him."

"The possibility of serious illness is just as likely as death by native assassins," Winifred Ringwood said with a shudder. "It's a good thing Captain Grant has been confined to his quarters. I dread to imagine what might have happened if he walked among us."

"Malaria is not catching," Gemma replied. "It's spread by mosquitoes."

"Well, thank the good Lord for that," Winifred said. "This voyage has been harrowing enough without catching a debilitating disease."

"I don't think we were ever in danger, my dear," Mr. Ringwood said soothingly.

"Tell that to Lord and Lady Blackstock," Winifred snapped. "I don't expect they thought they were in any danger when they set off on this ill-fated voyage."

"I do declare, I cannot wait to get off this ship," Marilyn Caldwell exclaimed desperately. "A spell on dry land is just what's needed, isn't it, Jeffrey?"

Jeffrey Caldwell nodded. "I think we should hole up at our hotel for a day or two. What do you think, Mary? A proper bed, fresh linens, and excellent meals."

"And clean laundry," Marilyn said, and smiled eagerly. "One never realizes the importance of laundry until one is forced to wear undergarments washed in seawater. I expect you will be glad to return to Oxford, Miss Hobson," she said in an obvious attempt to draw the silent woman into the conversation. "It will be nice to be reunited with your young man, won't it?"

Miss Hobson's expression could only be described as pained, and she stared into her plate in obvious mortification.

"Oh, dear. Did I get that all wrong? I'm so sorry," Mrs. Caldwell cried. "I thought there was someone special."

"Not anymore," Miss Hobson replied woodenly. It was obvious

she didn't want to talk about her private life, but the bored women at the table stalked her like hungry hyenas.

"My dear, but what happened?" Mrs. Ringwood pressed. "Was your intended upset that you had gone away for such a long time? Men are like children, aren't they, Mrs. Caldwell? They must be coddled and adored, or they grow petulant and resentful."

"No, that wasn't it," Miss Hobson muttered.

"Miss Hobson's young man is part of the quartet, Winnie," Mr. Ringwood said *sotto voce* to his wife, and Gemma wondered how he'd known that.

"Ah yes, of course. I should have known. You all spend so much time together, love is bound to grow."

"Wait, don't tell me," Mrs. Caldwell cried excitedly. "It's Mr. Pennington. Am I right? He cuts a fine figure, doesn't he, Mrs. Ringwood? Very dashing."

"Or is it Mr. Bennett?" Mrs. Ringwood asked, watching Miss Hobson like she was about to swallow her whole. Her expression seemed to suggest that Mr. Bennett, who was neither handsome nor dashing, would be better suited to the likes of Cora Hobson, who couldn't possibly hold the interest of a man like Ezra Pennington.

Miss Hobson looked like she would have liked to disappear, but she could hardly make a scene and stalk off in a huff. Gemma couldn't help but wonder if Cora Hobson had been the butt of speculation for the entirety of the crossing, or if the women were so desperate for a diversion that they had decided to pick on the poor woman now that the end of their ordeal was in sight, and they wouldn't have to see her ever again.

"I believe Mr. Pennington's affections were engaged elsewhere," Mrs. Caldwell said with feigned delicacy, and patted Cora Hobson's hand in a patronizing manner.

"Really? What makes you say that, Mrs. Caldwell?" Mrs. Ringwood asked, her attention instantly shifting to the other woman. She had the look of a hound who'd got its first whiff of a fox.

"He seemed very taken with Audrey Blackstock," Mrs. Caldwell said in a loud whisper. "And I don't believe she was indifferent to him."

"Was he, indeed?" Jeffrey Caldwell asked, looking up from his plate as if he'd just realized that a conversation was taking place right next to him.

"She had no interest in Mr. Pennington," Winifred Ringwood huffed. "Anthony Blackstock was an extraordinarily handsome man with an enviable pedigree. What more could a woman want, especially someone who was as thoroughly common as Audrey Blackstock?"

"There was nothing common about Audrey," Jeffrey Caldwell protested hotly, his eyes blazing with indignation.

"I only meant that she wasn't of noble blood, Mr. Caldwell," Winifred clarified.

She squared her shoulders and lifted her chin defiantly, as if to remind Jeffrey Caldwell that, as an American, he understood nothing of the ways of the aristocracy and couldn't comprehend the honor that Anthony Blackstock had bestowed on his wife.

"Lord Blackstock plucked her out of complete obscurity and raised her up to heights she could have never hoped to achieve. He could have had anyone, anyone at all, and they would have thought themselves heaven-blessed to have him."

"I thought Anthony Blackstock rather unpleasant," Mrs. Caldwell stated coldly. "And the way he attacked Jeffrey!" she exclaimed with a disbelieving shake of her head. The accusations clearly still rankled, even though Anthony Blackstock was dead and his opinion of her husband had died with him.

Mrs. Ringwood waved a dismissive hand. "He was upset. I expect he wasn't much accustomed to losing."

"Despite his noble upbringing, the man had no breeding," Mr. Ringwood stated flatly. "If he had, he would have offered his apologies to Mr. Caldwell, since there was absolutely no evidence of chicanery."

Mr. Ringwood cast a worried glance at Jeffrey Caldwell, as if suddenly coming to the realization that the man might have set out to avenge the slight on his character and he might even now be breaking bread with a multiple murderer.

"It's unkind to speak ill of the dead," Miss Hobson said, her voice barely audible. "And as it happens, Lady Blackstock and Mr. Pennington were acquainted before they met on the ship."

"Yes, they had met while in New York," Mrs. Ringwood replied. "Lady Blackstock mentioned that they had enjoyed a performance by the Bennett Quartet at a musical evening hosted by Lord Blackstock's acquaintance, who lives in Washington Square."

"I'm certain they had met before that," Mrs. Caldwell announced triumphantly. "There was something decidedly familiar in Lady Blackstock's dealings with Mr. Pennington."

"Mary, what on earth are you talking about?" her husband demanded. "Audrey Blackstock was the soul of propriety."

Marilyn Caldwell harrumphed and looked around the table, as if daring someone to invite her to explain herself.

"What led you to suspect Lady Blackstock of inappropriate behavior?" Gemma asked, unable to remain silent and unobtrusive in the face of this fascinating new revelation.

"I heard her call him *Ez*," Marilyn Caldwell divulged with obvious glee. "If that's not being familiar, I don't know what is."

"You are quite mistaken," Winifred Ringwood argued. She had clearly been deeply impressed by the Blackstocks and seemed to feel a sense of loyalty towards her countrymen. "Lady Blackstock never acknowledged that she had known Mr. Pennington before her marriage."

All eyes turned to Miss Hobson, who was staring at her plate, her hands folded in her lap.

"Miss Hobson, perhaps you can tell us? Did Mr. Pennington and Audrey Blackstock know each other before her marriage to Lord Blackstock?" Winifred Ringwood asked.

"I'm sure I don't know," Miss Hobson said, but Gemma was certain that she did. And there could only be one answer to that question that she would prefer not to divulge.

Seemingly random events suddenly slotted into place, and Gemma realized that Cora Hobson had unwittingly handed her the central piece of the puzzle.

"Please excuse me," she said, and pushed away from the table. She had to find Sebastian right away.

It was only once she was upright that she realized the ship was moving. Mr. Reynolds had said they had until noon, but the *Prince Regent* would reach the port of London at least an hour before that.

THIRTY-THREE

On deck, a white cloud of canvas had unfurled overhead, the sails snapping in the breeze as the ship moved upriver. Sailors climbed the rigging, agile as monkeys, and a general sense of urgency emanated from the crew as everyone prepared for arrival. Gemma spotted the tall figure of Mr. Reynolds and marched resolutely towards him.

"You said we had until noon," she said accusingly.

"I'm sorry, Miss Tate, but I simply cannot afford to wait any longer. I must take advantage of the favorable wind, and Captain Grant is in need of medical assistance." Mr. Reynolds smiled in a way Gemma found infuriatingly condescending. "Another few hours won't change the outcome," he added smugly. "If your inspector were going to solve this case, he would have done so by now."

"What makes you think he hasn't solved it?" Gemma retorted angrily.

Shep Reynolds had blatantly lied, and used Captain Grant's condition as an excuse to go back on his word. Gemma had given the captain enough quinine to last several days and allay his symptoms until he was able to procure more, so if there was a medical emergency it wasn't with the captain.

"You're angry on Inspector Bell's behalf," Reynolds observed, his sardonic smile making Gemma feel more aggrieved by the minute. "Whatever did he do to earn such loyalty from one so fair?"

"Kindly refrain from paying me insincere compliments, Mr. Reynolds," Gemma snapped.

"Insincere?" Shep Reynolds' hand went to his heart, as if Gemma had mortally wounded him. "I assure you, Miss Tate, I'm completely in earnest. I happen to admire capable, intelligent women. I was raised by one. And if I weren't shipping out in a few days, I would implore you to see me again."

"Your plea would be in vain since I seem to recall that you are to be married, Mr. Reynolds," Gemma reminded him sharply.

"So I am, but that doesn't mean I can no longer enjoy friendships with women. And until your inspector makes an honest woman out of you, I suggest you consider other men. Life is awfully empty without love, Miss Tate, even if it is not the kind of love that lasts forever."

"I expect you would know all about that, Mr. Reynolds. Good day to you." Gemma turned on her heel and walked away, still seething at the man's insolence.

It didn't take her long to locate Sebastian, who was striding towards her across the deck.

"We're bound for the port of London," Gemma announced unnecessarily. It wasn't as if Sebastian could miss the shoreline sliding past, but she was too angry not to comment on Shep Reynolds' perfidy.

"I don't have the authority to prevent the ship from docking, and I don't believe I need to."

"Do you know who the murderer is?" Gemma asked, wondering if Sebastian had hit upon the same theory she had.

Sebastian slid his arm through hers and drew her along the deck, away from members of the crew and the first-class passengers, who'd finished their breakfast and come up for a breath of air.

"Cora Hobson had feelings for Ezra Pennington, and I think

her feelings might have been returned until Ezra Pennington met Audrey Blackstock," Sebastian theorized.

"Ezra and Audrey had met before."

"Yes, in New York."

"No, before that. Audrey Blackstock was overheard calling Ezra *Ez*."

"Was she, now?" Sebastian asked, a slow smile spreading over his previously tense face.

Gemma nodded, pleased to be able to supply such an important clue. "And Miss Hobson all but confirmed that they had been acquainted before meeting again in New York."

Sebastian nodded slowly, as if the pieces were finally beginning to fit together.

"Ezra Pennington was the one to book the return voyage. He obtained tickets for the *Prince Regent* instead of the *Columbia*, as had been previously planned. He claimed there were no more second-class cabins to be had on the *Columbia*, and because of that the quartet's departure was delayed. If he knew the Blackstocks would be sailing on the *Prince Regent*..."

"Then it all fits," Gemma finished for him.

Sebastian nodded. "Ezra Pennington murdered Anthony Blackstock to free Audrey. Perhaps he'd intended to carry out his plan on the last night of the voyage all along, but fate had handed him a unique opportunity in the form of an altercation between Jeffrey Caldwell and Anthony Blackstock. By fitting the iron cage around Blackstock's head and carving *pig* into his chest, he implicated Jeffrey Caldwell, knowing full well that someone would mention the row, Mr. Caldwell's stance on slavery, and the insults Anthony Blackstock had hurled at Caldwell."

"I was introduced to Ezra Pennington on the morning Audrey Blackstock went missing. He didn't seem the least bit distressed," Gemma pointed out excitedly.

"Because he had no reason to be," Sebastian hurried to add. "Audrey was never in any danger."

"But Greta Van Kemp must have seen something that night."

"According to Lorna Thorpe, Greta went up every night at twelve-thirty to see to her personal needs. If Anthony Blackstock was killed around midnight or just after, she might have unwittingly seen or heard something."

"But Ezra Pennington waited until last night to silence her," Gemma reminded him.

"Greta Van Kemp found herself halfway round the world with no job, no character reference, and no money. She told Lorna Thorpe she intended to return to New York as soon as possible, which means she had a plan."

"So, when Shep Reynolds refused to help her, she decided to blackmail the killer to raise funds for the return voyage," Gemma concluded.

"And paid for her audacity with her life."

"That still doesn't explain what happened to Audrey. Mr. Reynolds and Constable Forrest searched the vessel and found no trace of her." Gemma suddenly recalled something Shep Reynolds had told her the day before. "Anthony Blackstock had bragged about his collection of medieval torture devices. One of them was called a drunkard's coat, which was essentially a barrel with openings for the head and arms. If he had used such a thing on his wife, she would know that she could easily fit into a barrel."

"There are too many barrels in the hold to search through before we dock, but I suspect Audrey Blackstock never went anywhere near the hold."

"Do you know where she is?" Gemma asked.

Their discussion was cut short by a series of shouted commands that instructed the crew to prepare to drop anchor. The *Prince Regent* turned into the canal that led to the St. Katharine Docks and sailed majestically into the central basin before turning into the Western Dock. The moment of reckoning had arrived.

THIRTY-FOUR

St. Katharine Docks were a beehive of activity. At least two dozen ships were at anchor inside the basins, their bare masts like a wintry forest against the summer sky. Some vessels appeared to be empty, while others swarmed with sailors, dock workers, and arriving and departing passengers. It was impossible to tell who was going where since everyone seemed to be in motion, the crowd heaving with purpose. The warehouses that lined the docks were massive, featureless buildings that dwarfed the walkways and made the basins look like puddles in comparison. Perishable goods, kegs and barrels of various sizes, and crated cargo were maneuvered by dozens of stevedores, who were sweating in the warm sun as they hefted their burdens to and from the warehouses. Servants and porters carried arriving passengers' luggage towards the exits that would take them into the streets beyond the docks, where they would either find their carriages waiting for them or avail themselves of other transportation options.

"It's best if I arrest Ezra Pennington as soon as he gets off the ship," Sebastian said. He looked tense, his jaw working as his gaze swept the docks in search of the optimal spot to make his approach. "If I try to apprehend him on board, he might try to fight his way out and hurt innocent people, but if he manages to elude me once he's off the ship he will lose himself in the crowd and make his escape."

"Surely he won't get too far with a cello."

"Wait on the aft deck until Pennington is in custody."

"But I—"

"Gemma, I need to know you're safe. If we've got this right, then Ezra Pennington has already murdered two people. He won't hesitate to kill again, not if his life is on the line. Do I have your word that you will stay out of the way?"

"Yes. I will do as you ask," Gemma promised reluctantly. "But what about Audrey Blackstock?"

"She won't be far behind Pennington, and Constable Forrest will be ready and waiting."

"How on earth did they expect to get away with these murders?" Gemma asked.

"Ezra Pennington is leaving the quartet. He has expressed a desire to relocate to New York."

"With Audrey," Gemma finished for him.

"Once they board a New York-bound ship, they will be free."

"But the *Prince Regent* is not due to sail back for several days, and Mr. Reynolds and Captain Grant will recognize them."

"They don't have to sail from London," Sebastian replied, his gaze still on the docks beyond. "They can make their way to Liverpool and sail on the Red Swallowtail line, which would render them completely anonymous."

"And they can be married by the captain if they don't wish to wait," Gemma said.

"They can. And once Audrey Blackstock is safely settled in New York, she can begin legal proceedings to claim her late husband's estate. If Lord Blackstock didn't have a male heir, I expect she'll be able to get the lot."

"Do you suppose they would have allowed Jeffrey Caldwell or Shep Reynolds to go down for murder?" Gemma asked.

Given that Ezra Pennington and Audrey Blackstock were liable for the deaths of two people, it didn't seem likely they'd suffer pangs of conscience, but Gemma found she was still horri-fied by the idea of framing an innocent person and sending him to his death.

"It would seem so," Sebastian replied. "Or perhaps they imag-ined that, as Americans, Jeffrey Caldwell and Shep Reynolds could request to be tried in the United States."

"Could they really do that?"

"I don't know. I've never heard of a similar situation, but I expect the American minister, George Mifflin Dallas, might step in if called upon by an American citizen."

"I suppose Mrs. Caldwell could testify that her husband had never left the cabin, but how much weight would a wife's testi-mony carry in such proceedings?"

"A wife cannot be called upon to testify against her husband and would only be asked to take the stand if her testimony could exonerate him. I don't imagine Mrs. Caldwell's statement would carry much weight with the judge or the jury since there's no way to verify its validity."

"And Shep Reynolds wouldn't have anyone who could testify for him, especially since it's impossible to establish a precise time of death."

Sebastian reached for Gemma's hand and brought it to his lips. "I must go. I will see you once I have Ezra Pennington in custody."

"Where are you going now?" Gemma exclaimed, reluctant to be left alone and worried that she would be unable to help should Sebastian encounter greater resistance than he anticipated.

"I must find Constable Forrest and apprise him of the plan."

Gemma would have liked to hold Sebastian close and ask him to be careful, but Miss Hobson was heading towards them, her gaze glinting with speculation, and Mr. and Mrs. Caldwell had just come up on deck and were talking excitedly as they watched the ship glide towards an open slip.

"Later," Sebastian mouthed, and then he was gone, leaving Gemma to wait in limbo while he faced a desperate killer.

THIRTY-FIVE

As Sebastian made his way down to second class, he did his best to push down the worry that had coiled itself around his insides like a snake. If he'd got this wrong, Gemma would be left alone and exposed, an easy target for a violent and desperate man. Since their first meeting, she had become Sebastian's greatest ally and his most trusted and cherished companion, but she was also his Achilles heel, that tender, exposed part of him that made him vulnerable and fed his deepest fears.

Gemma knew how to acquit herself, Sebastian reminded himself as he hurried down the stairs. She was clever, brave, and resourceful. He had to trust her instincts and focus on the job at hand, since he would have only one chance to get this right. He wished he had cuffs, but they must have fallen out of his pocket while he was climbing the rope ladder. And Constable Forrest did not have anything to hand save his truncheon. Once he'd descended into the dim passage, Sebastian looked around, but there was nothing but smooth walls, not even a ball of twine or a leather thong he could use.

There was nothing for the passengers to do but wait until the ship dropped anchor and the gangway was in place. They were congregated around the communal table, looking anxious and eager to be on their way. Sebastian nodded amicably to Lorna Thorpe and the members of the quartet as he walked past. It was imperative no one suspected that he was about to make an arrest. He needed everyone to vacate the close quarters of the ship and disembark in an orderly manner. It was also vital that he find Constable Forrest and make him aware of the plan. Unfortunately, he didn't see the constable anywhere, and he didn't have much time since disembarkation would commence at any moment.

Unlike the orderly anticipation of the second-class passengers, steerage was utter pandemonium. Everyone was on their feet, gathering their belongings, admonishing their children, and exchanging last-minute information with fellow travelers. Sebastian finally spotted Constable Forrest among the throng, the buttons of his tunic glowing dully in the light filtering through a skylight. Forrest was enjoying a mug of coffee and a chat with one of the stewards who'd come to take away the empty pots and mugs.

"What are you doing?" Sebastian hissed once he'd reached the man.

"I was offered coffee," Constable Forrest explained. "I don't do well on an empty stomach, guv."

Sebastian's stomach growled in sympathy, but he ignored his hunger, and spoke in a low voice since there was nowhere they could speak privately at this late stage. A deep vibration reverberated through the ship as the massive chain was unwound and the anchor dropped. After a few seconds, the ship came to an abrupt halt, and the passengers grabbed whatever was to hand to retain their balance. Once they were no longer in danger of falling about, the most eager travelers surged towards the stairs, desperate to get off. Everyone was so focused on their belongings and traveling companions that no one paid any mind to the two men.

"I need you to listen to me very carefully," Sebastian said, and proceeded to outline his plan. Constable Forrest periodically bobbed his head in understanding.

"Why not grab him now?" the constable asked, his eyes bright with excitement at the prospect of an arrest.

"These people are packed like fish in a barrel," Sebastian said, jutting his chin towards the surging crowd. "There are women and children who could get seriously hurt. We must allow Pennington to believe he got away with it."

"But what if it wasn't him?"

"Then I have made a gross miscalculation, and a killer will go free. Now, I'm going to get off with the first-class passengers. Wait until the second-class passengers are ready to disembark, then follow Ezra Pennington off the ship. We must trap him between us."

"Understood. You can count on me, sir."

Sebastian pushed through the crowd until he was out of the dank hold, and rushed towards the gangway that had just been lowered onto the quay. The gangway had sturdy wooden railings and was wide enough for two average-size people to walk abreast. Sebastian intended to position himself near the end of the gangway, or he'd never find Ezra Pennington in the melee once the cellist was off the ship and free to sprint towards one of the exits that would take him away from the docks and into London's busy streets. Pennington's path to freedom was clear, the only hurdle in his way an unarmed Sebastian.

Once the gangway was securely in place, the Ringwoods gingerly made their way towards the quay, followed by the Caldwells, and the first-class stewards, who were laden with the passengers' hand luggage. Their trunks would most likely be delivered by the crew once they were offloaded during the course of the day. Sebastian tore his gaze from the gangway and searched the aft deck for Gemma. He breathed a sigh of relief when he saw her, standing against the rail, her hands gripping the polished wood as she braced herself for the coming confrontation. Sebastian smiled at her reassuringly, then returned his attention to the gangway.

A middle-aged couple, presumably the Galens, were in the process of disembarking with their two daughters, followed by Lorna Thorpe. Her face was shadowed by the brim of her outmoded bonnet, and she clutched her satchel in one hand as she grasped the railing and made her way carefully down the ramp. Several people followed, and then Sebastian spotted the Hobsons, Michael Hobson's tall hat towering above his sister's flower-bedecked bonnet. Michael Hobson carried two carpetbags, while Miss Hobson held her violin case, her gloved hands clutching the instrument as if it were her most precious possession, which Sebastian supposed it was. A young sailor had been entrusted with Michael Hobson's viola and a hat box that he carried sideways to avoid banging it against the wooden sides.

After a moment, Clyde Bennett appeared at the top of the gangway, his ginger hair peeking from beneath a brown bowler that matched a well-cut sack coat. He carried his satchel in one hand and his violin case beneath his arm as he followed the Hobsons down to the stone quay. Sebastian watched carefully, scanning the faces of the passengers from steerage, who charged the gangway like a barbarian horde, but, even though he stared at the crowd until his eyes started to water, the minutes passed and he saw no sign of Ezra Pennington.

THIRTY-SIX

Gemma looked on in dismay as the stream of disembarking passengers thinned to a trickle, the crowd moving along the walkways towards the exits. A few passengers from steerage milled about on the quay as they tried to get their bearings while probably enjoying the fresh breeze, the sunny sky, and the feel of solid ground beneath their feet after being cooped up for two weeks. Several port workers had assembled near the newly arrived vessel, and members of the crew went about their business. There was no sign of Joseph Abrahms, but he was probably belowdecks.

Sebastian remained at the foot of the gangway, looking remarkably ill-tempered and more than a little anxious since Constable Forrest had not appeared either. Sebastian's thoughts had to be running along the same track as Gemma's; she was becoming increasingly concerned about the constable's safety. She thought Sebastian must be torn between remaining at his post and coming back aboard to search for Constable Forrest and Ezra Pennington.

Where could Pennington have gone? Gemma mused frantically. He couldn't have evaded Sebastian, not when there was no other way off the ship, so the only reasonable answer was that he was biding his time and waiting for the right moment. Or maybe he was down in the hold, helping Audrey Blackstock out of whatever hidey-hole she'd been concealed in. Was it possible that she had remained crouched in some barrel or a crate all this time? It seemed unlikely, but people had done more desperate things than that when their liberty was at stake, and a day and a half of discomfort and hunger was a small price to pay for doing what one pleased for the rest of one's life. Or maybe Audrey wasn't aboard at all, and her body would eventually wash up, carried along by the current and unceremoniously deposited on the banks of the Thames.

Shep Reynolds materialized next to her and Gemma sighed irritably. "Are you quite all right, Miss Tate?" he asked, his expression blandly solicitous. "I would have thought you'd be eager to join Inspector Bell on dry land."

She *was* eager to join Sebastian and saw little point in remaining on deck, but she had promised to follow his instructions and would await his signal. The worst thing she could do now was distract him and cause him to worry about her.

"I'm waiting for Constable Forrest," she replied.

"And where might he be?"

"Do you pay a premium to get your cargo unloaded so quickly?" Gemma asked, desperate to change the subject.

The crew were already fitting a wooden slide that would allow them to roll the barrels directly onto the quay, and lowering ropes with hooks into the hold. The hooks would be attached to the crates, which would be lifted out of the hold and transferred to the dock. Gemma had heard that it sometimes took weeks to get a ship unloaded once it had come into port, and perishable items were frequently lost and had to be disposed of when they finally saw the light of day.

"As I mentioned before, we're on a tight schedule, Miss Tate. The *Prince Regent* must be unloaded, loaded, and ready to depart in three days' time."

"How very efficient," Gemma replied absentmindedly.

She was still watching Sebastian, who was now scowling, his eyes narrowed as he seemed to weigh his options. He appeared to be about to step onto the gangway when a family of five arrived at the top, the father holding the hands of two small girls and the mother carrying a boy of about two. Both the man and the woman wore bulging leather packs on their backs and completely filled the gangway as they moved towards the dock. It was just as they finally reached the bottom and stepped onto the quay that Gemma spotted Ezra Pennington. His bowler was pulled low over his eyes, his satchel was slung over his right arm, and his hands firmly gripped the massive cello case as he carefully maneuvered the unwieldy instrument down the gangway.

Gemma was surprised the other members of the quartet had not waited for him or offered a hand with the case. The Hobsons and Mr. Bennett were halfway down a crowded walkway that led towards East Smithfield, where they might be able to find an available cab.

"A small wheel at the bottom of the case would make transporting the instrument much easier," Shep Reynolds remarked, and Gemma had to acknowledge the wisdom of his suggestion. Why had no one thought of that?

Ezra Pennington stopped halfway down the gangplank, pulled out a handkerchief, and wiped his sweating brow. It really was warm, and he was obviously struggling. Sebastian stood quite still, his gaze on the cello player. He didn't offer to help, nor did he shift from his spot. Ezra Pennington paid Sebastian no mind. All his attention was on the case, which had tipped forwards due to the downward slant of the gangway and would surely fall if Ezra didn't right it in time. He wrapped his arms around the case and inched down the ramp.

"Mr. Pennington, a word," Sebastian called out as soon as Pennington had reached the bottom.

Gemma couldn't see Ezra's face, but she noted the added tension in his neck and shoulders as he approached Sebastian.

"Of course, Inspector," he huffed. "I just need a moment to catch my breath."

Sebastian didn't step aside but shifted his right leg backwards, as if to brace himself. That decision prevented him from losing his balance when Ezra Pennington dropped his satchel and shoved the wooden case into Sebastian with all his might. Sebastian staggered backwards but remained upright. He grabbed the case with both hands and tried to wrench it away from Pennington, whose bowler had come off and was instantly snatched up by a scrawny lad, who snaked through the crowd and disappeared from view. Ezra's dark forelock slid into his eyes, but he didn't appear to notice. His eyes blazed, and he let out a roar of anger as he charged Sebastian again, throwing all his weight behind the case in an effort to take Sebastian down.

A crowd quickly gathered, the onlookers mostly sailors and dock workers, who were eager for a bit of excitement. They began to cheer the combatants on and call out words of encouragement as they urged the two men to let go of the cello and resolve their differences by way of fisticuffs. Sebastian was entirely focused on retaining his balance, and Ezra Pennington, just as focused, rammed the case into him again and again, seemingly determined to knock him to the ground.

"Well, that escalated quickly," Shep Reynolds announced. He seemed amused, as if he were watching a paid match and not a struggle between good and evil. "I'm afraid Mr. Pennington is quickly gaining the upper hand."

"Please, help Sebastian," Gemma begged. "Get someone to intervene. Ezra Pennington is the killer."

"I'm afraid I can't do that, Miss Tate," Reynolds replied, not bothering to take his eyes off the brawling men. "I'm responsible for the safety of my crew and will not risk American lives for the sake of two Brits. If that man is the killer, he has nothing to lose and everything to gain by disabling your inspector."

"Bloody coward," Gemma hissed, but Shep Reynolds chuckled with amusement. "Don't you care if Sebastian gets hurt?"

"It's never advisable to mix business and pleasure, Miss Tate. For obvious reasons. You end up betraying your true emotions."

Gemma ignored Shep Reynolds' cutting comments and

watched in horror as the two men continued to tussle, her heart in her mouth as Sebastian lost ground. Sebastian had the law on his side, but Ezra Pennington was fighting for his very survival. To lose was to face the gallows, and he seemed to have tapped into some hidden reserve of strength as he drove Sebastian towards the stone wall of the nearest warehouse. A few more feet and Sebastian would have a stone wall at his back and the solid wooden case in front. If Ezra Pennington continued to apply relentless pressure, he could crush Sebastian's ribs, which could in turn puncture the lungs or damage the heart, leading to a prolonged, agonizing death.

Just when Gemma was certain the situation couldn't get more dire, a glint of metal flashed in the midday sun, and she cried out in alarm when the object revealed itself to be the blade of a pocketknife clutched in Ezra Pennington's right hand. He must have realized Sebastian had been waiting for him and had hidden the weapon in the pocket of his coat. He had managed to get it out and open it, and, judging by his ferocious expression and bared teeth, he had every intention of using it.

The onlookers roared with shock, and several men bellowed in approval, thrilled that the conflict had escalated into a fight to the death. Ezra's face was contorted with rage, his dark eyes narrowed against the midday sun as he single-mindedly applied himself to bringing the confrontation to a tragic conclusion. He was now secure in the knowledge that no one would try to stop him and once he'd wounded Sebastian he'd be free to run, leaving his opponent to bleed and, if Ezra was lucky, to die.

Gemma looked around frantically. Constable Forrest was nowhere to be seen, and, even though every member of the crew appeared to be watching the spectacle and cheering their chosen champion, not one man was willing to intervene. When Gemma lurched towards the gangway, Shep Reynolds called out to her and grabbed her by the upper arm, but she yanked her arm out of his grasp and disregarded his entreaty to remain on deck. She trotted down the ramp as quickly as her skirts would allow, ignoring the wobble of the planks beneath her feet. She was panting with terror, and her heels pounded on the thick wood, but no one noticed her approach. The noise had reached riot levels, and she could no longer see what was happening since her view was blocked by a solid wall of wide male backs.

"Let me through," she begged, but no one paid her any mind. They were too enthralled by the spectacle before them.

Gemma was struck by an elbow, then shoved aside by a burly docker who'd just come up behind her. He muscled his way in, shoving onlookers out of his way to get to the front. Without bothering to consider the ramifications, Gemma followed, squeezing herself into the quickly closing gap the man had created. The cheering men didn't even notice her. They pushed and shoved as they craned their necks to get a better view and encouraged Sebastian to produce a weapon of his own. Someone brandished a blade, calling to Sebastian to come and get it, but there was no way he could reach the weapon, not without making himself vulnerable.

Sebastian had no choice but to use the cello as a shield. He forced it against his attacker's heaving chest and tried to twist out of the way as Ezra brought his arm around the side and stabbed blindly in the hope of finding his target. The only thing working in Sebastian's favor was that the blade of the pocketknife wasn't very long, but, solid and bulky as the case was, it wasn't nearly wide or deep enough to keep him entirely out of harm's way.

Sebastian grimaced with pain as the knife connected with his upper arm, and a crimson stain bloomed on the sleeve of his light-colored coat, the blotch quickly expanding as blood soaked into the lightweight fabric. Gratified by this victory, Ezra let out another bellow of rage and brought down the knife, angling the tip towards Sebastian's trapezius, between the neck and shoulder. Just in time, Sebastian managed to duck out of the way, but Gemma was certain that Ezra's frenzied jabs would eventually prove successful. The blade wasn't long enough to penetrate any major organs, but it was perfectly adequate if Ezra decided to aim higher and tried to sever Sebastian's carotid artery or stab him through the temple.

There was no time to lose, and Gemma didn't have the

luxury of considering the repercussions of her decision. She fought her way to the front, so focused on getting to Sebastian that she didn't feel any pain as the men shoved her or tried to elbow her out of the way, yelling at her to get away and keep well back. Her bonnet had come off and was hanging down her back, and she'd pulled off her ruined gloves, leaving her hands bare. Once she finally had an unobstructed view, she unclasped her reticule with shaking fingers and drew out her pistol. She prayed it was loaded and capped and that the gunpowder inside the paper cartridges wasn't damp, or the gun wouldn't fire. Holding the pistol with both hands, Gemma cocked, aimed at Ezra's back, and fired.

The kickback from such a small pistol wasn't significant, and the shot could barely be heard above the din of the crowd, but Gemma felt a tremor in her hands as the lead ball left the chamber and was propelled through the barrel. Had the target been further away or smaller, she was certain she would have missed, but Ezra Pennington was no more than three feet from her, and his back was as large a target as she was likely to get. He jerked when the bullet struck him just above the right shoulder blade, his head rearing back and his back arching.

Believing she had evened the odds, Gemma lowered the pistol, but Ezra righted himself and stabbed at Sebastian even more viciously, all the while snarling something unintelligible through his gritted teeth. If he was bleeding, it was impossible to tell since his coat was black and bloodstains wouldn't be visible. Gemma had four more rounds in the chamber, or she hoped she did, and she was just about to aim again when a man next to her screamed, "She has a pistol."

The crowd heaved, a few men hastily moving away from her while others surged forward, eager to witness what was going to happen next. A man of indeterminable age who was dressed as a laborer and smelled strongly of sweat, spirits, and tobacco tackled Gemma and pushed her to the ground, pinning her with his weight. Several men looked on, but the majority of the spectators, especially those who hadn't heard the warning, were more interested in Sebastian and Ezra and what they might do next.

Gemma's assailant reached for the pistol, his calloused fingers closing around her bare hand. Her face was pressed to the ground, the only thing between the grit and her cheek a loose lock of hair. She could barely breathe, both because the man was so big and because his breath was foul. She tried to twist away, but he was too heavy and too determined to subdue her. She suspected the only thing he was after was the pistol, since it would fetch a tidy sum if fenced, even without spare cartridges. Helpless and terrified as she was, Gemma was more frightened for Sebastian, who was now bleeding profusely, his face pale and clammy as he attempted to wrestle the cello case away from Ezra Pennington so he could disarm him.

Ezra had one arm wrapped around the case, his weight keeping Sebastian pinned against the wall. He continued to stab blindly with the other hand in the hope of inflicting more wounds. Gemma was petrified she'd wound Sebastian, but something had to be done or he would be hurt much worse. Growling with frustration, she gathered all her strength, maneuvered her right arm from beneath her attacker, aimed at Pennington, and squeezed off another shot. Then another. The first ball missed, but the second found its mark, this time in Pennington's left buttock. He jerked and momentarily loosened his grip on the knife, providing Sebastian with the opening he needed. The cello case crashed to the ground, the wood splintering as Sebastian tackled him, bringing him down on the ground and jumping on top. Despite his injuries, Pennington was still in fighting form and not about to surrender. Sebastian punched him in the face, then again, before Ezra managed to throw him off and tried to regain the upper hand. The men rolled on the ground, fighting for dominance and possession of the knife.

The odious man on top of Gemma shifted his weight to pin down her right arm and squeezed her wrist so tightly, she had no choice but to let go of the pistol. It slid from her grasp, falling to the stone quay. Gleefully, the man grabbed the pistol and shoved it into his pocket before leaning on her arm and yelling, "Fetch the police. She's an assassin."

"I *am* the police," Sebastian bellowed.

"Let go of me, you brainless brute," Gemma shrieked. "I'm with the inspector. And that's his pistol you just pocketed."

"Sure ye are," the man sneered. "Inspectors are not issued with firearms. Ye'd know that if ye were telling the truth."

Gemma had no hope in hell of convincing him or getting him off her. He was holding her down, his face a mere inch from hers as he regarded her with renewed interest. His meaty hand closed around her breast. He squeezed hard, and panic of a different sort flared in her chest. Everyone was so focused on the fight, he could do anything he wanted, and no one would notice or care.

"I can't breathe," Gemma panted. "Please... I... can't..."

She allowed her eyelids to flutter, like she was about to pass out. That frightened her attacker. He might have wanted to take the pistol off her and grope her, but he clearly had no wish to be charged with the murder of a gentlewoman. He reluctantly heaved himself to his feet and held out a hand to her.

"Let me 'elp ye up, miss."

Gemma didn't want to touch or smell him, but she didn't think she would be able to stand up on her own, so allowed him to help her to her feet. Her legs wobbled, and she couldn't seem to take a deep breath. The whalebone in her corset must have cracked, because it was digging into her side, and she could barely move her right wrist. The man had bruised it badly when he'd wrenched the pistol away from her. Her shoulder and arm were numb from being pinned down for so long, and there was a pricking sensation where circulation had been impeded. Gemma's right arm was so weak, she could barely lift it. She held the aching arm to her middle and embraced it with her other one, rubbing gently to restore circulation and ease the soreness.

"Give me back the pistol," she demanded of the man, who was watching her with concern. "It belongs to Inspector Bell."

The man glanced towards Sebastian, who had finally managed

to get the knife away from Ezra Pennington and tossed it aside. No one dared to pick it up now that they knew Sebastian was an inspector with the police. They still meant to enjoy the show, but didn't care to be accused of aiding and abetting a criminal. The tide had shifted, and the onlookers were cheering Sebastian, who had got the upper hand and had his opponent pinned to the ground. Ezra's face was smeared with blood-tinged mud, and he groaned when his wounded buttock met with solid ground. Both men were filthy and bleeding profusely, but they were still locked in combat, since Ezra clearly wasn't ready to give up.

He looked like a man possessed, and seemed to access some last reserve of strength as he bucked violently, threw Sebastian off, and managed to roll on top of him and get him in a headlock. Sebastian's eyes bulged as Ezra attempted to choke him and blood surged into Ezra's previously pale face. Furious, Sebastian bared his teeth and bit hard on Ezra's exposed wrist. Ezra screamed and loosened his hold. Taking advantage of the momentary reprieve, Sebastian pushed him off, scrambled to his feet, and kicked Ezra in the stomach. Ezra howled with agony and curled in on himself, protecting his midriff, but he didn't stay down for long. In moments, he was on his feet again, swaying and cursing, but ready to engage with Sebastian once more. All those years of lugging around his cello had made him strong and resilient.

The crowd was rapt, the onlookers clearly impressed with the tenacity of the combatants. Someone fought through the crowd and shoved Gemma's assailant roughly out of the way. The man staggered and went down on his knees just as someone else fell over, their shoulder colliding with the man's head. Gemma took the opportunity to reach into his pocket, grab the pistol, and squeeze between several onlookers to put distance between herself and the angry man, who was back on his feet and looking from left to right to see where she'd gone. Since she was the shortest person there, she decided to hide behind a wide-shouldered sailor, and hoped her assailant wouldn't find her. She kept one eye on the man and another on Sebastian, relieved to note that the man who'd parted the crowd the way Moses parted the Red Sea was none other than Constable Forrest, wielding his truncheon.

He came up behind Ezra and brought down his truncheon on the man's wounded shoulder, then hit him again and again, before tossing the truncheon aside. He wrenched Ezra's arms behind his back and tied them with a cord. Ezra's knees buckled, and Constable Forrest forced him to sit on the ground and warned him not to move. Ezra rocked back and forth, presumably to ease the pain. His face was white as a sheet, and his clothes were soaked with blood. He had to be hurting badly, having not only been shot twice but also taken an enthusiastic beating from Constable Forrest.

"Where the hell were you?" Sebastian roared.

He was bleeding, unsteady on his feet, and spitting mad as he confronted his errant constable. Someone picked up Sebastian's hat and handed it to him, and he took it without turning and plopped it on his head.

"I'm sorry, sir," Constable Forrest cried. "He knocked me down and locked me in his cabin. I had to break down the door to get out." He was clearly embarrassed to have been outfoxed by Ezra Pennington, which probably explained why he had battered him so hard.

Gemma supposed that explained why Ezra Pennington had taken his time getting off the ship. He had neutralized Constable Forrest in order to improve his chances of escape. Gemma was so focused on the spectacle, she hadn't realized her assailant had found her. He grabbed her by the shoulders and shook her hard.

"Give me the pistol," the man demanded.

"I will not. And if you don't let go this minute, I will have you arrested on a charge of assault," Gemma threatened, displaying considerably more courage than she felt. She realized she was trembling, and her teeth were beginning to chatter.

The man let go of her and tried to rip the reticule from her hands. Gemma held on for dear life. She didn't realize she was screaming until the man yelled back, "Shut up, ye stupid cow. Ye're lucky I didn't have my way with ye. Now give me that."

The words were barely out of his mouth when Sebastian's bloodied fist met with the man's jaw, and he went down like a sack of turnips at Gemma's feet.

"Sebastian, I'm all right," Gemma cried. "I'm fine."

"I'm not," Sebastian hissed, and struck the man again and again.

"I'll have ye arrested, ye filthy cur," the man screamed. "Constable. Help me!"

Constable Forrest ignored him but picked up his truncheon and slapped it against his palm.

"Get lost," Sebastian said, his voice dangerously low, "or I will arrest you for attempted murder." He turned to Gemma. "Are you all right? I'm so sorry I couldn't get to you sooner."

"I'm perfectly well," Gemma lied. She was still holding her arm, and her breath came in short gasps as she attempted to calm her racing heart and stop shaking.

"I have to get you home."

"You must deal with Ezra Pennington first."

Sebastian nodded and strode towards Ezra, who sat with his head bowed. His shoulders quaked, and Gemma realized he was weeping. She thought Sebastian would tell him he was under arrest, but instead Sebastian continued towards the cello. He squatted next to the case and unlatched the fittings, carefully lifting the lid.

Inside, curled up like an unborn child in a womb, was a woman. Her hair was loose, and she wore rolled-up trousers and a man's shirt. Her chin had been pressed into her chest, but she gingerly lifted her head and squinted as she opened her eyes to the bright light of the summer afternoon. Her hair was raven black, but her eyes were ice blue, her complexion pale as the moon. The woman's coloring was both striking and a little unusual, and the look on her face was one of pure terror.

"Lady Blackstock, I presume?" Sebastian asked archly.

"I'm sorry," Ezra whimpered. "Oh, Audrey, I'm so sorry."

"You're both under arrest for the murders of Anthony Blackstock and Greta Van Kemp."

"She didn't do it," Ezra cried. "It was all me. I killed them both."

"Now, why don't I believe you?" Sebastian said under his breath.

He offered Audrey his hand, but she refused his help and scrambled out of the case, moving awkwardly, like a wounded crab. Gemma couldn't begin to imagine what the poor woman had endured while the men had fought using the case as a weapon with her inside. Once she was finally out, she straightened to her full and not very impressive height. She really was slight, and very beautiful despite her disheveled appearance and bruised face.

Sebastian took Audrey by the arm while Constable Forrest helped a beaten Ezra to his feet and pushed him towards the walkway that led to the exit. Gemma brought up the rear. The five of them wouldn't fit into a cab, not even into two cabs, but Sebastian had other plans. He handed Audrey Blackstock over to Constable Forrest, then turned to Gemma, taking her gently by the shoulders.

"Are you sure you're all right?"

"I need a warm compress for my wrist and a cup of tea." Gemma's gaze strayed to Sebastian's blood-soaked sleeve. "Are you in pain? That really should be seen to."

"I'll be fine."

Gemma doubted that was true, but there was no arguing with him when he was like this. "Come back with me, and I will clean and bandage it. Constable Forrest can get those two to Scotland Yard."

Sebastian shook his head. "I'll have someone bandage it once I get to the Yard."

Gemma gave up arguing. "Make sure to clean it first," she reminded him.

"Yes, ma'am."

As soon as an empty cab stopped next to them, Sebastian gave the cabbie Colin's address and handed Gemma inside. "Get some rest. I will come by later."

"You promise?" Gemma asked tearfully.

She didn't want to leave him and go back on her own. She was badly shaken, and her wrist was throbbing, but Sebastian had a job to do and could hardly leave Constable Forrest to deal with two suspects on his own, especially when Ezra Pennington had already bested him once. Even with his hands tied behind his back, Ezra was a threat, and Audrey Blackstock was just desperate enough to try anything.

"I promise. All will be well."

Sebastian smiled at her reassuringly and squeezed her hand, and then the cab began to move. Gemma rested her head against the seat and shut her eyes as the shock of the past half hour reverberated through her entire body. She trembled violently as silent tears of fear and pain slid down her cheeks. But she wouldn't be able to put this case behind her until she got answers.

THIRTY-SEVEN

"What on earth happened?" Mabel exclaimed when she opened the door and beheld Gemma's soiled gown, crushed bonnet, and torn gloves.

"I fell," Gemma muttered.

"Where's Inspector Bell? Were you not with him?"

"He had to leave."

As much as Gemma liked and trusted Mabel, she couldn't bring herself to confess that she'd shot a man—twice—and had been accosted by another. All she wanted was to go upstairs, wash, change into a clean gown, and hide in her room until Sebastian arrived. He hadn't been truthful about his injuries. Judging by the amount of blood on his coat, the wounds Ezra Pennington had inflicted were deep and probably very painful. Sebastian clearly hadn't wanted to worry her, which, although thoughtful, just made her fret all the more. She was also worried about the damage she'd done to Ezra Pennington.

The man richly deserved everything he'd got and more, and would have hacked Sebastian to pieces had Gemma not intervened, but the thought of causing another human being grave injury distressed her, even if that person was destined to hang for his crimes. She was a nurse, a healer, not a killer. And although she had no regrets about helping Sebastian, Gemma still had to come to terms with what she had done and what she would be willing to do in the future. There would be new cases, fresh threats, and difficult decisions that would go against everything she knew and believed, and she would have to live with the consequences of those actions.

Gemma wholeheartedly supported the rule of law, but she had never signed on to become the instrument of that rule, unlike Sebastian, who had chosen his profession willingly and knowingly. What she really wanted was to become a surgeon, but women were not permitted to enroll in medical school or allowed to sit in on a surgery. A woman couldn't even apply for a license to become a chemist, even though some women assisted their husbands behind closed doors, like her friend Poppy's sister, and no one was any the wiser; the customers would probably boycott the shop if they learned the truth.

Gemma had witnessed plenty of surgeries in Crimea, but at the time her job had been to swab the blood, keep the patients sedated if ether was available, and hand the surgeon medical instruments. There had been no opportunity to ask questions or study the surgeon's technique. Colin sometimes allowed her to watch while he performed an autopsy, but only as long as his pupils weren't there. They would be none too pleased to find a woman among their number and would possibly even walk out and find someone else to instruct them. But if she hoped to learn, she needed to lay her hands on an actual body, and after today she was more determined than ever.

Gemma met Poppy on the landing and, smiling tiredly, stopped to chat. Poppy had just come out of Anne's room and had carefully shut the door behind her, mindful of disturbing her patient.

"Oh, good, you're back," Poppy said. "I must get ready for my shift." She looked Gemma up and down. "Goodness me, you look like you've been dragged through a hedge backwards."

"It's nothing. I tripped and fell over."

"Are you hurt?"

"No, but I would like to rest for a little while."

"Well, don't worry on Anne's account. She ate most of her lunch, I read to her for an hour, and she just fell asleep. I almost nodded off myself. Never been a fan of *Little Dorrit.*"

"Bless you, Poppy. I will make it up to you." Gemma was grateful for an hour's reprieve.

"There's no need," Poppy said airily. "You are doing me a bigger favor than you realize."

Gemma knew what Poppy meant. She wanted Gemma's job, but Gemma wasn't quite ready to leave Colin's employ, at least not permanently.

"I want to become a surgeon, Poppy," Gemma blurted out, verbalizing her cherished dream. She watched Poppy's face undergo a transformation from surprise to disbelief, then sympathy, and hurtful censure.

"You do know how improbable that is, don't you?" Poppy asked. "No man will allow you anywhere near an operating theater, and no patient will agree to be operated on by a woman."

"I know, but perhaps I can practice pathology. The dead won't mind so much," Gemma amended. She would much rather help the living, but she acknowledged the truth of Poppy's objections and knew her friend's lack of support was well meant.

"Why would you want to do something so gruesome?" Poppy asked. "Looking after living patients is difficult enough."

"I want to understand how the human body works. I want to be able to relay messages from beyond the grave."

"You'll be setting yourself up for derision and disappointment, and possibly lifelong loneliness if your inspector gets scared off by your mad notions. Gemma, you finally have a chance at a life. Marry Sebastian, have children, and practice your nursing skills on the people you love. Keep them safe and well; that's what a woman is best suited to."

"You are in no rush to marry," Gemma snapped, irritated by Poppy's typically feminine advice.

"Believe you me, Gemma, if a good man were to ask, I wouldn't hesitate."

"And by a good man, you mean Colin?" Gemma probed.

"Colin is kind and considerate. And I happen to think he's quite handsome. Don't you agree?" Poppy asked dreamily. She didn't wait for Gemma to reply before continuing. "And he's well respected and comfortably off. Oh, Gemma, I would give anything. Do you think he even notices me?"

Poppy's hangdog expression begged for reassurance, so Gemma jumped in to hearten her friend. "Of course he notices you. You are lovely."

"So is Mabel," Poppy announced grumpily. "And she's a really good cook."

"Are you jealous of Mabel?"

"No. Maybe. A little."

"Mabel is smitten with Jacob from next door. And she knows full well Colin would never look at her, at least not in that way."

"Why, because she's a maidservant? A nurse is not that much higher on the social register."

"No, it's not because she's a maidservant. It's because he simply doesn't see her that way."

"Does he see me that way?" Poppy asked carefully.

Gemma didn't want to give her false hope, but she thought Colin looked forward to Poppy's visits and was working up the courage to ask her to join him for a walk or a musical performance.

"Have patience. Colin is not an impulsive man."

"Is Sebastian impulsive?"

Gemma was about to say that he wasn't but suddenly realized that wouldn't be true. Unlike Colin, Sebastian acted on his feelings, and, although he had been the perfect gentleman since they had met, now that Gemma knew him better she realized he had probably known he would pursue her the very first time they'd met. Perhaps he hadn't fully realized it himself, let alone acknowledged it outright, but deep inside, he'd known. Just as she had.

Perhaps they really were two of a kind and God had put them in each other's paths because that was what they'd both needed.

"Tell him, Poppy," Gemma suggested. "Let Colin know you have feelings for him."

"I would never," Poppy protested. "Imagine if he doesn't feel the same, which he probably doesn't. I would never get over the humiliation."

"Then your only option is to wait."

"I think I'll have a better chance once you finally leave this house," Poppy grumbled as she moved towards the stairs.

"You must do what feels right to you."

"And so should you," Poppy said. "Even if it's madness and you'll probably regret it."

Gemma watched Poppy as she hurried down the stairs, then ambled towards her own room. As she removed her misshapen bonnet and muddy cape, she wondered what was happening at Scotland Yard and wished she could sit in on Sebastian's interview with Ezra Pennington and Audrey Blackstock. She could guess what had happened, but she needed to arrange the facts in a discernible pattern and determine who was guilty and who had been an innocent bystander in the tragedy that had unfolded aboard the ship.

THIRTY-EIGHT

"Well, I never," Ransome exclaimed when Sebastian knocked on the doorjamb and entered his office. "You're a sight."

Sebastian didn't think he looked that bad. He'd washed his hands, face, and muddy hair under the pump behind the building, and Sergeant Meadows, who wasn't nearly as skilled or gentle as Gemma but had done his best, had cleaned his wounds and bandaged them with strips of clean linen. Sebastian's suit was probably beyond salvaging, but Mrs. Quince tended to work miracles when motivated by the promise of profit, so not all was lost. His hat just needed to be brushed and it would be as good as new. He'd also had two mugs of strong, sweet tea, and a steak and ale pie Constable Hammond had been kind enough to procure from a nearby street vendor. On the whole, he didn't feel too bad.

Ezra Pennington hadn't been as lucky as Sebastian and had been given over to the gin-soaked ministrations of Mr. Fenwick as soon as he was brought to Scotland Yard. Sebastian wouldn't trust the man to operate on a dog, but Ezra was in no position to find his own surgeon, and the lead balls had needed to be removed before the flesh was stitched and bandaged. Sebastian hadn't heard any desperate screams coming from the mortuary, where Mr. Fenwick was tending to Ezra, so the doctor had either given him something for the pain or killed him already.

Once Sebastian was settled in the guest chair, Ransome shook his head in amazement, then a smile of gratification tugged at his lips, the points of his moustache lifting upwards. "You got your man."

"And woman."

"Please tell me they're not American," Ransome said on a sigh.

"They are not."

"That makes our life easier. Mind if I sit in on the interview?"

"Not at all, but you might have to wait a while."

"Oh?"

"The suspect is with Mr. Fenwick at present."

"Then may God help him," Ransome said with feeling. "In the meantime, you can fill me in." He extracted a bottle of brandy and two glasses from the bottom drawer of his desk and poured a generous measure for each of them.

"Here," he said gruffly. "You look like you could use it."

Ransome took a civilized sip, while Sebastian tossed back the lot and set the glass on the desk. The brandy wouldn't anesthetize his pain, but it would at least dull it a little and help him to make it through the rest of the day.

"More?" Ransome asked.

Sebastian shook his head. "I need to keep my wits about me."

Nodding, Ransome put the bottle away and leaned back in his chair, ready to hear and evaluate the facts of the case. Once Ransome was clear on the timeline of events and the suspects' motivations and had been apprised of everything that had happened since Audrey Blackstock's and Ezra Pennington's paths had serendipitously crossed in New York, the two men made their way to interview room 1, where a trembling, white-faced Ezra Pennington awaited their pleasure. Ezra's cuffed hands were chained to the iron ring affixed to the table, but Audrey, who sat next to him and kept stealing worried glances at Ezra's face, was unfettered, her delicate wrists poking out like twigs from the cuffs of the too-large shirt. She bowed her head when they entered, and her hair obscured her expression, but the slump of her narrow shoulders told Sebastian everything he needed to know. She was a broken woman, both physically and emotionally, and Ezra's fate would determine whatever future she may have left.

Constable Bryant was stationed outside the door in case Ezra made a miraculous recovery and decided to make a break for it, but the man looked in no condition to go anywhere. He was obviously in pain, and it probably hurt like the dickens to sit.

"Well, well, well," Ransome said once he'd shut the door and taken his place at the table. Sebastian sat next to him, taking the chair directly across from Ezra Pennington. "I imagine you two thought you were very clever."

"Clearly not clever enough," Audrey replied morosely.

She lifted her head and fixed Ransome with a look so scathing, a lesser man might have quaked in his boots. Now that Sebastian could see her clearly, he noted fading bruises as well as the new ones that Audrey must have sustained during the prolonged fight at the docks. Although the interior of the case was padded to protect Ezra's instrument, Audrey would still have been tossed around like a ship in a storm, her head and limbs striking the sides.

"You nearly got away with it," Ransome replied, and Sebastian thought he heard a note of admiration in the superintendent's voice. "And you likely would have, had I sent a different man."

Although he'd made no mention of Gemma, Ransome had privately acknowledged her role in solving the case and had asked Sebastian to pass on his sincere compliments. Gemma would appreciate that since, without her contribution, Sebastian would not have been able to complete the puzzle. Turning to Sebastian, Ransome silently invited him to begin. He seemed as eager as Sebastian to close the case on the *Prince Regent* murders and send the culprits to Newgate or Coldbath Fields to await trial.

Sebastian exhaled deeply. His wounds throbbed, and despite the bandage he could feel blood trickling down his arm and pooling in the crook of his elbow. He was suddenly very tired, and wished the interview had been postponed until the following day. Ezra could use some time to recover, and, if neither he nor Audrey Blackstock was ready to own up to their crimes, then Sebastian would need to build his case against them brick by evidential brick, and that could take hours.

"Lady Blackstock, would you like to start us off?" Sebastian asked.

"I expect you already know everything," Audrey replied quietly.

"Tell us anyway."

"May I?" Ezra interrupted.

He looked ten years older than he had that morning, and wore his defeat like a mantle. Audrey cast a grateful glance in his direction and bowed her head once again, as if she simply couldn't bear to hear the truth. Ezra clasped his cuffed hands and fixed Sebastian with a sorrowful stare.

"Audrey and I met when Audrey befriended my sister at school. We lived a few streets away from one another, so Audrey and Stella spent quite a bit of time together, especially during the school holidays." Ezra sighed heavily. "We were in love and planned to marry once Audrey turned eighteen. Professor Stack thought me a suitable match for his daughter. That is, until Anthony Blackstock turned up and showed an interest in Audrey."

Audrey raised her head, her gaze clouded with what were obviously painful memories. "My father became blinded by ambition," she said angrily. "He imagined marriage to Anthony Blackstock would elevate our family and provide him with opportunities for advancement. I didn't care about any of that," she confessed. "I only wanted to be with Ezra, but my father forbade me to see him and threatened to disown me if I refused Anthony's suit. I was devastated, but I was very young and believed my father had my best interests at heart. I told Ezra I intended to abide by my father's wishes and ended our relationship."

Tears shimmered in Audrey's pale eyes as her gaze met Sebastian's. "Before we married, Anthony was charming, solicitous, and seemingly besotted with me. He went out of his way to spoil me and promised me a life of ease and gaiety. I thought perhaps my father was right, and Ezra was just a girlish infatuation. This was real life, and I had a chance at something greater."

"But things changed once you were married," Ransome observed grimly.

Audrey nodded. "The first few months were difficult. Like any new bride, I had to become accustomed to living with a man I barely knew and accept the reality of sharing his bed. Anthony was no longer as gentle or solicitous as he had pretended to be, but my father told me this was normal, and no man could be expected to behave as he did during the period of courtship. I accepted this," she said stonily. "I was Lady Blackstock, and I had to learn to behave accordingly, but during that first year my husband became increasingly tyrannical. He set out rules of conduct for me, and, if I violated any of his edicts, he punished me."

Audrey seemed to draw in on herself, and her eyes swam with tears. "At first, it was the loss of personal freedom. He'd lock me in my bedroom for hours. I thought that was unnecessarily cruel, but after a time things got much worse. Anthony would lock me in one of his medieval contraptions and sit in the room with me, watching and enjoying my suffering. He said I had been given too much freedom and that I thought I had a say in my future. I needed to learn my place." Tears slid down Audrey's bruised cheeks. "He taught me to be constantly afraid and to consider my every word and action for fear of upsetting him. But no matter how hard I tried, I still displeased him."

Blinding anger burned in Sebastian's chest. He'd come across men like Anthony Blackstock before, men who were shielded from consequences by their wealth and position and believed they could get away with anything, even murder. Sometimes, all too rarely, these individuals got their comeuppance, but for the most part they continued to terrorize their wives and children, and abuse the whores they thought less than human and beat them to a pulp for the sheer pleasure of watching them bleed. If a prostitute died as a result of the man's temper, he simply paid off the madam and the whole incident was swept under the carpet, never to be mentioned again. For some, money wiped away all manner of sins.

"Please, go on," Ransome invited when Audrey went silent.

She angrily wiped away her tears and continued, her voice barely above a whisper. "When Anthony announced we were going to America, I allowed myself to hope for a reprieve. I didn't think he'd torture me in someone else's home. And he didn't. For the first time since we were married, I was treated as a wife should be. We went out, socialized with other couples, and Anthony treated me with courtesy and respect. But I knew it wouldn't last, not when Anthony purchased that hideous cage and extolled its virtues at the dinner table."

"And then you came face to face with Ezra," Sebastian concluded.

Audrey nodded. "It was at a musical evening we had been invited to while in New York. Our hosts were friends of Lord Lyons, the British envoy. They were kind, lovely people," she said with a wistful smile. "I wished I could remain with them forever, but as the date of our departure drew near I grew more and more fearful of what my life would be once we came home."

"I couldn't believe my eyes when I saw her," Ezra said, his gaze sliding to Audrey. "She seemed so mature and sophisticated, not at all like the girl I had known in Oxford."

"Was that when she told you about the abuse in her marriage?" Ransome asked.

Ezra shook his head. "Audrey and I spoke very briefly after the recital, and Audrey assured me she was content. Lord Blackstock seemed a good man. It was he who mentioned they would be sailing to London on the *Prince Regent*," he confessed.

"So, you made certain you booked passage on the same ship," Ransome observed.

"Yes. I was desperate to see Audrey again, and two weeks aboard would give us a chance to talk."

"Were you hoping to begin an affair?" Ransome asked.

"No. Maybe," Ezra admitted. "I just missed Audrey so much, and seeing her again…"

Audrey reached out and laid a hand over his cuffed wrists. "I wouldn't have dared to see Ezra once we were back in England," she said. "If my husband found out, he would have locked me up and thrown away the key."

"So, what happened when you met on board? Did you two hatch a plan to kill him?" Ransome asked.

"No," Audrey said wearily. "It wasn't like that."

"How was it, then?"

"I made certain to book a first-class cabin for Cora Hobson so that the members of the quartet would be permitted on deck," Ezra explained. "I told the others that Mr. Abbott had paid for it, but I covered the difference with my own money. I saw Audrey from time to time, but we rarely spoke. Her husband was always nearby. I had quite given up hope of ever speaking to her privately when I saw her, the night before we were due to dock. I had come up for a breath of air—this had to be just after midnight—and I found Audrey on deck. She was huddled behind the hatch, her face in her hands, her hair wild. She was in her nightdress, and her feet were bare."

"Ezra, no," Audrey moaned, but Ezra wasn't going to stop there.

"Anthony Blackstock and Jeffrey Caldwell had had a blazing row. Or, more accurately, Anthony Blackstock had accused Jeffrey Caldwell of cheating at cards and had insulted him and called him names. Jeffrey Caldwell did not rise to the bait, which made Blackstock even angrier. When he returned to his cabin, he took his anger out on Audrey. He gagged her so no one would hear, then brutalized and beat her until his anger was spent. Once he was satisfied, he fell into a drunken stupor," Ezra ground out. "Had I not come up when I did…" He wasn't able to finish the sentence, but the implication was obvious. Audrey had considered ending her life.

"I sat down next to Audrey and held her while she cried," Ezra went on quietly. "It took a long while, but she finally told me the truth of her marriage." He fixed Ransome with a dark, angry stare. "I hid Audrey in my cabin, then went to first class. I gagged Anthony Blackstock with one of my gloves, then locked him in the scold's bridle. He was so drunk, he didn't even wake, but I wanted him to know how it felt to be denied a voice and to find himself at the mercy of someone who had no compassion. I shook him awake and let him suffer for a little while, just watching the terror in his eyes and listening to his whimpering. And then I put a pillow over his face and held it down until he was dead. I carved *pig* into his chest with his shaving razor and let myself out," Ezra concluded. "I'm solely responsible for Anthony Blackstock's death."

"What did you do with the key and the razor?" Ransome asked.

"I threw them overboard," Ezra replied with a shrug, as if the answer should be obvious.

"Did you know that a man known to Mr. Reynolds had been murdered in the same way?" Sebastian asked. He was still curious about the connection between the two cases.

Ezra nodded. "Reynolds told Audrey about it."

"Why did he tell you that?" Sebastian asked, turning to Audrey.

"Anthony liked to take a nap in the afternoon, and that was the only time I was left on my own. I couldn't talk to Ezra, since the passengers from first class were always there on deck, watching. Especially Miss Hobson. But Shep made a point of speaking to me. He saw..." Audrey paused and drew in a deep breath. "He realized what sort of man my husband was. He said Cyrus Rutherford had been that sort of man and thought he had been murdered by a woman he'd abused."

"Did he offer to help you?" Sebastian asked.

"There was nothing he could do, but he just spoke to me, and that made me feel better. He treated me with kindness."

"Was that why you decided to set him up?"

Audrey shook her head. "I told Ezra about what had happened to that awful man in New York. I never intended..."

"Did you intentionally try to frame Mr. Reynolds and Mr. Caldwell, Mr. Pennington?" Sebastian asked.

Ezra shook his head. "No. I only realized how what I'd done might look once I had time to reflect."

Sebastian didn't know if he believed that, but he let it go. Whether Ezra Pennington would have allowed either man to get the blame was no longer relevant.

"You say this wasn't planned, but other passengers realized you knew Ezra," Ransome pointed out. "They saw you speaking to him, rather familiarly, I might add."

"I slipped up. Once," Audrey exclaimed. "I called him Ez when I spotted him, as I used to when we were courting."

"So, what was the splash the night watch had heard that night?" Ransome asked, but Sebastian already knew. He'd known since he'd seen Ezra excuse himself and take food back to his cabin. Ezra had thrown his cello overboard so he could hide Audrey until they were safely off the ship.

"It was my cello," Ezra said. "I wanted the night watch to think Audrey had killed herself, so they wouldn't search for her. I found an iron stanchion and wedged it beneath the strings to weight down the cello."

"Surely a new cello would cost you dearly," Ransome mused.

"It was a sacrifice I was prepared to make to keep Audrey safe."

"And Greta Van Kemp? Why did you murder her?" Sebastian demanded.

"She saw us," Ezra said. "She had no reason to be on the aft deck after hours, but she had decided to enjoy a breath of air before returning to her cabin since she wasn't permitted on deck during the day. I would never have hurt her had she not threatened to expose us."

"How much did she want?" Ransome asked.

"Five hundred dollars," Audrey said softly.

"I would have gladly given it to her," Ezra said. "But Anthony Blackstock only had fifty pounds in his purse, and Greta wasn't willing to accept a forged check since, by the time she presented the check, his bank would have been notified of his death and might turn her over to the authorities."

"Greta said fifty pounds wasn't enough and she would tell Inspector Bell everything she knew unless Ezra raised the rest of the money," Audrey said.

"Where did she expect you to get it?" Sebastian asked Ezra.

"Clyde Bennett was in possession of our earnings from the tour."

"But you murdered the woman rather than ask Mr. Bennett for the money," Ransome snarled.

"I wasn't about to tell Clyde I had murdered Anthony Blackstock and needed four hundred dollars to pay off my blackmailer," Ezra replied testily. "Nor was I going to risk revealing Audrey's hiding place. Unless I confessed, she would be accused of murdering her husband. And I didn't think it right to steal from my friends. Clyde, Michael, and Cora were relying on that money. I couldn't deprive them of their earnings."

"Surely you could have found a way to pay Greta Van Kemp once you'd disembarked and Lady Blackstock was able to access her husband's accounts," Ransome said.

"Greta wasn't willing to wait that long," Audrey said. "She thought we'd refuse to pay her once we were safely off the ship."

"And would you have?"

"We would have paid her," Audrey said, "but Greta was the sort of person who'd never let go. She needed money to get home, and it certainly wasn't her fault that she'd lost her position and had no means to return to New York. As far as she was concerned, she'd been handed an opportunity, and she would continue to exploit it."

"As long as Anthony Blackstock's murder remained unsolved, she'd be able to threaten us with exposure," Ezra said. "I had no choice, not if Audrey and I hoped to be free."

Ransome nodded. "It was a clever plan, I'll grant you that. Lucky for you, your lady love was able to fit into the case." Turning to Audrey, he said, "I expect you climbed inside whenever you feared you might be discovered?"

Audrey nodded.

"And Mr. Pennington here brought you food and drink and would carry you off the ship when the time came. What then, your ladyship? What was the plan?"

"We planned to return to New York, then make our way to San Francisco," Ezra admitted.

"Once you had claimed Lady Blackstock's inheritance," Ransome supplied.

"As his widow, Audrey is entitled to receive her husband's assets."

"Not if she's an accomplice in a double murder."

"Audrey is innocent," Ezra cried. "I murdered both Anthony Blackstock and Greta Van Kemp."

"All right, then," Ransome said. "As long as you're willing to sign a confession to that effect, Lady Blackstock will be free to go."

"Ezra—" Audrey Blackstock began, but Ezra cut across her.

"I will furnish you with a written confession." He turned to Audrey, his gaze growing soft with love. "Audrey, please, don't let it be for nothing. Go and live your life. Be free."

Audrey was unable to speak, the tears choking her as she tried to reply, but she nodded and placed her hand over Ezra's. "I'm so sorry," she whispered at last. "I'm so very sorry, Ezra. I wish I would have been brave enough."

"Brave enough to do what?" Ezra asked, looking at Audrey as if no one else were in the room.

"To follow my heart and run away with you when you first asked me to. We would have been so happy."

"Yes, we would have," Ezra replied, smiling through the pain. "I would have loved you for the rest of my days." They gazed at one another, acutely aware that Ezra's days were numbered. "Look after my mother and Stella," Ezra choked out. "They'll need support after I'm gone."

Audrey sniffed loudly, and Ransome handed her his handkerchief. "You are free to leave, my lady."

She made no move to stand. Sebastian expected she had no money for the train fare to Oxford or clothes to change into, since all her things were still aboard the ship. She could hardly make the journey in Ezra's shirt and trousers, even if she managed to find someone who was willing to lend her the money to get home.

"Is there anyone you can ask for assistance?" Ransome asked, having clearly deduced the same thing.

Audrey shook her head. "There's no one."

"I will see that her ladyship retrieves her possessions from the ship and find her a place to stay," Sebastian offered.

Audrey looked at him with wordless gratitude.

"Take my brougham," Ransome offered as his gaze swept over Sebastian's bloodstained coat and muddy trousers. "You're in no fit state to go traipsing about London."

"Thank you, sir."

Audrey staggered to her feet, but before she left she wrapped her arms around Ezra and held his dark head to her breast as she whispered words of love meant only for him. Once she finally let go, Ezra looked up at her, and all the love, longing, and regret they so obviously felt was like a stab to Sebastian's own heart. Ezra Pennington might be a remorseless killer, but Sebastian was self-aware enough to admit that, had he been in Ezra's place, he would have done whatever it took to protect the woman he loved. He hadn't been able to save Louisa, but he would kill anyone who meant Gemma harm and stand content as he faced his executioner, knowing that he'd kept her safe. He prayed he would never have to make that choice, but, given the life he'd chosen and Gemma's determination to share that life with him, he accepted that such an outcome wasn't unlikely.

Sebastian escorted a weeping Audrey Blackstock to Ransome's carriage and helped her inside. They rode to St. Katharine Docks in silence, each lost in their own thoughts, until the tall masts of the ships at anchor finally came into view, and they had to walk the rest of the way since the walkways weren't wide enough for the brougham to pass. Audrey walked slowly, like a woman in pain, her too-big trousers hanging off her slim frame and the white shirt doing little to conceal the camisole beneath. Sebastian supposed it would have been impossible for her to curl up inside the case if she had whalebone to contend with and her crinolines and wide skirts to tuck in. In Ezra's clothes, she could pass for an adolescent boy if she hid her hair beneath a cap.

The *Prince Regent* was still in the process of being unloaded, but the decks were empty, most of the crew probably on shore leave until they were needed back on board. Shep Reynolds was there, though, and came forward to meet Sebastian and Audrey when they walked up the ramp. He'd watched the fight from the ship and already knew what had happened. He bowed stiffly to Audrey, informed her that the stateroom door wasn't locked, then turned his back on them both. He probably thought Audrey had tried to frame him for the murder and had nothing more to say to her. As the saying went, the road to hell was paved with good intentions. He'd think twice about helping a damsel in distress ever again.

Sebastian walked Audrey Blackstock to the stateroom she had shared with her husband and watched her go inside. He left her to change and pack her belongings in private, then escorted her back to the brougham and delivered her to a small but reputable hotel near the Strand. Tomorrow, the stewards would forward her trunk to Anthony Blackstock's ancestral home, and the clerk at the hotel would help find her a cab to take her to Paddington, where she would take a train to Oxford, but by then she would no longer be Sebastian's concern.

He wished her a good evening, if such a thing were possible in her current state, and left her to rest. Sebastian was desperate to see Gemma and reassure himself that she was well after her ordeal and the brute who'd assaulted her hadn't caused her any lasting harm. He also knew Gemma would be anxiously awaiting news of the case, and didn't want to keep her waiting any longer than necessary, but he needed to stop at home first. His coat was crusted with dried blood, his trousers were filthy, and he needed to change his shirt, which was stuck to the bandage and reeked of sweat. He also needed to check on Gustav to make sure the cat had been fed. Sebastian would have found a cab, but was grateful to Ransome's driver, Davies, when the man offered to take him wherever he wished to go and promised to wait while Sebastian washed, shaved, and changed.

Sebastian woke with a start when the brougham pulled up before Colin's front door some two hours later. He thanked Davies and tipped him generously, then walked up the path and heaved his weary bones up the steps as he tried to ignore the throbbing in his arm and the livid bruises that covered most of his body. Most days, Sebastian was careful about his alcohol intake, and he'd already had a drink with Ransome, but he needed another quite badly and meant to have it, preferably with Colin and Gemma.

When Mabel opened the door, she didn't look pleased to see him and all but huffed in disapproval.

"Good evening, Mabel," Sebastian said as he handed her his hat.

"I suppose it is for some," Mabel replied cryptically. "I expect Miss Tate will be glad to see you, but after the way you sent her home you really should have had the decency to stay away."

"Mabel, I—" Sebastian began, then realized that Mabel probably knew nothing of what had happened, only what she had perceived when Gemma turned up looking like she'd fallen off a turnip cart. "Please tell Miss Tate I need to see her."

Mabel gave him the gimlet eye, then muttered under her breath, "Some people always turn up, like a bad penny."

"You've got some nerve," Colin exclaimed as soon as Sebastian walked into the drawing room. "The state of Gemma when she came back. Mabel told me all about it, and I have a good mind to ban you from the house."

"Colin, there's really no need for you to chastise me."

"There's every need. Gemma is an unmarried woman who's under my protection. You are here on my sufferance, sir."

Sebastian opened his mouth with a ready retort, but shut it and folded himself into an armchair. Colin was absolutely right. Sebastian had no claim on Gemma, and, as long as she lived under Colin's roof, he was, for all intents and purposes, her guardian. Well, if Sebastian had anything to say about it, that would soon change. He'd had enough self-loathing, crippling anxiety, and meddlesome Ramseys.

He tried to stand when Gemma walked into the room, but couldn't seem to find the strength and needed to rely on the armrests to push himself upright. Walking past Colin, Gemma crossed the room, and threw herself into Sebastian's arms, pressing herself to his chest as if she needed to hear the beating of his heart.

"Really, Gemma," Colin exclaimed, but was completely ignored.

"Thank God you're all right," she said. "Are you in pain?"

"Not anymore," Sebastian said, and wrapped his arms around her. "You're all the balm I need."

Colin snorted like a spooked horse but had the good grace not to say anything, and went to pour them all a drink. Once Sebastian had been offered a brandy and Gemma had accepted a larger than usual sherry, they settled around the unlit hearth, ready to dissect the details of the case.

THIRTY-NINE

Colin and Gemma listened carefully while Sebastian relayed the details of the police interview and told them about Ezra's confession and Audrey's release.

"Do you really think she's innocent?" Colin asked.

Sebastian looked thoughtful. "I've been asking myself that all the way here, and I'm honestly not sure."

Sebastian and Colin turned to Gemma, who gazed into her sherry as she mulled over the facts. If half the things she'd heard about Anthony Blackstock were true, the man had been a sadistic monster, but, although Ezra Pennington's account made sense, there was room for doubt. Audrey Blackstock was too slight to over-power Greta Van Kemp and hoist her up, but she wasn't too weak to smother an inebriated man who was in deep sleep. Perhaps, after Anthony Blackstock had beaten her after his row with Jeffrey Caldwell, she'd snapped. Anthony Blackstock would have only become worse as time went by and would have surely caused her irreparable harm, if he hadn't already, and seeing Ezra had probably reminded Audrey of how sweet life could be. But the sad truth was that no court in the land would side with Audrey even if presented with evidence of her husband's systematic abuse, so if she had been the one to kill him she'd be sentenced to death.

It was possible that Ezra had lost his temper when he'd seen the state Audrey was in and had gone down to the stateroom to mete out justice, but he wasn't likely to have known where the scold's bridle and the key were kept, nor did it make sense that he would wake Anthony Blackstock just to prove a point. If Blackstock had kicked up a fuss and the other passengers had come running, Ezra would have been caught red-handed. And why would a man in the throes of a murderous rage bother with the contraption at all, fitting though it might seem to give the man a dose of his own medicine?

The more obvious answer was that Audrey had fitted the cage around her husband's head and then suffocated him with a pillow. She had probably thought he was dead when she carved the letters into his chest, clearly inspired by the slur Jeffrey Caldwell had called him earlier in the evening and the story Shep Reynolds had shared with her. Which explained why Reynolds had felt no remorse about suggesting Audrey as a suspect. He'd thought she'd tried to frame him and saw no reason to protect her.

Anthony Blackstock might have beaten Audrey, just as she'd said, or she might have sustained the bruises as he fought for his life but hadn't been able to gain purchase in his intoxicated state. Perhaps the black fibers beneath his fingernails had come from Ezra's coat, or they could have just as easily already been there from contact with his own clothing, or from maintaining a grip on Greta Van Kemp while he raped her. That would be the more likely possibility, since Anthony Blackstock probably hadn't worn worsted.

When Ezra had found Audrey on deck, he'd likely made a spur-of-the-moment decision to shield the woman he loved from the law. He'd hidden her in his cabin, thrown away his cello, and intended to keep up the pretense until he got Audrey safely away from the ship. Unfortunately for him, Shep Reynolds had been instructed to involve Scotland Yard, John Ransome had sent Sebastian instead of a detective who might have bungled the investigation, and Greta Van Kemp had decided to blackmail Ezra, sealing her fate.

Gemma sighed and took a sip of sherry. She couldn't condone murder, but she could understand how an abused woman would be driven to kill. Gemma's parents had loved and respected each other, and Sebastian had come from a close-knit family, but there were many women who suffered daily at the hands of violent, angry men and had no recourse or means of escape. Perhaps Ezra Pennington had really murdered Anthony Blackstock, but it was just as likely that he'd forfeited his own life in one final act of devotion and had gifted the woman he adored a future.

"Ezra Pennington has made his choice," Gemma said. "Whether he committed both murders or just one, the outcome will be the same. The only difference is whether Audrey Blackstock will hang as well."

"Unless she's with child," Colin interjected. "Then they might wait until she delivers before hanging her."

Either way, she'd be dead, Gemma thought, and, if she was with child, who would love it or even care if it lived or died? *Don't let Ezra's sacrifice be in vain*, she added silently to Audrey as Sebastian met her gaze.

Gemma thought he knew exactly what she had been thinking and didn't think Audrey deserved the death penalty, but all he said was, "The only way that will happen is if Audrey herself speaks up. As it stands, the case is closed."

"Do you think Mr. Quince will fictionalize it for his next penny dreadful?" Colin asked.

"I'm certain he will try," Sebastian replied. "He tried to pump me for information when I stopped at the boarding house to wash and change, but he won't learn any of the details from me."

"He doesn't need to," Gemma said. "He can use the newspaper accounts and put his own stamp on the facts. He's done it before."

"And I'm in no doubt that someone will sell the story to the press," Sebastian added morosely. "The crew's shore leave is long enough for someone to find their way to the offices of the *Illus-*

trated News and give the editor all the information he needs to publish a shocking story."

"Such is the prerogative of authors," Colin said. "We are all here for their amusement."

He looked to Sebastian as if he expected him to leave, but Sebastian remained where he was.

"Colin, if Gemma and I might have a moment," he said when Colin didn't budge.

Colin looked at Gemma, and she nodded, desperate to spend a few moments alone with Sebastian. Reluctantly, Colin heaved himself to his feet and walked out the door, leaving it open behind him.

EPILOGUE

The house was quiet, Colin probably down in the cellar and Mabel in her own room in the attic. Sebastian stood and shut the door, then, once they were truly alone, turned to face Gemma. She got up and walked towards him but didn't touch him or speak. She sensed that he had something to say and didn't wish to interrupt.

Sebastian took a deep breath, and Gemma could see that he was nervous and maybe even a little frightened, and he was clearly in pain. She waited.

Smiling uncertainly, Sebastian began, "I was going to do this right, but I can't wait another day. I've waited long enough and spent enough of my life on misery and self-recrimination. Gemma, I love you, adore you," he said, his voice catching in his throat. He sucked in a quavering breath and went on. "If you'll have me, I swear I will do everything in my power to keep you safe without stifling you or crushing your dreams. Will you marry me?"

Gemma smiled into his eyes. "As if you have to ask."

Sebastian pulled a ring from his waistcoat pocket and slipped it on her finger. It sparkled in the light of the gas lamps, and Gemma was certain it was the most beautiful thing she'd ever been given—but she'd admire the ring later. Just then, she had eyes only for Sebastian.

"I love you so much, it hurts," she whispered.

And then he crossed the short distance between them and pulled Gemma to him, his lips crushing hers and igniting a longing that would torment her mercilessly for hours. He made to pull away, then changed his mind and pushed her up against the wall, kissing her urgently until Gemma thought her knees would give way and she'd slide to the floor if Sebastian let her go. She pressed herself against him, her hips grinding against his, until he tore himself away with a frustrated groan. Sebastian's gaze burned with desire, and at that moment, if Colin hadn't been in the house to keep them apart, Gemma would have gladly taken Sebastian by the hand and led him to her bedroom. She was done waiting, and, clearly, so was he.

"Set a date," Sebastian said hoarsely. "Please, set a date."

"September the first," Gemma replied weakly. "I promised Colin I'd stay until the end of August."

"Bugger Colin," Sebastian said under his breath, then nodded. "Of course. You must honor your commitment. And we have much to do before the wedding."

Gemma nodded joyfully. "Will I see you on Sunday?"

"Nothing will keep me away."

Famous last words, Gemma thought, but didn't express her doubt aloud. There would always be new cases and new impediments, but they would overcome them together, as man and wife. The thought gave her a shiver of pleasure, and once she'd seen Sebastian out she leaned against the door and whispered, "Mrs. Sebastian Bell." It had a nice ring to it!

A LETTER FROM THE AUTHOR

Huge thanks for reading *Murder on the Prince Regent*. I hope you were hooked on Sebastian and Gemma's latest case. Their adventures will continue. If you want to join other readers in hearing all about my new releases and bonus content, you can sign up for my newsletter.

www.stormpublishing.co/irina-shapiro

If you enjoyed this book and could spare a few moments to leave a review, that would be hugely appreciated. Even a short review can make all the difference in encouraging a reader to discover my books for the first time. Thank you so much.

Thanks again for being part of this amazing journey with me and I hope you'll stay in touch—I have so many more stories and ideas to entertain you with.

Irina

irinashapiroauthor.com